Du

·1·4

.....

.ß.

'2'

....

...

...

..

...

....

....

....

Plea
sho

# Guns of Jeopardy

# GUNS OF JEOPARDY
## A Western Story

# ROBERT J. HORTON

SAGEBRUSH
Large Print Westerns

Copyright © 2005, by Golden West Literacy Agency

First published in Great Britain by ISIS Publishing
First published in the United States by Five Star

Published in Large Print 2007 by ISIS Publishing Ltd.,
7 Centremead, Osney Mead, Oxford OX2 0ES
United Kingdom
by arrangement with
Golden West Literary Agency

**British Library Cataloguing in Publication Data**
Horton, Robert J., d. 1934
    Guns of jeopardy: a Western story. –
    Large print ed. –
    (Sagebrush western series)
    1. Vendetta – Fiction
    2. Ranch life – Montana – Fiction
    3. Cattle stealing – Montana – Fiction
    4. Western stories
    5. Large type books
    I. Title
    813.5'2 [F]

ISBN 978–0–7531–7760–0 (hb)

Printed and bound in Great Britain by
T. J. International Ltd., Padstow, Cornwall

# CHAPTER
# ONE

"Whoopee!" The traditional joy yell of the West sounded shrilly above the thunder of flying hoofs. A score of riders swung their big gray Stetsons above their heads as they swept into the main street of Pondera, nosing ahead of a golden, swirling cloud of dust. Flags and bunting fluttered brightly in the warm September sun. Throngs cheered them as they made their entrance. The vanguard of the KT outfit was in town!

"Hello, KT!" came the roar from groups of cowboy celebrants.

"Whoopee!" came the answer, and the KT cowpunchers whirled their horses in salute.

At their head rode Larry Owens, broad of shoulder, tall, blond, young, with more than passable looks — scion of the greatest cattle family on the north range and heir to the vast KT domain with its thoroughbred herds, its rich bottomlands, its substantial buildings and fine equipment. Just a few paces behind him, on the left, rode Stan Velie, general foreman of the KT, a bony, graying, blue-eyed man of soldierly bearing in the saddle. Behind them the cowpunchers whooped in the approved style and lustiness of range riders in for the big holiday after the beef shipment.

Off the main street and a rearing, yelling stop before the yawning entrance of the livery with Taffy Turner, old, slight, bowlegged, weather-beaten, singing in his high-pitched voice:

**All the good ones goin' out,**
**And the bad ones comin' in.**
**It's a great big country, boys,**
**And it's all full of sin!**

Out of the saddles, slicker packs first, then cinch straps loosening to the accompaniment of rough and ready banter. The liveryman approached Larry Owens with a smile of welcome.

"Guess you'll be beating it back to that Eastern college after the rodeo," he said. "We'll all be glad when you've got your book-learnin' and come back for keeps to get your real education."

The youth took this sally with the best of good nature. His laughter was real and spontaneous. He was bubbling with high spirits, glowing with health and vigor, carefree and reckless as sons of the open should be — independent, confident, friendly and happy, ready for fun or fight. "He's a dead ringer for what old Lafe must have been when he was in his twenties," said people who knew the Owenses.

"Don't worry, Ross," said Larry cheerfully, replying to the liveryman. "I'll be beating it back at Christmas time to ride a few blizzards and get my second wind for the books. And when I get that old diploma next year, I'll fire it back at 'em if it's a sheepskin!"

2

"That's talk for a cowman!" exclaimed Ross in high approval. "When will Lafe be along?"

"Won't be long now," sang Larry in parting. "He's on his way."

Larry and Stan Velie went first to the hotel to make sure that proper accommodations had been reserved for them and the more important members of the KT party soon to arrive. They found the rooms ready, and, after shedding their chaps and indulging in plenty of soap and water, they went down the street. Stan Velie departed on business of his own, and Larry was soon being greeted by friends on every hand. His course held true to that taken by the KT cowpunchers and he soon entered the Silver Dollar to stand a complimentary drink on behalf of the outfit.

"Whoopee!" cried a shrill voice at the bar. "It's a big country, boys . . . all full of sin!"

Some miles east of town, two spanking bays were leaving a ribbon of dust behind a two-seated buckboard. In the front seat, that old centaur, Lafe Owens, lord of the KT Ranch, known from Texas to the line and ruler of thousands of acres of open range, rode with his wife Sarah. A big man, Lafe Owens, physically, mentally, and politically, most powerful of the cattle barons, best liked and most feared of them all. He was president of the Teton Cattlemen's Association, big in face and stature, tanned, gray-eyed, iron-gray of hair and short mustache, hale and hearty. Lafe Owens was as substantial as the huge gold links of the watch chain that hung across his wide expanse of vest. Sarah Owens was a small, dark, nervous woman, some ten years his junior, who retained more than a trace of a former dazzling beauty. About the house, and in most of the affairs of the children, her tiny little finger ruled Lafe absolutely. Even when ranch business was importantly concerned, Lafe occasionally asked her advice, many times heeded it, and most times profited by it.

In the rear seat sat Molly Owens — impudent, vivacious, full of girlish fire, a veritable sprite of the prairies, much too wise for her nineteen years. At least, so thought the eligible youth of the north range country. Riding with Molly was Mary O'Neil, housekeeper at the big KT ranch house, who also had a determined nature as well as certain fixed ideas. She was a middle-aged Irishwoman who contended it was a blessing she was childless because it took every minute she could spare from her work to look after, or keep an eye on, her husband Pat.

It was well along in the forenoon when Lafe Owens drove into Pondera with his womenfolk. His reception was fully as enthusiastic as that accorded his son and employees, but it was more dignified as became his standing and station. Other stockmen waved to him, cowpunchers looked at him curiously and respectfully, businessmen nodded almost obsequiously. It was a triumphant entry, an impressive arrival in front of the hotel, where he helped the women down from the buckboard and turned the horses over to a flunky who had come posthaste from the livery.

"Now I reckon we can go ahead with the rodeo," greeted Sam Daniels, proprietor of the hotel, motioning

4

to a man who was serving as porter to load up with the Owenses' suitcases.

"That's not bad, considering that she's already one day gone," boomed Lafe. "Being in front of the public so long has got you to greasin' your words, Sam."

Others crowded about to shake hands with the stockman, while Molly and her mother and Mary O'Neil went into the hotel to go upstairs. All the greetings were cordial, whole-hearted, blustering in the way of such men, except one. When Jim Bolten, owner of the big Double B Ranch, which adjoined the KT on the east, came up a certain coolness seemed to linger in his salutation. A slight change might have been perceived in Lafe Owens's voice and manner, also.

"Heard you was goin' to Chi with your shipment," said Lafe.

"Changed my mind," Bolten returned. "Too much to look after at home."

With Bolten was a tall, dark, sinewy man who affected an ornamental black leather vest and gauntlets, with a black silk scarf and wide-brimmed hat. Cream-colored corduroys were tucked inside his spotless, shining boots.

"Ah, Fresee," said Lafe Owens, "I haven't seen you since spring."

"I've been kept pretty close on the east range," replied Fresee. He was Bolten's foreman and manager combined, and it was freely hinted that he occasionally served in a more sinister capacity. He was a gunman of repute. Now he turned aside, after a flashing glance of keen scrutiny directed at the KT owner, and vanished in the throng with Bolten.

Again the talk became free and soon Larry Owens appeared. Lafe beckoned to him. "Want you to take a little walk with me," he told his son.

"Time enough to run up and see Mother and Sis?" asked Larry.

"Go ahead." His father nodded. "I'll be somewhere here close."

When Larry returned, he found Lafe talking with some stockmen in the lobby. There were half a dozen in the little group and they were not laughing or joking but conversing seriously in guarded tones. The young man lounged against the cigar counter, rolled and lighted a cigarette, and waited.

His father finally left the others and they went out of the hotel and walked down the street.

"Boys all set?" Lafe asked.

"Off to an easy start." Larry grinned.

Lafe Owens's brows knitted a little. "Larry, put a bug in their ears to stay away from Bolten's Double B outfit. Tell 'em the old man doesn't want any run-ins this trip. Pass the word to 'em so they'll be sure to understand it. You know how to do it."

"Sure thing, Dad." Larry looked at his father with interest. "Are the Double B men wanting to start something?"

"Don't know, but I wouldn't put it past 'em," grumbled Lafe. "Anyway, I've got my reasons for not wantin' my men to rub against 'em. If I was sure of anything, I'd tell you. Let's drop in here."

They turned into the Pondera State Bank. The cashier nodded and spoke to both of them with great respect as Lafe led the way back to the little private office in the rear.

"Howdy, Brower," Lafe greeted as they entered unceremoniously.

Henry Brower, president of the bank, rose from his desk at once, holding out his hand. He might have been Lafe Owens's age, but, although his face and brow were lined, he was not gray. A smug little man, rather dark, who wore good clothes with distinction. There was a smart air about him that seemed foreign to his lot as a cow-town banker.

"I'm glad to see you, Lafe," he said. "I'm always glad to see both of you. You're a little wider and wiser than Larry, here, but he's a bit taller and he's got devils dancing in his eyes."

Larry's smile seemed to lighten up the room.

"I'm a little older, too," Lafe remarked wryly. "But you're too clever to mention that. We'll sit down."

The banker drew up chairs for them and resumed his seat at the desk.

"Larry'll be goin' back next week to finish his education," said Lafe. "I don't know what he's learning, but he's passed every year, and, if he makes this last squirt, he'll have a degree. That's more'n you and I had, but we wasn't handicapped by havin' too many smart people around. It isn't going to hurt him none to have a blue ribbon from a first-class university to fall back on, I reckon."

"Well, they haven't spoiled him," was Brower's comment.

"Nor have I," blurted Lafe. His voice was naturally of the carrying kind and it was likely he could be heard outside the thin partition of the private office. "I have always figured that I wanted Larry to have responsibility when he turned a man. I've waited a year since he was twenty-one. He'll be twenty-two in a few days and I'm not goin' to be bothered sending him drafts when he needs money. The KT has plenty of money, and, when we run short of cash, we'll borrow from you." His eyes twinkled and Brower smiled.

"We wouldn't mind carrying more of your paper, Lafe, if we could get it," said the banker.

"Well," Lafe drawled, "just give Larry a checkbook and make my account a joint one so Larry can draw same as me whenever he wants."

Larry Owens started in his chair. "Why . . . Dad . . . you don't want to do that!"

"Why not?" flared his father. "You're my son, are you not? You'll own the KT someday, won't you? You're honest, I take it. Next summer you'll step into harness to help run the ranch . . . not just ride around it. Oh, I know . . . don't look hurt. You've been workin' plenty, but my son has to be more than a cowhand. You've got to learn that signing your name means something. Just make out the papers, or whatever is necessary, Henry, and I'll put my mark on 'em in well-inked English."

"If you feel this way about it, maybe I'll draw a thousand to see how it feels, Dad," Larry bantered.

"You can draw more'n that and not be overdrawn," his father remarked dryly.

Henry Brower secured Larry's signature on the proper card, gave him a checkbook, and busied himself with some papers.

"Now you run along, Larry," said old Lafe. "Henry and I'll have a little to talk about. Get what you need from the cashier and step wide, free, and handsome so they'll know hereabouts that you belong to the KT. You're the entertainment committee chairman so far as our outfit is concerned, and look out a bit for your mother and Molly when I'm not around."

"All right, Dad." Larry laughed.

As Larry Owens left the private office, Fresee turned away from the cashier's window. Larry saw a look of annoyance on the cashier's face and sensed that the Double B foreman had prolonged his business in order to listen. He eyed the retreating figure with light contempt. Then he favored the cashier with his flashing smile as he cashed his first check.

# CHAPTER
# TWO

In Henry Brower's private office the talk no longer was loud or boisterous. Lafe Owens had hitched his chair close to the banker's desk and Brower was leaning forward with his forearms on its surface. Lafe was speaking slowly in a low, earnest tone.

"Some of the other stockmen on the west end of the range had been approached," he was saying, "and asked what they thought about it. I heard rumors this summer, and even as far back as last spring, but I paid no attention to 'em. But just today I got it straight from some of the boys who can be trusted to talk square, and I know there's something in it." He paused, nodding soberly at the interested banker. "Now, why does Jim Bolten want to oust me as president of the Cattlemen's Association?"

"Because he wants to be elected president himself," replied Brower without an instant's hesitation.

"Exactly!" exclaimed Lafe, slapping the desk top with an open palm. "Why?"

"That's easy." The banker smiled. "That's the most important office on this range. You know that, Lafe, without my having to tell you. It's more important than being sheriff, even though the sheriff's job is the best-paying job in any of the counties . . . and being president of the Association doesn't carry a cent of salary. But it is a signal honor in a famous cow country like this, and it carries a lot of weight and influence. The Association can elect sheriffs. It can control the votes. That is as it should be, for these towns all are dependent on the stock-raising industry. Farming is a long way off yet, Lafe, even if there is a dribble of homesteaders."

"But here's the point, Henry," Lafe said seriously, tapping the desk with sun-browned fingers. "Bolten's wanted to be president before. Every two years, when we elect a president, he's been a candidate. I've always beat him, but it has been closer of late years. I've been president ever since the Association was reorganized, and I don't see where any member has any complaint coming about the way I've conducted the organization's affairs."

"I should say not," said Brower firmly. "You've made the Association what it is . . . a genuine protection for every stock raiser, and for we men in business in the towns. You know how bad it has been in the past, and you know how long it has been since we had any big robberies or hold-ups or any considerable rustling. Why, any man who has any sense at all would give you credit for what you've done, and why should they want to change? Why change horses in midstream when everything is sitting pretty?"

"Don't ask me," said Lafe. "I'm just talking this over with you because you ought to know what's goin' on. Yours is the best and biggest bank in the district and you're entitled to know. But I can't get it out of my head, Henry, that there's more to this than we can get a line on."

"What makes you think that?" the banker asked with a look of concern.

"Because Bolten has always fought in the open," replied Lafe stoutly. "He's always come out square and always been ready to present his arguments in front of me. He's always said there was more territory in the eastern half of the range the Association protects than in the western half and that the eastern ranchers were entitled to a president once in a while. It was Bolten himself who made the boundary line between the KT and the Double B the dividing line between the east half and the west half of Teton range. I've never opposed any of his arguments for he has never questioned my proper filling of the office. I never campaigned for election. But the members have elected me time after time and I've done my best."

"And they'll elect you again this fall," declared Brower. "If there isn't as much territory in the west end, there are more stockmen and they control the vote. If it were all mine, I'd be willing to bet my bank they'll put you in again."

"That isn't the point," said Lafe impatiently. "I don't care if they elect Bolten. I would just as soon he would be president so long as things are running smoothly. And in this connection, I will say one thing. Now, Henry, you know me as well as any man on this range. You've seen me fight my battles from the time I had nothing and won 'em. I won 'em fair and square when those who were out after my hide fought fair and square. When they tried tricks, I showed 'em a few. But mostly we fought in the open. And I claim to be the man best suited for the president of the Association because I reorganized it along the lines it has worked on for the past sixteen years or so, and I have the experience. And you know me well enough to know that I haven't got a swelled head." The stockman banged his fist on the desk.

"I know more than that," said the banker. "I know you have more ability than any stockman on this range. Thanks to you and these west-enders, this very bank is here today and the range practically immune from bandits, long riders, and rustlers. You have my support, and I have some influence myself."

Lafe Owens waved a hand disparagingly. "Let's get back to where I started. As I explained, Bolten always has fought in the open for the presidency of the Association. Now honestly, Henry, the last time or two I would have liked for him to be elected. I even hinted around to some of my friends about it and got called down proper. They said . . . 'What you want to do . . . leave us in the hole after you've got things going all right?' That settled it. But this year, Bolten isn't fighting in the open. He's . . . well, there's no other name for it, Henry . . . he's sneaking around. He claims to have the east half of the range with him to a man, and he's trying to work on the west-enders, as you call 'em. That isn't altogether like Bolten. Since we had our worst trouble, years ago, he's been pretty much on the square. It isn't like him to change so sudden without being prodded by somebody."

There was a short silence after this as the men looked at each other.

The banker's brow wrinkled in thought. "Got any idea as to who might be doing the prodding?"

"Yes. Henry, I know men. I know men because I've tried to learn 'em. I can almost tell what a man is thinking about by the look in his eyes ... if he's thinking real hard. Bolten's got a man working for him who doesn't like me. I had to put him in his place once, when he first came here after our big trouble, and I've kept him there ever since. But he knows the cow business and he knows how to handle the kind of men he hired for the Double B outfit. He's spent ten years making himself what he is today ... Bolten's right bower."

"Fresee?" said Brower softly.

"Yes." Lafe Owens scowled. "I know the Fresee breed, Henry. He comes from 'way down in the border country where they have a good type and two or three bad types. He isn't the first type I mentioned. And he isn't the kind that forgets. Right now, here, during this rodeo, he's goin' to try to make trouble with my men."

"Are you sure of that?" Brower asked in surprise.

"Pretty near. He's got thirty of his outfit in town and outnumbers us. I've got too many cattle scattered around to bring in too big a bunch at once. His men have made some talk and a word or two has been slipped to some of the boys of the Association. They passed it along to me. Can't you see the play?"

14

The banker's brow wrinkled again. "All I can see is that he wants to make trouble for you. Wants to nag you, maybe."

Lafe shook his head. "More'n that to it. By gettin' my men mixed up in a row and managing, maybe, to throw the blame on 'em, it would react against me, and Bolten could say . . . 'Why, Owens is having trouble managing his own men.'"

Brower thought a spell. "Doesn't sound reasonable."

"No? Well, this Fresee is just clever enough to stir up my men and get 'em to rampaging just the same. And there's other ways he can make trouble for me. I don't know what he has been telling Bolten. I don't know what tricks he may have played. But I do know what I see in the man's eyes and that isn't complimentary to him, nor soothing to me. It would please him most powerfully to see me ousted as president of the Association, provided he could make me see *he* had something to do with it. Now, you begin to understand. Men of his breed can't be crossed, no matter how shady a deal they're mixed up in, without nursing a grudge that becomes hatred. They just exist for revenge. He's lightning and hot dynamite with his gun, and he'd try to rope me into gun play in an hour if he thought he could get away with it."

Brower was startled. "Lafe, I think you're imagining things. It seems too big an undertaking just to satisfy a personal grudge."

"Ah . . . and maybe it is," said Lafe Owens softly. "You know this is still wild country, Henry, and strange things are done in a wild country for more reasons than one. Maybe Fresee has another reason, some other object in view. It might even be that there is somebody prodding *him*. Half of my success has been due to playing hunches and outguessing the other fellow. Sounds foolish, and I reckon it wouldn't work in your line of business. But it has sure worked in mine." He nodded his head grimly.

"But who . . . why . . . ?"

"Don't ask me," Lafe interposed. "Don't ask me a thing. But just do this one thing for me as a favor, Henry . . . keep your eyes open. Notice any strangers who come to town, or anything unusual that might have a bearing . . . even by guessing . . . on what I've told you. I know I can trust you, know that you're smart and sensible. Just keep a friendly eye out for me here, will you?"

"Of course," Brower promised instantly. "I think your conjectures are a little far-fetched, but I'll do as you ask. Have you . . . said anything to the sheriff?"

"Certainly not," Lafe answered vehemently. "I've nothing to go to the sheriff about. What could I say to him in his official capacity, which is the only way I would go? I've been talking to you as a friend and one who doesn't have to have facts and evidence to see the point of my remarks. Oh, I don't want to sound like the advance agent for some coming disaster, or anything like that, but I want to be prepared for any move against me. And this time I *do* want to be elected president again of the Association. I merely asked you for a little help and don't you say anything to anybody."

**16**

"I won't," said Brower. "And I'll keep my eyes open, and my ears open, also. You can lay a bet on that. And I'm going to seal the promise by giving you a good cigar, for I don't believe in handshaking."

When Lafe Owens had gone, Henry Brower sat thoughtfully at his desk, looking out the little, barred window of his office into the brilliant sunshine of midday. He went to dinner late, and, instead of going home, where his housekeeper had a good meal waiting, he went to the Horseshoe Café, where a majority of the cowpunchers were accustomed to eat. It was his first experience in deliberate espionage.

Meanwhile, Lafe Owens went to the hotel, where he sat at the head of a table with his family and Stan Velie and Mary O'Neil. It was the second day of the annual rodeo that staged a four-day program the end of each September. It was not an important day in so far as the contests were concerned, as the semi-finals would come the third day and the great final exhibitions on the fourth and last.

In Pondera, as in all cattle country centers, the rodeo was a meeting time for stockmen and their employees, for family reunions, for an extended holiday — the biggest celebration of the year. So, in the afternoon, Lafe was busy renewing friendships and acquaintances, talking stock and range conditions with other cattlemen, transacting business. The others of his family went to the fairgrounds where the contests were being held.

Arrayed in colored shirts and scarves of purple, yellow, or pink with their holiday hats and best boots, the cowpunchers made merry in the resorts before and after the preliminary contests. That night would come the dark-to-dawn dancing, with fireworks as an added diversion, and gambling a competing feature.

At sundown the crowd in the largest resort, the Silver Dollar, was going strong. The place was jammed with as picturesque a throng as could be gathered between walls. Already the big hanging lamps were yellow moons in a sky of blue smoke. The medley of sound was indescribable. The mass of male celebrants weaved about the bar and gaming tables. Shouts and whoops and snatches of song. Above the backbar hung a sign:

**KEEP YOUR
HOLSTER FLAPS
TIED DOWN**

Among those who were enjoying themselves to the utmost were Taffy Turner and Pat O'Neil of the KT outfit. All afternoon they had held their place at the bar and they appeared none the worse for it. True, they were more than ordinarily jovial and in a very happy mood — a mood that at regular intervals broke loose in song. Taffy had taught Pat fifteen verses of his song, some of which the Irishman suspected had been made up on the spot, and he so stated.

"What of it?" shrilled Taffy Turner, whose high voice cut through the noise in the place like a knife. " 'S all right, ain't it?" Then:

**Smoke coming out,
Drinks goin' in . . .**

18

**It's a great big country, boys,
All full of sin.**

Then the two of them repeated the verse as loudly as they could sing, drowning the chatter and clamor at the bar. Ordinarily these outbursts were given a hand by other convivial spirits and drinks were ordered, but this latest effort drew a different response. A thick-set man, short, round-faced with puffed cheeks and small brown eyes that contrasted with yellow brows, forced his way toward the pair and, reaching out across the bar, hurled the fiery contents of a liquor glass into their faces.

"That'll grease your whistles so they won't squeak so much," he jeered, tossing away the glass.

Taffy Turner sputtered and blinked his mild blue eyes. Then he went for his gun. Several grasped him and held him. With Pat it was different. The Irishman had no use for guns. He relied on his strength and his fists. His great arms circled those in front of him and his huge hands flung men aside as if they had been made of straw. He wore no weapon. In a moment he confronted Bloat Simpson, the notorious Double B bully.

"Thanks for the grease, Bloat," he said loudly so all could hear in the temporary lull in the din about the bar. "What you need is some sand . . . you're slipping!"

He towered over the heavier man who leaned back against the bar on one elbow — his left — sneering. The lack of a gun as part of the Irishman's dress forestalled a shooting, but Simpson hunched his shoulders forward and his right fist started to describe a

**19**

parabola. It only started. Pat closed in like a tiger, shooting his right squarely into the pudgy face and bringing his left up in a short, vicious uppercut that cracked against Simpson's jaw like a pistol shot. The crowd backed away to give them room as the bully sagged against the bar.

But the outraged Irishman wasn't through. Again he drove his smashing right and it found its mark on Simpson's jaw. The man dropped as if his body were made of lead and he lay motionlessly, sprawled full length on the floor.

Now there was a new movement close at hand as members of the KT and Double B outfits pushed into the cleared space.

"Fair play!"

"Give him a chance to come out of it and he'll kill that harp!"

"You're guessing, guy!"

The cowpunchers jostled each other, a man shoved, a free-for-all mêlée seemed imminent. Simpson was stirring on the floor, looking up, dazed.

"Leave him to me!" cried Pat O'Neil. "He started the party, now let him finish it . . . if he's able."

Simpson's eyes cleared and blazed. He had heard and now he remembered. He started to his feet cursing, bethought himself of his gun, jerked it from his holster. But O'Neil's booted foot sent it spinning into the crowd. The Irishman didn't wait for him to clamber all the way to his feet but grasped him by the collar and drew him up, thrust him back against the bar.

"Ye'll fight with yer hands fer once, ye soap-faced bloater!" he shouted. "Ye don't see no gun on me, eh? But I've got bullets in me fist, and, if ye've got nerve enough to put up your mitts, I'll hand 'em to ye where they'll do the most good!"

In the sudden silence, Simpson snarled, his lips drawing back against his teeth. Then came an interruption.

"That'll do, Pat. Beat it!"

Pat whirled at the first sound of the voice and saw Larry Owens, standing close to him.

"He insulted me, Mister Larry," he complained. "Said me voice squeaked and fired a shot of white likker in me face, the . . ."

"Me, too!" shrilled Taffy Turner, wrestling himself free and pushing forward. "If he wants to shoot it out, let me at him!"

Bloat Simpson laughed jeeringly. "You better get these playboys out in the air where they can shake the fog out of their heads. It ain't safe to let a pair of KT half-wits circulate around men."

The youth's eyes narrowed. He flashed a quick look of warning to the KT men who he could see. Then, ignoring Simpson, he spoke to O'Neil. "Who started it?"

"There he is," O'Neil accused, pointing to Simpson. "The one with the greasy shirt."

"Hold court, rah-rah boy," came from a Double B man behind Larry.

"Give your college yell and we'll buy a drink!" called another while his companions laughed.

21

There was an angry muttering among members of the KT outfit close at hand. It needed a mere spark to touch off an explosion of wrath and combat. Larry Owens's eyes flashed fire, but he remembered what his father had told him about not wanting trouble and he remained cool, although it required effort. He stepped directly in front of Simpson. "You're not going to start a fight with our men," he said in a ringing voice. "If you want to start one with me . . . that's different."

"*Our* men?" jeered Simpson. "Has papa taken us into the firm before we get our sheepskin?"

A roar went up from the Double B men. "Rah, rah, rah!" they shouted in high glee.

Larry's face reddened with swift and uncontrollable anger. The KT men saw it coming and there was a rush — but not before Larry had smashed down Simpson's guard with his left and drove his right for a knockout. Almost in a wink of an eyelash, the Silver Dollar was the scene of a combat that was to live indefinitely in the memory of the spectators and remain a highlight in the strenuous history of Teton range.

# CHAPTER
# THREE

"No guns!" screamed the proprietor of the resort as he climbed up on the bar. "No guns, boys, for everybody's sake!"

The crowd took it up. "No guns!" everyone shouted, and there was a mad scramble to get out of the way, for none there but expected bullets would decide such an issue between the two largest and most powerful outfits on the range. But the fighting started with such suddenness and ferocity, at such close quarters, that the combatants would have found it difficult to use their weapons if they had been so minded. Neither outfit was represented by its full strength, but they fought with the savageness and barbarity that made up for lack of numbers. These were men whose normal lives required no knowledge of boxing. They grappled and wrestled, kicked and gouged, and even bit; guns and not fists were their usual weapons.

Atop the bar, the proprietor continuously shouted his warning. It must have been that even in the heat of the terrific encounter the men fighting realized the danger of an attempt at gun play. The first shot would mean the disintegration of the whirling, struggling knot

23

of men and the instant recourse to smoking guns. Dark, stark tragedy would certainly result.

Meanwhile, the news of the clash had spread through the town with incredible rapidity. The customers of other resorts left their glasses on the bars, or hastily cashed their poker chips, and rushed for the Silver Dollar. Soon the street was crowded.

Sheriff Rowan, big, square-jawed, a genuine fighting man, came on the run with regular and special deputies trailing him. They literally burst in upon the mêlée, the commanding voice of the sheriff carrying above the pandemonium like the roaring of a bull. Then came Lafe Owens himself, plunging into the fray and throwing men right and left regardless of who they were or of the side on which they fought. He was followed by Stan Velie and almost immediately by Fresee.

With the commands of the stockman, the shouts of the foremen, and the stern voice of the law ringing in their ears, the combatants ceased fighting and drew back, bloody-faced, their clothes torn, mostly stripped of gaudy scarves, and all hatless. The floor was strewn with guns that had been knocked or lost from holsters.

"Don't touch the guns!" shouted the frenzied proprietor from his place on the bar.

Silence fell over the big room as by a touch of a magician's wand, and in the stillness a man was heard whimpering. All looked to see Taffy Turner, a pitiful sight, sitting on the floor amid the débris of chairs and tables, cards and chips. He was bloody and rocked slowly to and fro in pain while he moaned. "My gun eye . . . oh, my gun eye." His thin, bony hand was held tightly over the right side of his face.

Larry Owens, breathing hard, bloody and torn as the result of having been the chief target of the attack, stooped over the thin, small figure.

"What's the matter, Taffy? You . . . hurt bad?"

The diminutive man shivered. Then he looked up and removed his hand. Larry started back with an involuntary cry of horror. A swift intake of breath came from all present. Lafe Owens swore with incredulity. Taffy Turner's right eye was missing! Blood streamed from the empty socket. Men turned away, sick with the dreadful sight of it.

Then Lafe's voice boomed shakily: "Get him to the doctor, Larry, quick as you can. One of you KT men help him. And bring him a drink first." The big stockman gripped his palms and swore through clenched teeth.

Larry lifted Taffy to his feet, while the sheriff's voice boomed. "Every one of you get out!" he commanded, indicating the circle of remaining spectators. They began to file out at once. "The rest of you," he shouted hoarsely at the torn and bloody group, "are under arrest . . . that means every one of you!"

At this point, Lafe Owens, his great shoulders straight, his eyes snapping, stepped beside the official. "I assume full responsibility for my men," he announced sternly. "Any time you want them to appear, I'll produce them. And since when, Rowan, have you been arresting everybody in a free-for-all fight, of which this town has had more than plenty?"

The sheriff frowned darkly. "I passed the word, and I passed it generous, that I'd stand for none of this business this year," he said loudly. "Your men and Bolten's haven't paid any attention to my warning. You . . ." He ceased talking as he met the old Trojan's eye. "Of course, you'll back up your men," he said in a less aggressive tone. "I'd expect that . . . wouldn't expect anything else." Then, to the crowd: "The KT men can go on Lafe Owens's word, but when I send for you, you've got to show."

Not a man moved. Larry, who was giving Taffy Turner a stimulant, caught a look from his father. "C'mon, boys," he ordered as cheerfully as possible. The KT outfit followed him as he and another left with Taffy Turner.

"I'll stand good for the Double B men," said Fresee crisply, waving a hand toward the remaining combatants.

"Just a minute!" rang Lafe Owens's voice as the men made to leave. He turned to the sheriff. "Since you've made this arrest, Rowan, do you want to let these men go just on the word of a foreman before you've investigated and found out how this thing started?"

"No," said Rowan shortly. "I'll have to have Bolten's word."

"I speak for Bolten," Fresee announced curtly.

"Not to me, you don't," flared the sheriff, who was getting mad. "And, Lafe, how does it come . . . since you ask me why I was arresting everybody in a free-for-all fight all of a sudden . . . I've got to investigate how it started? That's seldom been done before."

"Because I'm a citizen and a taxpayer and a voice in this county, and president of the Cattlemen's Association, and I want to know!" thundered Lafe Owens. "And don't forget that the oldest man in my outfit, who's been with me thirty years, has lost an eye!"

The sheriff was taken aback by the vehemence of the reply. He bit his lip and tugged at his mustache.

"I expect it's because he wants to put the blame on the Double B . . . if he can," said Fresee dryly.

Lafe Owens turned on the Double B foreman. "Did you instruct your outfit not to start trouble with my men?"

"I don't treat my men like babies when they're on their own in town," Fresee retorted coldly. "They know how to take care of themselves."

"That's fair enough," Lafe conceded. "I've never treated my men like babies, either . . . they wouldn't let me, if I wanted to. But I gave an order that none of my outfit was to start trouble with any of the Bolten crowd. I don't know how this started, but I do know my men well enough to bet ten-to-one that they would obey a straight order."

Fresee's mean eyes narrowed, but he managed a thin smile. "As I said," he told the sheriff, "Owens intends to put the blame on my men. If they started the row, you can bet they had good reason, and they'll stick behind it without any bellyaching."

"That's aimed at me," said Lafe sternly. "Look at me, Fresee! I told you where to get off once, and you took the hint. Now I'm tellin' you again. Don't start any trouble with me or my men. This is the first warning. Get it straight! For you'll never get another."

Fresee's eyes were beady jets of flame. Involuntarily his fingers twitched above his gun as the hate blazed between his lids, but he managed to hold back the hot challenge that was on his tongue. "I reckon the sheriff, here, will remember that threat."

"The sheriff is out of it, so far as you and me are concerned," was Lafe's grim retort. "And you won't have to wiggle those loose brains of yours much to guess the reason."

"Now there's no use in you fellows goin' on like this," the sheriff put in, addressing his remark more to Fresee than to the stockman. "And . . . I'm goin' to let these men go on their word to show up when I want 'em, Lafe. I can trust Bolten to round 'em up if necessary." But he was talking only to the Double B foreman for Owens was striding out the door.

As he expected, Lafe Owens found the men in the barn where cuts and bruises had been washed and in many instances bandaged. Stan Velie, who had followed Lafe, listened quietly while the KT owner assembled the facts. It was Pat O'Neil who did most of the talking, since the trouble had started over the song sung by himself and Taffy Turner. Taffy, of course, was not present. He had been taken immediately to the doctor's office by Larry. Moreover, it just so happened that Pat and Taffy had not been slipped the word to steer wide

28

of the Double B outfit, as other cowpunchers brought out in affirming the Irishman's account.

"It wouldn't have made any difference," said Pat, shaking his head sorrowfully. "No man can throw likker in my face and get away with it without a receipt. And now look what's happened to Taffy."

"I'm going to see him," said Lafe, frowning heavily. "It looks as if this business had been cooked up. I could see it in that Fresee's eyes when I called him about it. I had a hunch some such play was in the picture and that's why I sent word to step careful. I don't think they'll try it a second time . . . and this affair may have been a fluke . . . but I don't want any more trouble. Take it a little easy this trip, boys. I'm goin' to keep every one of you on the ranch this winter. Save a bunkhouse stake to play cards with till next spring's horse roundup."

After this, he went out with Stan Velie, leaving the men wondering and elated. It was customary for the big ranches to let most of their men go for the winter, which meant loafing in the towns or riding the line, usually broke. This was cheering news.

"Something's up," said a tall cowpuncher, peering at the faces of his companions in the lantern light. "The old man's got some kind of bug in his ear and it's got something to do with the Double B. I bet we won't be just playin' kyards all winter."

Lafe found Larry and Taffy Turner at the doctor's house. The physician had just finished bandaging

**29**

Taffy's right eye, or where his right eye had been and where now was an empty socket.

Lafe Owens pulled up a chair and sat beside him. The stockman's face was white. "Do you know who did it, Taffy?" he asked in a voice that trembled.

"No," said Taffy. "If I did . . ." He paused, biting his lip. "But it wasn't one of our boys, of course. We was in such a jam . . . maybe whoever did it, didn't intend to do it. Everybody was clawing. If it could only have been the left . . ." His voice trailed off in a whisper and died.

"An eye for an eye," Lafe Owens muttered, his face drawn into grim lines.

"What's that?" said Taffy.

Lafe put a hand on Taffy's knee. "You've worked for me for a long time, Taffy," he said tremulously, "and you've always been loyal. But I never thought it would cost you this much. Well, you don't have to work any more. That ranch of ours is your home just as much as mine or Larry's or any of us. You can do just as you danged please out there. And I'm not forgettin' what happened tonight. Somebody's goin' to pay . . . I promise you that. This hits me worse than you can realize." He gripped the old man's hand. "Larry'll take you to the hotel and put you in one of our rooms. Does . . . does it hurt much?"

"Shucks, Lafe, don't you go worrying about me. The doc's got it all doped up so it feels fine. The only medicine I need now is a few hefty snorts of likker and some tall sleep. But, listen, Lafe . . ." He leaned toward the stockman, his one eye glowing feverishly.

The doctor raised a hand. "You mustn't get excited, Taffy."

"Excited?" Taffy swore. "Lafe, I've rode the range a good many years, and I've seen some queer performances. This thing today didn't happen casual-like. It looked like it was done on purpose. And Simpson was just a tool . . ." He lowered his voice to a whisper, glancing swiftly out of his left eye at the doctor, Larry, and Stan Velie. "The man you've got to watch is Fresee. He ain't right in the first place, and he's got something up his sleeve. You allers said I could tell a storm three days off. Well, I'm tellin' trouble further off than that. Something's in the wind." He tried to nod his head.

"I know it," said Lafe. "Now you just rest easy and leave that part of it to me. The doctor says you've got to keep quiet, so you go along with Larry, and I'll be up after a while. Larry'll see you get your drinks and stay with you till I come in. I've got to look after the womenfolk."

When they had gone, Lafe instructed Stan Velie to circulate among the resorts and wherever the men congregated, and to keep both eyes and ears open. Then he started for the hotel himself.

# CHAPTER
# FOUR

Lafe found Jane Bolten with his wife, Molly, Mary O'Neil, and the wife of another stockman in the upstairs parlor reserved for his party. Jane was the same age as Molly Owens, and the girls were friends, for neither Jim Bolten, Jane's father, nor Lafe Owens permitted their rivalry, or past differences, to interfere with social activities of their womenfolk. The girls visited each other at the two ranches at intervals and often were found together much of the time when in town.

"I'm declaring myself straight off," said Jane to Lafe Owens. "I think it's terrible. I came up here to see your folks as soon as I heard about it. Poor Taffy! I think Father, and you, too, ought to read the riot act to the men!"

"Pooh, pooh," said Lafe, who was careful to appear normal in the presence of the women. " 'Punchers will get tangled up in town. They always have, and they always will. Taffy was unlucky . . . he sure was. But we can be thankful they didn't lose their heads and start shooting. Now . . . as soon as I've looked in on Taffy . . . we're goin' to the dance."

"Can I see him, Dad?" asked Molly anxiously.

32

"Not tonight. The doctor has given him some medicine and he must sleep. The men are goin' to take turns staying with him, and in the morning I'm going to send two men with him down to Great Falls where he can get the attention he needs. The bays will take 'em there in short order. There's nothing to worry about."

Healthy youth will not remain depressed for long, and, when Larry Owens entered the dancing pavilion some two hours later, he had decided to take his father's advice and try to have a good time, despite a darkened eye and numerous bruises. Larry danced first with his sister. Molly had much to ask him and he replied as best he could, for his attention was attracted elsewhere.

Jane Bolten was dancing with a stranger. This was not unusual, as Larry didn't know everyone on the range. For several years he had been away to school most of the year, and pretty much confined to the ranch when he was at home. No, the fact that Jane was dancing with a stranger was not unusual, but the stranger himself was unusual. Back to back, Larry and the stranger would have been within a scant fraction of an inch as tall as each other; their shoulders would have been about as broad, their lithe build similar. Larry estimated the fellow to be about his own age. He was dark whereas Larry was blond, but he was mighty good-looking, and frequently his teeth flashed white and even in a catching smile. Good talker, too, Larry decided, frowning. He certainly was entertaining Jane Bolten, and, whenever any other likely young fellow seemed to be entertaining Jane, Larry instantly became alert. Larry thought pretty well of Jane. What she thought of him, he could only guess — and she didn't help his guessing much.

"Who's that dancing with Jane?" he asked his sister.

"Oh, you've noticed, too?" said Molly impishly. "Must be some out-of-town friend of Jane's. I haven't met him."

"*Humph*. I thought you knew every fellow who ever hit this town."

"Most of them," mocked Molly, secretly amused by his irritation. "But I don't know this one, and, whoever he is, he's a dazzler. He can dress and dance, anyway."

"You find out who he is before you dance with him."

"Yes?" His sister tilted her saucy nose. "If we waited to be properly introduced at these affairs to every fellow who asked us to dance, we'd be off the floor a lot, wouldn't we?"

"You pretty ones wouldn't," growled Larry. "You or Jane never have to wait for partners."

"Thanks, Larry. I see it's going to cost me something for your birthday present this year, or would, if I hadn't already bought it. What do you care who dances with Jane?"

"You can't make me mad," Larry returned defiantly. "I never had any strings on Jane and she's certainly never had any on me. I'm . . . I'm just curious."

Molly laughed. "Larry, you're rich . . . funny, I mean. You're stuck as hard on Jane as a fly in molasses. I guess a little healthy competition would wake you up. But don't worry. I always speak a good word for you."

Larry lost his struggle not to flush. The number ended, and he led Molly to her seat. "Wish me luck," he said, and headed straight for Jane Bolten.

He had to cross the floor and it so happened that the stranger started on his way at the same time. Their eyes met in a flashing glance as they passed. There was nothing wrong with the stranger's eyes. He was well set up and mighty good-looking. Larry lost no time in getting Jane Bolten away from her ring of admirers. He could do this easily as the other men knew the two would have things to say to each other concerning what had happened that day, and they readily gave ground.

What they had to say about the trouble was taken care of by the time the next dance started. As they circled the floor, Larry gave vent to a smothered exclamation. The stranger was dancing with Molly Owens. Thus Larry was offered an opportunity to speak about him without Jane's being aware that he was overly interested.

"Who's that dancing with my sister? And didn't I notice you dancing with him last time?"

Jane looked about. "Why, I believe you did," she said airily, "that is, if you looked."

"I can't help seeing who dances with you when I always look for you on the floor," Larry blurted — and was sorry immediately.

"That's nice of you, Larry," Jane cooed. "He's a stranger up here from south somewhere. Doesn't know anybody and you know we girls are always sorry for strangers."

"Wasn't he even polite enough to tell you his name?" asked Larry foolishly.

"He said he was Harry-From-Nowhere," Jane returned tantalizingly. "I thought that was too novel to insist on a last name. He's a splendid dancer and talks well. Some rich rancher's son, probably. Anyway, I love mysteries."

As soon as the dance was finished, Larry hurried to his sister. The stranger had left before he gained her ear. "Did you find out who he is, Molly? You can't blame me for being curious about a fellow I don't know who dances with my own sister."

"Of course not," said Molly. "And I was careful to ask him who he is. You might know I'd do that."

"Well, let's have it," said her brother impatiently.

"He said he was Harry-From-Nowhere. It sounded so mysterious I didn't want to spoil it by pressing him any further."

Larry snorted and reddened. Then he caught sight of the stranger strolling into the refreshment stand at one corner of the pavilion. His mind was made up instantly. Without a word he proceeded in that direction.

When he entered the booth, he found the stranger at the counter, drinking a bottle of soda. He took his place beside him and ordered the same. He sensed the stranger looking at him, and turned to meet his level gaze.

"Howdy," he said, raising his glass with a faint smile.

"Likewise," returned the other, sipping his drink.

"First trip up here?" inquired Larry pleasantly.

36

"You're the first gentleman I've met," returned the other affably. "I assume you're on the reception committee."

"Not exactly. I have no wish to be rude, but I feel privileged to ask who you are."

"Yes?" The other's brows went up and his smile died. "On what grounds?" he asked rather sharply.

"I like to know who dances with my sister," Larry replied evenly.

"Don't blame you," said the stranger. "Good dancer, good looker, and witty in the bargain. I didn't ask her name. Oh, I suppose it would be easy enough to find out her name." The stranger shrugged slightly. "My name is Harry. Harry Jones." He put down his empty glass.

"Jones." Larry appeared puzzled. "I don't know of a Jones on this range."

"Don't let that bother you, my friend," was the dry retort. "Just put me down as one of the Joneses." With a chuckle he walked out of the booth, leaving Larry Owens scowling over his half empty glass.

# CHAPTER
# FIVE

In the gaily decorated pavilion the dance whirled on —
a boisterous merry-go-round propelled by the imported
orchestra. In the resorts every card table had its full
quota of players; roulette and craps, faro and blackjack
were patronized to the limit. The bars were thronged.
Crowds constantly circulated in the streets, cafés,
stores, hotels, and other business places. The celebrants
were jovial, happy, considerate, and remarkably
well-behaved. Pondera blazed with glory as Teton range
made holiday.

But there was an undercurrent beneath this joyous
exterior, a swift-flowing stream of conjecture, apprehen-
sion, and premonition that simmered in many minds of
varying intellect. There were whisperings and low-
voiced confidences, camouflaged by badinage and light
talk. The winds of rumor fanned a growing feeling of
unrest among those who sensed the portent of what
had taken place earlier.

Lafe Owens was at the dance, a great, boisterous,
hearty, jovial, blustering picture of robust health, a man
who in size, appearance, and personality typified his
calling, his power and prestige. Everyone welcomed
him, and, to a casual on-looker, it would have seemed

unlikely that he had an enemy in the world. But there were those who noticed with trepidation that Jim Bolten did not appear again after leaving earlier in the night. It was noticeable, too, especially to the womenfolk, that when the hour grew late, there were not many stockmen in the pavilion. Of the younger masculine element, there was ample representation, and of cowpunchers. Slowly the conviction that trouble was impending took hold.

"I'll be going out for a spell, Mother," Lafe Owens told his wife, squeezing her hand.

Her worried gaze followed him as he weaved in and out among the crowd to the big front entrance. Larry, too, saw him go and his dancing partner chided him for a lapse in bantering conversation. Another fact that weighed on Larry's mind was that the stranger who called himself one of the Joneses had danced but once after they had met and had then left the floor.

Lafe Owens made his way first to the hotel. It was by the merest coincidence that the first group of stockmen with whom he came in contact included Jim Bolten. A flashing survey showed that the men were both from the east and west ends of the range.

The Double B owner stepped forward quickly. "Lafe, I'm sorry our boys got mixed up today. I've told 'em if there's any more trouble I'd fire the lot."

Owens looked at him closely. "Better be sure Fresee understands that, Jim," he said with a significant nod of his head. The others about them were listening keenly.

Bolten frowned. "I reckon it wouldn't have happened if Fresee had been around, but he can't be everywhere at once."

"That's true," said Lafe. "I suppose he slipped you the word I handed him. Well, Jim, I wouldn't tell your foreman anything behind your back that I wouldn't say in front of you. He's had a mean look in his eye for me lately, looks like. Tonight he was almost belligerent. I told him where to head in and not to start any trouble with my outfit or me. I tried to make it plain that it was a warning and would be the last."

Bolten's lips tightened. "That looks like you were putting it up to me, Lafe," he said, "but I'm not goin' to take it that way. I don't want any trouble out our way if I can help it. I'm sayin' right here in public that I'm sorry for what happened to Taffy Turner and that whatever that fool Bloat Simpson said to Larry he said on his own hook, and, if you want it, I'll fire him tomorrow."

Lafe Owens could not overlook the fact that this was to all appearances equivalent to an apology. He didn't believe that Jim Bolten intended him to think it as such, knew he was speaking for the benefit of others present and to put a good face on his stand in the matter, but he had to accept it as an apology just the same.

"No, I don't want anybody fired, Jim. You know me better than that. And I understand Bloat got smacked plenty for his insult. I don't propose to have any trouble, either, and I guess you and I have got enough say to keep peace in our territory."

There was a murmur of approval at this from the other stockmen. "I should think you'd have," said one, laughing. "And pretty much on the whole range for that matter."

It was noteworthy that the remark brought significant looks. Then the topic was changed abruptly, for all present knew Lafe Owens and Jim Bolten were on dangerous ground. They remembered the feud of years before which had resulted from a boundary dispute. There had been a compromise. Both Owens and Bolten had yielded a point or two upon the insistence of the Cattlemen's Association's board of arbitration. But the yielded points still rankled in the breasts of each. It was the year after the ending of the controversy that Lafe had run for president of the Association, had been elected, had reorganized it, and had directed its activities ever since.

News of the meeting between Owens and Bolten spread about the hotel rapidly. Soon it would be known all over town, even to the words used in the conversation. Then the words would be twisted by members of the two factions — for it was beginning to be recognized that there were two factions, and that these factions took in the east and west ends of the range as well as the two big outfits involved — and, of course, members of these factions would arrange their reports so they would be favorable to the side they favored. This extraordinary and menacing situation arose in a few short hours!

Instead of returning to the pavilion at once, Lafe went to his rooms in the hotel. The dancers, as he well knew, would not hear the strains of "Home, Sweet Home" until the gray banners of dawn were afloat in the eastern horizon. It would be another hour, at least, more likely two, before his womenfolk would be ready to leave. Rodeo came once a year.

Lafe sat in an easy chair at a window overlooking the street. He had not been sitting long when there came a light knock at the door.

Lafe hesitated, then turned his chair. "Come in," he invited gruffly.

Henry Brower opened the door. "I saw . . . your cigar . . . and thought I'd take a chance on you being alone," the banker explained hesitatingly. "I don't want to intrude . . ."

"Come right in, Henry," said Lafe heartily. "I'm glad you're here. Yes, I'm alone . . ." He halted as Brower stepped into the room, touching a finger to his lips and closing the door softly.

Lafe Owens was openly surprised at the stealthy, furtive manner of the banker who stepped swiftly to his side, exercising care that his shadow should not be seen through the window. He drew up a chair and looked about the room.

"Damn it, Henry, you act like a horse thief only two jumps ahead of a posse. What's up?"

"I don't wish to be seen or heard," replied Brower. "I came up the back way. I've something important to tell you, and—"

"Wait a minute," Lafe interrupted. He rose and went to the door. He looked outside for a short space and, when he returned, spoke to the banker cheerfully.

"Don't worry. You won't be seen or heard. One of my men is staying with Taffy Turner two doors away and he has the door open so he can listen and act if necessary."

"Lafe, I'm going to tell you something and give you a piece of advice . . . if you ask for it," the banker said earnestly. "I did something for you last night and early this morning . . . I am doing something for you this very minute that I wouldn't do for any other man on earth, bar none!"

"Well, now, Henry, I sure appreciate that. And I've asked your advice more'n once and never refused to listen to you. And I hope you haven't been doin' anything for me that you wouldn't have me do for you."

"I don't know," the banker considered doubtfully. "In the first place, I've been stealing around, you might say, eavesdropping for you ever since you were in my office. That's not so good."

"In a way it isn't," Lafe agreed. "You're right there, Henry. And then, in a way it is. You see, what you find out might help you to prevent trouble around these parts. Trouble wouldn't be so good for your bank, would it? Suppose we take a business slant at this, Henry, and let the personal side of it slide."

"Just what I'm doin'," said Brower. "Just why I'm doing what I am." He spoke as if he was trying to convince himself as much as to impress the stockman. "Right now I'm practically violating a business confidence, although important bank business might come before you sooner or later as you are one of our directors. You were right, Lafe, when you said there was a scheme afoot. Now I'm not going to tell you how I got my information or where from, but this I know. Bolten is going to do everything in his power to split the range!"

"He started some time ago," Lafe observed dryly. "I expect that all the events that have taken place since I came to town were sort of planned in advance."

"Exactly," Brower confirmed. "You know Fresee was in the bank when you and Larry were there and I expect he heard what was said, although I can't see how it would do him any good merely to know that Larry can draw money when he needs it. Of course, he went out when Larry left the office and couldn't know what you and I talked about. But just the same I was approached in an effort to ascertain where I would stand if trouble arose."

"Neutral, of course," said Lafe promptly. "I don't expect you to take any chances with your business on my account, Henry."

"It would have to be that way, Lafe. I don't own that bank, as you know, and I cannot take chances with the investments of my stockholders or our depositors' money. I guess everybody would understand that the bank could not afford, morally nor legally, to be drawn into any controversy. Now, listen . . ." The banker leaned forward and tapped Lafe Owens on the knee. "Bolten is organizing the ranchers on the east end of the range to back him to a man for president of the Cattlemen's Association at the meeting the first of the month."

44

"Well," said Lafe, "it's underhanded work, in a way, but I suppose it's his right. The only kick I've got coming is because he doesn't work in the open."

"What's more," Brower went on, "he has sent word around for a secret meeting of the east-enders for tomorrow night."

"That's goin' too far!" exclaimed Lafe angrily.

"Just a minute," Brower warned. "Now don't fly off the handle, Lafe. You'll be roaring mad when you hear what's coming next but hold your head and keep cool." He continued to tap the stockman's knee as if to steady him. "If Bolten doesn't get the election, he's going to try to split the Association and form another organization for the east end!"

Lafe Owens knocked the hand from his knee, but Brower caught him as he was getting to his feet.

"By the . . ." Then the big man sputtered in a rage. "All aimed at me!" he cried with an oath. "Well, let me tell you one thing, Henry Brower, I'm goin' to be at that secret meeting! I'll show that sneaking, double-crossing . . ." It was impossible for him to go on, so consuming was his wrath. The scheme now was laid bare.

"I wouldn't go to their meeting, Lafe," said Brower quietly.

"No?" stormed the stockman. "You'd let him try to pull a thing like this and me sit and twiddle my thumbs? Not by a—"

"Just a minute," the banker interrupted, "don't you see that, if you were to put in an appearance, it would bring matters to a head at once? You would be bound to

45

have your say, and I know you well enough to know that you'd say it in such a way that none would be liable to misunderstand you. It —"

"That's my style," Lafe broke in. "I'm no bush-beater."

"But there is a possibility that all the east-end stockmen are not convinced that Bolten is the best man for president of the Association, and are dubious . . . or would be . . . of any plan to form another organization. Those are the men you do not want to offend. You want to keep them on your side. They might think you were brow-beating them as well as the others . . . I'm talking plain, Lafe . . . and it would only make matters worse by helping Bolten."

"You were always a plausible cuss," grumbled Lafe. "I was thinking just before you came up of goin' straight to Jim Bolten in private and putting it up to him square between the eyes, but that might look as if he had me groggy."

"I wouldn't do that, either," said Brower. "It might, as you say, be construed as showing weakness. Any time you should want my advice, Lafe, I'll be glad to tell you what I would do in your place."

The banker took out a cigar and carefully bit off the end. Lafe Owens fidgeted in his chair while the other applied his light.

"Well, let's have it," he said irritably at last. "You know I'm curious enough to ask it sooner or later, anyway."

"I'd lay low," said Brower without hesitation. "I wouldn't let on to Bolten that I knew a thing or cared a

**46**

whoop if I did. But . . ." Brower regarded the glowing end of his cigar thoughtfully . . . "I'd mix around the west-end crowd all I could and, in a way, get things lined up."

"You mean it's necessary for me to start organizing, too?" demanded Lafe in amazement. "Why, I'm solid as a rock on my side of the fence. I made this range, Henry."

The banker shrugged. "That may all be, but matters have been running smoothly for a long time now and, when men are . . . ah . . . contented, imbued with a sense of security, they are apt to be lax in many ways . . . open to argument, for instance."

Lafe Owens laughed. "Henry, do you mean to say that you think Bolten would have a chance to promote himself in the west end?" he asked scornfully.

"Why not?" Brower retorted shortly. "You're not doing anything so far as anybody can see. Just taking it for granted . . . in a superior way, at that! . . . that you'll be elected again. Somebody might trick you and think it was a good joke. I'd look after my fences, just the same. I'd meet Bolten at his own game. But all this is merely my opinion . . . what I believe I'd do. I've never played range politics . . . can't afford to. I've told you what I know and now I've got to go, Lafe."

# CHAPTER
# SIX

Larry Owens had noted the long absence of his father and he decided to go out and have a look around. He headed for the hotel where he thought he might find him. As he neared the hotel, a shot rang out from the direction of the livery near at hand. Larry stopped short. This was bad business, for the sheriff had issued a strict mandate against the use of firearms as a means of noise-making. He had caused this order to be posted conspicuously in the resorts and other public places. As the youth was considering this, another shot broke above the other sounds of carnival. He started on a run for the livery, and, as he reached it, a figure danced in the lantern light flooding the entrance.

Larry leaped forward as he recognized the stranger who had styled himself as one of the Joneses. "Put up that gun, you fool!" he cried, seizing Jones by his right arm and wrestling the weapon from his grasp. "You'll have a flock of deputies on your back in a wink and the next thing you know you'll be in the cooler."

The other staggered back and Larry was amazed to see that he was unmistakably drunk. So soon? He had been sober, clear-eyed, alert in the dance pavilion. Had he deliberately gone out and got thoroughly drunk?

"My gun's for hire!" shouted Jones loudly. "Got to advertise and . . . show . . . off my wares." He leaned forward and stared intently at the astonished Larry. "Why, it's our frien' with the sis-sister!"

The liveryman approached hurriedly.

"How'd he get here?" Larry asked him bluntly.

"Wanted to see his horse. I knew he had some inside him, but I didn't know he had such a skinfull as all this."

"My gun's for hire!" came the thick exclamation again from Jones, steadying himself on Larry's arm.

"Shut up!" Larry commanded. "There! Somebody's coming! Tell 'em you don't know a thing, Ross," he said quickly to the liveryman. "Steer 'em away. I'm going to take care of this fellow since he says he doesn't know anybody here."

As he was talking, he pushed Jones back into the barn to the stall where his own horse was quartered. He spoke to the animal and entered the stall, dragging Jones and keeping a hand closed over his mouth so he couldn't shout. He could hear the sound of voices in the front of the barn. Jones struggled futilely and the voices died away. Suddenly Jones went limp in Larry's arms.

"Told 'em some fool 'puncher got gay and I kicked him out," said the liveryman, coming up as Larry got his burden out of the stall.

"He's all in," said Larry wonderingly. "Got it mighty quick. Looks to me, Ross, as if this fellow wasn't used to prairie likker. What're we going to do with him?"

"I'll put him up in the office in front. There's a bunk in there. Looks like a good sort and got a hoss that's a sight for any kind of eyes."

Larry suddenly made up his mind. "We'll take him in the hotel by the back door and up to my room. Said he was a stranger and everything points to it. If I was caught in the same fix, I'd sure appreciate somebody doing as much for me. Help me along with him."

Some minutes later Larry stood, surveying the figure of the stranger on his bed. He had taken off the heavy gun belt and pulled off the man's shoes.

"What a head he'll have when he comes out of it," Larry muttered aloud, and turned to the door just as one of the KT men who had been sitting up with the injured Taffy Turner appeared.

The man was greatly excited. "Larry!" he exclaimed in a hoarse whisper. "Come and look. Something's happened to Taffy!"

Larry pushed past him and turned into the room where the old cowpuncher lay. One look at the cold blue features, pinched and set, and Larry hastened to feel the pulse and listened with his ear against the breast.

His face was white as he drew back. "Run downstairs! Get Dad, the doctor, Sam Daniels, anybody . . . Taffy Turner's dead!"

Shock and the weight of years had done for Taffy Turner, the doctor told the little group that quickly assembled in the room. Yes, the loss of the eye, the attendant pain and perhaps an unexpected effect of the opiates, were prime causes. But Taffy had lived a

50

strenuous life, he was a very old man — none knew his exact age — and he might be expected to go in some way such as this. Thus the man of medicine disposed of the case. But not the members of the KT outfit.

Taffy Turner had been murdered and Bloat Simpson had started the events leading up to Taffy's demise. This decision sobered the men. The news of Taffy's death spread with incredible swiftness and soon the KT crew was gathered to a man in front of the hotel.

"Don't be severe with them," Lafe Owens told Stan Velie. "But they've got to keep their heads, and it won't do any good for them to hang around the hotel. Everything's over here. Tell 'em for me that, if they start anything, it'll only make things worse and the old man wants 'em to keep cool."

Lafe Owens's face was pale and had set in stern lines. The death of his oldest employee, a man who had been loyal through the long years of hardship and struggle before the dawn of a peaceful prosperity affected him greatly. It wasn't as if an ordinary cowhand had died or been killed; it was losing an old friend.

Larry hurried to the dance pavilion for the womenfolk. It wouldn't do for the Owens family to be making merry at a time such as this, as if they would want to! When he was leaving with his mother and sister, Mary O'Neil having left sometime before, Jane Bolten slipped to his side and put a hand on his arm. She drew him into a shadow of the building.

"I'm so sorry, Larry," she told him in a low, earnest voice, reaching up to put her hands on his shoulders.

"Honestly I am, Larry. It's just as if old Taffy had been one of our own men. And . . . Larry, I didn't mean to quarrel with you . . . tonight."

He brought her hands down within his own warm grasp. "Are you telling me this just because poor Taffy had to go?"

"Why . . . I had to tell you that I feel sorry," she evaded.

"But, Jane, listen to me a minute," he said tremulously. "We are both sorry about Taffy. It's too bad that he had to suffer because of the . . . the feeling that seems to have sprung up between our outfits. It isn't just because ours are the two largest outfits, and naturally rivals. There seems to be . . . oh, I can't explain it. But nothing that could happen would make any difference to us . . . you and me . . . would it, Jane?"

"Larry, I don't understand you," she answered calmly.

He tightened his grasp of her hands. "I mean, Jane, that if our outfits should get to fighting, if there should be real trouble on the range, we wouldn't let it interfere with our . . . our friendship, would we?"

"You're so mysterious, Larry. Our outfits have fought before. Why should a fight start trouble on the range? Don't be foolish. I know all our men will be sorry because of what has happened and won't want any more trouble."

"But you don't understand," said Larry desperately. "And I can't tell you because I do not understand it all myself. Only I can feel it coming. There is going to be trouble, Jane, and I don't want it to come between us."

Jane's eyes were wide and luminous as she looked up at him under the fading stars. Her hair trembled in the light breeze of approaching dawn. Her soft cheeks and glorious lips were close to him. He forgot and folded her in his arms, holding her tightly, and kissed her.

It seemed an eternity before she struggled free, her face flushed, eyes dark, her lips parted. She clenched her palms and there was a breathless moment of indecision. "You shouldn't have done that, Larry," she said quietly. And before he could speak she was gone.

Larry hurried to overtake his mother and sister and escort them to the hotel. He was dazed by the abruptness of his act. In the antithesis of feeling that followed he found himself experiencing no thrill of realization or of memory. What had happened to him in that impetuous moment? Why, he didn't love Jane in the least! What had come over him? He had shown himself to be a fool and, what was worse, a silly cad. Jane had resented his overt act in just the dignified way to put him thoroughly in his place, shelved and labeled. He would feel a sense of shame, rather than guilt, every time he saw her in the future.

When he got back to the hotel and up to his room, he found the stranger was sleeping peacefully. The white curtain fluttered at the window. All was quiet. His folks had gone to bed. Two of the men would be in the room with Taffy. Everything seemed strange —

changed. In a few hours the celebration had turned to tragedy. In a few hours more?

He threw his hat on the bureau, took off his coat, pulled off his boots, and lay down beside Harry-From-Nowhere. It was a peculiar coincidence that he could think of nothing save the look in Jane Bolten's eyes when she had gazed into his own after he had kissed her, could think of nothing else until he fell asleep.

The room was flooded with sunlight when he woke. He sat up, rubbing his eyes, staring. But in a moment he remembered. It was Jones, sitting there in the chair, looking at him through a veil of cigarette smoke. Jones nodded coolly, continuing to gaze at him curiously.

"How do you feel?" Larry inquired with a scowl, swinging to the edge of the bed.

"Who hit me?" Jones asked coolly.

"What . . . say? The old White Demon hit you and knocked you out. It was the hay or jail for you, and I brought you up here out of the goodness of my heart. Man, you were drunk. Popping off your six-gun in front of the livery barn against the sheriff's pet order. I shoved you into a stall in time to beat the deputies to an arrest. Liveryman steered 'em away. Then you passed out cold."

"Thanks," said Jones dryly. "Reckon I'd have done the same for you."

"I had some such idea in the back of my head. You said you were a stranger, or words to that effect, and I took it on myself to look after you. Where'd you get it so quickly?"

Jones waved a hand. "Where can't you get it around here?" he countered with a faint smile. Then he frowned. "I was lonesome."

"Well, from what I saw, you didn't have to leave the dance for company. You had 'em all interested with that Harry-From-Nowhere line."

"Yeah?" Jones grinned. "Comes just about being a true line, at that," he said, sobering. "And I can't stand much fire-water. It isn't in my line. I noticed my gun was empty when I found it on the stand there this morning."

"You emptied it, all right, and wanted to rent it," said Larry, looking at the other keenly. "What was the idea in saying your gun was for hire?"

"Did I say that?" Jones inquired blandly.

"You didn't say it," Larry snorted, pulling on his boots, "you shouted it. You wanted the world to hear."

"*Humph*. White Demon you mention must have been talking. Let it pass. I'm much obliged to you, just the same, Owens. Oh, I learned your name and something about you, which was no more than to be expected."

"You know more about me than I know about you," Larry accused.

The other rose, drew his gun, and loaded it leisurely. Then he twirled it, dropped it in his holster, and drew again, this time with such lightning rapidity that Larry gasped at the exhibition.

"Testing my nerves," drawled Jones, sheathing his weapon. "They're not so bad, although I can feel their edges. A few cups of strong coffee will fix me up. Yes, I know more about you than you know about me." He eyed Larry speculatively. "But that isn't my fault. You're well known around here. People talk about you and your outfit. How's that old codger who got hurt yesterday?"

"He's dead."

Jones whistled softly. "That'll make it bad, won't it?"

"What makes you think so?" Larry demanded angrily. He didn't like the air of mystery about the man, nor did he fancy the display of overwhelming confidence.

"I circulated some last night," Jones confessed. "Heard a lot of words passed. They didn't all pass over my head. Things on this range aren't any too smooth, I take it. This'll make it worse. Let me tip you off to watch that big blow-hard from the Double B outfit."

"Shucks!" exclaimed Larry in disgust. "Look here, Jones, I don't want to seem to be trying to pry into your affairs, but you say you don't know anybody here, and . . . well, now you know me. Can't you tell me something about yourself?"

"Harry Jones from somewhere south. That's all I can tell you now, Owens . . . on the level. It's as much as anybody else knows about me. Perhaps, later on . . . But you did me a favor last night, and I'm thanking you. Understand? I really appreciate it and I'd be poor tripe not to. Any time I can repay you . . ."

"Don't mention it," Larry broke in, putting on his coat. "If you're around, I'll see you later."

"Fair enough," said Jones as he went out.

Lafe Owens made it clear at noon that so far as the KT was concerned the rodeo was over. The men received the mandate in silence and without objection. They were to take Taffy Turner back to the ranch that afternoon for burial in the bottoms behind the ranch house.

Sheriff Rowan sought out Lafe at the hotel. "What did you want me to do, Lafe?" he asked.

"Do?" The stockman's gaze was cool between narrowed lids. "I don't want you to do anything. Nothing at all, understand?" He said it in a voice that sent the official away with a worried look in his eyes.

Jim Bolten and his foreman, Fresee, wisely stayed away. In the mid-afternoon a procession passed down the main street at Pondera. Lafe Owens and his family, and the men of the KT outfit, rode behind a spring wagon on which rested a box with a single wreath of flowers held secure by a branding iron. The tumultuous voice of the carnival was momentarily stilled. The crowd stood uncovered. There was only the sound of horses' hoofs, pounding a dirge into the dust of the street.

Henry Brower stood at the window of his bank, his face white, listening to the silent thunder of invisible guns. He alone, perhaps, understood the grim, frozen expression on Lafe Owens's face.

# CHAPTER
# SEVEN

They buried Taffy Turner under the weaving cottonwoods next morning. The minister had ridden out from town to conduct the service. Brother Van, as this prairie man of the cloth was known, admonished the men for wearing their guns at the ceremony. "Just a matter of form," Lafe Owens had told him, but Lafe was uneasy in his mind just the same.

After dinner, Lafe and Stan Velie went into conference in the little ranch office at the front of the great, rambling ranch house. They were closeted together for an hour. When they came out, the foreman hurried to the barn and ordered his horse and Lafe's mount saddled. Five minutes afterward, Lafe Owens and his foreman rode swiftly away in the direction of Pondera.

Half an hour after his father's departure, Larry Owens, grim-faced, determined, also was riding across the sun-burned plain to westward. On this ride he was wearing his gun. The sun was poised for its drop behind the western mountains when Larry rode into town. He avoided the main street and took a roundabout way to reach the livery. He did not wish to see his father until he had had a chance to look about a little and perhaps ascertain the purpose of Lafe Owens's visit.

As he took charge of Larry's horse, Ed Ross peered at him curiously. "Didn't expect to see you in today," he ventured.

"No?" Larry appeared surprised. "Why not, Ed?"

"Oh . . . just a notion, I reckon," Ross replied in confusion.

Larry felt puzzled by the man's manner. When he reached the crowded street, the first person he met who he knew was Jones.

"Hello!" the strange youth greeted, stopping in his tracks. "C'mon with me, Owens. I want to see you."

"What's up now?" Larry asked, scowling.

"Let's get off the street," said Jones quickly, grasping Larry's arm. "Too many people, too many ears. Here, we'll lose ourselves in this place."

He turned into a resort that was seething with hilarious humanity. "We'll slide along back," he told Larry, and began pushing through the crowd.

A man at a gaming table tipped back his chair just in time to come in contact with Jones's surge forward. Jones veered and Larry caught the back of the player's chair, preventing the man from falling backward. It was all the work of an instant, but the man leaped to his feet in a flash. As he did so, Jones and Larry were separated by the chair, and the player confronted Larry alone.

"Oh, see who's here!" roared the player in a thick, hoarse voice. "The rah-rah boy! Goin' to tip me over, eh?"

Larry bit his lip with vexation. The speaker, by the most unexpected of all coincidences, was Bloat Simpson. Larry caught sight of Jones struggling to reach him, shaking his head wildly. Larry had no desire for an encounter with the Double B bully. He tried to step aside, but those nearby had heard Simpson's bellowing voice and had crowded forward to see what was going on. He was hemmed in. When the crowd recognized him, a silence fell over that portion of the big room.

"I wasn't trying to tip you," said Larry coldly. "I merely caught your chair to save you from a fall."

As he was speaking, Larry's gaze wandered about and he met the cold gleam of Fresee's eyes across the table. One word from the Double B foreman would end the altercation. But the word did not come. Fresee's lips tightened against his teeth in a mean grin.

"Yeah?" sneered Simpson. "Sure you wasn't goin' to help me over, playboy? I've a good notion, now there's a chance for a square deal, to hand you a good spanking!"

The crowd started to back away, jamming against tables and causing a general uproar. Larry had seen Bloat Simpson's gaze fasten on the weapon he wore. During the altercation of the day before, Larry had not been armed. As he heard Simpson's last words hissed hoarsely, his face went white.

"I don't want trouble with you, Simpson," he said, striving to keep anger out of his voice. "So we'd best let well enough alone."

"Yeah?" Simpson thrust his leering face close. "You don't want trouble when you ain't got your gang behind you, eh? You're yellow! Give us your college cheer or dance, you son-of-a-bitch."

As the epithet came from the coarse lips, Larry drove it back with a slap that echoed in the place like a pistol shot. He saw Jones leaping toward Simpson, saw two orbs that blazed red fire, heard the snarl, and caught the move in the other's eyes. The room rocked to the blast of guns. Larry leaned to the left and Jones caught his arm, jerking him away as Bloat Simpson went down, sending a wild shot into the hanging lamp that rained glass on the frantic crowd.

"Out the back!" Jones yelled in his ear.

They pushed through the crowd, Larry unwittingly keeping his gun in his hand and striking out with it as they struggled free of the jam. They squeezed through the open rear door and Jones started on a run behind the buildings with Larry following.

"Make for the barn!" cried Jones.

They dashed between two buildings, and, as they reached the street, the thunder of pounding hoofs came from just below them. Then they were caught in a maëlstrom of pedestrians in full flight to avoid a score of horsemen speeding through the dust. Larry recognized the KT riders, arriving in town to a man!

"That's your outfit, isn't it?" Jones shouted in Larry's ear above the din.

Larry nodded. Events had taken place with such startling rapidity that he was dazed. He thrust the gun he still held into its sheath and caught his breath with the realization that he had probably killed Bloat Simpson. This left him cool; his brain cleared as if by magic. Simpson had forced the issue and left him no alternative but to protect his own life.

"Come along!" cried Jones hoarsely as he grasped Larry by the arm and pushed through the crowd into the dust of the street. "The best place to get right now is the barn where your men are going."

This struck Larry as sensible and as good a move as any for the time being. They ran up the street, plunging through the cloud of dust that trailed the KT riders. Looking over his shoulder, Larry saw men running after them. His face hardened and his eyes glinted. They reached the barn as the KT men were dismounting.

"He's shot Bloat Simpson!" Jones called.

A tall, blond cowpuncher was the man to take immediate command of the situation. "In the barn, Larry!" he ordered. "Out in front, boys, here they come. Larry's shot Bloat!"

The men all had heard Jones's shout and they understood their leader's order without any need of further explanation. Ed Ross and his helper, with one of the cowpunchers, were hurrying the horses into the barn to lead them out the rear into the corral. The street was in turmoil with a great crowd hurrying in the wake of a dozen men, led by Fresee, the Double B foreman.

The KT outfit quickly gathered in front of the barn entrance. The Double B men were coming from the street, while others were closing in from either side behind the buildings. The air was a bedlam of shouts and yells as cowpunchers and other men of the range rushed to witness what promised to be a deadly clash between the two biggest outfits in the territory.

Fresee was well ahead of the men who followed him. As he drew close, Larry pushed through the KT phalanx. "Let me handle this, Blondy," he said sternly to the cowboy leader. "See that the bunch keeps their guns where they belong."

He stepped forward as Fresee came to a halt. Jones moved up to Larry's left elbow. Instead of the hot words Larry expected to flow from Fresee's mouth, the Double B foreman turned on his own men and held up his right hand, palm outward.

"Take it easy, boys!" His words were sharp and clear with the force of command. "No rough stuff. Keep your hands off your guns!" He turned about with his men muttering angrily behind him. Instead of addressing Larry, he looked directly at Jones. "You get out of here!" he ordered peremptorily, waving a hand as if to dismiss the stranger automatically, and finally.

"Huh?" Jones shot the word in a way that caused Larry to look at him quickly. Larry was startled by the change in Jones's expression. His eyes had narrowed, his face set. He stepped in front of Larry to confront Fresee.

"You prodding me?" he asked. Before Larry could start a move to prevent it, Jones's right hand flickered at his side and his gun covered Fresee. "You leave me out of it," he said curtly. "Just make your little talk and forget about me being here, if you don't like it. It happens I'm goin' to stay, you four-flusher, and, if you don't like it, you can lump it . . . it's all the same to me."

Fresee's face had gone white — not with fear of the menacing gun, but with anger. His lips tightened to a white line and his eyes flashed ominously. "This man belong here?" he asked Larry, striving to hold his composure.

"A new hand," said Larry with sudden inspiration, touching Jones on the arm. "You better order your men off, Fresee. We've had trouble enough." He put his left hand on Jones's gun, pushing it down toward its holster.

"I'm givin' you your orders!" flared Fresee, momentarily losing control of himself. "Just because that old pensioner of yours got the worst of it in a fight he started himself, you come prancing into town to get even. You've killed Bloat, and, if you've got any sense in that soft head of yours, you'll beat it fast . . . and take your outfit with you!"

"You're not giving any orders, Fresee, and we're not leaving town because of any threat of yours," Larry retorted coolly, looking about at the great circle of spectators. "I shot Bloat in self-defense and you know it. You could have stopped the fuss if you'd wanted to."

"I suppose I could have stopped Bloat after you tried to spill him on the floor and make a fool of him," jeered Fresee. "You wanted gun play and you had your hand on your gun when you started things."

"That's a sweet lie!" Jones put in with a short laugh.

**64**

Fresee's lips were white and trembling with rage. "It's a scheme to get our outfits tangled up again!" he shouted at Larry. "Well, you're not goin' to do it! I've ordered my men to lay off. You can't start trouble with the Double B, for I won't let you!"

Lafe Owens, Stan Velie, the sheriff, and a number of deputies arrived on the run and burst through the crowd just in time to hear Larry Owens's ringing reply to the Double B foreman.

"You should have ordered your men to lay off in the first place." He was standing squarely in front of Fresee. "You framed the first fight and you let this thing go through this afternoon when you could have stopped it with a word. I saw you grinning at the table where Bloat was playing when he jumped me. Now that there's people around that can hear you blat, you're trying to crawfish. I'm calling the turn! If you don't want trouble, keep your men in hand, or send 'em back to the ranch. The KT isn't starting trouble, but if you want it, we're not running away!"

In the silence that followed this speech, the murmurs of approval from the KT men were clearly heard. Larry Owens and Fresee stood in the center of the semicircle with their men at their backs. All about were strained faces. Then came a series of exclamations as Jim Bolten stepped forward dramatically, waving an arm at Fresee.

"Clear out!" he commanded sharply. "Take the men away." He turned to Larry. "Listen, you young whippersnapper," he said, his face dark with anger, "if you wasn't a brainless kid, I wouldn't overlook what you've just said. But don't forget you've just killed one

**65**

of my men. You seem to overlook that. There's such a thing as going too far on this range, and you've got one foot over the line. If you get the other one over, I won't be responsible."

"I stand behind what I said," Larry retorted stoutly.

"Will you shut up and get out of here?" roared Bolten.

"Just a minute, Jim," came a drawling voice. "I reckon this is public range." It was Lafe Owens who had spoken, and he waved Larry and the members of the KT outfit back. "Maybe you better talk to me," Lafe added as Bolten faced him in a fury.

"You're not deaf!" thundered the Double B owner. "You heard what was said and you know what's happened. If this is a trick of yours, Lafe Owens, it's the dirtiest piece of work ever seen on this range!"

"If it's a trick, I reckon I'll play it through, Jim," said Lafe calmly. "I guess you're excited. From what I hear, Bloat Simpson got just what was comin' to him and I'm standing behind Larry."

Sheriff Rowan stood by helplessly. It wasn't his part to interfere with this face-to-face meeting in the open between the two cattle kings of the Teton. But he saw the reopening of the Owens-Bolten feud and the splitting of the range being enacted before his very eyes.

Jim Bolten realized at once that with Lafe Owens taking the matter with composure, holding his temper and keeping cool, he was making a favorable impression. For Bolten had one eye on the spectators who were watching this drama. He therefore waved a hand as if to dismiss the part Larry had played that afternoon.

"I expect you to stand behind your son and your men. Right or wrong." He looked quickly at the sheriff.

"We won't argue that part of it, Jim," said Lafe. "It looks as if our outfits couldn't get along this trip. Have you noticed it?"

Bolten's brows wrinkled for a moment in perplexity. "What're you gettin' at now?" he demanded, his lips curling slightly.

"I'm thinking we ought to keep them separated, since they seem to be a little heated up," Lafe explained. "Suppose you keep your men on the south side of the street and I'll try to keep mine on the north side." There was a flicker of a smile on Lafe's face.

Bolten stared at him. Then his anger blazed forth again as one or two of the spectators laughed. "Are you aiming to make a fool out of me?" he cried, taking a step toward the older stockman.

"Stop right where you are, Jim Bolten!" came Lafe's stern command. "Larry spoke the truth! Your men have been wanting trouble with the KT ever since we came to town yesterday morning. That sneaking foreman of yours" — he pointed to Fresee, who was sneering openly — "made Bloat Simpson the goat on your side. You're overlooking the fact, it seems to me, that I've also lost a man, and Taffy Turner was worth a hundred of Simpson's stamp! I'm not trying to make any fool out of you. I'm giving you a chance to show some sense. If you want to prevent further trouble, keep your men on the south side of the street. I guess I can still guarantee that my men will obey my orders."

Jim Bolten saw that the issue had been squarely put up to him. In the matter of diplomacy he could not hope to match Lafe's cleverness. Yet this realization only served to increase his anger. He looked about, undecided as to his next step. Then his gaze riveted on Jones.

"Who is that man?" he demanded. "He threw his gun on my foreman and I've a right to ask."

Lafe looked at Jones, but it was Larry who replied to the Double B owner's question.

"I told your foreman he was a new hand," he said quietly. "That's enough for him. I'll tell you, he's a friend of mine. He was with me when Bloat started his ruckus."

"You hear that?" shouted Bolten, shaking a forefinger at Lafe. "An accomplice! Another young gunfighter! The two of 'em makin' sport with hot lead! Now who's startin' the trouble?" Even as the words came from his mouth, Bolten sensed their lack of logic. He had spoken foolishly and the thought maddened him.

Lafe Owens was smiling. Many of the spectators were smiling with him. "That doesn't sound like sense, Jim," he said amiably. "I have no gunfighters in my employ. If any of my men can handle their guns right smart, it's something I never asked them about or took notice of. There hasn't been any occasion . . . our range being peaceful."

He stepped toward the KT men, knowing that he had made his point and turned the edge of Bolten's accusation. "Listen!" His right hand went up as he addressed his men. Spectators craned their necks to see and strained their ears to listen. "I order you men to stay on the north side of the street. That's the side you're on now. Do not cross! Those of you who intend to obey this order, hold up your hands."

There was a tense interval, fraught with excitement and expectancy from the big crowd. Then the blond leader chuckled aloud and raised his hand. As if it were an awaited signal, every KT hand went up.

"That's all!" sang Lafe Owens in a voice of triumph. "My men will keep their word, Bolten. So far as the KT is concerned, our little misunderstanding is over."

He waved a hand in dismissal to his men and deliberately turned his back on Jim Bolten.

The Double B owner swore. He whirled on Fresee. "Back to the ranch!" he roared. "Every one of you . . . just as fast as horse and leather can take you. I don't want a Double B man in town at sundown. That's my order and I don't need any raising of hands. Beat it!"

Then he, too, strode from the scene, leaving the sheriff and deputies to watch the outfits separate and the crowd dissolve. But every stockman in Pondera knew the damage had been done.

# CHAPTER
# EIGHT

Larry Owens took Jones into the little front office of the livery barn. "It's a showdown," he told the stranger who had so unexpectedly injected himself into the troubled affairs of the KT. "You heard what my dad and Jim Bolten had to say to each other and I guess you can listen between the lines. It's war sure enough from this very minute, and they've got it in for you proper. I saw that in Fresee's eyes, plain as the nose on his face. I don't want you to get mixed up in this business on my account. Maybe you better . . ." He paused, studying the look Jones gave him.

"Better what?" drawled Jones, rolling a cigarette.

"Well, if you hang around here, you're going to run up against the real thing sooner or later," said Larry rather lamely. He was beginning to like this stranger — and the way he could draw a gun!

"Say, listen here," said Jones with a scowl. "What was your idea in tellin' that Double B foreman I was a new hand?"

"So he couldn't say you were just butting in," Larry retorted bluntly. "There had to be some reason for your siding with our crowd."

"All right. Just let it stand as it is."

Larry shook his head. "It won't work. And it'll make it all the worse for you when they find out we tricked 'em. You don't know that outfit as I do. Fresee picks his men for toughness in the first place and sticks behind 'em no matter what happens."

"Fair enough." Jones smiled. "Maybe it's time you folks started pickin' men the same way. You made the statement publicly that I was a new hand. Now I'm holding you to your word. You're licked, Owens."

Larry flushed angrily. "I said what I did for your own protection."

"And now you're asking me to beat it?" said Jones pointedly.

"If you do, that will also probably be for your own good."

"But if I don't beat it . . . that's the point. I'm not the kind that wishes trouble on himself and then runs away. If I hadn't known you were up against a frame-up, I wouldn't have meddled in this business. I was going to warn you when I asked you to come with me. I'd heard some of the Double B bunch talkin' and I heard this Bloat party declaring himself this morning. How you goin' to get away from that?"

Jones had talked fast, looking Larry squarely in the eyes. Larry was nonplussed. If this were true — and he had no cause to doubt the other's word — Jones had become involved while trying to do him a favor. But there was no place for another man on the ranch with winter coming on. No stockman would think of hiring at the start of the long dull season. Larry found himself in a real predicament.

"I appreciate what you did, Jones," he said. "I didn't intend to be sharp about things. Maybe I shouldn't have told Fresee what I did. In fact, we wouldn't think of taking on a man just before winter, and I don't know as I've any right to hire a hand in the first place, although I guess Dad would stand behind me."

Jones's smile came instantly. "That's straight talk," he said, holding out a hand that Larry took with relief. "Tell you what you do. You let things stand as they are at present." His eyes became several shades darker. "Fact is, I need an excuse for being around here besides the rodeo because I may want to stay a while after it's over. I can say I came up here looking for work and found it. You don't have to put me on any payroll. Is that all right?"

"It'll have to be," Larry decided on the spur of the moment. "We'll let it go at that, then." It was not until some time afterward that Larry wondered why Jones would need an excuse for being in Pondera.

A number of men came trooping into the barn, talking loudly, some cursing. Then came Fresee's sharp, commanding voice.

"You can take everything back with you that you want and finish up in the bunkhouse, but you're goin' back if you're goin' to hang on at the Double B. Curse your thick heads off, but you're mindin' orders as long as I'm bossin' this outfit!"

The men stamped on through the barn to get their horses out of the stalls or the corrals. They were grumbling and swearing because they had to leave the celebration; none answered Fresee's dictum. It was evident that his word was law, but his tone also betrayed his own dissatisfaction with Jim Bolten's order. Perhaps he thought it looked too much like giving in to the KT, especially after Bolten had been routed in the play of words before the crowd.

As Larry and Jones left the barn office, Fresee was standing alone a short distance away. He whirled on them and his eyes burned with malice. Both Larry and Jones ignored him and this was too much. For once Fresee lost his wily composure. He drew a cartridge from his belt and caught Larry by the arm. Before Larry sensed what he was about, he had pressed the cartridge into his hand.

"Give your new gunman my card!" sneered Fresee.

Quick as a wink, Jones grabbed the cartridge from Larry's hand and threw it in Fresee's face. "There's your receipt!"

"And here's yours!" yelled Fresee. His right hand whipped back before he was yanked backward, hitting the barn floor with a crash. Jones's gun was glinting in the subdued light in the barn. Fresee's gun was in his holster. Larry and Jones were both staring at the tall, soldierly figure of a man who had appeared on the scene as if by magic and had jerked Fresee back at the very instant of his attempted draw. It was Stan Velie.

But it was a new KT foreman who faced them and looked down at Fresee. The latter lay motionless upon the barn floor, staring upward with a look of incredulity in his snapping eyes.

"Get up!" Velie commanded. "You won't look very good before your men in that position." The Double B outfit was trooping back into the rear of the barn as Fresee rose to his feet, a queer smile on his lips.

"I'm sure thankin' you, Velie," he got out. "I lost my head after all that's happened today . . . and havin' my outfit ordered back to the ranch, and . . ." He turned a mean eye on Jones. "This fellow drew on me outside. Have you taken him on?"

"You are not to ask me questions," said Velie in a voice none present ever had heard him use. "From where I was standing, I heard and saw everything. There's no question as to who started this. I saved you from killing a man where you couldn't plead self-defense. You thanked me and we'll let the matter drop there. If you don't want to let it drop, you'll have to go at it with me!"

Fresee's eyes glinted, then, suddenly to the astonishment of all, he smiled. "I guess, Stan," he said amiably, calling Velie by his first name for the first time, "we've all put on enough of a show for today. So long." He waved to the Double B men gathering in the barn. "On our way, boys!" he shouted, and left with a little, smirking bow.

The men obeyed, and Stan Velie turned to Larry and Jones. "Your father wants to see both of you upstairs in the hotel, right away," he told Larry in his usual quiet, incisive voice. The old Velie had returned.

"That foreman of yours is some bear-cat," said Jones to Larry as they left the barn. "And if I hadn't seen him in time and known what he was goin' to do, Mister Bolten would be looking for a brand new foreman."

74

"I suppose so," Larry returned dully. He was marveling at what he had seen, the extraordinary and unprecedented change in Stan Velie. Had the man been drunk? But Velie didn't drink at all to speak of. And how had Fresee lost his head? Had he deliberately sought an opportunity to kill Jones? Larry smiled, remembering Jones's draw. Yet the memory of that draw and what Fresee had said about the "new gunman" worried Larry no little.

They entered silently the room where Lafe Owens awaited them. Larry was startled at the look his father gave him. It was as if the old gentleman was seeing him for the first time. In that glance were commingled curiosity, conjecture, perplexity, and perhaps a very small measure of self-reproach. But there was no deliberate admiration, no hint of censure, no remorse. Lafe turned away, staring at the checked cloth of the table. There were two other chairs in the room, a bed, bureau, washstand. It was just one of the ordinary rooms in the old hotel.

"Sit down," Lafe invited.

Larry and Jones sat down, conscious of a strange atmosphere in the room; it was almost electrical. Lafe had turned his back on them, but now he turned suddenly and his face was gray.

"How do you feel, Larry?" he asked in a throaty voice.

"Why . . ." Larry hesitated, and then realized like a flash what his father meant. "I'd rather not answer now," he said stoutly. "I haven't had time to think."

Lafe Owens shook his great white head slowly. "It's a serious business to kill a man, Larry," he said huskily.

"I'm ready to take the consequences," bristled Larry. "I've proof —"

"Oh, they won't even indict you," his father broke in impatiently. "Everyone knows Bloat was on your trail, and a good many of our own crowd saw what happened in there. It isn't that I mean, but just how does it feel to know in your heart that you have taken a human life?"

"I wish it could have been avoided," Larry evaded.

"Answer me!" Lafe Owens thundered in a voice that shook the lamp.

Larry's eyes flashed. "Bloat Simpson was no good," he said slowly, choosing his words carefully. "He was a braggart, a bully, and a cheat. He indirectly killed Taffy Turner. He would have killed me. I'm not sorry he's dead!"

His father stared at him as if he couldn't credit his hearing. "Your conscience . . . doesn't . . . bother you any?" he mumbled, gripping the edge of the table, leaning forward.

The youth looked the old stockman straight in the eyes. "No!" he answered bluntly. "Don't you think it's too soon to talk about this, Dad?"

The elder Owens kept his eyes upon him thoughtfully. "You mean the excitement . . . the . . . ?" He broke off abruptly, and his manner and expression underwent a change. "I had hoped you would never have to kill a man, Larry. And I had hoped, and still hope . . . oh, what do I hope? I'm getting old, but not too old. We'll let it rest." He took out a huge cigar and

76

lighted it with care, although his hand shook a little. Not once had he looked at Jones. Now he asked: "Who is this man who was with you when . . . when it happened?"

"Jones . . . Harry Jones," said Larry with a glance at his companion. "He had been trying to tell me he thought there was a frame-up, but he didn't have time."

"Where is he from?" asked Lafe.

Larry squirmed uneasily in his chair. "I don't know," he confessed.

"*Humph!*" For the first time Lafe turned his penetrating gaze full on the third man in the room. Jones returned the look gravely.

"Good Samaritan, eh?" he said.

"I admire to see fair play," Jones returned soberly.

"You drew on Fresee," Lafe accused. "Why did you do that?"

"He insulted me," was the ready reply.

"Yes?" Lafe's brows lifted. "How did he insult you? It was when the two outfits came together in front of the barn, wasn't it?"

"Yes," said Jones laconically. "He prodded me."

"He . . ." Old Lafe held his cigar motionless, studying the man before him. "He prodded you, and you threw down on one of the worst gunfighters in the country and threatened to tickle him in the ribs with a bullet. Is that it?"

"Exactly!" The word cracked in the room. "But I had him covered and knew he wouldn't try to draw. Later, he tried to beat me to it, and . . . he was lucky."

Lafe Owens's eyes widened. "Where . . . when was this?"

"I'd rather Larry would tell you," said Jones dryly.

Lafe looked at Larry. "Fresee got proddy in the barn when the Double B was saddling up," the latter explained casually. "Went off his head and gave me a cartridge as a souvenir for my new gunman. Harry . . . that is, Jones . . . grabbed it and threw it in his face. He started for his gun, but Stan Velie jerked him back and he went down. Stan told him any further trouble would have to be with him."

Old Lafe sat down. "Eh? What's that? Stan called him, do you say?"

"Called him proper, I'd say," Larry returned. "I never heard Stan talk in such a voice, Dad . . . and the look in his eyes was a caution. Seemed like a different man."

"Yes, yes!" exclaimed Lafe in great agitation. His face had turned gray. "And Fresee . . . what did he do?"

"Laughed it off, backed down, and left."

Lafe sat drumming his fingers on the table. Both young men were silent in the face of the old man's agitation and concern. It was plain that Lafe's thoughts were racing. It was as if old events were being pictured before him. He regained composure with an effort and raised his cigar in a shaking hand. Then he looked long at Jones and steadied. "You really wanted to help Larry today?" he asked curiously. They were so much alike — this able pair of youths.

"Sure thing," returned Jones nonchalantly. "He did me a favor once when I . . . no matter. We won't mention that. And don't forget, Mister Owens, that anything I do, I do on my own."

"*Humph!*" grunted Lafe. "I suppose the old can't always have charge." He appeared to be ruminating. Certainly at this moment he had little thought of Larry and Jones. "But old Stan . . . means something." His brows puckered. "Fresee sort of showed his hand, eh?" He spoke to no one in particular.

"I'd say he did, and it was all black cards, if you ask me." It was Jones who spoke.

Lafe roused himself and scowled at the speaker. "Larry, do I understand that you hired this man?" he asked.

"I told 'em he was with our outfit as a new hand. Yes, I guess I did."

"Oh, that's all right," Jones put in with an airy wave of his hand and a flashing smile. "Larry said that to help me out. I'm not holding him to it. We'll just forget it. I'm going to blow town, anyway, I reckon. Larry says it'll be healthier . . . No! I didn't mean to say that. I . . ."

"That's enough!" said Lafe Owens sternly. "When Larry hires a man for the KT outfit, it goes! As far as I can make out, it was all right with you, and, when the KT hires a man, he stays hired until there's a good reason for him to go. You'll take your orders from Velie or myself. That goes for both of you, understand? Now the Double B bunch has left town, so I hear. I'm going to send a certain message to the KT boys and they'll leave soon, too."

Lafe paused, drumming the table with nervous fingers. "I want you two to circulate among our boys and tell 'em everything's all right with the old man, and not to drink too much, and to expect some important news from me, and to keep it under their hats. And watch yourselves close. That's all."

He rose, and, as they reached the door, he stopped them. He put a hand on Larry's shoulder. "Get word to Stan Velie that I want to see him at the bank within an hour," he said.

# CHAPTER
# NINE

A dim light shone from the windows of the bank long after sunset, when the night sky had preened itself with stars. It came from above the partition of Henry Brower's private office at the rear of the cage. In the office were three men: the banker himself, Lafe Owens, and Stan Velie. Brower was seated at his desk, leaning his elbows upon it, his chin cupped in his right palm, an unlighted cigar in his left hand. Lafe sat across from him, drumming restlessly on the desk with the fingers of his left hand. Stan Velie occupied a chair near the lower end of the desk.

Lafe was staring thoughtfully at his foreman. Velie had met him outside the bank and had shaken his head slightly. Lafe had looked at him closely and then turned away with a tightening of the lips. He, too, had glimpsed the change in his foreman.

"Doesn't look so good, Stan?" he had asked.

"It's the finish," Velie had replied grimly, "and the beginning, if I can still read sign."

Lafe had nodded thoughtfully. "Let's go in and see Brower. He knows we're coming." He had spoken quietly, and they had entered the building practically unnoticed in the excitement of the celebration in the street.

Now Lafe glanced impatiently at Brower. "Why in thunder don't you light that cigar . . . and offer me one?"

Brower started, handed Lafe an open box of cigars. Lafe selected one and passed the box to Velie. All three lighted up.

"Yes," said Brower nervously, "it was bad business today."

"It was worse than that, Henry," said Lafe Owens. "Bolten practically laid down his cards and I called 'em. Now I'm goin' to force his hand . . . his big hand. It's war, Henry. It was war from the instant Jim Bolten and me looked into each other's eyes. Don't overlook that, Henry."

Lafe's speech was soft and measured, but his tone was ominous, fraught with dire foreboding. He stared gloomily at Stan Velie, and the KT foreman nodded.

Brower rose and paced the space behind his desk, chewing his cigar. Finally he stopped and glanced at each of them. "Oh, it can't be that bad," he addressed Lafe. "You've both got too much at stake. And everybody knows Larry drew last and was forced into that gun play. Simpson had it coming. He invited it. He wanted it . . . and he got it. Even the Double B men know that, Lafe."

Lafe shook his head. "Larry's affair has nothing to do with it . . . not in the least. Bolten didn't care a snap of his finger for Bloat Simpson, dead or alive. It furnished an excuse, that's all. The thing was done when I called

82

him there in front of the barn. We understood each other when we parted. This range, Henry, is goin' to be torn so wide apart that you could drop the Rocky Mountains in the crack."

Brower frowned. "But it's all so foolish, Lafe. There's no need for a range war just because of . . . of . . ." He paused.

"Because of what, Henry?" Lafe asked quietly.

"Well, because of this ruckus in town," replied the banker lamely.

"Henry, don't be a fool. You know as well as I do that what's happened in town was all part of a game, and the cards were out long ago. The big feuds and wars in any range country are started over trifles . . . a foot of boundary, an acre of ranch, and such. We've had peace here on the Teton a long time now, but my being president of the Cattlemen's Association always has rankled in Bolten's breast. That's the trifle that this war is starting over." Lafe mopped his brow with a big bandanna and nodded vigorously.

"But it hasn't started," Brower objected.

"Hasn't it? I've lost a good hand and friend, and Bolten's lost a man . . . a bad one, but a hand just the same. My boy's killed a man! There's been a free-for-all fight between my outfit and Bolten's with men from the east end of the range, and others from the west end, takin' sides."

"I know it," said Brower hastily. "It's bad . . . very bad. But there's still a chance it will all blow over."

Lafe laughed scornfully. "Jim Bolten wants to be president of the Association. He wants the election this year. If he had gone about his campaigning on the square and in the open, he could have had it, if he could have won it. But he's been playing dirty politics and . . ." Lafe sputtered, then leaped to his feet and brought his great fist down on the desk. "Now, I say he can't have it!" he shouted.

The banker and Stan Velie both looked at him, startled.

But the stockman quickly recovered himself. "No, Henry," he said tremulously, "it's too late to stop it . . . and I'm not going to try. I can read the signals. I've had Stan in my employ a good many years . . . so many that the only man who had worked straight along with him was poor Taffy Turner. And you've known Stan a long time."

Brower nodded. "Of course."

"Well, Stan called the turn on Fresee today," drawled Lafe.

The banker's brows went up and he looked quickly at the KT foreman. "Gun play?" he asked. "I mean . . ."

"Might have been," said Stan Velie coolly. "He brought it on."

"So you see?" said Lafe, his eyes narrowing. "We're in for it."

"We?" said Brower vaguely.

"All of us," Lafe explained impatiently. "This thing will affect everybody on the range. Oh, Bolten will have a chance to lay down, but I know Bolten well enough to know that he won't do that . . . 'specially with that rat-faced Fresee pushing him on. I've nosed around a

84

bit and I know the west end is solid. What I want to know is if Bolten has the east end solid. I'm goin' to call the turn on him and find out. The best way to get the drop on a man is to beat him to the draw. I'm goin' to try to lick him at the start and stop this thing."

Brower sat down abruptly, his face showing concern, his eyes worried. He sensed that in some way this all had something to do with him — with his bank. "What are you going to do, Lafe?" he asked in a low voice.

"I'm goin' to call a special meeting of the Association for Saturday afternoon," Lafe announced.

"But . . ." Brower was on his feet again. "That's only day after tomorrow, Lafe. You couldn't get them together in that time, and . . ." He stopped as he saw the look on Lafe's face and sat down.

"They're all right here in town at the rodeo," Lafe said calmly, "or most of 'em are. A few members from the far east end aren't here, but there's always a few members missing at a meeting."

Brower couldn't conceal his admiration. Lafe was keeping certain members he believed favorable to Bolten from attending and thus beating Bolten to it. But to what? "What's the purpose of the meeting, Lafe?" he asked amiably.

"That will be brought out at the meeting, Henry. I just wanted to ask . . . and this is really why we're here . . . what would your position be in case certain things happened?"

The banker's brows puckered. "I don't believe I understand you, Lafe. My position . . . in case what certain things happened?"

Lafe shot a meaningful look at Stan Velie. "In case, say, of an open split, or more trouble between Jim Bolten and me. Say in one of those cases. How would you stand?"

Henry Brower's eyes widened. "Why, I'd be neutral!" he exclaimed. "I'd have to be. All this was understood before."

"Before the open break, Henry," corrected Lafe, his gaze hardening. Suddenly his manner and voice changed. "Listen, this is goin' to be the last war on this range. I'll see to that. As long as Bolten wants to re-open old wounds, I'll throw salt in 'em. I'm not as young as I might be, but my head can still tick. There's a lot of things I can overlook, but I can't overlook the fact that it was through Bolten's trickery that my boy had to kill a man. I can't and won't overlook that. What do you think I sent Larry to college for? Answer me!" The old stockman rose to his full height and his anger seemed to fill the room with menace.

"Why . . . why, to educate him," Brower faltered.

Lafe swore. "That was partly the reason. The *real* reason was that I had an idea in my old fool head that I could get him to look down on the rough stuff. I've killed a few men in my day . . . had to . . . but I wanted Larry to get along without having any such memories to nurse. Bolten has spoiled that. Larry's changed. I can see it in his eyes. I . . . I suppose I wanted him to be a gentleman stock raiser." Lafe laughed scornfully. "I'll admit I was a fool. And blood will crop out sooner or later. The Owens blood showed in Larry today . . . this afternoon. You should have heard him answer my questions over at the hotel and seen the look in his eyes. I'm not goin' to send him back to that school. His place is here where he can help his dad fight this battle. Bolten wanted a fight and he's goin' to get it!" The stockman paused, glaring fiercely at the two who listened. No one spoke. "And there's goin' to be no neutral side!" thundered old Lafe. "Not for a man of your importance, Henry Brower! You're goin' to side one way or the other!"

Brower's face went dead white. "But my bank, Lafe!" he cried shakily. "If I side with you, the east end will break me, and —"

"And if you side with the east end, *I'll* break you!" roared Lafe. "Just make up your mind. Figure which end has the most resources, and the least paper. I'm a director of this bank and I know pretty well how things stand." Lafe smiled while Brower stood, trembling and white. The banker knew this was an ultimatum. "You see, Henry," Lafe went on in a softer voice, "money is goin' to play a part in this game. And I aim to have the money on my side. I reckon Bolten hasn't even thought about that. And if this split comes at the meeting, I want you to do something. Bolten has been tryin' to build up his ranch to where it'd be as big as mine. He's gone in deep. I know. If this thing comes, I want you to call every cent of Bolten's paper!"

"Lafe!" cried Brower. "It would ruin me! He'd transfer his paper to Helena . . . easy enough! And maybe all the east-end paper! It's well secured and I'd lose the interest. You're using me as a . . . a tool!"

"Don't talk foolish," said Lafe scathingly. "You know they cannot get as liberal loans off this range. Bolten probably can transfer his paper to Helena. The others can't! If you call their paper, they're done . . . the little ones, especially. I aim to keep the whole east end out of this fight, except Bolten. I'm not using you as a tool. I'm using money as one of my weapons. Your bank is safe. Let Bolten take his paper to Helena and do what damage he can, and . . ." The old centaur paused and fixed the banker with a gleam of triumph in his eyes. When he spoke again, his voice fairly rang. "I've spent twenty long, hard years putting myself in the clear. I'm not using you as a tool, Henry, as I said, but I'm using money. I'll throw the KT into this thing . . . every acre I own, every head of stock, every penny of cash. If it is necessary, I'll go to Helena . . . and I'll bring back a quarter of a million in cash and make this bank as solid as the Rockies!"

Henry Brower sat spellbound and Stan Velie leaned forward in his chair, his eyes sparkling.

"That's all, Henry," said Lafe smilingly as he took the banker's limp hand. "We'll go now, Stan and me. You know where you stand so go home and have a good night's sleep. Let us out the back way."

For an hour after Lafe Owens and Stan Velie had gone, Henry Brower sat motionlessly at his desk. Then he found himself staring curiously at an envelope on the chair that had been occupied by the KT owner. He went around the desk and picked it up. It was not sealed, bore no address. The banker thought for a few moments, balancing the envelope in his hand. It might just be that Lafe Owens had left the envelope purposely. Brower opened it forthwith, took out a small printed sheet, and read:

**NOTICE**
**A SPECIAL MEETING**
of the
**TETON CATTLEMEN'S ASS'N**
is called for
**SATURDAY, SEPTEMBER 24**[TH]
At 2p.m.
**IN I.O.O.F. HALL**
**All members please attend.**
**LAFE OWENS, President**

It was the notice being sent to members of the Association and doubtless would be posted in all public places in the morning. Lafe Owens had worked fast. Henry Brower folded the paper, put it back in its envelope, and tossed it on his desk. Then he took his hat, put out the light, and let himself out the front door.

# CHAPTER
# TEN

On the night of the conference in Brower's office, Larry Owens and Harry Jones went to the dance. As soon as they entered the pavilion, every eye was turned upon them. But Larry noticed at once that instead of friendly greeting, the looks focused on them were frankly curious. He had heard the rumor going the rounds to the effect that Jones was KT's hired gunman, had denied it, but had seen it was generally accepted as a fact. This disturbed him and amused Jones who seemed to be getting a lot of fun out of it. Neither wore his gun.

Larry had come to the dance for the single purpose of having a word with Jane Bolten. He saw her almost immediately in the swirl of dancers and caught her eye. She stared at him with a startled expression, looking at him as long as she could before other couples intervened. When the dance was ended, he followed her to her seat, while Jones remained talking with a KT cowpuncher near the door.

As Larry approached Jane, the little group of admirers about her dissolved, and it seemed to him that a hush fell over those who were near them. A youth vacated a chair beside her.

"Why, hello, Jane," Larry greeted soberly.

The girl merely looked at him. Her distress was evident. She did not know what to do. Jane loathed anything hinting of a scene. If she rose and walked away, snubbing Larry, it would cause more talk, for almost everyone there knew they had been good friends since childhood. The memory of his embrace and kiss came with a rush, but her flush paled with the recollection of the momentous events of that day. Then her mind functioned normally.

"Sit down, Larry," she invited dully.

"That's nice of you, Jane," he said, taking the seat beside her. "You could have made it hard."

"I . . . cannot dance with you, Larry," she said decisively.

"I know that, Jane, and I didn't intend to ask you to dance. I couldn't dance tonight to save my very life."

At this juncture the orchestra struck up and soon the floor was alive with whirling couples.

"Let's go out on the airing porch, as they call it, back here," Jane suggested. Without waiting for an answer, she rose and led the way, her face white and her eyes dazzling, ignoring the looks directed at them.

On the shadowed platform outside, swept by the cool prairie breeze, she made sure they were alone, and then she turned on him in a fury. "You had to come here!" she cried fiercely. "You had to finish your day of glory by humiliating me!"

"No, Jane," he said firmly, "I had no such intention . . . and no one could look at it that way. It is simply natural I should seek you out after . . . after what's happened. Everybody knows that. We've been friends since we were kids, and you and Sis are chums. I could not find you anywhere else, and I had to see you tonight since I don't know what may happen from one minute to the next."

"I should say you don't," Jane said scornfully. "Anyway, you didn't pack your gun. I hate you, Larry Owens, and now I know what you meant when you said you hoped anything that happened wouldn't have any effect on our . . . on us. You intended to kill Bloat Simpson! You wanted to square yourself in advance. It is detestable!"

Larry's face was white as death in the light of the stars. "Nothing was further from my thoughts than that, Jane," he declared. "Look in my eyes and believe me. You know I do not lie. What I meant was . . . well, in case of trouble between the ranches. And that has come. It has been coming . . . oh, I don't want to talk about that. Anyway, I don't know much more about it than you do. I'm entitled to defend myself to the extent of saying that what happened today was forced upon me. But I didn't come to make excuses . . . to try to square myself, as you say."

She had been watching him closely. She knew in her heart that he spoke the truth. But she saw a new light in his eyes, a new firmness in his bearing. He had in some inexplicable way changed — seemingly, right before her eyes. She was at a loss for words, her anger having evaporated as suddenly as it had come. Then she said the very thing she wanted to keep back. "You've killed a man, Larry."

His lips tightened, and a glint that might have been pain came and went in his eyes. Then they were steady and grave and brilliant. He merely nodded. "I suppose it changes things," he said in a voice that seemed to come from the cold, swinging stars. "I came to tell you, Jane, that I am sorry for what I did the other night. It was . . . never mind. If for no other reason, I'm sorry because it hurt you to have me act so. But . . . things are taking place over which you and I have no control. So I won't say goodbye. I won't follow you inside. People will know that I just came to speak to you a moment and then left. And our kind of people will understand."

He placed a hand on the railing of the platform as if he would vault over it, but she grasped his arm.

"Larry!" she exclaimed impulsively. "Turn around so I can look in your eyes."

He looked at her. She was holding both his arms now.

"Larry . . . you haven't . . . turned gunman . . . have you?"

For the first time that day he smiled. "No, Jane. I reckon I couldn't do that if I tried. Whatever made you ask such a question?"

Jane took a long breath. "They say it's in the blood. Oh, Larry, I didn't mean that . . . honestly. People talk when they're excited like today. Oh, Larry, forgive me . . . as I forgive you?"

Her arms suddenly went up about his neck and her head leaned against him. He held her and knew she was sobbing softly.

"I'm so sorry it happened, Jane," he said gently. "I don't understand it all. Everything seemed to come so suddenly. I had to do it or get it myself. Somehow it has changed me. Don't feel bad . . . there's nothing to forgive. No one wants this world to get right again more than I do. Everything will come out all right."

For some moments she was still. Then she drew back. "I must go, Larry. Don't do it again . . . if you can help it." With that she disappeared into the lighted pavilion.

Couples came out on the platform and Larry vaulted over the rail. As he hit the ground, red fire streaked against the shadows, and a bullet whined its message. He flung himself flat on his face with the sharp report of the gun ringing in his ears.

There were cries from the platform above, a scuffle of many feet. Larry scrambled into the shadow of the pavilion wall, rose to his feet, and ran quickly to the street. Then he walked in the entrance and caught Jones's eye.

"Let's slope for the ranch," he said. "Mother and Sis are there, and I don't know what menfolk."

"It's a go with me," sang Harry-From-Nowhere cheerily.

As they started for the livery, Larry decided not to say anything about the shot from ambush for the present. He realized he had narrowly missed death, and it brought home with poignancy the seriousness of the

94

clash between the two outfits and the tactics that might be expected. Moreover, the man who had fired the shot had undoubtedly overheard the words spoken by Jane and himself. This last bothered him even more than his narrow escape. It was Jane of whom he was thinking.

He asked Jones to look after the horses while he stopped at the hotel, where he hoped to have a word with his father before leaving for the ranch. The hotel lobby was crowded with stockmen, and, as Larry entered, he sensed tension in the air. He attracted considerable notice, also, as he edged his way through the throng. Then he stopped in his tracks as a well-known voice boomed loudly.

"I tell you, you can't call a special meeting of the Association for Saturday!"

It was Jim Bolten who spoke.

"But I've called it," came the cool rejoinder of Lafe Owens.

The KT owner had worked fast. Even while he and Stan Velie had been closeted with Henry Brower in the banker's office, the work of distributing the notices to the stockmen and the posting of them in public places had been carried on by the printer and his aides.

Larry pushed through the crowd to a place behind his father, who was facing Bolten. It was the second meeting of these two that day, and this meeting, if anything, was even more dramatic than the first, for the gauntlet had been thrown down. Larry started as he saw the mean face of Fresee behind Bolten. Fresee hadn't gone back to the Double B! Instantly Larry's thoughts reverted to the shot in the dark. Had it been instigated by Fresee? His conjectures were cut short by Bolten's angry voice.

"You know very well, Owens, that all the members can't get there by day after tomorrow for a meeting. This is a trick!" The Double B owner's face was black with rage and he made no attempt to conceal his feelings.

"It is not a trick, Bolten," said Lafe slowly and distinctly so that all could hear. "Most of the members are in town. I know we have far more than a quorum here because I have met them and talked with them. If I didn't know how many members I could raise, I sure wouldn't be callin' any special meeting."

"There's some from the east end that aren't here!" shouted Bolten. "And you know they can't get here!"

"There are some who can't get here," Lafe conceded, "but I have a quorum and the majority rules, so they're protected. Anyway, there's nothing of importance to be voted on and I can't remember that we ever had a meeting with every member present."

"You haven't any right to call a meeting on such short notice," stormed Bolten.

"If you'll take the trouble to read the bylaws, you'll run across a clause that gives the president the right to call a special meeting at any time," Lafe pointed out.

"What's coming up at the meeting?" Bolten demanded.

"Whatever it is, it will come up at the meeting," Lafe replied coldly.

"There . . . you see?" Bolten waved a hand about at the assembled stockmen. "It's a trick, I tell you. He won't even say what the business is!"

"That's my privilege," said Lafe. "Anyway, you'll be there. Why all the fuss? It isn't causing anybody any trouble, for we'll all be in town. If there's any trick to this, it's catching the crowd together in one spot while the catching is good."

There were smiles and chuckles at this and Bolten became infuriated.

"All right, I'm goin' to put my cards on the table . . ."

"Mine have been there all along, and for the last twenty years!" Lafe Owens said in a ringing voice.

Bolten bit his lip to keep back the hot words that were on his tongue. "It's a funny thing," he sneered, "that you didn't think of this until you knew I'd sent my outfit back to the ranch. I notice you're keeping yours in town, and . . ." He cut off his words with a black scowl as he realized how senseless this remark sounded; also, it smacked of the ominous.

"I'll send mine back if you say so," Lafe volunteered.

Bolten seemed to be pondering a reply to this, scanning the faces of the stockmen gathered about them. A dead silence hung over the little lobby. Then Bolten looked Lafe Owens straight in the eyes.

"It seems a little unusual, this meeting, and I've said what I've said because I sort of represent the east end of this range and the boys out there expect me to see that they get a square deal. I'll be at the meeting." With this, he turned away.

A sharp intaking of breath came from the crowd. Bolten had declared himself.

Pondera seethed with excitement as the news of the special meeting of the Cattlemen's Association and the second clash between Lafe Owens and Jim Bolten spread like wildfire. Lafe took Larry and Stan Velie upstairs in the hotel and issued crisp orders. "Keep the men in town," he told Velie after they were seated. "Tell 'em to go where they please, but to keep themselves in hand. Put that Blondy Robbins in charge. I can't bring in any more men from the ranch. You say they came in as a matter of protest? Well, I'll let it go at that. I've got too good a crew to fight with 'em. Tomorrow morning I want 'em all out by the corrals to tell 'em a few things."

"I put Blondy in charge an hour after they came in this afternoon," said Velie dryly. "You leave the men to me, Lafe. You've got enough to attend to without bothering with them. And there's no need to talk to 'em. They'll obey my orders."

Lafe looked keenly at his foreman. It was many months since Velie had seen fit to assert himself so forcibly. Well, he was a good man, and Lafe was appreciative of his ability in a crisis. "All right." He scowled. "But I want 'em to hold their heads, Stan. Remember that."

"They'll understand it," Velie assured him. "Since Bolten's sent his outfit back to the Double B, I've given 'em the run of the town. But not a man in the outfit is wearing his gun."

"Good," said Lafe, very much pleased. "That was a good idea, Stan. I hadn't thought of it. Well, as you say, I have plenty to think about. All right, the men are in your hands, and that settles that end of it."

"I'll chase along," said Velie, rising. At the door he turned. His eyes were gleaming between narrowed lids as he spoke to the KT owner. "You know we're in for it, Lafe . . . as it looks. I called Fresee today. I just want you to know . . . that call goes." Then he went out.

Lafe Owens sat looking at his son speculatively. "I don't want Stan to mix guns with Fresee," he said as if to himself. "I don't suppose I could stop it, if it was to come. But Fresee would get him just as sure as there'll be daylight tomorrow. Stan hasn't the speed he once had, although I haven't got the heart to tell him that . . . not now, anyway. He might get Fresee, but if he did, the two of them would go home together."

Larry was struck by his father's look, words, and manner. But he could think of nothing to say. In the years he had been so much away from the ranch, he had become detached from these two men. They were more or less of a mystery to him. For the first time he realized that he knew his own father none too well.

"I'm not going to send you back East this fall, Larry," Lafe announced soberly. "You'll have to stand by. Tonight you better go back to the ranch. Mother and Molly are there. Take this Jones with you. Have you . . . heard any talk . . . very much talk, I mean?"

Instantly Larry remembered Jane Bolten's words: *They say it's in the blood!* Should he tell his father? Should he tell him of the attempt on his own life that night? Surely his father had enough on his mind. "I've only heard what you must have heard, Dad . . . that the old feud between the KT and the Double B has been renewed . . ."

"It's Bolten's fault!" Lafe interjected angrily. "But he's bucked up against the wrong party. Maybe he thinks he's strong enough now to beat me to it. Larry, I . . ." He paused, eying his son closely. "Go on, Larry."

"Well, that's been going the rounds, and they're saying that Bolten is organizing the east end and proposes to use that as a club to get himself elected president of the Association. Then they're hinting that the east-enders may form an organization of their own, if Bolten doesn't make the grade. Of course, my being your son, I'm handed many compliments about you."

"Naturally," grunted Lafe. "Most of 'em are trying to put themselves in right with both sides. But what do you hear about the . . . shooting?" He squinted under his grizzly brows.

Larry stiffened. "Folks on our side . . . I mean some folks . . . say Bloat had it coming, and all that. I don't listen to 'em. There isn't much talk about that to me. Then there're hints I've turned gunman, and that's a lie. One told me . . ." He halted abruptly. He had almost let it out.

"Yes, yes," urged Lafe, "go on."

"Oh, nothing," said Larry lamely. "There's a lot of loose talk of no consequence going around."

His father leaned forward. "Larry," he commanded sternly, "what did this person tell you? Answer me!"

Larry's lips tightened. *Well, why not?* "That it runs in the blood!" he said slowly.

"Ah," said Lafe, drawing out the word. "So there's some skunk enough to spread the report that I'd made a gunman out of my son! That's the sort of low lizard we're up against, Larry. Low, mean, despicable skunks."

Larry flushed, remembering the source of the remark. "But . . ." He realized instantly that he could not protest without naming the person. He must throw his father off the trail. "Somebody shot at me tonight, Dad," he said in a matter-of-fact way.

This information had the desired effect. His father leaped to his feet, his eyes blazing. "From ambush?" he demanded.

Larry nodded. "Up near the dance pavilion. But I guess it was just somebody celebrating."

"You know better than that," his father said hoarsely. "If . . . well, that settles it. By . . ." He sputtered, inarticulate with rage. Then he calmed. "You must be careful, Larry. Watch yourself every minute." It was as if the possibility of harm suddenly befalling his son was suddenly brought home to him.

"Don't worry, Dad. I can take care of myself."

There was a shadow of worry in old Lafe's eyes. "Keep away from alleys and dark places," he advised, although his words sounded foolish. "Shake on home, now. Keep your eyes open . . . but I don't really have to tell you to do that. But, Son, don't say anything to your mother or your sister. Tell 'em I'm detained in town on business . . . which is a fact. Jolly 'em along. This isn't a woman's game."

When Larry rose, his father took his hand. "So long," he said in a serious tone.

Larry went downstairs and met Jones in the hotel lobby. "We'll go on out to the ranch now, Harry," he said.

"Sure thing," said Jones, who had been waiting for him. "But, listen . . . know what I just heard?"

"No idea," said Larry, noting that his friend appeared a bit excited, which was not usual for him.

"I don't know if this is so or not," said Jones, "but I heard that Bolten's sent to bring his men back into town."

"What good will that do him? They can't get into trouble with our outfit . . . the KT men are not armed, and, what's more, they've got their instructions and have agreed to obey orders. They're not to get in trouble, no matter what is said to them or what happens."

Jones shook his head doubtfully. "I'm not so sure there won't be trouble, Larry. These 'punchers . . . well, I've worked the range, you know . . . and . . . do you know what they're calling us?"

"Nothing good, I'll bet."

"They're calling us the KT twins." Jones said it with a broad grin.

Larry grinned, also. "They won't find us such a soft pair if they rub our hair the wrong way. Well, Harry, let's get going. There's one thing you must remember.

Don't say anything about this at the ranch, understand? Dad's staying in town on business, and let it go at that."

"Listen, partner, there are a few things I've had to learn . . . and learn hard. One of them is to keep my mouth shut."

They went to the barn for their horses and in half an hour were on the road, riding at a swinging lope for the KT. For a distance of ten miles, the road led across the open plain. The stars hung in clusters from the curtains of the sky and the moon drifted, white and cold, laving the land with a soft gray light in which the shadows danced. There was a breeze and the air was scented with the faint perfume of autumn grasses and foliage. It was a magic landscape, stretching into the distance where the stars fell behind the horizon. Larry and Jones rode, happy and free. It was impossible for them, because of their youth, to worry or think seriously with good horseflesh beneath and such a world surrounding them. But this could not last, as the road that turned off to the KT ranch house, situated in the bottoms, soon encountered rises and swells and tumbled country, and finally reached the trees, where it crossed a little creek.

"We want to keep an eye out down here," Larry told his companion now that they had entered the bottoms, and brought his horse down to a walk.

"You'll have to show the way, that's all," said Jones.

They entered the trees and his words might have been a signal, for they were hardly out of his mouth when red fire flamed in the shadows of the trees, and mad bullets whistled.

"An ambush!" Larry yelled, raking his horse with the steel so that the animal fairly hurdled the next space of road.

Jones was at his side, leaning low over the saddle, his gun streaming bullets at the place where the bursts of gunfire had been seen. But accurate shooting under the circumstances was impossible for either side. Larry and Jones swept on at top speed, reloading their guns. They pushed their mounts to the utmost, knowing that the horses would keep to the road in the semidarkness. There might be another ambush ahead, in which event their safety would be assured by speed. But they broke out of the trees without having been fired upon again.

In the open of the bottoms, Larry reined in. "Harry, do you think they could have hit us if they wanted to?" he asked.

"Well, we were walking our horses and made pretty big marks," replied Jones. "What're you driving at?"

"Just this," said Larry grimly. "I think they were trying to throw a scare into us."

"Might be. Yes, it looks like it. But we couldn't take any chances . . . what's that?"

"It's at the ranch!" cried Larry. "Ride like hell!"

In a moment they were off, racing their horses across the bottoms toward the KT ranch house from which had come the sharp reports of guns.

# CHAPTER
# ELEVEN

As they sped around the fences enclosing the fields where the limited crops of oats were grown, two more shots rang out, and then a third. If one man only were shooting, he had emptied his gun. This thought occurred to both Larry and Jones as they spurred their mounts to greater efforts. It seemed inconceivable to Larry that a deliberate attack would be made on the ranch house where there were only women. So far as he knew, the only men at the ranch at present were Jerry, the barn man who had taken the place of Taffy Turner, Ned, another older hand, and the cook.

Soon they saw the lights of the ranch house through the windbreak of cottonwoods, and in another minute dashed into the courtyard. Just as they arrived in front of the barn, Larry saw a figure stealing around the rear of the house from the side opposite the courtyard. He thought he saw Jerry in the courtyard, his form outlined by the light from a window. Larry lost no time. He flung himself from his horse and dashed for the figure at the rear of the house, closely followed by Jones. In another moment Larry had knocked the man down and wrested his gun from him. Then he took him by the collar and dragged him into the light in the courtyard as Jerry came running and Molly called in a frightened voice from the front porch.

Larry handed Jones the gun he had taken from his captive, and Jones spilled six empty shells on the ground.

"He was shootin' at me from the other side of the house," Jerry panted, "and I couldn't see him to get a crack at him."

"Never mind," said Larry crisply. "Help me get him into the bunkhouse, Harry. You sure there's only one, Jerry?"

"So far as I know," replied the barn man. "If there's any more around, they ain't showed themselves."

Larry and Jones carried the intruder into the bunkhouse where a lamp was burning and placed him on a bunk. Then they stepped back and saw that he was conscious and staring at them.

"I can't place him," Larry said. "Ever see him, Jerry?"

"I could tell that twisted nose a mile off. He's one of the Double B crowd and was traveling with Bloat Simpson's gang."

"What were you doing around here?" Larry asked.

"Wha . . . wha . . . ?" the man stammered. He tried to grin.

Larry stepped forward and shook the man fiercely. "Don't play drunk. You're in a bad way, taking shots at the house and one of our men. What was the big idea?"

Again the man tried to talk and merely hiccupped and sputtered.

**106**

"Jerry, bring a pail of cold water," Larry ordered, and turned to Jones to wink.

Jerry returned from the bunkhouse kitchen shortly with a pail of water, and Larry dashed the contents fully in the face of the man on the bunk. He started up, and then lay back, rubbing the water out of his eyes. "Wha's matter?" he mumbled, staring blankly.

Larry nodded to Jerry and a second pail of water was administered. This time the man cursed.

"That's more like it," Larry said. "Listen, you're not as drunk as you pretend. But if you are, you're coming out of it, and don't think you're not. I'm going to stand right here and throw pails of water into your face until you snap out of it. And we've got plenty of water on this ranch. Jerry, bring another."

Both Larry and Jones thought the man's eyes flashed. He sat up unsteadily. "Gimme a drink," he muttered. "Gimme a bracer. I . . ." His brows knit as he peered at Larry and Jones. "Am I home?"

"You know you're not home," said Larry scornfully. "No trouble for you to tell the difference between the Double B bunkhouse and a strange place. We've got the goods on you, and I want to know what you were doing here, trying to pot our barn man."

The man scowled heavily and slowly swung about so that his feet were on the floor. "You might give me a drink to sober up on," he said resentfully.

Larry considered, then turned to Jerry. "Tell the cook to give you a good-size snort and bring it here." He drew up a chair in front of the captive.

107

When Jerry came in with the liquor, the man downed it in two gulps, shivered, and then smacked his lips. "That's more like," he said in a stronger tone. "I recognize you now, Owens. How did I get here?"

Larry and Jones exchanged a significant glance. Both sensed the man's game. He would plead intoxication and claim he did not know — could not remember — what had happened. Yet both were convinced that his presence at the ranch had some connection with the ambush in the river brakes.

"You know how you got here . . . Twisted Nose . . ."

"My name's Casey," the man interjected angrily.

"All right, Casey, we're glad to have the information, although we would have gotten it later on, anyway. You sneaked in here tonight in your right mind. No drunken Double B man on the way to his home ranch would stumble in here. Why'd you do it?"

"I tell you I don't know how I got here," Casey insisted. "I know the location of this place and in my befuddled state probably came here instead of goin' home. That's all I know."

"All right. What was the idea of the shooting?"

Casey, who had a disagreeable habit of shaking his head to one side and sniffing, glared at Larry out of mean eyes. "Don't try to hang something on me I didn't do."

"Here's Jerry to prove it, and Harry and I heard the shots. You remember me knocking you down well enough. I took your gun and Harry emptied the spent shells."

"Here they are, Casey," Jones put in, holding out his hand with the empty casings in the palm. "Feel your holster and grab some air where your gun should be."

Casey did so instinctively, then quickly withdrew his hand. "This is a frame-up!"

Larry laughed. "No man could have been drunk as you pretended and sober up so suddenly as you did. Your hand is steady as a pitchfork handle."

"I'm used to hard liquor," Casey snarled.

"Casey, this play won't get you a thing. You planted that ambush to scare me, and you sneaked in here to see what I'd say when I got home . . . or to pot-shoot me."

"It's a lie!" yelled Casey, jumping to his feet.

"Isn't he active," drawled Jones.

This drew a look of hatred from the captive. "You're another young upstart who's goin' to get what's comin' to him."

"That's the stuff, Casey," said Jones amiably. "You've proved that what Larry said is true. If Larry has any sense, we'll test a rope on this ranch when daylight shows us a good limb."

Casey sat down, his manner changed. He looked apprehensively at the two of them. "I'm entitled to a square deal," he said.

"You can have everything but a minister . . . you're not entitled to that," said Jones.

Larry looked narrowly at the man on the bunk. "Casey, there's something in what Harry says. The outfit is sure to be back tonight. When they hear about this . . . well, after the trouble Bloat Simpson made . . .

Taffy Turner losing an eye and then dying . . . I don't think I'll be able to control 'em. Then there's the fact that I was ambushed in town, and both of us were ambushed riding through the brakes. Add all that to your play here tonight." He shrugged, seeing the beads of moisture on the captive's brow. "No, Casey, they'd hang you sure . . . and they could get away with it, too."

"I demand protection!" Casey said hoarsely. "If I'm in the wrong, Owens, it's your duty to turn me over to the sheriff."

Jones's lips curled in contempt. This man was yellow.

"I'm going to turn you over to the men," Larry concluded.

"No!" Casey fairly screamed the word. "Fresee planned that ambush to throw a scare into you, but he told the men they could use their own judgment. They could have shot you down and he wouldn't have cared . . . but they didn't. They didn't want to . . . wouldn't do it. And I came here of my own accord. I'm tellin' you the truth, Owens. I was drunk and I felt like spyin' around a little. I shot to scare that man of yours away so I could get to my horse. I don't know a thing about what happened to you in town. I wasn't there. Honest. Now I've told you. Turn me over to the sheriff, Owens." He was whining. "I've got that much coming . . . now."

Larry looked at Jones and the other nodded slightly. The man in his cowardice had told the truth. "Yes, I guess you've got it coming. There's a place in the barn where I can lock you up for the night, and we'll take you to town in the morning."

"But suppose your outfit comes back tonight?" asked Casey with fear.

"I won't say anything about your being here," Larry promised. "Come along. Jerry, where's the lantern?"

With the yellow rays of the lantern splashing about their feet, they took Casey into the barn and locked him in the harness and saddle room. But Larry did not stop there. He instructed Jerry to remain for the rest of the night where he could watch the locked door. He was taking no chances.

"Well, what do you think of it all?" he asked Jones once they were in the courtyard.

"I think we've had a streak of luck," Jones said shortly.

"Harry, it looks like we're going to make a good team. It was you who dragged in the rope." He grinned. "Now we'll tell the womenfolks that . . . that . . ."

"That a drunken 'puncher strayed in here from the celebration and forgot he still wasn't at the rodeo," Jones supplied. "We've put him to bed in the barn."

They walked rapidly to the house and into the kitchen where Larry found his mother and sister and Mary O'Neil, the housekeeper. All wore looks of concern, but Larry noticed that Molly's eyes flashed over his shoulder at Jones.

"What was it, Larry?" Mrs. Owens asked anxiously.

Larry told the story just as Jones had suggested.

"I thought it might be Pat," Mary O'Neil said grimly. "If it had been, I'd break his neck. What was he doin' in town, Mister Larry?"

"Pat's as sober as a judge," Larry told her convincingly. "Mother, this is Harry Jones." He turned to see Jones bow, sweeping his hat in a gesture worthy of a chevalier.

"Hello, Harry-From-Nowhere," said Molly flippantly.

"Harry-From-Somewhere, you mean," said Jones gravely.

"Oh, good, he's going to tell us where he's from. Where are you from, Harry?"

"The KT Ranch," replied Jones. "Ever hear of it?"

"Harry is now with our outfit," Larry announced. "What's more, he's my friend, so don't get fresh with him."

"Fine chance I'd have to get fresh with *him*," was her scornful rejoinder.

"The truth is that Harry's got a lot on his mind," Larry told her.

"Including supper." Jones nodded.

This brought a general laugh.

"Just you folks go in the living room, and I'll have supper on the table in short order," assured Mary O'Neil.

"Short order?" Jones queried. "This bein' a cattle ranch, I'll take a porterhouse steak smothered with bacon and eggs, garnished with potatoes, string beans, peas, corn on the cob, with fried cabbage on the side."

Mary O'Neil pointed to the door leading out of the kitchen to the front rooms. "Go in there and spend the rest of the time guessing what you're going to get," she said severely.

As they left the kitchen, Mrs. Owens put her hand on her son's arm and stopped him in the dining room, while Jones and Molly went into the living room.

"Is your father going to stay in town tonight?" his mother asked Larry.

"Yes, he told me to explain that he had to stay in on business."

"What kind of business, Larry?" Her tone was worried.

"He has called a special meeting of the Association," Larry answered. "He called it because so many of the members . . . practically all of them . . . are in town for the rodeo."

But his mother knew there was more significance in this move than Larry was admitting. "What business is there for the Association at this time, when the regular meeting is so near?" Seeing Larry's reluctance to answer, his mother then put her hands on his shoulders and looked into his eyes as she said: "Larry, before you left this afternoon, the men went into town, as you know. Is there trouble?"

With her looking at him like that, Larry couldn't dissemble, not even to tell a white lie, so he told her what he knew, leaving out only the shot fired at him from ambush in town and the shots fired later at Jones and him near the river. It seemed to satisfy her.

"I just hope there is no more trouble," she said, giving him a little hug. "I'll go to the kitchen now and help Mary."

Meanwhile, Molly Owens and Harry Jones had seated themselves before the fireplace where coals were glowing against the chill of the fall night.

"How'd you happen to work for us?" Molly asked him.

"It didn't happen," Jones drawled. "It occurred. Larry asked me just how good a cowhand I was, and, when I told him, he hired me on the spot." He snapped a thumb and finger. "Just like that."

"Why is it you are always trivial with me?" she demanded, nettled.

"I do it to conceal my real feelings," he replied, looking at her intently.

Molly colored slightly and for a few moments was confused. He was the first man who had made her feel that way and she was irritated by it. "What do you mean?"

"Just this," he said soberly, leaning toward her. "When a fellow meets a girl for the first time, a likable, jolly girl, I mean, he should be careful what he says. If he says this, she may think he's fresh. If he says that, she may think he's cold and reserved. So I find it best to jolly 'em along." He nodded for emphasis.

Molly nearly gasped. "So you sit here beside me and tell me you're jollying me along?" She arched her brows.

"Exactly. But I wouldn't dream of jollying you along if you weren't worth it."

Molly nearly gasped again. "Well, you're not jollying me . . . you're being fresh."

**114**

He looked at her with increased interest. "Am I to understand that we are having a quarrel at our second meeting? Why, I'm making progress."

"In the wrong direction," she said stiffly. "At first, I thought we were going to be friends, but you . . ."

"Not *going* to be friends," he corrected. "We're friends already."

This was too much for Molly. "You only think so. It takes two to make friends."

He smiled his irresistible smile. "Thank you for limiting it to two. I come out here in a cheerful frame of mind, contented and happy, a new hand proud of his job, anxious to please, and now see what a state of mind you've got me in. I thought that because of my culture, ability, and social standing on my first day at the KT I would be considered a guest. This is no way to treat a guest, Miss Molly . . . now, is it?"

Molly could not resist the impulse to laugh, and he joined her. At this point Larry entered the living room.

"What's the joke?" he asked, looking from one to the other.

"No joke," Jones said, rising. "It's our way of taking exercise before meals."

Jones had heard hoof beats sounding out in the courtyard. So had Larry. The two exchanged looks and then left the room, heading outside. They were soon in the courtyard where two riders were now sitting their horses.

"Howdy," said one of the horsemen. "We're from the Double B. Sorry to bother you, but did one of our men happen to stray down this way tonight? We're shy a man and are afraid something might have happened to him."

"You know none of your men would have strayed down this way," Larry replied coldly.

"Well, we didn't know . . ."

At this moment a clamor arose that caused all four men to look toward the barn. Casey had heard and was shouting at the top of his voice. Jerry put out the lantern light. Then the riders spurred their horses toward the barn, and Larry and Jones ran after them with their guns glinting in the moonlight.

As they ran toward the barn, Larry upbraided himself for not having closed the barn doors. Casey surely had heard the pound of hoofs in the courtyard and, fearful that the KT riders were returning, had glued an ear to one of the numerous cracks in the harness room and listened. The voice of the Double B rider had carried clearly in the night air. Casey had heard what was said and now was shouting his head off, hoping to gain his freedom.

"Keep 'em covered," Larry told Jones as they neared the open door of the barn.

The Double B riders drew up just outside the barn, where the moon shone fully on them. Larry and Jones, with their guns in their hands, stopped, each at the horse of one of the men.

"Are you in there, Casey?" called the rider who had acted as the spokesman.

"I'm locked in!" shouted Casey. "Get me out of here! They've got my horse! Get me out!"

116

"What's the big idea?" demanded the spokesman of Larry.

"Listen, you two . . . keep your right hands on your saddle horns," Larry ordered sharply. "You're covered, and you're going to stay covered until you get out of here. That rat in there was shooting at Jerry, our barn man. I reckon you knew he was here. He's even told us how Harry and I came to be ambushed by Double B men tonight. That skunk stays where he is until we can turn him over to the sheriff. Now, I'm ordering you off this ranch!"

"We'll take Casey with us," snarled the spokesman, starting to dismount.

Larry's gun spit flame and the report broke sharply on the still air. The spokesman brought his right foot and leg back on the right side of his horse with a curse.

"Reach!" Larry commanded. "Reach . . . or I'll take it for granted you're trying to draw and slip you a KT souvenir."

The spokesman raised his hands.

"You, too," Jones told the second rider. "I'd rather shoot you than not. Be quick about it!"

"Harry, I've got 'em covered," said Larry. "Take their guns."

The spokesman cursed again, and Casey yelled from his locked room as Jones lifted the guns from the riders.

"Now, then, get down off your horses!" Larry ordered.

When the men were on the ground, he had Jones cover them while he went toward the barn.

"Nothing would please me more than for one of you to start to run or something," Jones drawled. "It'll give me a chance for a little target practice. If you can't oblige, stand perfectly still with your hands at your sides like the dummies you are."

"There's always a second time," the spokesman snapped out.

Jones took a step forward. "Open your trap again, and I'll split it from ear to ear."

Jerry had lighted the lantern, and presently Larry came out of the barn with ropes. He quickly bound the men's wrists behind their backs. "Looks like we're going to have a regular jail here, Harry," he said lightly. "Now, move on to the bunkhouse, you two. You can see the light yonder."

In the bunkhouse, Larry quickly bound the ankles and legs of the two riders, while they muttered curses. Soon they were helpless on two bunks. The cook had come in and stood grinning as he watched the trussing up of the men. Each wore a stubble of beard and showed plainly the effects of the wild dissipation in town.

"Doesn't look like we caught much," Larry observed.

"Just Double B range trash," Jones said, lighting a cigarette.

"There'll be more to this," snarled the spokesman.

"Sure thing," said Larry dryly. He turned to the cook. "Get your gun and keep an eye on this sweet pair. I'll send Jerry over shortly to play cards with you the rest of the night and keep 'em amused. Give 'em nothing but water or lead . . . whichever they want."

118

When Larry and Jones were outside, Larry said: "I'm going to take that Casey into town tonight. You'll have to stick around in case some more of these *hombres* show up. Use your own judgment."

"That's perfect," Jones agreed. "Going to eat first?"

"Reckon so."

In the early hours of the morning Larry rode into Pondera with his prisoner riding ahead of him. Sheriff Rowan was in his office, keeping vigil in the wee hours when fights were likely. He slept only a few hours a night during rodeo week.

"Lock this fellow up," said Larry curtly, indicating Casey.

Casey bristled. "He hasn't any right to lock me up," he declared. "This is spite work by the KT, Sheriff."

"Lock him up," Larry repeated. "We'll talk afterward."

Rowan hesitated, then called the jailer, who led Casey away to a cell, cursing and whining by turns.

"Caught him out at the ranch last night," Larry explained to the puzzled official. "Peeking in windows. Took six shots at our barn man. Jones and I were ambushed in the brakes and this fellow confessed Fresee put them up to it. Most likely, Fresee sent him to spy on the house. Two Double B men came after him and that shows they knew where he was. They're trussed up in the bunkhouse. Harry Jones is going to let 'em loose at dawn. Had to keep 'em there so I could get this fellow in without being followed. That's all . . . except that Dad will make the complaint."

The sheriff was shaking his head, a worried expression on his face. "Don't like having a Double B man in here just now," he said. "It might start trouble."

"Listen, Sheriff, how about my business yesterday . . . about Bloat, I mean?"

"The coroner's jury will exonerate you," Rowan replied, "but for the love of Mike be careful, Larry! It makes it hard for me."

Larry looked at him scornfully. "I suppose you think I'm going to let somebody plug me, eh?"

"Don't get smart with me," flared the sheriff. "I don't care if you are Lafe Owens's boy."

Larry paused in the doorway. "I didn't mean it the way it sounded, Sheriff," he said slowly. "But, you see, you're not the only one with a lot on his mind these days. I guess you understand. I'm going over to the hotel."

"Forget it, Larry," said Rowan, smiling.

Lafe Owens received Larry's report in cool silence. "I won't shove this Casey," he decided aloud after a moment. "It wouldn't do any good, and I believe it was probably drink that put the idea of such a fool stunt in his head. Maybe the others knew about it, but I don't believe Fresee ordered him to spy on the house. Bolten wouldn't stand for it, because we've always kept our home ranches apart from any other activities. Bolten will give them thunder when he hears of it. But we'll leave this Casey in there a spell."

This was the only comment his father made, but Larry could see that Lafe was doing some tall thinking, that his eyes glinted strangely. Larry rode back to the ranch that morning and found that Jones had released the prisoners and sent them on their way with empty guns and cartridge belts and a few well-chosen words of advice. Then they rode out on the range, pursuant to Lafe's orders, and brought in half a dozen cowpunchers to stay in the bunkhouse.

The next morning Larry and Jones rode to town. The rodeo proper was over, but big crowds remained for the last day of the week, many staying over because of the Association meeting. There was considerable excitement in town, although the cattlemen were calm, discussing range matters among themselves and transacting such business as was required to prepare for the winter season. There was a sensation before the calling of the meeting, however, when the entire Double B outfit rode into town at noon.

Whether this was a piece of dramatics on the part of Bolten or not, it created an unfavorable impression and disapproval was freely voiced by businessmen and others. The stockmen were silent. The feud between the KT and the Double B was, to all appearances, none of their affair, and certainly it had, on the exterior, no bearing on the meeting or connection with the Association. Yet, within twenty minutes of the arrival of the Double B outfit, the order for all KT men to remain on the north side of Main Street was in effect.

A big crowd assembled in the street before the entrance to the stairway leading to the hall where the meeting was to be held, which was over the largest of the general stores. At two o'clock the members began to file up the stairs. Lafe Owens was among the first and Jim Bolten among the last.

Old Lafe sat behind a small table on the raised platform at the rear of the hall. The secretary of the Association sat at another table to keep the minutes. When the preliminaries had speedily been dispensed with, Lafe rose. He was a fine figure of a man, towering above the table, his eyes flashing, every line in his features denoting strength of purpose, soundness of mind. His keen gaze roved over the sea of faces before him, most of them the faces of seasoned stockmen with records of many years on that range. The newer members, all from the far east end, could readily be segregated. Jim Bolten sat in a front seat to the right of the platform. As Lafe walked out from the table to the edge of the platform to speak, he was greeted by tremendous applause. He waved a hand and smiled. His face beamed with pleasure.

"Men, I've called this meeting for a very simple purpose. If you hadn't all been here in town, and able to spare half an hour, I wouldn't have called you together. Most of you I know. Those of you who are new members should know that I've been president of this Association for the past twenty years. I reorganized it, put it on its feet with the help of the members, and we have prospered ever since. There has been peace on the range, rustling has been wiped out, all of our problems have been solved to the satisfaction of the Association, its members, and the whole range in general, with its several towns, the largest of which is Pondera." He paused, noting with satisfaction the looks

122

of approval on the faces of most of those in his audience. He was choosing his words carefully. "A certain discussion seems to have developed lately." The audience held its breath, knowing he referred to the KT/Double B feud, and expecting an outburst, perhaps, from Jim Bolten. "This, however, has nothing to do with this organization or the range in general. It will be adjusted in time. I've been president of this body for many years, as I've said, yet I've not made an active campaign for election to that office in fourteen years." He paused to let this sink in. "This year we again elect a president. He should be a man familiar with the business of the Association, well acquainted with range affairs, in close touch with market and financial conditions, and . . . an able executive. I leave it to the members to decide if I have shown those qualities in the past. I now announce my candidacy for election as president of the Teton Cattlemen's Association for an eleventh term."

There was a short period of silence, and then the hall rang with cheers. But Lafe noted that this cheering was not as loud as that which had greeted his preparation to speak. He resumed: "This time I propose to make an active campaign. Members of the Association, I stand on my record. I start my campaign here and now . . . in the open and above board!"

Again the cheers burst forth. "That's aimed at me!" shouted Bolten, leaping to his feet. Instantly there was silence. "Somebody has been circulating the report that I'm organizing the east end, the east half of the range, to make trouble. It's a lie! I want you all to know that

I'm a candidate for president of the Association. If I can organize the east end to vote for me, that's my privilege. The east end is entitled to a president once in twenty years. I'm out in the open for president just as much as you are, Lafe Owens!" Bolten shouted the last words hoarsely and shook his fist at the figure on the platform.

"That's what I wanted to know," rang out Lafe's voice, "and that's what I wanted the members to know. I want a fight in the open and I'm goin' to have it!"

"You insult a member of almost as long standing as yourself in this Association!" shouted Bolten, his face purpling.

"I am insulting no one," Lafe retorted sternly. "I am bringing this campaign to an issue, so that there cannot be any misunderstanding on the part of our members. Now that you have declared yourself, we know where we stand."

Older stockmen appreciated what they considered a brilliant move on the part of Lafe Owens. Already he had some doubtful members, whose votes he had stood to lose, guessing now, and he had scored on Bolten. But Bolten wasn't through. "This whole business has been planned to hurt me in my attempt to be elected president," he accused harshly. "If this is a sample of the kind of tricks you're goin' to play, Lafe Owens, I'll play some tricks of my own!"

Lafe nodded and looked out at the sea of faces. "This is a sample of my tricks," he said calmly, "played in front of a majority of the members of the Association."

124

Before Bolten could frame an adequate reply, Lafe dropped behind the table, brought the gavel down with a smashing impact, and announced: "This meeting is adjourned!"

It might have been a signal, for more than half those present rose instantly and started to file out. Bolten's protest was drowned in the clamor of loud voices, cheers, moving of chairs and shuffling of booted feet. The meeting was over.

Jim Bolten came thrashing down the stairs like a charging bull. His face was a dark red, his eyes were blazing. Behind him came virtually all the stockmen from the eastern half of Teton range. They had waited until the west-enders had left and heard Bolten tell them in thunderous tones to stick to a man for east-end rights. Bolten was fighting mad after his second defeat at the hands of the old centaur of the KT. All thought of fairness was banished from his mind. Trickery, chicanery, threats, cajolery, brute force — anything to lick Lafe Owens. Momentarily he had thrown discretion to the winds. At his elbow, when he reached the street, was Fresee, his black eyes snapping with triumph.

The crowd gave way before them, fell back at the enraged looks that Bolten cast about. Gradually the crowd left the scene as the principals disappeared. But already the rumor was afloat that Lafe Owens had played another trump, had made a masterstroke in forcing Bolten into the open and in an unfavorable light at that. A slogan began to be whispered: "East for east." It spread and increased in volume until it fairly thundered through the town. It was countered by "West means the West," and Pondera was split into two factions in an hour. A difference was noted now in the attitude of the stockmen. They appeared more alert, animated by some inward quickening of spirit, and, when the groups gathered, they were either all west-enders or all east-enders. Thus the word went out that the Association had split! As the Association was the most important factor in maintaining the prosperity of the range, this rumor created a tremendous sensation.

In the lobby of the hotel Fresee spoke a few words in Bolten's ear that caused the rancher to whirl on him and put a question.

"Framed him," said Fresee in an undertone. "The boys are milling around, mighty sore. Casey was pretty drunk, they claim. He ain't much, but he belongs to the outfit, and . . ."

"No Double B man gets in jail in this town," said Bolten, his anger swelling. Here was an opportunity for an outlet of his feelings. "Tell the boys I'll be over there in a minute."

He was overheard, and the word spread among the KT outfit in an incredibly short time. They had heard about Casey's spying and shooting at the ranch house the night before and naturally they were incensed. Heretofore, a house had been held inviolate. The Double B had broken this unwritten law; at least, so they looked at the incident. Within fifteen minutes the entire outfit was armed.

Meanwhile, Lafe Owens had made a formal complaint against Casey, to hold him until he could ascertain more facts in the matter and question the prisoner himself. Now he intended to hold him because of Bolten's aggressive stand in the matter. He would show the Double B owner who it was in the county controlled the votes, if necessary by dictating to the sheriff. Practically the entire Double B outfit had gathered in the vicinity of the jail. The sheriff recognized the storm signals and gathered his deputies. He had the complaint in a drawer of his desk, and he proposed to hold his prisoner at all costs. He would not be dictated to by Bolten or anybody else. It was a tense moment for him, for he had received word that Bolten was coming shortly to his office to demand Casey's release.

When Bolten had finished with his conference at the hotel, he left and walked briskly along with Fresee to the jail. Gathered on the north side of the street were the KT men, while the Double B outfit crowded the south side. Scores of spectators were in the street itself. It was a fit setting for the drama that was to ensue. Stan Velie had given strict orders to his men, but he was doubtful of the outcome.

Bolten strode unceremoniously toward Sheriff Rowan's office. The sheriff, seated at his desk, looked up with a frown as the door was thrown open and Bolten made his entrance with Fresee behind him. He realized that this was the first issue of the rumored split and the feud, and he proposed to remain neutral.

"Have you got one of my men here?" Bolten demanded belligerently.

"I don't know," said the sheriff. "What's the name?"

"You know his name as well as I do, and you don't have to ask it," said Bolten harshly. "Look here, Rowan, what're you tryin' to pull?"

The sheriff's eyes were cold. "That doesn't sound like sense to me, Bolten. You know I'm not trying to pull anything. I'm doing my duty as sheriff."

Bolten cursed. "Since you see fit to tie a lot of red tape around that tin star of yours, I'll tell you the name. It's Casey. Trot him out!"

The sheriff's gaze hardened. "Have you got papers for his release?"

"I don't need papers for his release," Bolten fumed. "He's one of my men and I'm responsible for him."

"Just now he's my responsibility," Rowan said coldly. "He's my prisoner, and, so far as I know, no bail has been set."

"You mean to tell me you won't release him on my word?" Bolten thundered, bringing his fist down on the desk in a smashing blow.

Rowan leaped to his feet. "Not on anybody's word!" he exclaimed. "When the proper papers are in my hands, he can go, and not a split second sooner."

Fresee's mean laugh was heard. The sheriff's eyes flashed. He strode around the desk, confronted the Double B foreman, and pointed to the open door. "Get out of here!" he commanded. "Get out of my office, or, so help me, I'll lock you up, too."

Fresee hesitated, his eyes narrowing dangerously. Several deputies advanced toward him from the outer office. "Get out!" Rowan repeated. Fresee caught a look from Bolten and went out. Rowan slammed the door. Then he turned on Bolten. "What're you trying to do? Make a lot of trouble for me? I'm not mixed up in this thing, and you damned well know it. I'm sheriff of this county. When a prisoner is delivered for safekeeping with the proper papers, I've got to keep him. I haven't the authority to let this Casey go. See the county attorney or the justice who has authority in such cases. You can't come in here and try to bully me, Bolten. I have the law behind me." Rowan walked back around his desk.

"Who made this complaint?" Bolten asked.

"I don't have to answer that, as I see it, but I will. Lafe Owens made the complaint."

Bolten nodded. "What is the complaint?"

"Casey was prowling around the KT ranch house and took six shots at the barn man out there. Assault with an attempt to kill, and trespassing. He can be put away for that."

"Casey was drunk," said Bolten harshly. "Worse stunts than that have been pulled around here and nothing said. It's just a scheme of Owens to get one of my men out of the way. Rowan . . . which side are you on?"

"I'm telling you, I'm neutral. I'm not taking sides because I can't afford to."

"You're a liar!" cried Bolten. "You're siding with Owens and you know it. That's why you're holding Casey."

Rowan's face was white. His whole body trembled. It was some time before he could control his voice to speak. "Bolten, get out of here," he said huskily. "Get out, Bolten, for heaven's sake, because I'm not responsible. If you open your mouth again, I'll drop you in your tracks."

Bolten saw a look in the sheriff's eyes he had never seen there before. It was a flickering, maniacal light. The official was shaking and he leaned on his right hand, gripping the desk. Bolten turned abruptly and went out, closing the door behind him. He was calmer now. As he reached the head of the steps leading to the sheriff's office alone, a hoarse cry went up from the Double B men, packed around the bottom of the steps. Bolten shook his head and made a gesture to indicate that his mission had proved futile. Silence fell over the crowd, then there was a rush past the Double B owner and, before those in the outer office realized what was happening, the room was crowded with men. Only one shot was fired before the attackers fell upon the deputies, knocking them down, piling up on them, and disarming them.

"Get the keys!" cried a commanding voice.

As the sheriff jerked open the door of his office, two men hurled themselves upon him, throwing him to the floor. It was the suddenness of the attack that caught the lawman unawares. His gun was wrenched from his hand before he could pull the trigger, and he was held face downward so that he could not see his assailants.

It took but a few seconds to secure the keys from the jailer, and then some of the men ran into the cell-block.

130

Meanwhile, the street outside was in a turmoil. Spectators were running in all directions, raising a cloud of dust. Through the choking veil the KT men dashed across the street. As they reached the foot of the jail steps, there came a veritable roar of guns and they split, crowding to each side of the steps as the Double B men came plunging down. Other cowpunchers, deliberately taking sides, closed in, and instantly there was a fighting, milling mass raising a dense fog of dust in the street.

Sheriff Rowan, who had been liberated when the Double B men left the jail, stood at the top of the steps, white-faced, with his arms outstretched on either side of him, holding his deputies back. From the direction of the hotel Larry and Jones came on the run. Bolten had disappeared. The street was clear except for the swirling mob in the dust. Jones ran to one side of the ring of combat, Larry to the other, calling: "KT, break away!" Stan Velie, in the thick of it, was throwing men right and left in an effort to single out KT men and wave them out of the fray. The dust and the press of closely packed combatants made gun play impossible. Men went down, others stumbled over them, wrestling in the thick dust of the street. Three forms lay motionlessly at the foot of the jail steps.

As Jones circled the human whirlpool, a figure came reeling out of the dust. Jones caught sight of the gun leveled at him just in time. His right hand snapped into action and his gun barked sharply. The man went to his knees and toppled onto his face. It was Casey.

By now the dust was so thick it choked and blinded. Men staggered away on all sides. Shots rang out, but the firing soon ceased. The sheriff was in the street now, and at his side was the tall, commanding figure of Lafe Owens. The sight of them seemed to bring the combatants to their senses. They ran in all directions. As the dust settled, two more forms were to be seen lying inert, mute testimony to the deadly seriousness of the encounter.

Stan Velie, wounded and torn, approached the sheriff and old Lafe. He was shaking his head and his face was the color of chalk.

"How many?" asked Lafe shortly.

"Two, and one wounded, and I don't know how many broken heads," the foreman replied hoarsely. "Fresee's missing."

Lafe noted his foreman's look. Fresee, then, had instigated this outrage and had then fled the scene. Bolten, too. Lafe's lips curled. He turned to Sheriff Rowan, who appeared dazed by the scene he had witnessed.

"I guess you know where you stand now," Lafe said grimly.

"What can I do?" said the sheriff, looking about vaguely.

"Nothing," Lafe answered curtly. He turned to Velie. "Where's Larry?" There was the suggestion of a tremor in his voice.

"Gone with the men," replied the KT foreman. "I ordered them to saddle up . . . the whole outfit. They'll come back . . ." He looked at the forms lying in the dust, and Lafe understood what he meant.

"Might hope this'll settle it," Lafe said to the sheriff, and turned away with Velie.

At sunset the town of Pondera was quiet. The street was clear; the sidewalks practically deserted. The KT and Double B outfits were gone. Most of the stockmen and their outfits had left. Clouds scuttled across the high western skies so that funereal lights played on the mountains. The wind whined in naked branches. Rodeo had spent its term.

# CHAPTER
# TWELVE

The courtyard of the KT group of ranch buildings was swarming with men. The outfit had returned from town, to be followed by Lafe Owens and Stan Velie. The cowpunchers were smoking in the cool air of evening after having had supper in the bunkhouse eating room. They talked in low tones of the tragic happenings in town. Jones had won their respect and was one of them. They had always been loyal to Lafe Owens and Larry. They admired Stan Velie. But they felt that the present trouble was not merely a feud between old Lafe and Jim Bolten, but also a feud between the KT and Double B outfits. They had particularly resented the intrusion of Casey at the ranch house. It amounted to spying on the womenfolk, and the very thought made their blood boil. Jerry had told his story, and told it well. It had the effect of making the KT outfit more dangerous even than the Double B crew. But the situation was ruled by Stan Velie who now was boss in every sense of the word. The men welcomed this new attitude of stern authority on the part of their foreman. He had been lenient, generous, somewhat easy-going, but when the trouble started, he had reverted to the Velie who the old-timers had known and respected. The men were satisfied with their leader, which is nine-tenths of any battle so far as morale is concerned. As night came on, they went into the bunkhouse. But no cards were played, for they were to bury two comrades on the morrow.

Inside the big, rambling ranch house, Lafe Owens and his wife sat before the fire in the living room. Molly was upstairs. Larry and Jones were in Larry's room.

"But did Larry have to do it?" Mrs. Owens asked.

"I reckon he did," replied Lafe. "In fact, I know he did. Larry isn't the kind to pick a fight, and this is his first gun play. Bloat was out to make a fool of him. It would have been all right if he had stuck to that. He'd only have got a beating. His big mistake was in going for his gun." He paused, his eyes sparkling. "They tell me Larry is powerful fast on the draw."

His wife leaned toward him and put a hand on his arm. "There's the big danger, Lafe. Men who are slow on the draw don't attract attention, and they don't get into trouble, usually. It's the fast ones who get into mix-ups. This will affect Lawrence, I don't know how much. And I don't want our boy to turn into a killer."

"There's no danger of that," her husband assured her. "I know Larry pretty well . . . better than he thinks."

"But Lafe . . . he may have inherited . . . he might . . ."

"That's story stuff," Lafe broke in scornfully. "He got his draw by practice. You don't inherit such things. I taught him a trick or two because I wanted him to be

**135**

able to protect himself in any emergency, that's all. There's no need to worry, Mother."

"Who is this Jones? No one knows anything about him. How did you come to hire him?"

"I didn't." Lafe smiled. "Larry told Bolten he was a new member of the outfit when Bolten made a fuss about Jones. They've done each other a favor or two, and I thought Larry might as well have a friend here this winter. So Jones is staying on."

"This winter, Lafe? Isn't Larry going back to college?"

Lafe shook his head but looked away. "He doesn't want to go, and I guess it would be better if he stuck around. I'm getting old, and now . . . this trouble . . ." He ceased talking with the abruptness of one who thinks he has said too much.

"Oh, Lafe, don't go on. I know the old feud is on again. The cook gets the news from the men and passes it on to Mary O'Neil. Little by little I get the facts from her. It makes me cold all over to think of it. Think of the times when Larry and Molly were born. It's a wonder they are healthy children, with me bearing the burden of worry that I shouldered then. The night Jim Bolten shot you through the left arm, he was aiming at your heart. Lafe, he meant to kill you."

"He was lucky that night," Lafe said grimly. "I can outdraw and outshoot him, even now. He knows better than to make it too personal."

"There it is again. Guns . . . always guns. And now once more they will jeopardize our very existence. If it was a reign of terror before, what will it be this time

**136**

when your resources and Bolten's have multiplied a hundredfold, almost?"

"I'm fighting him with different weapons. I'm not depending on guns, although they'll be handy."

There was an interval of silence before Mrs. Owens spoke again. "Lafe, why don't you let him have the Association presidency and avoid all this trouble? You can keep peace on our range with almost a single word, if you would speak it to the stockmen . . ." She paused as she saw his look.

"Give in to him? At the cost of my honor? After what I told the members today? Never! If he had gone about things in the right way, I wouldn't have made the slightest effort to be elected president again. But he's been sneaking around behind my back, with that Fresee at his ear, urging him on. No, I can't backwater now. And I'm convinced there's more to this than just heading the Association. Fresee's got something in the back of his head. He hates me and wants revenge, so he thinks. Where would I be if I let them start riding me on this range?"

His wife sighed. She knew it was useless to try to persuade Lafe to give in. She could not resist a feeling of pride because of his sturdy stand for his rights, but she knew, as all women of the range knew, what ramifications could result from a feud. "That fight in town today was just the beginning, Lafe. It shows what they are ready to do."

"We had to show them that they couldn't bring trouble into our very dooryard. Casey was a skunk, anyway. They can't tell me he just stumbled in here drunk. He was sent here, for what purpose I do not know." He did not see fit to mention the ambush or the shot taken at Larry in the dark.

"This young Jones is the one who shot Casey after they got him out. Tell me, is he a gunman, too?"

Lafe swore under his breath. He would see that the cook did no more talking! "He's fast, but I have no gunmen . . . as you call them . . . on this ranch. Things may settle down after the regular meeting of the Association, dear. Bolten may be elected, after all. I don't feel any too sure of myself. I'm still banking on Bolten having too much sense to start big trouble, a range war. For one thing, I'm going to fight him with dollars, not bullets."

"Lafe!" His wife sat up, startled. "You wouldn't jeopardize our property, would you? Think of the children!"

"I won't jeopardize any property or any stock. But I'll use 'em as a club, and Bolten will find out mighty quick that it isn't stuffed."

Sarah Owens was worried. "There's another thing, Lafe, that you must do for my sake, and the sake of Larry and Molly. You must be careful of yourself, for if anything was to happen to you . . ." She left the sentence unfinished.

Molly came down the stairs, ending the conversation.

When Larry and Jones came down later, they found Molly alone in the living room. Larry hurried out, but Jones tarried as Molly spoke to him. Jones was uneasy and apparently not prepared with his customary line of friendly badinage. He wore his gun. It seemed to Molly

**138**

that she could not keep her eyes off the weapon, and Jones noted this. "We're going out on the range," he said in explanation.

"Tonight?" Molly asked in surprise.

"Merely for a ride, I think," he said with a slight frown.

"Mister Jones, tell me about what happened in town today," she invited, motioning to a chair.

Jones shrugged but did not take the chair. "You heard about it?"

"I heard there was a terrible fight and that four or five men got killed, including that . . ." She bit her lip as she stopped short.

"They tried to break him out of jail and we helped the sheriff. That was all. It was our duty."

"Was it your duty to shoot that prisoner?" Molly asked in a queer voice.

"I get a certain amount of satisfaction out of living," Jones replied stiffly. "It was shoot or pass in my harp ticket to be punched. I think you can understand that."

"You gunmen all have an alibi," Molly observed soberly, shaking her head. "It's a dreadful thing to kill a man, Mister Jones. Why, Larry's experience already has changed him."

Jones's eyes flashed. "Larry could no more have evaded that business than he could have disappeared into thin air. I reckon he would rather have vanished . . . anything . . . than have had that thing happen. You mustn't blame Larry a bit, Miss Molly. That outfit is dangerous and hung on a hair-trigger. It's as bad-acting a crowd as I ever saw, and I've trailed around some."

Although Molly admired him for standing squarely behind her brother and sticking up for him, she was troubled and doubtful. She wondered if this friend, this new friend, would be a good influence in Larry's life. "I guess you like Larry."

"If I didn't, I wouldn't be here."

"You seem to have had more experience than he's had. I know he likes you. You can have a good influence on him, if you choose."

Jones's brows lifted. "Meaning, perhaps, that I haven't been a good influence? I'm ready to take the blame for everything, Miss Molly, if it'll ease your mind any."

"Oh, I'm not asking that. And I'm not really blaming you. It's just that . . ."

She seemed on the verge of tears. Jones sat down on the edge of a chair near her.

"This isn't a tame country by a long shot," he said seriously. "Just because Larry . . . yes, and myself . . . had to do something we didn't want to do is no sign we'll have to do it again. But a man has to protect himself. Self-preservation, and all that." He paused, and then continued, looking now toward the fire. "I've had to shoot a man twice before. It wasn't a pleasant sensation the first time. It was worse the second. Tonight I feel none too good. I hope you don't think any less of me . . . if you think of me at all . . . because of what happened today. There was no other way out."

Molly was staring at him in fascination. A veil seemed drawn over his eyes. He appeared almost dejected. She had heard, though, of gunfighters being

**140**

afflicted with remorse after a killing. Many times they took to drink for a spell. Could Jones be one of the breed that kills for pleasure? It seemed ridiculous and she put the thought from her mind. Yet the killing of Casey had thrust something between them. And she looked at Larry, too, in a new light. "I've hardly been able to speak to Larry since he came back from town," she said dully. "I . . . I don't know what to say to him. That's one reason why I . . . I wanted to talk to you."

"Don't say anything about his trouble," Jones counseled. "Just give him a pat on the shoulder. That'll make him feel better. What's done is done, and you can't change it. It won't do any good to talk about it. Menfolk like to have peace in their homes, especially when they have relatives and . . ." He paused, then rose.

Molly rose, too. "Haven't you any relatives, Mister Jones?" she asked innocently and then, seeing his change of expression, added hastily: "I didn't mean to ask that. Of course you have, and it's none of my business, anyway."

"The only relative I know of is in jail this minute," he said laconically, and walked out of the room, leaving her alone in front of the fire.

Unwittingly she had hurt him, and, in pure disgust probably, he had told her a secret. It was a secret she would keep. But suddenly she felt a wave of sympathy sweep over her. Jones, then, had no home but this. She flushed, for no reason she could determine. She went out onto the porch. The moon was riding high in the sky. Clouds were drifting among the stars, like sails of vagrant, celestial ships. The last yellow leaves of the cottonwoods spiraled in the night wind. From somewhere on the bench road came the dull, echoing pound of flying hoofs. Molly Owens shivered in the cool atmosphere and went back into the house. The night gave her a feeling of loneliness she could not understand.

In the meantime, Lafe Owens and Stan Velie were conferring in front of the barn. Larry and Jones were in the bunkhouse with the men. Lafe and Velie both heard the horse come trotting down the road and moved into the courtyard to see who arrived. Jerry came out of the bunkhouse, and, as the horse came to a walk at the upper end of the courtyard, the KT owner and his foreman heard the barn man cry out and run for the horse.

"He ain't got a rider!" Jerry shrilled. "Reins wrapped around the saddle horn! KT brand, too."

Velie sprang forward and men came pouring out of the bunkhouse door through which the yellow lamplight streamed.

"Come here, you 'punchers!" called Velie. "Take a look at this horse and see if you know whose string he's out of."

The men crowded about the horse that with the reins tied about the saddle horn had returned to the ranch. If the reins had been left dangling, the animal would have stood indefinitely. Therefore, it seemed apparent that its rider had purposely tied the reins to the horn and started the horse for home. This could mean but one thing: the rider was in trouble.

142

"That's Bud Davis's horse," said one of the cowpunchers who had been called in to guard the house when Larry and Jones had gone to town that morning. "We left him alone over on the east range by the cut-off corner. There's a bunch of three-year-old shorthorns down there."

"Make sure of that," Velie snapped, looking the saddle over.

The man who had spoken walked around the horse slowly and examined the bridle and saddle. "He was riding that horse with that saddle and bridle when we left him," he said in a convincing voice. He called two others who had been riding herd down there and they confirmed his opinion.

"Eight of you saddle up," Velie ordered. "Davis has sent his horse in because he's in trouble. I'll go with you. You three who were working with Davis, come along."

In a moment the men were running to the corrals for their best mounts.

"We'll go along, too," Larry told Velie, indicating Jones at his side.

Velie nodded and turned to Lafe Owens who had come up and had listened to the identification. "It may be that Davis had a fall and sent his horse in so we'd know he was in trouble," Velie told Lafe. "Maybe he got hurt some other way. There's bad ground down in that southeast corner by the brakes, even if the grass is good. It won't take us an hour to get there."

"Send a man back as soon as you find out what's up," Lafe ordered. "I want to know." He turned into the house, frowning. "I don't think Bolten would meddle on my range at present," he muttered. Stan Velie hurried to the barn where Jerry was saddling his horse. In another five minutes the eight cowpunchers, with Larry and Jones, rode out of the courtyard for the bench road with Stan Velie at their head.

Those left behind in the bunkhouse talked in low, excited tones. It was significant that Velie had taken men toward the cut-off corner.

# CHAPTER
# THIRTEEN

The cut-off corner, as it was called, was the extreme south-eastern section of the KT range. The corner was, indeed, cut off by a high ridge that was the beginning of the river brakes. To the east was Double B range. No one had claimed the range south of the river for many miles. The cut-off was fenced to prevent the cattle straying into the wilderness of brakes and badlands and the dividing line between the KT and Double B ranges was fenced from the brakes twelve miles north. It was this line that had precipitated the feud years before. The grass in the corner was particularly good and was saved annually for the shorthorns that were to be shipped as beeves the following year. This portion of the range was good for wintering a sizable herd of shorthorns, cattle that are poor rustlers. The Herefords did very well farther north and, in an emergency, were the last cattle that had to be fed. Thoroughbred horses were kept mostly in the bottoms.

Although Stan Velie gave no indication of what was going on in his mind, he was worried. There was prize stock in the corner, where three or even four men were often riding herd. If the cattle broke through the fence and got into the brakes, there would be slight chance of ever rounding all of them up and getting them out. They would scatter through a labyrinth of trails made by strays and game, get into the soap holes — treacherous patches of quicksand with an alkali crust — and, if a third of them were recovered, it would be a matter of pure luck.

The KT foreman set the pace at a ringing gallop as they reached the benchland and swung southeast. He didn't wish Bud Davis any hard luck, but he hoped it was a case of an injury or of protecting a break in the fence rather than of the loss of cattle. And if Davis had been hurt, he had at least been able to stand up and tie the reins of his bridle to the horn. His horse was not an ordinary cow pony and had been bred at the ranch, kept in pasture there. It was his prize mount and he had bought it out of his wages. Therefore, it was a more intelligent animal than the average range pony.

In a little over half an hour the dark dots that appeared on the plain denoted bedded cattle and Velie sighed with relief. They swept on until they reached the herd. Then Velie gave orders to his men to spread out and keep a sharp look-out for sign of Bud Davis. They were to converge near the shack where the men who worked this section of the range lived while on duty. With Larry and Jones, he rode for the shack that was situated some distance east of the corner proper.

As they rode through the cattle, Velie looked about with a practiced eye. The cattle were a good distance from the fence shutting off the badlands and did not appear to have been disturbed. Horses were off to the right. If Davis had wanted someone to come out from the ranch quickly, he could have sent in his good horse and ridden one of the others. But his horse had necessarily borne his saddle and Velie didn't know if there were other saddles in the shack or not. Anyway, no horseman was in sight except those men Velie had brought along. The clouds were gathering now; the wind was shifting to the northwest and freshening — true harbinger of a storm. It might prove to be the first blizzard of the approaching winter. It was growing colder. The light filtered through the banking clouds in fitful gleams and grotesque shadows scampered over the plain. This weird effect of cloud and moon and shadow, and the whistling wind in sere grasses, made the cattle uneasy and they soon were all on their feet and bunching. With the onrush of the storm they would begin to mill.

Leaving the cattle behind, Velie and the two youths rode straight for the shack that now was a square blot of shadow directly ahead. They had almost reached it when Stan Velie cried out and brought his horse to a rearing stop. Larry and Jones halted beside him and for a few moments looked at the dark form on the ground. They all were out of their saddles in a twinkling and Velie was bending over the prostrate form of Bud Davis.

"It's Davis, all right," said Velie. "There's so much blood on his face I couldn't recognize him at once. Here, Larry, help me get him on my horse. Ride ahead and make a light in that shack, Jones."

As Jones sped away, Velie and Larry got the unconscious cowpuncher across Velie's saddle. Velie then mounted behind and they rode in to the shack. Jones had a lantern lighted by the time they arrived and they put Davis on one of the lower bunks in the shack.

Velie made a careful examination. "He's hit in the head," he announced. "Up over the left ear. I can't tell you how deep it is. Get some water, one of you. I've got two extra handkerchiefs that are clean, thank goodness. Help me off with his shirt, Larry."

Further examination showed that another bullet had hit the cowpuncher in the left collar bone. Velie could find no other wounds. He went to work at once, cleansing and bandaging the wounds as best he could and giving orders during the process.

"Jones, ride back to the ranch as fast as you can and report to the old man. Tell him I don't know yet what this shooting was about, but that I think you'd better race right on into town for a doctor. Tell him I'm sending Davis in as soon as I can and will stay here to investigate."

Jones was off at a mad gallop as soon as the words of instruction were out of Velie's mouth.

"Larry, tell the men who're coming in to wait for further orders," Velie directed. "And ride back there . . . better take some of the men with you . . . and see if you can find Davis's gun. It isn't on him."

Velie worked over the unconscious form on the bunk for some little time. Then he got the shirt back on and called one of the men outside to help him put a Mackinaw, that was hanging on a nail behind the door, on Davis as a protection against the cold wind.

He had hardly finished when Larry returned with a six-shooter. "Found it right about where he was lying," Larry explained.

Velie took the gun to the light. There were bloodstains on the barrel and cylinder. He was careful not to touch these as he broke the gun and took out the shells, one by one, replacing them immediately. Every cartridge had been fired!

"There's been trouble here all right," the foreman muttered grimly. He wrapped the gun carefully in a newspaper that was on the table, thrust it into his side pocket. But in a moment he thought better of this and took it out, handing it to Larry. "Put that in your pocket and take it back to the ranch. Give it to your father." He paused, frowning. "I guess you better take Davis in yourself, Larry. Keep his head up, whatever you do. He's lost a lot of blood. I'll send a man with you in case you need him. You better start right away. Tell your father I'm goin' to inspect the fence, and, as soon as it's daylight, I'll start counting the cattle. Not that I think any are gone," he concluded hastily, "but I intend to make sure."

They got the unconscious Davis on Larry's horse. Larry climbed up behind to hold him, and Velie delegated a man to go with them. As the pair started for the ranch, Velie ordered the other men to ride the fence in the cut-off, along the east side, and he himself rode with two others to inspect the wire along the south side, between the range and the brakes.

For two hours they rode back and forth but could discover no break in the wire. Then Velie called his crew in to the shack. "If the wire's been cut and joined again, we could never find it in this poor light," he said. "Three of you can take another look in the morning. There's coffee and bacon and enough stuff here for your breakfast. I'm goin' in to the ranch, but I'll be back at daybreak. Let me see." He looked at them, considering for a few moments. Then he turned to Blondy Robbins, who had come along and who had chosen the others. "I make you range boss," he said shortly. "There are seven of you. Have your six men stand guard two at a time in two-hour shifts. Keep the herd well in for we'll count 'em in the morning. I'll bring out more men. If there should be any sign of trouble, send a messenger to the ranch at once."

"I've got you," said Blondy. He turned to the men. "You, Lawson, and you, Williams, take the first guard."

As he left the shack with Blondy, Velie was plainly puzzled and very much concerned. "What do you make of it?"

"There you got me. If it was a cattle raid, you'd think the fence would be punctured. They couldn't very well drive 'em north without some of our men seein' 'em up there. I don't see how they could make away with a bunch of steers through the badlands, either. It looks to me as if some of the Double B crowd had come down here to make trouble and there'd been gun play."

Stan Velie nodded. "It looks very much that way. It all depends on Davis regaining consciousness so he can talk. If he doesn't, we'll never know what happened probably. Keep an eye out the rest of the night, although, if the Double B did this thing, there's small likelihood of any of 'em showing up again."

Velie rode away with an eye to the weather. The scuttling clouds now obscured the moon entirely and most of the stars. The wind was blowing stronger and colder. Velie didn't like this at all. The years he had spent on that range had made him more or less sure of weather indications and he expected snow to be riding on that blast out of the northwest by morning. The snow would cover any tracks. If any of the cattle had been taken, it was likely the rustlers had also recognized the storm signals and were depending on the snow to cover up the evidence of their operations. If it had, indeed, been a case of running off stock, and Davis had fallen, presumably dead, the rustlers would not have expected him to get up and manage to tie his reins and send his horse back to the ranch. Davis had probably done this by sheer willpower, and then dropped in his tracks, or he might have done it before the bullet struck him in the head. He was shot twice and there might have been two attacks. But Velie realized that these conjectures were futile and he sent his horse toward the home ranch at its fastest pace.

Meanwhile, Larry had reached the ranch with his unconscious burden. At this new development, Sarah Owens was cool and collected. She had Davis taken to the spare guest room, which had been occupied by Jones, and immediately set about giving first aid with more at hand to work with than Velie had had in the little shack in cut-off corner. Molly and Mary O'Neil helped her.

**151**

"I expected it," said Sarah, "only I didn't think it would come so soon. I know what these range feuds are. There will be more injuries, maybe more killings, and we women must keep our nerve and bear it."

That was all Sarah Owens had to say. She gave her whole attention to nursing the wounded cowpuncher.

Downstairs, in the living room, Larry delivered Stan Velie's message. His father listened, his face frozen into gray, stern lines. When Larry had finished, Lafe merely nodded. "There was no use in my going out there . . . I knew that. I put Jones on the fastest horse we had in the barn and saw him on to town for the doctor. You better get a few winks of sleep and go back in the morning."

Larry went to the bunkhouse where the men all were up and eager for news. He told them what he knew and lay down on a bunk. He did not hear Stan Velie when he arrived, or Jones, when he came back from town. The doctor was driving out in his buckboard.

Velie reported briefly to Lafe Owens who remained in the living room, awaiting the arrival of the doctor.

"We won't know anything for sure until Davis is able to talk," said Lafe slowly. "But if the Double B did do this, I don't want any reprisals by our side . . . remember that. Not yet, anyway. Our time will come. But I can't believe that Jim Bolten would allow anything like this, not after what happened in town yesterday."

"He might not have known anything about it," Velie pointed out.

"Don't worry," said Lafe sharply. "He knows where his men are at a time like this, just as I know where my men are. He left town with his outfit and you can lay to it that none of 'em strayed on the way back home."

Velie took this as a dismissal. "I'll snatch thirty winks before morning. I'll be in the bunkhouse if you want me."

Lafe nodded and resumed his pipe, looking steadily into the glowing embers of the fire.

Toward morning Sarah Owens approached her husband. "He's muttering," she said slowly. "I believe he's badly hurt, Lafe. Suppose . . . suppose he should die. We don't know anything about his people, you know."

"Must be something . . . a letter or something . . . among his things."

His wife sat down. She was struggling to keep back the tears. "He's so young. It . . . it might be our own Larry."

"Now, Mother, you mustn't take things this way. That bullet didn't go into his head, so far as I could see. His head was grazed. I'm not worrying about the other wound. But I know that any man who's hurt in my employ, protecting my property, is going to have the best medical and surgical attention that money will buy. He's carrying a fever and he'll most likely be delirious. Listen to anything he says. He might say something that'll give us a hint as to what happened. You better lie down for a spell. The doctor will be here soon. He has a good team and he'll make time, knowing it's me that wants him."

Sarah went back upstairs and Lafe resumed his vigil. Although he had talked bravely to his wife to reassure her and quiet her fears, he was worried. It hit him below the belt, as he thought, to have a man dangerously wounded while protecting his stock, or upholding the cause of the KT. He looked at the gun that Larry had left on the table and stirred uneasily in his chair. Jones returned and reported briefly that the doctor was coming as fast as his team could bring him.

Lafe went upstairs to the sickroom. Bud Davis lay flat on the bed, his face below the bandages the color of old celluloid. He was picking at the covers and his lips were moving but emitting no sound. His eyes were closed. Lafe went back down to his chair by the fire and filled his pipe nervously.

At an early hour the doctor arrived. Jerry was waiting and took charge of his team. Lafe let him in the back door and took him in to the fire.

"Starting to snow," said the doctor. "If it turns into a blizzard, I may not get home for a week." He took off his gloves, overcoat, muffler, and hat. "Who's hurt, Lafe?" he asked, rubbing his hands before the fire.

Lafe explained, and then the doctor took his case and went upstairs. Lafe followed him. The physician made his preliminary examination and took off his coat. For an hour he worked over the wounded man, his face serious, eyes keen, fingers deft. Then he administered a hypodermic.

Lafe had sat quietly in a corner of the room. Sarah Owens had been the doctor's assistant. Molly and Mary

O'Neil were outside the door. Davis was uneasy and muttering constantly.

"How about it, Doc?" asked Lafe.

Dr. Moore pursed his lips and shook his head slightly. "Pretty deep," he said. "Pretty deep. Skull may be cracked."

Lafe started from his chair. "You mean he might not come out of it?" he asked anxiously.

The doctor looked at him and nodded. "Too early to tell. I'll have to stay here a while."

"Maybe we better get him to Great Falls to the hospital," Lafe suggested.

The doctor shook his head. "Not yet. And we can't take him anywhere as he is now."

Suddenly a single word came shrilly from the sick man's mouth. "Bianco!" He turned and clutched the covers, and then again lay still.

Lafe stared at him and wet his lips with his tongue. Then he looked at the doctor. "You heard?"

"Delirium," said the doctor. "It's to be expected."

"But the name," said Lafe, greatly excited. "You heard the name?" He stared again at the white face in the pillows. "Bianco," he whispered.

"Somebody you know?" queried the doctor casually.

"Someone I never hope to know or meet," said Lafe, frowning. "I wonder . . . Davis must have met him somewhere. Bianco! I wonder . . . no, it couldn't be, Doctor, it couldn't possibly be. But why should he call that name?"

"You better go downstairs," the doctor decided, taking him by the arm. "Come, I'll go with you, and, if

**155**

you've got it around the place, we'll each take a good, strong, hot whiskey. Then I guess you'd better go to bed. You can't do any good staying up. And you, Missus Owens. There's nothing for you to do now. Molly can stay up. She's young. You will need your strength later on."

Sarah Owens promised to lie down, and Lafe and the doctor went downstairs. Lafe gave an order to Mary O'Neil who went to prepare the hot drinks.

"Davis comes from some place south," Lafe said as if speaking to himself. "He might have met him down there somewhere."

"Met who?" the doctor asked irritably.

"Bianco. The name he called up there."

"Who is this Bianco?"

Lafe smiled as if he pitied him. "You've never heard of him? Well, he's the devil . . . nothing less. Gunman, killer, and rustler king. But he's never worked north of the Wyoming line that I ever heard. Davis has only been with me three years. He came from somewhere south. Maybe he knew him down there, eh?"

"Probably . . . or heard of him. Folks sometimes go back for years when in delirium."

"Yes, that must be it," Lafe said, nodding and filling his pipe with trembling fingers. "That's probably it. He's going back, as you say. There couldn't be any connection, do you think, between that name and what happened down in the corner?"

"I don't know," replied the doctor bluntly. "But I do know that it won't do you any good to get worked up like this. Next thing I know, I'll have two patients on my hands. Here come the drinks."

Mary O'Neil brought in the hot drinks in tall glasses with a slice of lemon floating in each. The doctor took a sip and smacked his lips. Lafe took several swallows. The windows shook with the force of the wind. Lafe went to the front door and opened it a bit. A flurry of snow swept in.

"Blizzard weather," he said, closing the door and returning to the fire.

"I knew it was coming," said the doctor. "The air's had the feel all day. Liable to get three days of it, maybe more. Lucky I haven't got any tough cases in town."

The two gray-haired men resumed their drinks. The house shook with the force of the blast. Lafe called to Mary O'Neil to put more wood on the fire.

"Bianco!"

The word cut through the stillness of the house like a keen-edged blade. Lafe dropped his glass on the bricks before the fireplace where it shattered into pieces. The doctor came quickly and took him by the arm. Lafe slumped in his chair, staring at his pipe. It had gone out.

Day dawned upon a world of white. The wind was driving the snow before it in a steady veil, but there were no gusts, no sudden bursts of fury, for the full force of the blizzard was yet to come.

Stan Velie had the men up and breakfast was eaten just before daylight. Then with ten men, Larry, and Jones, he rode to the cut-off corner range to count the cattle there. Two crews were set to work, each counting half the herd. The work was well under way an hour and a half after dawn.

In the ranch house Lafe Owens slept on a couch in the living room. The doctor was getting some rest in Larry's room upstairs, where he was near his patient. Sarah Owens had been persuaded to lie down and Molly had remained in the sickroom.

All through the early hours of the morning, Bud Davis had tossed and clutched the bedclothes in his delirium. More than once he had spoken the name that Lafe hated to hear. But his other ravings had been of the past — of range life and wild celebrations in the towns. Bessie. None knew of her. She might have been his sister.

Mary O'Neil had breakfast ready an hour after dawn by which time both Lafe and Dr. Moore were up. The doctor's face showed concern. "Temperature of a hundred and five and a tenth," he said laconically when Lafe asked about the patient's condition.

"Dangerous figure, isn't it?"

"Well, it isn't safe."

Lafe went into the living room again after breakfast while the doctor went upstairs. Lafe no longer worried in the hope that Davis would recover consciousness so he could tell what had happened. His whole concern now was for the cowpuncher's life. A man shot down in town or on the range was one thing; a man lying in the shadow of death in the house was another. It brought home poignantly the seriousness of the situation — the uncertainty, the danger, and the tragedy of it all. Lafe was visibly affected. He wandered aimlessly about the lower part of the house, stole up to the stairs occasionally. Once he went out to the barn for no reason at all, then looked into the empty bunkhouse. But always he returned to the chair before the fire to fuss with his pipe and stare vacantly into the blaze.

Sarah Owens was soon up, relieving Molly in the sickroom where the doctor remained at the bedside of his patient. Hours passed and the sick man's eyelids fluttered. The muttering ceased. The doctor spoke softly to Sarah Owens. "Call Lafe," he said. "He's gaining consciousness."

Lafe came quickly up the stairs and stood by the bedside. Suddenly Davis's eyes opened wide and stared fully into old Lafe's face. Lafe leaned over and took one of the sick man's hands. Davis seemed to be trying to remember. Then in an instant the eyes cleared. The lips moved and Lafe leaned low to catch the whisper.

"It . . . was Bianco . . . the cattle . . . shot me . . . missed him . . ."

The veil of delirium dropped over the eyes again and Davis began to laugh a croaking laugh in his throat that was horrible to hear.

Lafe straightened, his face white. He nodded to the doctor who motioned him out of the room. Lafe stumbled down the stairs and dropped into his chair. Bianco on the north range! He had shot Davis, probably because he had recognized him. Davis must have known him somewhere or he wouldn't know his name at once. Davis had emptied his gun at him and missed. Could Bianco have heard about the trouble on

**159**

the range? Did he propose to take advantage of it to ply his nefarious trade of rustling, stealing anything he could, gun play, and rapine? Had he raided the Double B range, also? These questions flashed through Lafe's mind unanswered, and he asked himself how this notorious bandit had gotten to the north range so soon, if he had heard of recent events. Perhaps Bianco had been working north anyway. Doubtless he found it pretty hot in the south where thousands of dollars in rewards were on his head.

The house shook with the sudden gust of wind and the snow strained against the panes. Lafe went to the door and looked out. He couldn't see the trees in the swirl of white flakes. Another gust and then there came a lull with the air suddenly lifeless. Lafe looked at his watch. It was an hour past noon. Velie and the men were due, he thought. If they got caught in the corner when the blizzard broke, they would have to stay there.

Down from the benchland came a billow of white. Then there was wind and snow — a force that rocked the house. Everything was blotted out in a moment. The wind shrieked in the trees and about the buildings. It was an icy blast. Lafe exerted himself in closing the door against the power of that wind. Then the blizzard broke in all its fury.

The fierceness of the storm caused fresh worry for Lafe. If Velie, Larry, and the others had started for home, they could easily become lost. There would be no telling the direction of the wind by wetting a finger in that maëlstrom of swirling snow. One could hardly see his hand before his face in the courtyard, and it

**160**

would be worse on the open prairie where there was no protection of any kind whatsoever from the full force of the raging blizzard.

The doctor came down to dinner in a taciturn mood. Lafe did not have to ask about Davis's condition. He knew by the physician's manner and the constant attention he was giving his patient that the sick man was fighting for his life. The doctor was using every known means to fight the fever that continued to rise in an alarming manner. This information Lafe obtained from his wife, for the doctor refused to talk.

Dinner was a depressing affair. Lafe found his appetite was gone. The others ate little. Sarah Owens was worried about Larry. Lafe was worried himself. Outside, the wind howled and shrieked and blast after blast hurled the snow against the rattling windows until it was impossible to see out of them. The thermometer had dropped to zero at noon. It would go lower, as Lafe knew. He again was restless, going every few minutes to the front windows although he could not see the road where it entered the courtyard.

Then, at two o'clock, he breathed a long sigh of relief as he was peering through a window. Dark shadows appeared suddenly and the riders came thundering into the courtyard, the pounding of their horses' hoofs on the hard ground beneath the thin, shifting layer of snow sounding above the tumult of the storm.

Almost immediately Larry and Stan Velie came in the rear door and Velie entered the living room while Larry paused in the kitchen to arrange for dinner. Lafe saw at once that Velie had important news. The foreman's face was serious. Velie pulled off his gloves and rubbed his hands. "It's blowing pitchforks," he said. "We were lucky to make it. I left it to the horses. How's Davis?"

Lafe shook his head. "Looks bad. Hit deeper than we thought. May not pull through, the doc says."

Velie's brows went up with concern. "So? I'd call that tough if he was to . . . to . . . but he won't. He's got an open-range constitution, that boy. Said anything yet?"

"Let's hear what you have to report first," Lafe suggested.

"Not so good," said Velie. "Lafe, we're a hundred and one head short on the tally down in the corner. The fence was cut at a post just east of the shack down there, and repaired so you could hardly discover it. That's why we couldn't find it last night. And this snow has covered every track, and we can't go hunting for stolen cattle in this weather. We're up against rustlers." The foreman was surprised that Lafe should take the news so calmly.

"I suspected as much before you got here," Lafe said. "Davis came to for a half minute or so this morning and named the leader. Said the man shot him twice while he missed. You remember his gun was empty, so he must have tried mighty hard before he went down."

"Who was the leader?" Velie asked quickly.

"Bianco," said Lafe softly. "But don't tell the men . . . yet."

Velie was staring, open-mouthed. "Bianco?"

"The one and the same," Lafe affirmed grimly. "Davis called his name several times last night, and I thought maybe he was raving about his past when he had met that cut-throat rustler. But this morning he named him straight in his right mind, looking me square in the eyes and knowing me. Bianco has come north."

Velie dropped into a chair, shaking his head and biting his lower lip under his mustache. "That's bad, Lafe . . . worse than bad."

"And worse than that. That man won't stop at anything! As near as I can figure it out, he learned there was only one man with those cattle. He probably raided the herd around sunset, or before. More'n likely he knew we were in town. He must have deliberately rode in and shot Davis down and helped himself to the stock. The worst element of half a dozen tough ranges ride with him. He'd have taken more cattle . . . the whole herd . . . if he could have handled them in the badlands."

Velie nodded. "The brakes are pretty well protected. He might even be able to move cattle in there during this storm, although I doubt it. And we can't make a move until this blizzard has blown itself out."

"We can't make a move then," said Lafe. "He'd shoot down our whole outfit . . . ambush 'em and kill 'em like rats in a trap. Bianco never works a territory until he is familiar with it. He, or some of his men, must have been here for days. What do you make of it, Stan?"

"Don't ask me," said Velie, wrinkling his brow. "This is like the bolt out of a clear sky they tell about. Maybe . . . do you suppose he knew trouble was brewing up here?"

"Just what I'm wondering," said Lafe. "He might take advantage of conditions to pull his raids . . . but he'd raid the Double B, too, wouldn't he?"

"I should think so. And Bolten's got a lot of fine cattle close to the brakes. If he's raiding Bolten's stock, too, then the Double B will most likely want to join with us and try to run him down."

Lafe looked up quickly. "That's so, Stan. I hadn't thought of that. Why, this might wake up what brains Bolten's got and end the trouble. He's got to give in sometime."

"I hope he does," said Velie moodily. "I'll have to tell the men something. They're pretty much worked up. They think this rustling and shooting of Davis is the Double B outfit's doings."

"Tell 'em straight that it isn't," Lafe ordered. "Explain to 'em that you can't tell 'em any more at present. Keep 'em in hand, and, if they get too excited, I'll talk to 'em myself. Now you better get something to eat. I see Larry fussing around out there and you two must be hungry. Where's Jones?"

"He'll likely be a minute . . . but, say, Lafe, there's a good man, even if he is pretty young."

Lafe waved him away and went upstairs.

The doctor was sitting at the bedside with his fingers on the wounded man's pulse. Lafe looked at the strong, young face, white now, although burning with fever. Davis was talking incoherently.

"Bessie!" The cry echoed hollow-like in the room. "No . . . tomorrow . . ." The lips moved silently. "Bianco . . . you rat!" The breathing was labored.

**164**

"Then . . . she'll come back . . . to me . . ." The voice trailed off. In his delirium Bud Davis was trying to sing. "Give us another, Ed!" The sick man tried to sit up, and fell back on the pillows, picking at the bedspread — always picking — picking . . .

The face flushed momentarily and the doctor leaned back. He did not take his eyes from the face in the pillows as he shook his head slowly. He rested his hands on his knees. Sarah Owens stood beside her husband with a hand on his arm. Lafe understood.

"Bianco! Take it . . . I know you!" The sick man's right hand moved back on the coverlet — his gun hand. "Take it and like it . . . Bessie!" He turned his head to the right. Sarah Owens left the room hurriedly. "Let 'er ride for the chunk! Play your luck when you've got it. Play . . . play . . ." The voice died into mutterings with only a distinctly spoken word now and then. The flush came back to the face. "If I'd known in time, Bessie . . . if . . ."

The blizzard's blast shook the house. It was as if the storm exulted in the wounded man's plight as he lay there at the edge of the eternal shadow. A throaty chuckle came from the bed. "Larry did right. Gimme a napkin and . . ." Again that chuckle that sounded as if the sick man was choking. Lafe went out of the room and slowly descended the stairs.

Larry met him in the living room. "The men want to know just how Davis is, Dad. What shall I tell 'em?"

"Tell 'em he's riding the line," said Lafe dully.

"Dad, is it that bad?"

165

"It's that bad, Son. Yes . . . it's that bad. You . . ." He hesitated as to whether to tell Larry about Bianco and then decided against it. "You can tell the men," he concluded.

The KT outfit received the news in silence — a silence that was ominous because of its intensity. The men merely looked at each other. Larry could see that every one of them believed the Double B responsible for the cattle rustling and the shooting of Davis. He was in the dark himself, for neither his father nor Stan Velie had enlightened him any further than to tell him what had been told the men, that the Double B had had nothing to do with it. Larry would have insisted that his father tell him all he knew had it not been for the condition of Davis. He knew his father was very much worried. But the wounded man evidently had recovered sufficiently to say something during the day. Larry determined this by his father's and Velie's manner.

"It's a tough break." It was Jones who spoke and the others looked at him. He was rolling a cigarette. "We don't want to forget he was a KT man and he left an empty gun."

The men exchanged startled glances. Did Jones mean that he thought Davis was going to die? He had spoken in the past tense. Larry, too, was struck by the cool manner in which Jones had put his words.

Jones noted them looking at him with queer expressions on their faces and he said: "I mean, we must stick behind him to the last one of us. I'm hoping he comes out of it. If he doesn't . . ." He shrugged.

"Well, we'll stick all right," said Blondy Robbins.

**166**

Nevertheless, Jones's words had served to bring home the fact that Davis was liable to die, and these men were not accustomed to men dying in bed. Death at the point of flaming guns seemed natural, but this other — perhaps it was the suspense. From this time on, the men talked in hushed tones and gloom permeated every nook and corner of the bunkhouse.

The doctor slept little this night and Lafe merely dozed in his chair by the fire. All night the blizzard raged; the wind tore at trees and buildings; the snow whipped the last of the leaves from branches and drifted high in the bottoms. Bud Davis shouted hoarsely, whispered and moaned in the throes of his delirium — riding the range, working cattle, playing the dance halls and gambling hells, and always coming back to two names: Bianco and the girl, Bessie. There was no sound sleep in the house this night.

The storm continued with unabated fury at dawn. It was ten degrees below zero — a record for that time of year. The doctor looked haggard and worn as he sat at the sick man's bedside. Davis seemed to be in a coma. His delirium was gone.

The doctor was sipping a cup of strong, black coffee when his patient suddenly opened his eyes. He put the coffee aside quickly and leaned over him to ask a question. But Davis's lips were moving.

"Where's . . . the priest?" he whispered.

The doctor bent his ear low to catch the next few whispered words. Then the young cowpuncher again lapsed into coma.

The doctor hurried downstairs. Breakfast was just finished and Larry was in the living room with Lafe. The doctor spoke to them briefly, and again went upstairs.

"I'll go," said Larry in a determined voice.

His father shook his head. "You never could make it in this storm, Larry. And probably he wouldn't come."

"I can't lose the trees along the river," said Larry. "I'll follow 'em till I get to Pondera Creek and turn up that into town. I've got to go, Dad. Somebody's got to go and I'm the one."

His father hesitated. "You probably could make it all right, going as you say. Go call Blondy Robbins in here. He knows the country as well as any man on the ranch."

Larry went for Robbins and on the way gave curt orders to Jerry. Twenty minutes later, Larry and Robbins rode forth into the storm.

Jerry entered the bunkhouse and looked about at the men. "They've sent for the priest," he said in an awed tone.

The men received this news in silence and looked at each other stupefied. The priest? Then Bud Davis was going out. It was inconceivable. A cowpuncher who sat on a bunk with his hat on, instinctively took it off. The cook stepped in and stood, open-mouthed, holding a big mixing spoon in his hand. The silence weighed down like some material thing.

"Who went?" asked one of the men, although all knew.

"Larry and Blondy," Jerry answered. "They're goin' to follow the river."

The men nodded. "They'll make it," said Jones, relieving the tension. Then they talked in low tones, and smoked, and listened as the storm unleashed its furies.

Hours passed. The doctor remained constantly in the sickroom. Sarah Owens went downstairs and sat with Lafe before the fire. Molly went about on tiptoe. In the kitchen, Mary O'Neil crossed herself and wiped her eyes. It was the first time the gaunt specter of death had stalked through that house.

Noon came and none cared for dinner. The food went untasted. The storm seemed to be lessening in ferocity. The wind was blowing more moderately. Miles to westward, Larry and Blondy and Father Boucher were battling their way toward the ranch, following the river by keeping the shadow of the trees in sight. But they were on the blizzard-swept open prairie on the north side, where they received the full force of the icy blast. As the wind began to abate, they made better time, and finally they dared a short cut that saved two miles of river bend.

It was three o'clock that afternoon when Larry and Blondy reached the ranch with the priest. The last went upstairs at once and the doctor came down. He had exhausted every means of his medical science and now slumped in his chair, defeated.

After a time the priest came down. Lafe and his wife, and Larry and Stan Velie went upstairs with the man of the cloth. The doctor was in the sickroom again. Molly came in. Under the influence of the powerful stimulant the doctor had administered, Bud Davis's cheeks were flushed. He opened his eyes and smiled. His lips moved slightly and his fading gaze sought the window.

Molly drew aside the white curtains. The wind had all but died, and the snow had ceased. Almost with her move a ray of brilliant sunlight streamed across the white mantle below, scattering diamonds and rubies in iridescent profusion on its surface. Bud Davis saw, and then closed his eyes, and sighed. The priest bent over him.

Larry Owens entered the bunkhouse. The men rose when they saw the look on his face. He cleared his throat.

"Boys, Bud's crossed to the big range." It was said with simple finality.

Then he turned and went out, leaving them standing there in silence.

# CHAPTER
# FOURTEEN

The KT buried Davis the next day, with the snow gone and the world golden with sunshine under a sky of flawless blue. The priest rode back to town, accompanied by Larry. In the late afternoon, Lafe spoke to the outfit in the bunkhouse, disclosing what Davis had said about the cattle raid. He told them he did not want an encounter with Bianco and his men at this time, and announced that the cattle would be moved out of the corner at once. He told them he would keep all the stock closer to the home ranch, even if he would have to feed hay. If necessary, he would buy hay, although there were three full sheds behind the corrals. He ordered Velie to post guards at the shed lest the rustlers should try to fire them and thus drive the cattle farther out on the open range until hay could be hauled in. Lafe made it clear that, in dealing with Bianco, they were not up against any ordinary rustler; he impressed this upon the men, and then turned them over to Stan Velie for further instructions.

The next morning all the men, including Larry and Jones, were out on the range. Lafe had decided not to try to locate the stolen stock for the present. Bianco would expect him to send men into the badlands. He

**171**

would fool the arch-rustler — puzzle him — compel him to make the next move. He had heard much of Bianco's tactics. Sooner or later, he would have a visit from the outlaw. Although he said nothing about his plans, Lafe was studying how he could lay a trap.

Three days later, with the promise of fair weather for some time, Lafe started for the extreme eastern end of the Teton range in the interests of his campaign for the Association presidency. The KT owner felt certain he would receive the solid west-end vote. But he needed some support in the east end. In the west the ranches were larger and there were fewer members than in the eastern part of the range. He had talked with many east-enders and had decided to make a bid directly for the votes of a group of ranchers, raising stock on a small scale at the extreme eastern end. These men had a leader in the person of a man named Steve Amberg who was of Dutch and Scot ancestry, and, in Lafe's opinion, both fair and wise-minded. He was going to see this man.

He rode eastward in the early morning, mounted on his favorite saddle horse, a big iron-gray gelding that easily carried his weight. He followed the road that crossed the KT and the Double B ranges. Reaching the fence, he passed through the gate, fastened it behind him, and struck eastward at a lope that his horse could maintain for hours.

The road ran a scant half mile north of the Double B ranch house, situated in the bottoms. As Lafe approached the intersection of the road leading down to the ranch house, Jim Bolten came suddenly into view, riding at a gallop up the road. He waved to Lafe, and the KT owner reined in his mount with a frown on his face. He had intended going to see Bolten on his way back, and this abrupt appearance of the Double B owner suggested that Bolten had in some way known he was coming and had ridden out to intercept him. Lafe detested being spied upon. He was beginning, also, to detest Bolten, whereas before he had merely looked on him as unfriendly, and later as an enemy.

"Nice mornin'," Bolten greeted, searching Lafe's face keenly as he rode up. "You're out early."

"We never figure it's early after the sun's up over at our place."

"Owens, I was sorry to hear about that man of yours," Bolten said. "And I was afraid maybe you'd think some of my men had something to do with it. If you've got any such idea, you can drop it, because every man in my outfit came straight back to the ranch with me and stayed there all night. I can vouch for every one of them."

"I'm not packing any such idea," Lafe informed him.

Bolten looked at him sharply and a bit suspiciously before he made further comment. "I'm glad of that," he said finally.

There was a pause during which Lafe said nothing.

"I suppose you held your men in that night?" Bolten asked pointedly.

"Not all of them. I had to send some to the cut-off to keep an eye out down there. What makes you ask?"

The Double B owner looked into the gray eyes of his rival and shifted uneasily in his saddle. "Something happened on my range that night," he replied.

"Yes? And you thought my men were over here? Bolten, here and now I want to ask you if we're going to raid each other's cattle?"

"I never had any such intention," Bolten flared. "But I lost a hundred head the night the blizzard started, and I haven't been able to find a trace of 'em. I ordered the count after the blizzard because the man down there was missing. I don't know where he is, either, although I know he couldn't run off a hundred head by himself and make a clean job of it."

"So you thought he'd thrown in with my men and helped 'em steal your cattle, is that it?" Lafe said with contempt.

"No . . . not exactly," Bolten conceded. "But there must have been some kind of trouble on your corner range for your man to get shot up, and I'm wondering if you've lost any cattle."

Lafe considered this an important bit of news and didn't doubt Bolten's word. How much should he tell him? How far could he trust him? "Yes, I've lost some stock. Lost it the same day you lost yours. Davis was shot twice trying to protect my cattle from rustlers. I lost a hundred and one head of shorthorns."

Bolten whistled softly and looked at Lafe in perplexity. "It's the first time any cattle have been stolen on this range in years. I can't understand it."

His sincerity was apparent and Lafe came to a decision. "If you knew what I think I know, you'd understand it."

"Do you know who did it?" Bolten asked eagerly.

"I have a strong suspicion, and, if my hunch is right, we're both in for trouble. We have the best bred cattle on the range. A first-class rustling band could get fat off us . . . if they can get away with it."

Bolten scowled. "I don't propose to let 'em get away with it on my range. If you want to tell me what your hunch is, I'd be glad to hear it. Rustling is one thing we've . . . we've sort of got to work together against."

"I'm glad you look at it that way. I can tell you something, but you'll have to be the best judge as to what to do with the information . . . I mean, whether to spread it around yet, or not."

"I'll use my best judgment to protect my cattle. You can lay to that."

"I'll tell you provided you give me your word to accept my suggestion in the matter."

"Go ahead. That's agreeable."

"Before Bud Davis died, he recovered consciousness once when I was in the room. He mentioned a name . . . a very formidable name, Bolten . . . and said this man had shot him and he'd shot back and missed. But even in his delirium he kept calling the name of this rustler. Must have known him from somewhere and recognized him."

"What was the name?"

"The man he named was Bianco."

Bolten's eyes popped. "No! Why, he's never worked up here. It couldn't have been him."

"That's what I thought, but now that I hear how slick somebody made off with a hundred head from you, I'm sure Davis named the right man. It was a clever piece of work, Bolten. My south fence was cut and patched so that it was hard to find where it had been done even in broad daylight. And you say your man is missing?"

"Yes, George Remy is missing. Disappeared as completely as the stock."

"Undoubtedly taken prisoner. Maybe you'll have to pay to get him back. An old hand?"

"Been with me fourteen years. Fresee trusted him and so did I."

Lafe smiled wryly at mention of Fresee. He knew the kind of men the Double B foreman was in the habit of hiring — gunmen first, cowhands second. "It may be that Bianco wanted to take Bud Davis prisoner, too, but he shot him down when he realized that he had been recognized. Right now I'm banking on Bianco's thinking that Bud was done for and that we don't know he's in the vicinity. I've got him guessing, too, because I didn't send out any men looking for my cattle. He might even think we don't know the fence was cut. The less he knows, the more our advantage. That's why I'd be careful, if I was you, not to talk too much about this. Bianco'll make another move, and it may be a false one."

Bolten seemed stunned by what he had heard. "He's got those cattle hid in the badlands, that's what. If we could get enough men to comb 'em . . ."

"We can't. Too many have tried that in the south. If Bianco is caught, he'll be caught by a trick. I refuse to send any more men into the brakes. I've lost several men as it is." He flashed a look at Bolten that caused the man to shift his gaze. "I'm not going to give this Bianco a chance to ambush my men and shoot 'em down like dogs. Play it careful."

With this, Lafe shook out his reins and rode away eastward. He had given Bolten no information about his mission. Bolten could think what he wished, and he was a fool if he could not see that Lafe was invading what he claimed was his own territory. With the regular meeting a little more than a week away, this was the only trip Lafe planned to make to the east range.

As he rode, Lafe took careful note of the country about him. He had not been on the east range in months. He found Bolten's range in as good a condition as his own. Beyond the Double B boundary, conditions were not quite so good. He stopped by a little creek at noon to water and feed his horse and eat his lunch. He was soon off again.

It was nearly sundown when he reached the Amberg Ranch. Here he found the range in good shape, the bottoms fenced for fields and pasturage, the buildings in excellent repair. Amberg was a good stockman and a farmer as well. The ranch bore an air of prosperity. As he rode into the courtyard by the ranch house, Amberg himself came out of the house to greet him.

" 'Lo, Steve," Lafe said. It was the first time he had ever called the stockman by his first name, although he had met him and talked with him many times in the nine years Amberg had been there. However, he had not seen him at the rodeo.

"Hello, Owens," said Amberg heartily. "Frank, come and take this horse." This was addressed to the barn man who hurried to obey the order. "Come in the house," Amberg invited. "I don't know where you're going, but it's too late to go any farther anywhere tonight."

"Thanks," said Lafe, pleased by the other's manner. "I came out to see you."

It was the first time Lafe had been in Amberg's house. He found it tidy and comfortably furnished. He met the stockman's wife who evidently was somewhat flustered in the presence of the most influential cattle baron on that range. Amberg himself was about forty, a tall man with dark eyes and hair, high cheek bones, and a close-cropped mustache. They went into the living room where a fire burned in a big, barrel-type heating stove. "You came out to see me?" Amberg said amiably.

"Yes, I want to have a little talk with you, since you're the leader of this bunch of comers out here. Maybe you'll pass on what I have to say to your friends."

"We'll talk after supper," said Amberg. "I always listen better on a full stomach . . . think better, too, I guess. My woman says my brains are in my stomach, and, if that's so, she's given me a good set of brains." He laughed, and his wife left them, pleased with the compliment.

Lafe and Amberg talked of range conditions and Lafe spoke of the rodeo, passing lightly over the trouble

178

in town, but not neglecting to hint of trouble between the KT and the Double B. He wanted Amberg to know everything, for here was a man with whom one had to be square and above board to keep his respect. It was a good supper and Lafe proved to be an entertaining guest. He also divulged much of his knowledge of the cattle business, to which Amberg listened carefully. When they had filled their pipes by the stove in the living room, Lafe acquainted his host with his mission.

"Now, I don't want you to make any promises, Steve. I want you to use your own judgment for what you think is best for this range. You've only been here nine years, but you have a good start. You're going to win out, and I hope all you fellows win out. There's room for all of us here, but I reckon you can see for yourself . . . that the east end and the west end of the range must co-operate and work together, since the west end is so much more powerful and can be a real help to this end in a pinch."

"That's providing they want to be of real help," said Amberg.

"You have my word for it, and my word is good. I've been president of the Cattlemen's Association for twenty years. As to how good a president I've been, I point to my record. There's trouble brewing down my way, but I'm going to settle it once and for all. I promise that. I won't permit personal affairs to involve the Association. The point is this . . . should the Association change horses in mid-stream, or let well enough alone?"

"Things have gone along all right since I've been here," Amberg confessed. "I don't mind telling you that Bolten's been out here talking."

"I knew that. I've come out here to see you because it's the smaller stock raisers this thing will affect the most. Bolten has virtually threatened a division of the range. I called that special meeting in town after the rodeo to bring him out into the open. If the range is divided, that would mean disaster. For one thing, Steve . . ." — Lafe paused, ostensibly to light his pipe — "the financing is done from the other end." Out of the corner of his eye, Lafe saw that this shot told. Amberg pursed his lips and Lafe sensed that he was thinking hard on a point he had overlooked. The bank in Pondera held a considerable amount of Amberg's paper, as Lafe well knew. It was well secured, to be sure, but then Amberg was getting a good rate of interest and he was half Scottish. Some of the other ranchers in that section were originally of the same nationality. "You see, Steve, I'm not boasting, and I've worn the same size hat for twenty years, so my head is staying normal, but it's up to you fellows out here to determine whether Bolten can do you more good than I as head of the Association. Remember, I ask for no promises and I don't want you to commit yourself to anything. This is the only trip I'm going to make to the east end. The thing is personal animosities should not enter into the affairs of the Association. All I ask is that you fellows out here all come to the annual meeting and use your best judgment in deciding what stand to

**180**

take. Those who cannot possibly come should send proxies. I want a full vote."

"You're entitled to that," Amberg commented. "But suppose Bolten was to be elected president. Would the west end bolt?"

"Certainly not!" Lafe replied spiritedly. "We're wise enough out there to know that this range isn't big enough for two organizations. But if you were to ask me if the spirit of co-operation would be the same, I couldn't say to that."

"Suppose rustling started on this range?" Amberg asked suddenly. "What would the Association do?"

Lafe started and looked at him sharply. "It would stamp it out." He was tempted to tell the smaller stockman that rustling had started, but he decided against it because he didn't want it known widely as yet. "We've stamped it out before."

"So I've heard," Amberg said. "There's been none since I've been here. But you mentioned the financing being done at the other end. Is that bank in Pondera a strong one?"

"I'm a director," said Lafe. "And every acre I own, every head of stock that is mine, every dollar in cash I've got is behind it. There are others who feel the same way."

Amberg, apparently satisfied, rose from his chair and called his family into the room. His daughter had learned a new piece to play on the piano and Amberg asked her to perform it for their guest. Then Amberg went out and returned, with cigars and two modest drinks. They drank a silent toast as the girl began to play.

Early the next morning, Lafe Owens started back to his ranch. He had been well entertained, had enjoyed a good night's sleep, had eaten an excellent breakfast, had inspected Amberg's new bull, and talked a little shop with the east-end stockman. As he rode homeward, he could not keep his thoughts from reverting to the theft of cattle from the Double B and the disappearance of one of Bolten's men. It hardly seemed like Bianco to take a prisoner. What purpose would it serve? What's more, it seemed unlikely that the outlaw would take a man into his camp and then let him go. Bianco was too smart for that.

He had eaten his lunch at the little creek and was riding again when a horseman appeared, coming at a swift gallop. When the rider was some distance away, Lafe recognized him and cursed. It was Bolten again — riding east to learn what he could about Lafe's visit out there.

The Double B owner drew up with a flourish of his hand. Lafe stopped and his gaze narrowed. "Losing no time to tag me, eh, Bolten?" he said sarcastically. "Or maybe some of your stock has strayed out this way."

"I don't have to explain my movements in my own territory," Bolten retorted in a mean voice. "We won't discuss that. My man came back to the ranch yesterday noon."

Lafe showed immediate interest. "What did he say about the cattle?"

182

"Didn't know they were gone. Says the blizzard caught him on the south side of the herd and he couldn't get back to his shack or the ranch. Didn't know where he was till he struck the fence. Cut the wire and went through into the brakes for protection against the storm. Did I tell you our wire was down? Says he got lost in the badlands and just got out. I think he went daffy in the storm, for he doesn't talk right."

"Cut the wire, you say? How come he was packing wire cutters?"

"He'd been ridin' fence and still had 'em on him. Says he didn't see a soul before the storm."

"Looks mighty queer to me," Lafe observed, his lips tightening. "That man with a horse all this time . . ."

"He lost his horse," Bolten interjected. "Came back afoot. Nobody knows where his horse is . . . Say, listen, you don't think my man had anything to do with the rustling, do you?"

"I don't know much about your men, but from what I've seen of 'em, I wouldn't put much past 'em."

"That's an insult!" Bolten snapped, growing red in the face.

"You asked my opinion . . . and got it. I've got enough to do looking after my own affairs without bothering over yours. I'll tell you straight, Bolten. If we have that cut-throat rustler up here, I don't look for any great help from you driving him out, killing, or capturing him."

"Going to use it as an issue and promise protection to everybody, I suppose," Bolten sneered. "That's the

**183**

message you've likely carried out east to those tenderfeet who can't think for themselves. Well, you better think of something else, because I'm going right out there and spike it. I reckon your brain's getting tired with too much scheming."

"The man who flies off the handle is always at a disadvantage," said Lafe. "That's one reason why you'd be bad to head the Association. You'd have us in hot water all the time."

Lafe's insolent coolness fairly maddened Bolten. "You're a conceited, foolish old man, Owens!"

"I wasn't fool enough to tell 'em out there about the rustling," said Lafe in the same moderate voice. "If you've learned to think in anything except a circle, you won't tell 'em, either. So long."

Again he left Bolten cold, galloping westward while the Double B owner fumed, turned his horse as if to make after him, thought better of it, and resumed his ride east.

That evening Larry and Jones rode in from the range. Larry reported that Velie had put the cattle in positions where they would be virtually immune from raids unless the outlaws came in full force and ran off stock in a pitched battle.

"I don't want any pitched battle," said Lafe. "I don't want to lose any more men. Larry, I want you to go to town and round up twelve more good men. If you can't get 'em in Pondera, go up to Shelby and around. For that matter, we can use fifteen. Don't look surprised. I want this ranch manned. You can take Jones along."

"That's a big order, Dad," said Larry, his eyes shining, "but I'll fill it. Any particular qualifications?"

"They shouldn't be afraid of the dark," growled Lafe. "We'll go in tonight."

He and Jones had a late supper served by Molly. Midway through the meal Larry put down his knife and fork and scowled at his sister. "You must think that Jones, here, is pretty weak the way you keep fussing around, keeping his coffee cup overflowing and pushing the dishes toward him. He had something to eat already today that I know about."

"When I'm in the house, I'm in the capacity of a guest," said Jones in a superior tone. "Miss Owens is merely doing her duty."

"Yeah?" jeered Larry. "You mean you've got her goat! Well, it's about time somebody got it. She's been dragging it around loose ever since I can remember."

"You're not so bright, Lawrence," said Molly, drawling out his real name in a way that always angered him. "Sometimes I wonder what you think with."

"That's one of his secrets," Jones said carelessly.

Larry gave him a look. "I suppose it's only a question of time when we'll have to make regular hours for you two to hold hands," he said with biting sarcasm.

"We're capable of making our own hours."

Molly left the room exasperated and didn't return. Larry grinned and said no more. Jones looked about at the walls. "I thought there wasn't," he said absently.

"Wasn't what?" Larry demanded.

"Any brotherly love mottoes hanging up."

Half an hour later they rode away for town. Lafe watched them go. He had sent Larry on his first important mission in connection with the ranch. He wondered about the men the youth would hire. He wanted more men and he wanted the right kind. He believed Larry knew the kind he wanted. Well, there was nothing more to do about it until they came. Velie would ascertain their mettle in short order. He spoke casually to Jerry, the barn man. Jerry and the cook were the only two men left on the ranch, except for himself.

Lafe went around to the front porch. There he surveyed the gaunt branches of the trees, robbed of their leaves unusually early. The moon was swinging westward. He could not see it from his position, but the dark velvet canopy of the night sky was splashed with stars. A cool wind whispered about the buildings. To the left was the shadow of the bluffs below the benchland; to the right was the shadow of the trees that studded the banks of the river. Between lay the silent fields. Lafe went into the house to his pipe and his place by the fire.

He was tired and he fell asleep. Ordinarily Lafe didn't dream. It was only when he was very tired that he dreamed. He dreamed now. He was riding — riding at a heart-breaking gallop across the Double B range. A big form loomed in the saddle on a horse that thundered closely behind him. Others followed — riders as far back as he could see. And the man just behind was Bolten. He began to shoot. *Crack, crack, crack, crack, crack.* Lafe opened his eyes with a start. Someone was knocking at the front door — a soft,

**186**

persistent rapping on the panel of the door. Lafe rose, went to the door, and opened it. He found himself looking squarely into the black bore of a six-shooter. His eyes shifted at once to the face above the gun. It was a round face, smooth-shaven, dark, with a seam on either side down the cheek from the corner of the eye. The eyes were a greenish-black. Lafe had never seen eyes like them.

"Is there anyone in that room?" The voice of this visitor was moderate and not unpleasant.

"No," said Lafe. "Come in."

He glanced beyond the man in front of him and saw men on horses. He heard hoofs stamping in the courtyard. His dream was explained and now he believed he knew the identity of his visitor. "Come in, Bianco," he invited, taking a step aside. "If you want to see me, the place to talk is in my office."

The eyes flashed as the man stepped forward and looked into the room. Lafe pointed to the open door of his little office at one side of the front window next to the front door. His visitor motioned him inside and, as he complied, closed the front door and stepped inside the office, closing that door, also.

The barrel of the big gun slid into the holster like a snake. The eyes glittered and shot green sparks as they contemplated Lafe's face. The gaze took in the room at a glance. "Sit down," came that purring voice.

Lafe dropped into his swivel chair by the roll-top desk and rested a hand on the table between himself and the visitor. Over the desk hung a six-shooter in its holster and Lafe smiled grimly at the irony of it.

"You called me by a name," said the visitor softly, sitting down and leaning on his elbows on the table. "Why did you do that?"

Lafe was trying to place the man's nationality. Mexican? — no. Spaniard? — hardly. Italian? — well, perhaps. "That's your name, isn't it?" he said, frowning. "Don't you want to be called by your name?"

"How did you know?" persisted the mild voice.

"I guessed at it. If you're not Bianco, you've no business here."

"Ah!"

Lafe could have sworn the green-black eyes twinkled. This man did not look like the ruthless killer and all-around badman he was reputed to be. There was something jovial in his look at the moment. Then Lafe got a shock. The whole expression changed in the wink of an eyelash. Now the eyes were narrowed and hard, the lips were pressed tightly, the face was cold and stern and brutal. Here was a glimpse of the true Bianco.

"You must not play with names!" The tone was not loud, but it throbbed with menace. "You must not repeat the one you spoke. You're smart enough to take a hint when you get it from the proper party. So?"

"I've been called smart, at times," replied Lafe curtly. There was something about the outlaw that inspired immediate dislike — a dislike that came near being a loathing.

"We'll see, now, how smart you are," said the outlaw with a trace of a sneer. "You're running a big ranch here. Plenty of stock. You want to get that Cattlemen's

188

Association job again. Bah!" He snapped a thumb and finger. "I know the system. But you buy cattle, eh?"

"I buy some cattle . . . yes," said Lafe. The bandit had had his spies in town as well as on the range.

"I have some cattle to sell," purred the outlaw. "I have a hundred and one head of shorthorns to sell. What would you give for a hundred and one head of shorthorns, Mister Smart Man?"

Lafe smiled wryly. So this was the way it was done. Bianco was about to give Lafe a chance to buy him off by selling him his own cattle at a big figure, a polite and original form of robbery. "I'd have to see 'em first. And I don't buy stock at the point of a gun." The hoofs were stamping continuously in the courtyard outside the window. Bianco must have brought a lot of men. It was a bold stroke, one worthy of his sinister reputation.

The outlaw ignored the last thrust. "You know very well what a hundred and one head of shorthorns are," he said slowly. "Now . . . I will sell them to you." He nodded and smiled; the smile matched the look in the eyes.

Lafe started to speak, and then he felt a hot wave of anger surge through him. Here was a rustler, a bandit and killer who had stolen 101 head of his prize stock having the effrontery to order him into his office at the point of a gun and coolly state that he would sell the KT its own stock! "I'm not buying stock at present," said Lafe crisply. "And I'm not buying my own stock at any time."

The glittering eyes never shifted their gaze from his face. "I will sell the cattle to you for twenty thousand dollars," said the outlaw softly. "I can't take time to deliver 'em, but I'll turn 'em over to three of your men, including yourself, in good condition. I'll have to have the cash."

The cool, confident insolence of the man caused every nerve in Lafe Owens's body to tingle with anger. He bit his lip to keep control of himself. He must keep a hold on himself. This man was dangerous. "And what do I get for the twenty thousand dollars . . . which I haven't got . . . in cash, I mean?"

The outlaw made an impatient gesture. "You can get it quick enough. You get a hundred and one head of shorthorns. Isn't that enough?" Again that smile and the green daggers in the eyes.

"You mean you want to bulldoze me out of twenty thousand and give me back my own cattle . . . maybe . . . and then probably turn around and try the same stunt again! That's what you mean, isn't it?"

"I don't have to say what I mean!" This was a different voice. Every word constituted a threat. "You're not smart enough to be a good guesser . . . that's flat. You heard my proposition. Now what have you got to say to it?"

"I turn it down!" exclaimed Lafe, his anger getting the better of him at last. "And that's flat!"

The outlaw got to his feet quickly as a cat. His eyes gleamed, and Lafe thought afterward that they had gleamed with satisfaction.

"You are not smart enough to see a bargain when it's hung under your nose," said the outlaw through his teeth. "You won't get a crack at that bargain again. Now you'll pay full price! Your cattle are down in the corner."

Bianco turned to the door, then whirled, his gun appearing in his hand as if by magic. "Stay in that chair!" he commanded sternly.

Next moment he was gone. Lafe sat in his swivel chair, staring at the closed door. He heard sharp orders given outside. There was a clatter and pound of hoofs and the riders swept out of the courtyard. As the echoes of the flying hoof beats died away, Lafe still sat motionless. His cattle in the corner? Pay the full price? Great guns! Had he made a mistake in defying Bianco?

The door opened softly and Sarah Owens looked in. "Who was here, Lafe?" she asked.

"Some men from the east end, where I was today," Lafe replied, turning to his desk. "They're going on to town. Don't bother me, Mother. I'm going to clean up this desk a bit."

"I'll leave the door open so it'll be warm in here," said his wife.

But Lafe was thinking of another kind of door. Had he closed it or left it open? He went into the living room to get his pipe.

# CHAPTER
# FIFTEEN

When Bolten had told Lafe Owens about the return of his cowpuncher, George Remy, from the badlands after the blizzard, he did not paint conditions quite as serious as they were. Remy's ears had been frozen; he was starved, weak, footsore, and ragged. When he had been put to bed, given some hot soup and light food, and a hot drink, he talked incoherently about his experience. He still was sleeping in fits and starts when Bolten started out to ride to the far east-end ranchers.

When Bolten returned about midnight, in bad humor, Fresee met him at the barn and told him he better go in the bunkhouse and see the cowpuncher. "I've stayed in at the ranch, after puttin' the men out on the range, because this fellow knows something," said Fresee.

"Has that cook in there got any hot coffee?"

"Plenty, and a good supper, if you want it," Fresee assured him.

"Well, I want it, and I want it quick," Bolten snapped out. "I'll be there in a minute. Looks like they're all asleep in the house."

It was Fresee's policy to humor Bolten in all his moods. This was no inconsiderable asset. For years he had handled Bolten with rubber gloves, so to speak, but the important point was that he had handled him. Fresee's position as manager, rather than foreman, of the Double B was solid as granite. With the men his word was absolute law, but it could be said for him that he knew how to handle the men, as well as Bolten. They respected his prowess with his gun, for they were all of a class that would do this. Fresee had a hard crew under him.

Bolten went into the kitchen at the end of the bunkhouse and ate his second supper while Fresee drank a cup of coffee with him.

"What's Remy got under his hat?" Bolten asked between mouthfuls.

"Thinks he knows something about the cattle we lost," replied Fresee. "I think he's a little off his nut, since he wouldn't talk to me. Bound to see you soon as you come in. I didn't know whether to bother you or not, but I thought, you being the big boss, you better hear his ravings."

"That's right. Anything like this should be brought to my attention at once. If he is cracked, we can't keep him around here. That's a purple-painted cinch."

"That's the way I looked at it," said Fresee suavely.

Bolten drained his third cup of coffee in big gulps, wiped his mouth with a blue bandanna, and rose from the table. "We'll go in and see him."

Remy, a tall, thin cowpuncher with mild blue eyes, who had been employed by the Double B for many years — years before Fresee came — looked at Bolten eagerly. He sat up on the bunk weakly.

"Well, George," blustered Bolten, "did you want to see me about something?"

"About the cattle," said Remy in a frail voice. "Some's been stolen, I hear. I didn't know it until they told me. They might have strayed through the gap I made in the fence in the blizzard, but I doubt it. I had to cut the wire, Jim, and get into the brakes for shelter. It caught me all of a sudden . . . just as I —"

"Yes, yes," said Bolten with a show of impatience. "What about the cattle?"

"I think they were stolen," said Remy slowly, appearing hurt because of Bolten's interruption. "There are men in the brakes, Jim."

"Eh? You saw men down there?"

"I saw men, and they took my hoss," said Remy stoutly. "That hoss never would have left me. I saw a big man with a round face and eyes like hornets. They blazed right through the flyin' snow. I heard him say . . . 'Oh, let him go, he'll freeze to death, anyway!'"

Bolten looked at Fresee, and Fresee stared back at him with no indication of his thoughts.

"Are you sure you know what you're talking about?" Bolten asked the cowpuncher.

"Of course I do," Remy asserted in the strongest voice he could muster. "I know what you're thinkin'. You're thinkin' what I went through has knocked me coo-coo. Well, I'm all right now, and I was all right when I saw those men down there. I don't remember so much afterward, except that I crawled into a cave and went to sleep. It was protected enough so I didn't freeze. I was there two days. I don't know what I operated on, but I managed to get back to the ranch, and I remember gettin' back. Then things went blooey again, but I'm all right now. I've worked fourteen years for you, Jim, and you never heard of me seein' things or lying. And I know more'n what I told you, too."

Bolten was frowning and biting his lower lip. He believed Remy. "All right, tell me the rest of it. Be sure you remember right, George."

"I will, you bet. I'll remember right and hard. I'll remember back quite a few years to the winter I went down into Wyoming. Guess you'll remember the time, too. And when I came back, I told you about seein' somebody down there . . . somebody few folks got a chance to see. Everybody was scared of him and he rode right into town for what he wanted and stayed there three days. Remember?"

Bolten was looking at him intently now. He nodded for reply.

"Well," said Remy in some excitement, "that same person was the man I saw in the brakes in the blizzard before I holed up!"

Bolten started from his chair. "You was crazy and seeing things!" he exclaimed. "The storm blew you daffy!"

"You can think that if you want to," said Remy, sinking back on the pillows. "But I'm tellin' you I saw him. And that's all I've got to say." His words were utterly convincing.

Bolten settled in his chair again and looked at Fresee with a strange expression on his face. "If he isn't crazy, he's told us something," he said grimly.

"Who does he think he saw?"

"Bianco," came the hushed reply. "Ever hear of him?"

Fresee nodded and his brow wrinkled as he frowned heavily. "He would be the last man in the world to come up here. Why, he doesn't know this country, does he?"

"I wouldn't think so," said Bolten. "But he might have had some of his gang scouting around. If what Remy says is true, it's bad business. Listen, Fresee, Owens told me he had lost some stock, too."

Fresee's eyes widened in surprise. "Was that what the shooting was about in the corner down there?"

Bolten nodded. "Bud Davis came out of it long enough to name Bianco as the man who shot him. And now George, here, says he saw Bianco in the brakes. It took a mighty clever rustler, Fresee, to sneak off a hundred head from both ranches as slick as it was done."

"Yes . . . that's so," Fresee agreed. "I'll have to bring more men south." His eyes gleamed with the light of battle. "I've got an outfit that can ride and shoot, and we'll give him a run for his money . . . if he's here."

But Bolten was shaking his head slowly. "We don't want a run-in with that fellow. He'd squash us flatter than a pancake, and I don't want to lose any more men, if I can help it. Instead of movin' the men, we'll move the cattle where they're harder to get at, and guard 'em better. You attend to that tomorrow. I'll bet that's what Owens has done. Have one of the men take a ride along the road across the KT range tomorrow and see what he can see. I don't like this at all."

"You're the boss," Fresee acquiesced. "I'll see that your order is carried out." He paused, thinking. "But, if you hear anything more, let me know," he added. "I've got to look after the range stock, you know."

Bolten nodded, and rose. "You stayin' here tonight?"

"Till daylight," Fresee answered. "I'll have breakfast at the Deep Springs camp, I guess."

Bolten went out into the clear, cool night. Like Owens, who some time before that night had stood looking at the stars and the playing shadows, so Bolten now did the same thing. A few minutes later he entered the house by the rear door. Shortly afterward a light shone from the window of his office. Feeling somewhat heavy after his late meal and the strong coffee, he had decided to smoke a cigar before going to bed. He took a box of Perfectos from a drawer of his desk, chose one, and lighted it carefully. He leaned back comfortably in his chair, smoking lazily, thinking sluggishly. The house was still. Everyone was asleep except himself. That was as it should be, for he had time and again instructed his family never to wait up for him. It annoyed him to come home late and find them sitting there, thinking something may have happened to him.

A light rapping sounded on the front door. Bolten grunted and rose. "Wonder Fresee couldn't think of everything he had to say when I was out there," he grumbled as he went into the living room and opened the door.

There was a dim light shining from the open door of his office at the rear of the living room. But this was enough to enable him to see a large form, a round, dark face, small, glittering eyes above the smooth cheeks. Then he saw the gun and started back.

"Easy," said a low, warning voice. "Just edge along back to your office where we can talk without disturbing anybody." The visitor stepped aside and closed the door behind him. Bolten went back to his office, his heart pounding. The man holding the gun at his back resembled the notorious outlaw George Remy had described.

Bolten resumed his chair and looked intently at his visitor as the latter took a chair across from him. Yes, this was the man!

Bianco leaned on the arms of his chair. "Do you know who I am?" he asked in his softest voice.

"Not for sure," Bolten replied nervously.

The outlaw could tell by his manner and answer that Bolten had heard something. "It's just as well. I come to sell you some cattle."

"Sell . . . cattle?" Bolten appeared puzzled. A light of uncertainty flickered in his eyes.

"A hundred head," purred the rustler. "Herefords."

A great light broke upon Bolten. Here was the arch-rustler, as he had suspected, and the scheme was to gorge money out of him for protection. As had been the case with Lafe Owens, his anger flamed, but it soon gave way to a cunning thought. Had the outlaw approached Owens? Had it been this man who had also stolen the KT stock? Bolten was inclined to think so.

"I lost a hundred head of Herefords in the blizzard," he said in a surly tone.

"Then you will want to buy a hundred head to take their place," Bianco suggested.

"How much do you want for them?"

"Twenty thousand dollars," replied the outlaw softly, never once taking his eyes from Bolten's face.

"That's a new way of doing it," said Bolten shortly. "Then you'll leave my stock alone, I suppose."

"I'm offering you a bargain!" The tone and the look of the rustler changed. "You can take it or leave it, but you'll have to make up your mind pretty quick. And I don't have to make promises. You'll have to guess your way out."

"I see. But that's what it amounts to just the same. Twenty thousand to buy you off. You're as good a businessman as a cow thief, Bianco."

The gun was out like a flash of light. The outlaw tapped his knee with the barrel, his narrowed gaze holding Bolten's as though in a spell. "Those are two words you'll forget," said the voice in a sinister tone of meaning. "I didn't come here just for a conversation. If you've got a mind, make it up . . . one way or the other." This last conveyed an unmistakable threat.

Bolten suddenly leaned forward. "Owens of the KT has lost some cattle, too," he said in a lowered tone. "Did he make a deal with you?"

The outlaw's eyes flashed dangerously. "You've got all you can do to attend to your own business. I don't know anything about any cattle that's been lost. And

I'm not going to go make my proposition again. I'm being as patient as I can. Understand?"

Bolten thought he understood several things and of one thing he was sure: he didn't want this man making war on his range. It would hurt his credit. He couldn't afford to lose any cattle; he didn't want to have both Owens and Bianco to fight at the same time. He would be between two fires, unless Owens also had to fight the outlaw. If they combined the Double B and KT forces to fight off the rustlers, Bolten knew it never would work. Bianco was clever. His visit and his proposition proved this.

"I'd like to consult my foreman," he said wryly. "I ask his advice on all important matters like this. Not that I always take it," he added hastily, "but two heads are better than one, and he's a good man. He's the only man here, except for a sick 'puncher, the cook, and a man looking after the barn. He's in the bunkhouse." He had not seen fit to mention Remy as yet.

"It wouldn't make any difference if your whole outfit was here," said Bianco scornfully. "Do you think I travel alone? We'll go get him." He rose and opened the door, keeping his eye on Bolten the while. "Tell him to leave his gun behind," he warned as they went out with Bolten in the lead.

"We'll go the back way," whispered Bolten.

They went through the dining room and out the kitchen door. In the courtyard, the outlaw whistled softly, a queer note. Almost instantly men stepped out of the shadows. Bolten stopped in his tracks, astonished

200

at the number. He felt the muzzle of the rustler's gun in his back. "Just call him from the door," was the order.

The outlaw stood to one side as Bolten opened the bunkhouse door and called softly. Fresee came, coatless and bootless. Bolten told him what to do and he came out of the bunkhouse in a few moments, wearing his boots and coat. He had discarded his gun. The three of them returned to Bolten's office.

There, while Bolten explained the nature of the night visit, Fresee and Bianco eyed each other keenly. When Bolten had finished, he looked at one and the other of them nervously. All in all he was glad Fresee didn't have his gun. He felt tremors of trepidation as these two men looked at each other through narrowed lids.

"You heard what he said," remarked the outlaw. "He made a play about wanting your advice. Give it to him."

"Don't be so rough," snapped Fresee. "What do we get for the twenty thousand?"

"You get a hundred head of stock," purred Bianco.

"We'll take the stock for granted," said Fresee curtly. "What else do we get?"

"A receipt, if you want it," the outlaw hissed between his teeth.

"And if we don't fork over, you figure on raidin' us all winter, eh?" Fresee scoffed. "You can't get away with it! We've got some tough weather comin'. If you killed off every man on our range and ran off every head of stock, you couldn't get clean away with 'em! And this range isn't as soft as you think."

Bolten nearly gasped as he listened to this speech from Fresee. He was throwing defiance into the other's teeth.

But Bianco merely laughed in his throat. "You talk like a fish," he sneered. "Listen!" His eyes snapped with green fire. "My men need work. I have to keep 'em busy or they'll go stale. You don't know what I can do, and I'm not telling you. I offered Bolten a bargain. He wants your advice. Give it to him, and shut up! You run off at the mouth too much. You're itching to have your loose tongue shot out."

"Tell me what you think, Fresee," Bolten put in. "I don't want a lot of trouble on the range at this time. I —"

"I wouldn't give him a cancelled stamp!" Fresee exploded.

The outlaw turned his blazing eyes on Bolten. "And you?" he said sharply.

Bolten thought he knew what would happen if these men clashed. He imagined many things — his cattle raided, men shot down, the ranch buildings in flames — this man would stop at nothing to gain his ends. He remembered the outlaw's followers outside. He must have made the same proposition to Owens — or he would make it. Owens could easily afford to buy him off. He probably would, to keep peace on his range so far as rustling was concerned. And, if Bianco began operations at once, what effect would it have on the Association election?

"I . . . I think you'd better go, Fresee," he said. "I want to talk with this . . . this man alone."

Fresee swore. "You're giving in!" he snorted, rising.

"Sit down!" the outlaw commanded. "There isn't going to be any more talk. I've heard enough talk, and I can't remember when I've humored a man like I've humored you, Bolten. I'm giving you a break because you're slow-witted. Now kick in with your answer!"

"I haven't got that much money here," said Bolten with a frown. "There isn't two hundred dollars in cash on the place that I know of."

"You can get it," Bianco flashed. "I'll give you until tomorrow night."

"Where . . . where would you meet me?" asked Bolten.

"I'll take care of that," was the sharp rejoinder.

Bolten didn't look at Fresee. All his doubts and fears seemed to bunch in his brain. He could feel the outlaw's eyes boring into him. He was between two fires — three fires. If he took Fresee's advice, Fresee would certainly be shot down in the first clash. He had seen that in Bianco's eyes as the outlaw had listened to Fresee. He needed Fresee and couldn't afford to lose him. His mind snapped to a decision.

"I'll take you up on your bargain," he said slowly, meeting the outlaw's gaze. "You can send the cattle back when you wish. I'll be back from town tomorrow afternoon with the money."

Fresee sneered as Bianco rose. "It's settled," said the latter. "Stay here for five minutes."

In another moment he was gone, leaving Bolten and Fresee in the office. A whistle sounded, then the pound of hoofs — then silence.

★   ★   ★

Jim Bolten started for town early in the morning. He had told Fresee where to get off at after the rustler king had left the Double B the night before. It was worth twice $20,000 to protect his range from Bianco, he had asserted. Bolten would attend to financial affairs connected with his property. Fresee's place was out on the range, except when he was needed at the home ranch or in town. And so on. To all of which the crafty foreman had listened patiently, simulating a contriteness he did not feel. Finally Bolten had dismissed him angrily and Fresee had gone to the bunkhouse and to bed with a queer smile playing on his lips.

Then, at dawn, a rider had come in from the north range, in great excitement. The 100 head of stolen Herefords were back inside the fence and the fence repaired. It had been repaired after Remy had cut the wire — at which time no other break had been discovered, as it was assumed the cattle had been taken through that break — but it had been necessary for the rustlers to cut the wire again to drive the cattle back. And, in order to get them back so soon, the cattle must have been close to the fence when Bianco visited the ranch. It was all puzzling to Bolten; it impressed him with Bianco's cleverness. But the great surprise was to come on his way to town.

He had hardly passed through the gate in the fence and ridden onto KT range when he saw a herd of about 100 shorthorns being driven northward. They were coming from the cut-off corner. Now Bolten was aware of the fact that Owens had taken his shorthorns out of the corner range, and Owens had said he had lost 101 head. This small herd looked as if it contained that number of cattle. Bolten reined in his horse as a great light broke over him. Then he thought better of riding down to put a question or two and went on toward town, following the road at a ringing gallop. He was smiling a smile of satisfaction. The cattle being driven northward were the cattle Bianco had stolen from the KT. Plain as dust under his horse's hoofs! Owens also had accepted the outlaw's proposition, probably paid the cash right out of his safe for Owens was better than well-fixed financially. Wait until Bolten told Fresee about it. He could gloat over his foreman now. He had done exactly the right thing in accepting the outlaw's proposition. With $40,000 cash in his and his men's pockets, Bianco could afford to go his way and leave this range unmolested in the future. Well, it was worth the money, and the value of the returned cattle had to be taken into consideration. They represented considerable money. Moreover, Owens's action in buying Bianco off showed that he, too, didn't relish the idea of outside interference in the trouble between the Double B and the KT factions. Bolten never thought of this trouble as a feud. He was merely out to get what he thought was coming to him — to avenge a wrong that he fancied had been done to him in the past — but in his heart he hated Lafe Owens.

Henry Brower was alone in the private office of the bank at noon. He heard Bolten's blustering salutation to his teller and clerk as the stockman came in and strode down outside the cage to the door of the private office. The banker's lips tightened, but he smiled amiably as he looked up when Bolten came in without knocking.

"Hello, Henry," Bolten greeted in his booming voice. "You're sure fixed pretty snug here for blizzard weather. We've had our first taste of what's coming out on the range." He didn't propose to tell the banker anything about the rustling or the deal he had made.

"That's what I hear," said Brower smoothly. "Well, we've had to go through a good many winters before this. Sit down, Bolten."

Bolten eased himself into a big chair across the desk from the banker. "What's my cash balance, Henry?" he asked in a casual voice.

Brower rose and went out into the cage where he busied himself with a book for a minute. "Your balance is fourteen thousand, eight hundred, and sixteen dollars, and twenty-two cents," he announced as he returned to his desk.

"More than I thought, for this time of year," said Bolten. "Well, let's see. I don't really need that much cash. May not have to buy any hay this winter. Got some left from last winter, in fact, besides my crop this year. I can spare five thousand of that, and I need twenty thousand in cash, Henry. Take five thousand from my balance and make out a note for fifteen thousand. That'll make it nicely. Make the note for six months." He took out a cigar and bit off its end, nodding condescendingly at the banker. He struck a match but let it burn until it was down to his fingers without lighting the cigar. He stared at Brower with a puzzled expression.

The banker's manner had undergone a change. He was not looking at Bolten, but looking down at his desk with his brow wrinkled, and he was moving some papers, fussing with articles on his desk. When he looked up, he shook his head slowly. "I can't make the loan, Bolten."

"Can't make the loan!" Bolten exclaimed. "Are you crazy? That isn't much money . . . fifteen thousand . . . for me. You've got a number one, gilt-edged security, and you know it."

"That may be," said Brower quietly, "but I can't make any loans in any such amount at this time, not for even one-third of that amount." He looked Bolten straight in the eyes.

Bolten's hand, with the cigar between his fingers, came down. "Is the . . . is the bank in bad shape?" he asked in an anxious voice.

"The bank is as sound as a dollar," Brower asserted with a trace of annoyance. "Here's the September statement of our condition." He took a small printed slip from a drawer and passed it over to his client.

Bolten merely glanced at it with a frown. "Don't you think my security is OK, Brower?"

"I believe it's all right, but you know we're carrying a sizable amount of your paper as it is."

"And you mean to tell me that I'm not good for a measly fifteen thousand more?" Bolten thundered, angered.

"Any such loan at this time will have to be passed upon by three members of our board of directors," said Brower in slow, distinct tones.

"Yeah? And have my other loans been passed upon by three members of the board?" the Double B owner demanded hotly. "You know very well that I've come in here and got money when I needed it, and a lot more than fifteen thousand. And I've put every cent I've borrowed, almost, into breeded stock and improvements at the ranch. You haven't got a note in your safe that's better secured than mine. How does it come that all of a sudden my application for a loan has got to go to the directors?"

"Because those are my instructions regarding all loans of over a thousand dollars at present," replied Brower. "I don't own this bank, Bolten. Lots of folk think I have the controlling interest, but I haven't. I am president . . . yes. But I'm practically here in the capacity of manager. Of course, I have considerable influence" — he toyed with a penholder — "but I'm responsible to my directors, and they are responsible to the stockholders."

"You bet you've got influence," said the irate stockman. "You can make this loan to me here and now, and you can fix it with the directors afterward . . . providing you have to do that, which I doubt."

Henry Brower looked up instantly. "Do you think I'm lying?" he asked coldly.

"Oh, I wouldn't say that," returned Bolten with a heavy frown. "Now look here, Henry, I've got to have this cash today. It's very important. It might even affect your security!" He bit his lip. He shouldn't have said that, but it was out and the banker was looking at him with interest.

"What do you want the money for?" Brower asked curiously.

Bolten twisted in his chair. "That's it, Henry," he said with a trace of nervousness. "I can't tell you what I want it for. But I want it for a legitimate purpose, for it is to my interests and to the bank's interest. You'll just have to take my word for it, and I've got to have the money!"

To Brower's certain knowledge, this was the first time the stockman ever had made such free use of his first name. In a way, he didn't like it. "If you will think back," he said slowly, "you will remember that this bank never extended a loan to you without knowing what the money was to be used for . . . and we've never made any loan without knowing fully all the details as to the reason for the borrowing and the purpose to which the money was to be put."

"If I wanted to throw it away on a big time for me and my family, or to take a trip, or to gamble with it, or burn it up, my security would be good for it!" Bolten flared.

"You couldn't obtain a loan for any of those purposes, regardless of your security," said Brower coolly.

But Bolten had been thinking hard. Now he leaned his elbows on the desk and looked at the banker narrowly. "Has this trouble between Owens and me got anything to do with it?"

"I don't have to answer that question," said Brower sharply. "But I'll tell you this. Any trouble you get mixed up in isn't going to make your security any better. You can depend on that."

"Owens is a stockholder, isn't he?" Bolten persisted. "As a leading customer of the bank, I'm entitled to know that."

"You already know it."

"And he's a member of your board of directors, isn't he?"

"You know that, too. You'll find the names of the officers of the bank and the directors at the bottom of that statement I gave you."

"That's it!" exclaimed Bolten, his face darkening as he brought his fist down on the desk. "Lafe Owens has given you your orders! By Jupiter! I'll take my business away from you and all the business of the eastern range with me! I'll break your bank! I'll show it up for the tin can that it is. I'll . . ." He sputtered in the hot wave of anger that swept over him.

Brower rose from his chair. His face was pale and his eyes were flashing. Few men ever had seen Henry Brower's eyes flash like that, and, when they had, they regretted it. "I guess you're through, Bolten. You can go."

But Bolten had cooled as suddenly as he had given rein to his rage. "Just one thing, Brower. If I get Lafe Owens's OK on this loan myself, will the loan be made without my having to tell you what I want the money for? I can tell Owens, but I don't feel called upon to tell you . . . or anybody else in town, for that matter."

"If Lafe Owens and two other directors approve the loan, you can have the money at once. And that's the only way you will get it. Furthermore, now that you've indirectly brought Owens into the matter, I require his approval." The eyes still were flashing.

"I reckon it won't be hard to get two dummies to follow his lead," snorted Bolten. "He'll attend to that himself. So long."

Henry Brower didn't answer him as he strode out of the office.

It was Jerry who came into the house in the late afternoon with the word that Jim Bolten was in the courtyard and asking to see Lafe. In the living room Lafe was enjoying a pipe before the fire, having just returned from the range. "Take him into the bunkhouse," he told Jerry. "If it was any other stockman, I'd invite him in here."

A few minutes afterward, Lafe entered the bunkhouse to find the Double B owner seated at the table. They nodded to each other coldly. Bolten was confident that his mission would be successful. It would not help Lafe's candidacy any if it got noised about that he had paid Bianco $20,000 to leave his stock alone.

"You wanted to see me about something?" Lafe asked as he sat down.

"Yes." Bolten decided to come to the point at once. "I went in to the bank today to borrow fifteen thousand on my note and Brower turned me down cold . . . me, the best customer the bank has, I guess. I pay in money enough, anyway."

Old Lafe's brows lifted and he looked perplexed. "Yes?" he said. He had seen through the reason for

Bolten's visit before the Double B owner had ceased speaking.

"I need twenty thousand at once," Bolten announced, looking hard at Lafe. "I'm taking five thousand out of my cash balance in the bank and borrowing fifteen thousand. The security is gilt-edged. Brower acknowledged that. But . . . for the first time since I've been doing business with the bank, and that's some long time . . . Brower said the loan would have to be approved by three of the board of directors. That's why I come here to see you, Lafe Owens. I need this money within twenty-four hours at the latest."

"Well," said Lafe, puckering his brow, "the next meeting of the directors isn't till December First."

"Oh, bosh!" Bolten exploded. "A meeting isn't necessary, and you know that as well as I do. All I need is your OK on a piece of paper and a couple of the others will follow your lead without question. You can write 'em a short note, if necessary. I wouldn't tell Brower what I want the money for, and that made him sore. But I told him I would tell you."

"You needn't do that," Lafe drawled. "And we rather depend on Brower's judgment a lot . . . a whole lot, in fact. But I don't feel that I want to take the lead in anything like this. I'd prefer to have it come before the directors in the regular way."

"Well, maybe you'll change your mind," Bolten snapped out. "I reckon you've already guessed what I want this money for, and it's to your interest as well as mine, and the bank's."

"I'm not guessing at anything," Lafe shot back.

212

"Then I'll tell you," Bolten barked. "I'm going to do the same thing with this twenty thousand that you did with that much, or more, last night."

"You seem to think you know a whole lot about my affairs," said Lafe. "You don't know a thing. You can't even spy out anything!"

"Don't I?" There was a sneer in Bolten's voice. "Listen! Bianco came to see me last night. He offered to sell me back my own cattle for twenty thousand dollars. Of course, he's just levying that for protection. I saw through it at once. I did some swift thinking and decided it was worth buying him off and getting my stock back. He's a dangerous man to have around. I figured that he'd stole your cattle, as you thought, and that he'd been to see you with the same proposition, or would come to you later."

"He was here." Lafe nodded.

"I thought so!" Bolten cried in triumph. "I agreed to pay him the money. That's the money I need now. And this morning my cattle were all back on my south range near the brakes."

"Fast work."

"Sure. And then what? This morning, when I was riding to town, I saw your men driving a hundred head or so of shorthorns out of the corner range. My men saw the herd that was down there driven out, so those cattle this morning must have been the stock that Bianco stole. He returned 'em about the same time he returned mine."

"Probably," said Lafe.

"So they were the cattle! Then you met that rustler's terms, too. And now you don't want me to get the cash to give him to protect myself. You want him to bother me, eh? You want to use that outlaw on your side, is that it? It's a dirty piece of business."

"You don't know what you're talking about," said Lafe calmly.

"I guess not! You want this Bianco to raid my ranch, and maybe make more trouble on the range so you can tell the Association members that they need you to help 'em stop the rustling, or some such thing. You know how to feed 'em the soft soap! You accuse me of working under cover. What'll they think when they hear about this?"

"It's a good thing you've got a big hat," said Lafe dryly. "One big enough to soak up all the talking you do through it. Bolten, I didn't pay Bianco a cent."

Bolten stared, and then laughed. "I suppose Bianco just returned your cattle out of the goodness of his black heart."

"I don't know why he returned 'em, but he returned 'em . . . and without getting so much as a red penny," said Lafe convincingly, looking Bolten straight in the eyes. "Regardless of how much you dislike me, Bolten, you know I don't lie."

"And I know that outlaw wouldn't send back your cattle unless you'd made some kind of a deal," Bolten said angrily. "If it wasn't money, it was something else."

"It wasn't money, and it wasn't anything else. I made no deal of any kind whatever. I turned him down flat."

"I don't believe it!"

214

"I'll pass that over. You'll believe it when you calm down and think things over. But I'm going to surprise you. Just wait here until I go to my office a minute."

He rose and left the bunkhouse. Bolten had never been so puzzled in his life. If Lafe had defied the outlaw, why had Bianco returned the cattle? Because he couldn't take care of them in the brakes and couldn't easily get away with them? Never! The outlaw would have driven them into a soap hole before he would have given them back! But . . . but what? In his heart, Bolten knew that Lafe had never been caught in a deliberate lie. He worried his brains for the answer to the problem until Lafe returned.

Lafe held a sealed envelope in his hand. It was sealed with wax that bore the impression of the KT owner's signet ring. He handed the envelope to Bolten.

"Take that in to Brower," he said briefly, "and Brower will make the loan."

"I thought so," said Bolten, to conceal his surprise. "I'm much obliged, of course."

"Don't mention it," said Lafe curtly.

A few minutes later Bolten rode homeward with the envelope safely stowed in an outside pocket. He would get the money in the morning. He was jubilant. He had caught Lafe in a lie at last! For he firmly believed that Owens never would have arranged the loan for him if he hadn't himself paid a bunch of money to Bianco. He had Owens on the run!

# CHAPTER
# SIXTEEN

After supper that night, on his return from town and the KT, Bolten called Fresee into his office. In great elation he told the foreman exactly what had happened. "That sealed envelope does the trick," he concluded, displaying the envelope Lafe Owens had given him. "And if Owens hadn't bought Bianco off himself, he never would have fixed it for me to get the money. Of course, I could get it in Helena, maybe in Great Falls, but I'd have to do a lot of explaining and lying, and this and that because they'd want to know why I didn't get it from my regular bank and so on."

Fresee, who had listened intently, nodded and cleared his throat. "I don't see how Owens came to fix it for you, just the same."

"You don't? Why, to protect himself, that's why."

Fresee shook his head. "He didn't have to do that. We couldn't prove a thing . . . not a thing. You're the only man he told about the cattle and he could deny every word of it if he wanted to. He could have let Bianco ride us and be safe himself, if he had paid the money. Seems like he'd want to do that . . . make us all the trouble he could . . . since he's out to get us."

216

Bolten stared at him. "Why, now with Bianco out of the country, nobody will know a thing. It wouldn't help me any to say that I'd bought that rustler off, and it wouldn't help him any for it to get out that there was rustling on the range. He's running for the Association job on his record."

The dubious look did not leave Fresee's face. "There's a trick to it somewhere. You know, boss, I've studied that man a lot."

"And maybe you think I haven't studied him a lot," Bolten said irritably. "Whatever you've got in your head, I probably know . . . but spill it just the same."

"I've got a hunch that Owens told you the truth."

"You mean . . . say, Fresee, are you crazy? You mean he didn't pay any money to Bianco? Then how did he get his cattle back?"

"I don't know," said Fresee, shifting his gaze. "That's a trick, too. That's Bianco's trick. Don't forget that Bianco is smart. Anyway, that's my hunch, that Owens didn't kick in with the cash. He's just the kind that would tell Bianco to go to the devil if it cost him his ranch. If he did that, it's all the better for us. We'll be safe, I suppose, but Bianco will make Lafe Owens wish he'd shelled out the money."

Bolten's eyes glowed. "Maybe there's something in what you say, Fresee. But if he didn't shell out, why did he fix it so I could pay without further trouble?"

"That's it. That's just what I would like to know. That's what makes me think it's a trick. But I haven't got a thing to back up my hunch, except the fact that it gets stronger every minute. And he may have paid Bianco, after all."

"I think you'll come around to see it that way," said Bolten. He was annoyed to find that, after what Fresee had said, he didn't feel so sure of it himself. "Do you think Bianco will come for the money tonight? I'll have to stall him off until tomorrow . . . there's no way out of it."

"I don't know when or how he'll come. I don't suppose he comes the same way twice. He's too smart for that. Maybe you better let me talk to him when he comes."

"No!" Bolten exclaimed decisively. "I don't want you two anywhere near each other. I could see your trigger fingers itching last night and I don't want you killed. I'll handle this myself."

"Well, I'm not afraid of him. And, if he comes on our range again, after this deal, he'll find it pretty hard sleddin' . . . if we see him." He rose to go.

"He may head north for Canada across our range, and, if he does, don't bother him," Bolten ordered.

The Double B owner remained in his office until after midnight, but no tapping was heard on the door. When Bianco had failed to show up by one o'clock in the morning, Bolten put out the lights and went to bed.

He rode to Pondera in the morning and tossed the envelope on Brower's desk. More than once he had been tempted to tamper with it to read what it contained, but the seal stopped him. "I guess that'll tell you what to do," he sneered. "And it didn't take three directors, either."

The banker examined the envelope, recognized the handwriting in which it was addressed, broke the seal, and took out the note. When he had finished reading it, he folded the note and put it in his pocket. Then he took a note blank and a check blank out of a drawer and filled them out. He passed the slips across his desk to Bolten with the pen for his signature.

"There's a check for five thousand on your account and a note for fifteen thousand," he said, very business-like. While Bolten was signing, he called the teller and told him to bring fifteen thousand dollars in cash — large bills.

Bolten looked at the note after signing. "Look here, Brower," he said roughly, "this note is payable at sight."

"That's the way I made it out," said Brower crisply.

"But I said six months," Bolten protested with a scowl.

"Most of your paper is made out the same way, if you'll remember." The teller brought in the packet of banknotes. "However, you do not have to take the money under the terms if you don't want to."

Bolten swore and shoved the two slips across the desk. He counted the money and thrust it into an inside pocket. "I suppose I'll have trouble with this bank from now on because you got riled yesterday," he said pointedly.

"You won't have to bother with us long if you're going to put us out of business. I guess that's all for this morning."

Bolten went out swearing to himself. He took dinner at the hotel and started back to the Double B immediately. When he reached the little stream at the western boundary of the KT range, where the short-cut trail turned off toward the bottoms above the brakes, a horseman suddenly dashed out of the trees and closed in beside him. It was Bianco.

"Did you get it?" the outlaw demanded, his gaze boring into Bolten's.

For answer Bolten unbuttoned his Mackinaw with nervous fingers and reached into an inside pocket. There was something in the way that the rustler looked at him that gave him the creeps. He was suddenly convinced, too, that Bianco knew every move he had made from the time they had parted at the Double B ranch house until now. He drew out the packet of bills and handed them over. "You could do me a big favor, if you wanted to," he said unsteadily. "I'd keep it to myself, too."

"What's that?" the outlaw asked, keeping his eyes on him as he stowed away the banknotes.

"Just tell me if that damned Owens kicked in."

"Keep your eyes straight ahead on the road and start moving," came the sharp command in a terrible voice.

Bolten spurred his horse, half expecting a bullet in the back. He did not breathe freely again until he was halfway across the KT range. Then his feelings exploded in a burst of profanity as he stole a look over his shoulder at the empty plain behind.

The blizzard had ushered in the month of October. Now Larry Owens's birthday was but three days away. With Lafe Owens's consent, Molly and her mother had planned a surprise party. Molly had sent invitations when one of the men had gone to town for the mail. Mary O'Neil was preparing a big birthday cake on which there would be twenty-two candles. Lafe had entered into the spirit of the thing, thinking that such an affair would cheer up the spirits of the women and provide a diversion for the men. A five-piece orchestra had been engaged. With Larry away looking up men for the ranch, making arrangements for the party had been easy. But now it was a question of whether he would return by Wednesday.

"Don't worry, he'll be here for his birthday, whether he's finished what I sent him to do, or not," Lafe assured his wife and Molly.

But when he hadn't arrived by Tuesday afternoon, even Lafe began to feel uneasy. It wasn't so much on account of the projected party — which would have been carried out in any event — as it was because of the fact that Larry and Jones had had time enough to complete their mission.

At sundown, Lafe's concern vanished and the worries of the womenfolk were washed away as Larry and Jones galloped down the bench road at the head of fifteen men and thundered into the courtyard in a cloud of dust. Lafe went out through the barn and watched as the men unsaddled and turned their horses into the corrals. They were a good-looking crew physically; hardly a man was under six feet in height. All were bearded, unkempt, displaying flying signals of having had one roaring time after having been let go for the winter. One man, taller than the others, slim-waisted, with gray moustaches that hung low on either side of his mouth, was giving orders and bantering the crew. "Take your packs into the bunkhouse," he said, "and don't take more'n one drink before you eat. We're damned lucky to have a winter job and we've got to take care of it."

Lafe looked at Larry as he came up. "How do you like the looks of 'em?" Larry asked with a grin.

"Where'd you get 'em?" asked Lafe.

"Shelby. They rode down from Lethbridge. Were going to work on the Great Northern snow sheds or a big cut or something. I grabbed the lot. They're all from the PT outfit across the line in Alberta."

Lafe pursed his lips. The PT Ranch was one of the biggest and best known in western Canada. Moreover, it was noted for its hard crew. A PT man had to be tough and he had to stay tough to hold his job. No willy-nillys, these men. Lafe frowned. "They'll have to toe the mark here. I reckon Stan can get that into their heads."

At this juncture, the tall leader approached. He glanced at Larry, and then looked at Lafe appraisingly. "Are you the old man?"

"I own this ranch," replied Lafe shortly.

"Fair enough. I'm Sid Tyler. I've sort of been ridin' herd on this ornery bunch since we left the PT a while back. We went broke just in time for this young buckaroo to hire us." He indicated Larry. "He's seen us in action." He looked at Larry again, and Larry grinned broadly. "We're hard-workin', hard-ridin', hard-shootin', and, when off the range, hard-drinkin'. We

222

need a man-size meal, a hefty nightcap . . . that we're packin' with us . . . and a good night's sleep. And we'll be ready for orders at daylight."

Lafe Owens liked this man immediately. He was one of the old school. He knew full well, without having to be told, that this man would have been a foreman were it not for a propensity to go on sprees. He looked over the others who were grouped behind the tall leader. Half of them had black eyes; all of them bore the signs of battle royal. Court plasters and bandages were not lacking. And Larry had seen them in action — seen them and hired them to a man as soon as the smoke had cleared away! Lafe felt a thrill. Unless he was mistaken, this was just the kind of a crew he needed.

"Take your men to the bunkhouse, Tyler," he said. "Larry, you tell the cook to take a look at this patched-up outfit and feed 'em accordingly. If you've got your own nightcaps, it saves me that much whiskey, Tyler. My foreman, Stan Velie, will talk to you and give you your orders in the morning. I know your outfit and your old man, Frank Baldwin. I expect you to be as loyal to the KT this winter as you'd be to the PT. That's all."

"That's enough," said Tyler. "I reckon we'll get along."

He led the men through the barn to the courtyard and turned to the bunkhouse at once. Later, when their horses had cooled off, they would look after them.

Larry and Jones became busy at the wash bench. Lafe drew near. "What was this action Tyler says you saw 'em in?" Lafe asked Larry.

"Double action," said Larry through the swirling towel. "We watched 'em play around for a day or so and then saw 'em take a joint apart and put it together again with about half its liquid refreshments missing. I'd found out where they were from and had managed to talk a little with Tyler. I thought they'd do, and, when things were top side up again, I hired the lot of 'em."

Old Lafe went on into the living room with a satisfied smile.

Stan Velie came in off the range that night and talked for some time with Lafe after supper. In the morning he spoke to the men after breakfast. He explained conditions exactly as they were, omitting no details, and even warned them of the presence in the vicinity of Bianco. He saw their eyes sparkle with excitement as they looked at one another. They were mostly clear-eyed after their night of sound sleep.

"This is a good outfit to work for," Velie concluded, in concise tones. "If there's trouble, we'll pay a bonus for any . . . extra work." He paused to let the statement sink in. "And now, if there's any of you that want to shave and fix up a bit, go to it. After dinner we'll all go out on the range. I'm going to bring a bunch of the regulars in because this is young Larry's birthday and I think they've got something framed up for him. You can keep it under your hats."

"Talks like the goods," was Tyler's comment when Velie had gone. "Looks like a good winter berth with something besides snow to keep us warm." This seemed to be the general impression and the men set about

224

shaving, washing, getting their packs in shape, looking after their guns, and making small repairs to saddles or bridles.

Larry hadn't thought of his birthday, so he said, until his mother kissed him in the morning and gave him her best wishes.

"Must be terrible to be so old," was Molly Owens's comment as she presented him with a splendid watch chain. "I should have got a pair of carpet slippers, but I was bulldozed into buying that out of my allowance. Dad's put the other half of it under your plate."

At breakfast Larry attached the $300 Hamilton to the chain and winked at his father. "All I need now is one of those round, glass charms with a lock of hair in it."

"Horse hair is about your speed," Molly chided.

"If I'd known this was to be your day, I'd have brought some kind of trinket for you, Larry," said Jones.

Larry looked at him, saw he meant it, and smiled. "Wish me luck, Harry. I seem to need lots of it."

"I've got it!" exclaimed Molly. "Give him an old horseshoe, Mister Jones."

Jones looked at her gravely. "Chop off the mister, girlie. I hate to feel dignified at breakfast."

Everyone laughed at this sally. But Larry had to be sent away from the house before any of the guests arrived. As some of them were coming from quite a distance, they would start early and might arrive after noon. An invitation to a party at Lafe Owens's ranch was not to be taken lightly on that range.

Consequently Larry and Jones were dispatched to the north range on a pretext soon after breakfast. Stan Velie rode away with the new men after dinner, intending to put them in the places of men he would send back to the ranch to be present at the party. Lafe was set on doing the thing up right and was bubbling with enthusiasm. He helped with the decorations and bothered about the kitchen until Mary O'Neil put her hands on her hips and told him to clear out and stay out!

During all this, Lafe had forgotten conditions on the range, forgotten to anticipate any results of his defiance of Bianco. Larry was twenty-two, strong, healthy and able, and, as Lafe had finally decided, home to stay.

At two o'clock the first guests arrived. They were the Fowlers of the west end. Fred Fowler was the largest stock raiser west of the KT. They brought their son Billy.

"That's what we want," boomed Lafe, shaking Billy's hand and speaking to the stockman and his wife. "We need young people to make this old ranch sing today and tonight, and I'm getting younger every minute myself."

The Fowlers were speedily followed by others. Young men and girls came horseback while their elders came in buckboards and even in spring wagons. One who knew that range would have noticed that all who arrived early were from the west end. At sundown, George Robertson, a powerful stockman from the east end, arrived with his wife. Later came Amberg with his wife and two children. Henry Brower came out from

226

town and with him was Sheriff Rowan. The Norths, who were a power on the west range, came, and with them were the Vaughans and Pattens. Then came the Tibbetts and Burns families, the Russells, the Lees, the Fullers, the Hills, and Percys, followed by the Welches and others, until the big ranch house seemed filled to overflowing.

"Jumping coyotes, Mother!" said Lafe Owens, looking about at the familiar faces. "I don't believe we invited all these folks . . . we haven't got room enough!"

Men were coming in off the range, helping with the saddle horses and teams. The courtyard was crowded. Lafe passed the word and the men repaired to the bunkhouse eating room where a great bowl of Tom-and-Jerry, containing the proper proportions of sherry and rum, reposed majestically in the center of the long table.

Jerry, the barman, attired in one of the cook's white shirts, about six sizes too large for him, and a white apron that was wound around and around his waist and legs like a winding sheet, mixed the hot, creamy drinks.

"Where's the other half of the team?" asked a jovial stockman. "We've only got Jerry here."

"Tom's mixing up another bowl," boomed Lafe Owens promptly. "Dog-gone if it doesn't look like we've got an Association quorum here! But this isn't part of my campaigning, boys. This is just Larry's birthday, and that's enough for me."

Larry arrived with Jones and Stan Velie just after dark. He was taken from his horse and carried on the shoulders of KT men to the living room to be the center of a throng of well-wishers, all of whom shook hands with him. Almost everyone had brought a gift, and these were heaped on a table. "I hope there's a pair of home-knit wool socks in that pile," Larry said, overwhelmed by his reception. From the surprise angle, the party already was a huge success.

"Clear out, all you men!" Lafe thundered. "There's got to be tables set, and, if some of you didn't bring your own eating tools, you'll have to use your fingers, for our supply is limited!"

"Lafe," his wife reproved, "somebody's liable to believe what you're saying."

"Well, I hope they don't think I'm foolin'. Personally I only remember inviting the sheriff as a safety measure, and look at this outfit."

But Sarah Owens pushed him out the door amid the laughter.

An hour later, or a bit less, the announcement was made that supper was ready. Larry managed to elude the scores of guests and was standing in the yard in front of the house in the shadows. He was tremendously affected by the friendly good wishes that had been heaped upon him, but he knew that these people of the range also were honoring his father. He wanted to get his sister aside to ask her a question — a question that had to do with the only tinge of disappointment that he felt. He heard hoof beats on the bench road. A single horse. A lone late arrival.

Larry saw the horse and the rider round into the road for the house. He could see plainly in the light of the stars and moon. As the rider came on, his heart gave a bound and he walked quickly to the side of the road. No need to ask Molly that question now!

"How'd you ever run the blockade?" he said joyously as Jane Bolten reined in her horse beside him. He was hatless, and the wind was tossing his hair. His eyes were sparkling.

"That's about what it amounted to," said Jane as she let him hand her down. "Father didn't want me to come."

"Well, you just forget all that," said Larry, taking the reins from her hand. "You're here and more than welcome. I was thinking of asking Sis if she'd forgotten, but I ought to have known better."

They stood looking at each other in the silvery light while the thoroughbred stamped and neighed.

Larry took her hand. "Come on. I'll turn this horse over to one of the men and we'll go inside. I reckon this party is going to be a big success, after all."

Already a man had spied them and came running to take the horse. Larry turned it over to him. Then he and Jane Bolten entered the house. There was a pause in the laughing and talking, then came a mighty cheer, and Molly Owens hurried to welcome the belated guest.

# CHAPTER
# SEVENTEEN

Tables had been set in both dining room and living room. On a small table midway between the others, the birthday cake rose in a mound of white topped by twenty-two colored candles, the one in the center being a bit taller than the others. In a few minutes the guests and hosts sat down to the birthday feast. Lafe Owens was at the head of the table in the dining room. Larry was at his right with Jane Bolten beside him. Henry Brower sat at his left. Sheriff Rowan, Fowler, and Robertson were also at his table. Sarah Owens sat at the head of the table in the living room and with her were Molly and Jones. Young people and their elders were interspersed in the other chairs. The orchestra played in the hall at the head of the stairs leading from the living room. It was the first time this feature had been introduced during a meal on the range. It created something of a sensation, but the merry-making at the tables nearly drowned the music.

"Funny I should find myself sitting next to you," Jones told Molly. "There are so many good-looking future cattle kings here for you to pick from."

"Yes, but you don't know anybody very well here, and I thought you would feel more at home beside me."

Jones grinned at her. "It must be my personality. I can't think of anything else."

"You needn't be ashamed to eat all you want."

"I don't feel a bit hungry when you're so close and amiable," was his retort. "Miss Molly, you're no slouch at this thing they call repartée."

Molly found it necessary to speak to the man on her left.

"Does Larry think he's going to blow out all those candles with one breath?" Jones inquired when she turned to him again.

Molly laughed. "Why not?" she said in an amused voice.

"Because, judging by the hectic conversation he's carrying on with Miss Bolten, he won't have any breath left," said Jones soberly.

Molly looked through the door at Larry and Jane. She looked for some little space. Then she glanced at Jones with a queer expression. "Larry has to be nice to Jane," she said, lowering her voice. "She's my friend, for one thing, and . . . her folks were not invited. I guess you understand."

Jones understood. It was a subject that would not allow a bantering remark. "Sure, I know. I didn't think of it just at the time. I'm pretty dumb, anyway."

"No, you're not dumb. You're a smart boy, Harry Jones. But you've got to watch your step on this range, just the same."

He knew what she meant. "Just so I don't slip when you're around, I'll take my chances."

There was a faint glow of color in Molly's cheeks. "You must try not to slip at any time."

"When's your birthday, Miss Molly?" he inquired.

"You can leave the handle off my name. I don't fancy it any more than you like the mister. And I'm not going to tell you when my birthday is, and we mustn't talk to each other so much, for there are other people here."

"But you see, it's like you said, Molly, I don't know 'em." Jones grinned.

"Well, you don't know me very well."

"I know one thing about you," he said so she alone could hear.

Molly couldn't keep back the question that was on her tongue. "What's that?" she asked — and then was furious with herself.

"You're awfully nice," he said, looking at his plate.

Molly's assumed dignity collapsed as a giggle gurgled forth.

"Sounds funny, doesn't it?"

"It's the way you said it," Molly got out. Then she laughed so heartily that the others at the table laughed with her. Jones scowled and drew down the corners of his mouth.

"What's the matter out there, Harry?" called Larry.

"I've been insulted," Jones called back in a lull in the merriment.

"Don't worry," sang Larry gleefully. "She'll think of a way to twist it around into a compliment before the night's over. Don't give her back her goat on account of any insults. It's just a scheme!"

Molly's face flamed as the laughter burst forth again. There was a flash in her eyes as she looked at Jones. "You're just naturally mean," she said vehemently.

"I'm not responsible for what Larry says," said Jones calmly.

Nevertheless, there was little talk between them during the rest of the meal. When all had finished, Lafe Owens rose. "Now, folks, we're not going to have any speeches. I think I can say for Larry that he thanks you all for this surprise and for your remembrances. But there is an important function that must be observed on an occasion like this. Cast your peepers on that birthday cake. If all the eggs that went into that cake was laid end to end, they'd reach around what fence I've got! We're going to cut it presently . . . that is, Larry is going to cut it. But first he has to blow out the candles in one breath. Molly, light the candles."

"There's so many of 'em I'll need a torch," said Molly.

When the candles were lighted, Larry rose and stepped behind his chair. "Just a word, folks. I can thank you on my own hook for coming here today, and I do . . . thank you very much. Of all the remembrances, this show of goodwill and friendship is the best. Now I'll try to blow out those dog-gone candles."

He stepped to the table where the glorious cake reposed, the glowing candlelight casting flickering shadows on its snowy crown. He leaned down until he was even with the points of flame. A deep silence of anticipation fell over those at the tables. Larry drew a long, deep breath. Then it happened in a wink — the sharp report, a burst of glass, screams. The top of the center candle had been shot away!

Larry leaped back. Every man was on his feet in another instant. The lights went out like magic, leaving only the candles burning. In a moment Larry had blown them out and the rooms were in darkness, save for the glow of the fire and the light from the kitchen. The music stopped.

"Keep away from the windows!" rang Lafe Owens's voice.

The men were crowding to the front and rear doors. Larry and Jones ran upstairs for their guns. Few of the men were armed, but all ran out into the courtyard. Then, from the head of the courtyard, the yard in front of the house, and from the open space to the left of the barn, toward the bottoms, came the staccato of pistol shots and darting tongues of flame. An attack!

KT men, fully armed, poured from the bunkhouse. Then guns blazed in the courtyard as those who were possessed of weapons shot blindly into the shadows from whence the volley had come. There were no answering shots. Shouts and the pounding of hoofs could be heard in the bottoms. Men started to run from the courtyard in pursuit.

"Stay where you are!" thundered the commanding voice of Lafe Owens. "KT men get your horses!"

There was a dash for the corrals. Larry and Jones coming out the rear door joined in this. Lafe called loudly to Jerry to saddle his horse. Even as he did so, he felt that any attempt of pursuit would be useless.

"Have you got any extra horses here, Lafe?" asked a voice beside him.

Lafe turned and saw Fowler. "I think so, but you fellows don't mix in this. It's a . . . personal matter."

"It's more than that," Robertson, the east-ender, put in. "We're here, and our folks have been endangered."

Fowler already was striding toward the barn. Robertson followed him. And then came other stockmen and every young blood on the place. Soon the courtyard was swarming with horses, men were mounting — all were armed by now.

Lights shone from the windows of the ranch house. Lafe entered the living room where the women were gathered, frightened and pale.

"Nobody's been hurt," he said loudly. He was not sure of this but was under the impression that the attackers had fired high. Otherwise, men would have been hit and he had seen none fall, had heard none cry out as if wounded.

"Now just calm down," said Lafe in a reassuring tone. "Somebody or some outfit has been playing a joke on us. But we don't think it's such a joke, and we're going to see if we can find out who did it. There's no danger, and we'll be back in a minute. Hey, you fellers up there! That's what you're here for . . . to play!"

The music started before he went out and the women and girls had calmed down. There had been no hysterics, for these were range women. When Lafe had gone out, Molly suggested that they play cards.

Jerry had Lafe's horse at the front porch. The other riders were milling about the big courtyard. As Lafe swung into the saddle, he checked his horse so suddenly and hard that the animal reared.

"Listen!" he cried.

But there was no need for his warning. Everyone heard. On the wind from the north came the sharp echoes of shots. There was trouble on the bench. Lafe rode out of the yard with the others thundering after him. Sheriff Rowan moved swiftly up to his side. The visiting stockmen had heard swift remarks passed between the KT cowpunchers, but were only cognizant of the fact that whatever was up, it was not a joking matter. The same thought came to all of them: the Double B outfit had raided the ranch. But some of the remarks they had overheard had dealt with rustlers. They might not have felt called upon to join in the chase if it was merely a clash between the two outfits. If rustlers were about, that was different, and, if the raiders had really meant business, then the families of the visitors and their own lives had been imperiled. At any rate, they were Lafe Owens's guests, and they rode forth ready to stand behind him. If the Double B had staged the raid, it had showed poor judgment as to the selection of the time for it.

Counting the sixteen-odd men brought in from the range, Lafe, Stan Velie, Larry, and Jones, and the visiting stockmen and young men, the KT owner was leading a large force of men up the bench road. The shooting indicated that there were KT men where it was taking place. A wild hope swelled in Lafe's breast. He might be able to corner Bianco and his men, or to run them down. For Lafe didn't doubt for a moment but that Bianco was the man responsible.

The riders had hardly gained the bench land when they saw black dots moving swiftly on the moonlit plain in the northeast. Lafe reined in his horse and brought the cavalcade to a halt.

"Stan, take the KT men and strike straight across . . . clear to the fence," he ordered. "Head 'em off, if they start south for the brakes."

The KT cowpunchers started to follow the order immediately, and galloped eastward.

Then Lafe shouted to the stockmen and others. "I've reason to believe this is a rustling outfit, and a dangerous bunch. Take no chances, but if you shoot, shoot to *hit* something. Let's get up there!"

They raced northeastward at top speed. Moon and stars were shining brightly, laving the rolling prairie with soft white light. Soon riders were distinguishable from cattle. Red tongues of flame darted and the reports of the guns broke on the air like firecrackers. As Lafe and those with him neared the scene, horsemen swung out and started south. They were bunched, but Lafe's experienced eye told him there were close to twenty of them.

"Head them off!" he shouted, and swerved eastward.

Velie had also seen the break and he now was leading his men at a furious pace straight east in an effort to cut off the flight to the brakes. Behind the oncoming riders was a much smaller bunch of horsemen. These were KT men; so Lafe rightly assumed. The situation was unusual. The score or more of riders, fleeing like mad

237

for the shelter of the badlands in the south, were considerably nearer the fence than Velie's men and to the northeast of them. They would soon be directly ahead of Lafe and his men. They were leaving the handful of riders pursuing them rapidly behind. It became a matter of horseflesh with each man calling for the best his horse could give him. Soon riders were scattered all over that section of the range. Then came two startling new developments.

In the south, beyond Velie's men, appeared another bunch of horsemen, spurring their mounts toward Velie from that direction. These riders, Lafe concluded immediately, were the men who had raided the ranch house. Velie saw he was in danger of being caught and turned northeast. In doing this, he forfeited the chance to cut off the rustlers racing down for the cut-off corner where the wire undoubtedly was down and the way into the treacherous brakes open.

At the same time that Velie made his shift, Lafe swung his followers to the southeast to join him. And now the second development brought shouts from the men of both factions. In the east, and slightly south, appeared a sixth group of riders, racing from the direction of the fence! At this startling juncture, Sheriff Rowan took a hand. He had followed Lafe's orders because he didn't know the circumstances, and events had crowded each other with amazing swiftness. But he had heard the mention of rustlers and now he believed he knew what was up.

He spurred his horse into the lead, a neck ahead of Lafe's mount. "Straight at 'em!" he shouted. "That must be the Double B outfit! Straight at 'em and let Velie come along!"

Lafe accepted the order and they raced for the fleeing band. This brought the rustlers between two fires, providing the riders coming from the fence were Double B men, and friendly.

With this new move, the raiders stopped their pursuit of Velie's men and shot toward the east and the fence to meet the force coming from that direction. But the rustlers' horses were tiring as the result of the mad spurt. Soon all factions drew close, and then the fireflies of death began to wink as the guns cracked. Lafe and the sheriff swept in with their men from the west, the KT men who had been with the cattle dashed down from the north, Velie and his men were closing in below, and a score of riders were coming from the east. It looked as if the rustlers were to be surrounded.

Lafe shouted to the sheriff in a frenzy of excitement and hope: "Shoot 'em down like dogs! It's Bianco and his gang . . . do you hear? It's Bianco!"

Others heard his thundering voice and the cry went up: "Bianco!"

The rustlers ahead made a final spurt. Little they cared if they killed their horses! They passed between the riders to eastward and the two bunches of horsemen led by the sheriff and Velie in the west. Then the Double B riders raced down, joining in a general pursuit. Lafe recognized the slim form of Fresee at their head. They were firing at the rustlers, but there were no hits. Not a man or a horse fell. Some of the Double B riders on the left surged ahead. Fresee and others were shooting. A Double B rider toppled from the saddle, his horse running free. The raiders from the south had closed in and joined the rustlers from the north. The combined force might have been fifty men, maybe more. Bullets whistled and men on both sides went down. Lafe's horse went to his knees in a death plunge throwing him over its head. He fell in a black void — senseless. Horses behind him reared, darted aside, or stumbled over the body of his horse, piling up. It was his fallen horse that saved him from being trampled to death.

Other riders swept on, the Double B men swerving off to the left, their horses apparently spent. Velie's forces were trailing the fleeing outlaws but had to give way before a withering fire. Six of his men were down. Here Sheriff Rowan assumed full charge. The pursuit was halted as useless and the outlaws disappeared in the dark shadow of the tumbled river brakes.

Larry bent over his father, unconscious on the ground. In a few moments, the sheriff, Fowler, and Robertson were with him. Velie ordered the others to stay back and to look after the other men who had been shot down or thrown when their horses were hit.

Jones was swearing. Someone had taken his horse in the excitement at the ranch house and he had drawn a poor mount. "Behind every foot of the way!" he raved. "Lickin' up the dust! Who's got my horse?"

Men were too busy and too excited to pay any attention to him, and the name of the rustler chief was running through their brains.

Lafe Owens, still unconscious, was put across Larry's saddle and he started back with his father, accompanied by some of the stockmen. He called to Jones: "Hustle on to the ranch, get Jerry, and rope a fast horse in the lower pasture! Jerry'll know. Get the doctor."

Jones swept ahead as fast as his mount could carry him.

Behind were scattered groups, looking after dead and injured. It had been the first clash of the kind on that range in twenty years and one of the worst in its history.

Fresee was speaking to Sheriff Rowan. His eyes were sparking fire, it seemed. "We heard the shots and came over," he said. "My men will take your orders."

"Look after your own men," the sheriff snapped.

"I was lucky," said Fresee. "I only lost one. Poor George Remy got it in the back."

# CHAPTER
# EIGHTEEN

There had been no card playing at the KT ranch house. The orchestra had played lively selections and the women and girls had kept up an appearance of cheerfulness. But this is a trait of women of the rangelands when they know or think their menfolk are in danger. When Larry and the others rode into the courtyard, Sarah Owens was the first to meet them. Her face was white, for she knew instinctively, when she saw the form in Larry's arms, that it was Lafe.

The unconscious cattleman was carried upstairs and put to bed. The orchestra was dismissed. The women spoke in hushed tones and arrangements were begun to start home. The party was over.

Old Lafe had been thrown flat on his back apparently, for that was the position in which he was found. Those who examined him could find no exterior evidences of his injury. There was a swelling, however, at the back of his head, but Sarah Owens said that it was a natural formation.

In a short time all the visiting cattlemen had returned and were gathered in the bunkhouse. Their faces were grave. The events of that night had come like thunderbolts. The knowledge that the notorious rustler, bandit, and killer, Bianco, was on the north range stunned them. They could not understand it. Had Lafe been keeping something from them and, if so, why? Didn't he want it known that the range was threatened by cattle thieves until after the regular meeting of the Association which was scheduled a week from this day? Did Lafe feel himself slipping — unable to cope as of old with this dangerous situation? Had he kept quiet for that reason? The stockmen frankly discussed this among themselves, including Robertson and Amberg from the east end. Fowler and North, the most influential stockmen from the west half of the range, insisted that Lafe must have had a good reason for keeping his knowledge to himself and, in any event, he would not have been likely to tell them what he knew before the party and thus set them thinking about such a serious matter at a time when he wanted everyone carefree and merry. To the surprise of the west-end ranchers, both Robertson and Amberg sided with them.

They were discussing this when Larry came in. Without waiting to be asked, he told them briefly of the first raid, and Bud Davis's identification of the desperado. He knew nothing, however, of Bianco's visit to his father in the night and could not explain the return of the cattle. However, what he told them was enough. Bianco was on the range. The stockmen looked at one another. The same thought was in the mind of each. Did the re-opening of the feud between Lafe Owens and Jim Bolten have something to do with it? Was Bianco taking advantage of this disturbed condition? Had Lafe kept silent for this reason, because he believed that only his range and that of the Double B was threatened?

"How is Lafe now?" asked Fowler.

"He's still unconscious," Larry replied gravely, "but his breathing is regular and his pulse strong. I've sent for the doctor to look after him and the other men who have been hurt. I think the best thing we can do right now is start out there with a couple of spring wagons to bring back the injured and . . ." He didn't finish the sentence but the others understood and nodded.

"You'll have to stay here at the house," Robertson told Larry. "We'll look after this business. I think your father will come out of it all right, although I've seen men knocked out by a fall like that for twenty-four hours."

Larry nodded but vouchsafed no comment. Soon teams were hitched up and two spring wagons started out on the range. Larry had just entered the house and his mother was calling to him softly from the head of the stairs, when he heard newly arrived horsemen in the yard. "I'll be there in a minute, Mother," he told her, and went out to see who had come.

He found Stan Velie and the rest of the stockmen and some others dismounting. Then, to his astonishment, he caught the flash of Fresee's dark eyes as the Double B foreman swung from his horse. What was he doing there? It occurred to him immediately that Velie must have brought him along.

He turned back into the house and his mother met him at the head of the stairs. "Your father is conscious," she said in a low tone. "Now he mustn't get excited and he cannot get up as he wants to. Your father is no longer young, and the doctor should examine him before he leaves his bed."

"I'll go in and see him, Mother," said Larry, pushing past her. "Don't worry."

He found his father with a puzzled frown on his face. "My horse stumbled," he said, "and the next thing you know, I'm here. What happened?"

"Your horse was shot from under you, Dad, and you had a bad fall that knocked you out," said Larry, standing over the bed.

"Well, I feel all right now, except my back and head are a little sore," grumbled Lafe. "I can't stay here in bed with those visitors here, and there are a few things I want to find out. I've got to get up." He sat up in bed, but lay back at once with a groan.

"You can't get up, Dad, till the doctor sees you," said Larry in a determined voice. "You know very well that's sense. Where do you feel the worst?"

"Must have lit on a rock," Lafe muttered. "My back got a crack somehow. How'd I get home?"

"I brought you in on my horse. Harry Jones has ridden to town for the doctor."

"Doctor be hanged!" exclaimed Lafe. "I haven't had one since I broke my thumb and that was before you were born. I'm too tough to be kept in bed long. What happened after I went out of the picture?"

Larry told him briefly of the subsequent events. His mother came in with a cup of tea.

"Is Stan Velie back?" asked Lafe. "I heard horses below."

"Velie just got in," said Larry. He decided not to tell his father of the presence of Fresee.

"Bring Stan up here," Lafe ordered. "If I've got to stay in bed to humor you two, I'm going to talk anyway. My tongue isn't hurt any."

Larry looked at his mother who finally nodded. He went down, found Velie just coming out of the barn, and escorted him to the room where Lafe was lying.

"Got clean away, did they?" Lafe asked with a scowl.

"All but three," said Velie. "And those three will never ride on any more raids. Lafe, they were all hit more than once, and I believe Bianco made sure they wouldn't be taken prisoners."

This was a serious charge, but Lafe wouldn't put it past the outlaw to finish any of his men who were wounded and liable to be captured. Even the toughest rustler can be made to talk under certain conditions.

"How about our side?" Lafe asked quietly.

"Well . . ." Velie looked at Sarah Owens.

"You better go out, Mother," said Lafe, noting his foreman's glance. "I'll tell you everything later. There are some questions I want to ask Stan and maybe he'd rather we'd be alone. Larry, you take your mother downstairs. Tell our guests everything is all right and I'm just resting . . . which is the truth, by gad."

When Sarah Owens and Larry had gone, Velie resumed: "We've got five men hurt, but not seriously. That's what I call luck, although we weren't as lucky as the Double B. And we lost nine horses, with yours in the bunch."

246

"Best horse I ever had," said Lafe with a deep frown. "That's another mark against that cut-throat. How lucky was the Double B?"

"Lost one, none wounded, no horses shot," replied Velie.

"The twenty thousand fixed that" — Lafe had taken Velie fully into his confidence — "but why did they come over? That's a poser, eh, Stan?"

"The man they lost was shot in the back," said Velie. "And it was George Remy, the 'puncher that got lost in the badlands after the Double B cattle was stolen."

Lafe tried to sit up, grimaced with pain, and lay back again. "Got a twist in my back from that fall," he said. "Shot in the back! Say, Stan" — his voice dropped — "I saw that rider go ahead of Fresee . . . ahead of him and a little to the left. Next thing Fresee was shooting. The rustlers were pretty far ahead for a hit by Fresee, and they couldn't very well shoot in a semicircle and hit this Remy in the back."

The two men stared at each other. Remy had been ahead and Fresee had been shooting. Remy now was dead with a bullet in his back. Velie wet his lips. "You mean . . . ?" He didn't finish the question.

Lafe nodded slowly. "That's what I mean, Stan. I don't know why, just yet. And don't speak of this to anyone, understand? Have you heard what the stockmen think of it all? Where's the sheriff?"

"I let him take charge," said Velie. "He went down to the corner to investigate. You know what that amounts to. He's got my men and some of the young fellows.

He'll be back pretty quick. Larry told the stockmen of the other raid and why we think it's Bianco's work."

"What about the cattle?"

"Didn't get a single head. I think this raid down here was staged to draw the men off the range and that something went wrong, so their plans misfired. Might have been a question of time or . . . they must have known there was a party on here, if they're keeping any watch, as I suppose they are. Bianco wouldn't do anything without good reason. Maybe he figured a stunt like this would hurt you with the rest of the west-enders. There's something behind it. Fresee says they heard the firing and came on over. Funny he'd have so many men in one spot at this time."

"Fresee's a liar and a double-crosser," said Lafe harshly. "I think he's double-crossing Bolten himself some way, but I'm not even going to hint of it till I'm sure. You better get Fowler and Robertson up here. I want to talk to 'em. One's from the west and the other's from the east, and they can tell the others."

"But, Lafe, do you think you're able to . . . ?"

"Don't worry about me," Lafe broke in impatiently. "I'm all right, except my back hurts when I move and I've got a wee bit of a headache. I've got to tell 'em something before they go . . . that's certain. If they don't come up here, I'll have to manage to get up and go down there, that's all there is to it."

"All right," said Velie. "I'll bring 'em up."

While Velie was gone, Lafe thought about the death of Remy. He now believed that the story Remy had told when he returned from the badlands was true. He hadn't known anything of the rustling, but he might have seen something in the wilderness of brakes. He might even have seen Bianco or some of his men, and told about it. He might know more than was good for him. About what? Lafe was positive that Fresee's gun had sent the fatal bullet in the cowpuncher's back. What had first been a wild conjecture, now was a definitely formed suspicion. Why should Fresee want to kill Remy? Lafe thought he knew, and the conviction put him in an excited frame of mind that lasted until the appearance of the two stockmen he had sent for.

"How do you feel, Lafe?" Fowler asked.

"I'm all right," said Lafe with spirit. "Got a crick in my back where I hit a rock or something, that's all."

"I had a man who was knocked out for twenty-four hours by a bronc'," said Robertson. "You'll be all jake in a day or two."

Lafe nodded, but winced as he did so. "Sit down, boys, I want to tell you something. I hear Larry told you about the raid on my shorthorns a while back. Bud Davis died from wounds he received in that fray. He was shot twice. But he came to long enough to tell me who the ringleader was. It was Bianco, and I don't have to tell you anything about him."

The two stockmen shook their heads. "We know too much already," said Fowler wryly. "We was wondering if maybe he didn't think the time was ripe for working up here because . . ." He paused as if he thought better of his words.

But Lafe Owens had read his mind. "Because of the trouble between me and Jim Bolten. Maybe so. But I expect that trouble will be all settled for good a week from today after the Association's annual meeting. If Bolten can get what he wants, I'm through . . . so far as heading the organization is concerned. If I win, I'm banking on Bolten's having some common sense left. If he hasn't, I'll put some into his head for once and for all. That's enough about that angle." The old stockman looked quizzically at his listeners. "I know all of you are wondering why I didn't say something about Bianco being up here before. Now, it's like this. I had very good reason to believe that he only intended to work the KT and Double B ranges. I now have reason to still believe that is his intention. I do not think he intends to molest the rest of the range. And I have one or two things under my hat that I'm not going to let out, not before the meeting anyway. And I'm going to ask you and the others to keep this whole business quiet until the meeting. You've trusted me before and you needn't have any doubts this time. I'm going to get Bianco!"

Lafe's tone and the fire in his eye convinced them. He knew more than he would tell them. They thought of his record as head of their Association and it cemented the conviction that he knew what he was talking about.

"Now . . . suppose you shouldn't be able to get to the meeting, Lafe?" said Robertson. "I mean . . . well, a sprained back isn't reliable. It's apt to play tricks and keep you in bed a couple of weeks."

Lafe frowned. "Then they'll have to carry me there on a stretcher," he said grimly. "Don't you worry, I'll be there!"

**250**

"Here's another thing, Lafe," said Fowler. "How about the sheriff? He's carrying on out there in great style. Mad, too."

"I don't care how much he carries on out there on the range," said Lafe. "It's how he carries on in town that interests me. But there, again, you don't have to have any misgivings. I'll take care of the sheriff and see that he doesn't make a fool of himself. I suppose he's all for rounding that outlaw outfit up and jailing 'em." Lafe smiled as the stockmen nodded. "Now wouldn't Rowan look sweet, rounding up Bianco? And in the badlands, at that! Why, that dirty rustler knew every foot of this country in here before he came. He's had his men up here and has half a dozen exits picked for a quick getaway. I think he sent my cattle back because he didn't want to bother with 'em. He doesn't want cattle. He wants cash!"

"I'd think as much," said Robertson.

Lafe nodded amiably. He liked this tall, raw-boned, square-jawed stockman and believed he was square. But, nevertheless, he was a close friend of Bolten's. "Another thing," Lafe went on, "is that we don't know how long Bianco has been up here. He's been here long enough to know the ropes, and that's a cinch. He never goes blind in anything he does. We've got to remember that he's smart. We've got to give the devil his due. Now . . . and this is confidential between the four of us . . . I've got a dish framed up for that *hombre*. But I won't tell a soul what it is. I'll need some help later, and, when I do, I'll ask for it in the right quarters. As I said to start with, you've got to trust me and wait for the meeting next week. Caution the womenfolks and the young people, if they know. If they don't know, don't tell 'em."

The others nodded. These men respected Lafe Owens.

"Stan, were any of our new men mixed up in this?" Lafe asked.

"No. I put 'em 'way up the range. I hardly expected trouble so near the ranch, or so soon."

"I've got fifteen good men . . . new hands," Lafe told the two stockmen. "They're all from the PT outfit up in Alberta." Lafe grinned as he saw his listeners' eyes widen. "Larry picked 'em up." He sobered and his eyes narrowed a bit. "I'm not taking on new men for nothing," he said significantly.

He looked away and appeared tired. Sarah Owens came in with a determined look on her face. "You've talked enough for now, Lafe. Your face is red from the exertion and you've got to rest."

"We'll be going, Missus Owens," said Fowler as he and Robertson rose. "And Lafe, we'll keep in mind everything you said. It's our turn to tell you not to worry. We hope you're up and out again tomorrow."

The two stockmen shook hands with him.

"Say so long to the rest of the boys for me," said Lafe, his voice trembling somewhat, "and to the womenfolks. I don't see why you people can't go on with the dance, even if I'm not there. It isn't so terribly late yet, and I didn't figure on the party breaking up before dawn."

252

"I don't think many of us feel like dancing." Robertson smiled. "Most of us rode harder tonight than we've ridden in . . . I was goin' to say years, but I'll say a long time. And the women are nervous. It'll be a little while before we can get started home anyway."

When the stockmen and Stan Velie had gone, Lafe turned to his wife. There were small, glistening beads of sweat on his brow. "It was an effort, Mother," he said, "but I couldn't let 'em see I felt worse than I made out. There's too much at stake. I want a lot of cold water, and then maybe I can get some sleep."

He closed his eyes while Sarah busied herself, arranging his pillows and trying to make him more comfortable. Then she went for the water. She paused at the head of the stairs, startled. Larry and Jane Bolten were below, and Larry had one of the girl's hands in his. Sarah Owens coughed lightly and went down as if she had seen nothing.

The living room was deserted, save for the youth and the girl. Most of the women were in the kitchen, where their voices could not be heard upstairs, and the young people were outside. The party was over.

In the bunkhouse, Fowler and Robertson were explaining to the other stockmen, telling them what they themselves had been told. The chief interest, however, was Lafe's condition. They knew fully well that the cattleman would make a terrific struggle to appear in better shape than he actually was; he would make as light of his injury as possible.

"Bad place," said one. "A sprained back doesn't half begin to bother till the second and third day, sometimes. We'd better clear out and give him all the peace and quiet he can get."

This was the general opinion and preparations to leave the ranch were begun at once. Larry came out, as he now was acting as host. Jane and Molly were together with the older women in the kitchen. Men went for the horses and lanterns glowed about the barn and corrals as saddles and harness were picked by their owners.

In the midst of the orderly confusion, Larry found himself facing Fresee, who had slipped up beside him unnoticed.

"Is Miss Jane ready to go home?" asked Fresee.

"I don't know, I'm sure," Larry retorted shortly, and turned away.

Fresee put a hand on his arm. "Will you please find out for me?" he purred. "Tell her I have a message from her father."

Larry scowled. "I'll give her the message. What is it?"

"I'll have to tell her myself," said Fresee coldly.

"I hope you're not in a hurry. I'm pretty busy right now seeing these people off."

"I'll ask at the house so as not to bother you," said Fresee.

"Wait a minute!" Larry barked sharply. "You don't go near the house, understand? You've no business here, anyway, that I can see. I'll go and ask if she wants to see you."

Larry found Jane without difficulty. "Fresee is out there and says he wants to see you."

"Well, I don't want to see him," said Jane. "What does he want to see me about?"

"I don't know. I told him I'd deliver the message, but he said that wouldn't do, and that it isn't a question of what you want, it's your father's orders. I'll order him off the ranch if you say so."

Jane's face flushed angrily. "Where is he? I'll speak to him."

What was this? Was her father trying to humiliate her? She was really angry as Larry led her to Fresee.

"What is it you want to tell me?" she demanded.

"That I'm here to take you home," said Fresee with his twisted smile. "But there's no hurry, Miss Jane."

"You'll call me Miss Bolten, if you please. And I'm perfectly able to ride home alone. I know the way. You needn't wait." It was plain to Larry that she didn't like Fresee.

"Your father said to see that you got home safely," said Fresee. "You'll understand that I have to obey orders."

"You can go home and watch for me to see that I get there all right," said Jane in a tone of authority. "And you can tell Father those were my orders."

"Please don't make it hard for me, Miss Bolten. I can't do that. There's been trouble and you'll have to go home with the outfit, that's all. But we can wait until you're ready to go, even if it's daylight."

"You're dictating to me!" exclaimed Jane, stamping her foot in aggravated annoyance.

"That's all right, Fresee," Larry put in. "I'll see that Miss Bolten gets home safely."

"She might be safe enough," said Fresee curtly, "but you might not be so safe. Bloat Simpson stood pretty well with the outfit, and I can't be responsible for you on our range. We'll wait until Miss Bolten is ready to go."

"You'll do nothing of the sort!" Jane was indignant. "And I accept Larry's invitation to take me home!"

"That lets you out, mister," said Larry, stepping in front of Jane. "And is that how you happened to be on hand tonight . . . you were coming with a bunch of men, not knowing anything was wrong, to get Miss Bolten?"

Fresee's manner changed instantly. "If you've got any business of your own, glue on to it!" he shot through his teeth. "I'm here on orders and you're not goin' to take that girl home. And I've got a bunch of men here to back me up."

"But you haven't got nerve enough to back yourself up in another way!" shot back Larry. "Take your men and get off this ranch!"

"You can wait for me at the fence," said Jane. "After what you've said, I wouldn't trust Larry on our range with you around."

At this moment Stan Velie approached.

"I've ordered this man off the ranch," Larry said sternly. "Come, we'll go to the house, Jane."

Fresee explained to Velie in crisp sentences while Larry and Jane entered the ranch house. Velie listened attentively and, when Fresee had finished, he thought a few moments. "I guess you'd better go," he decided.

"You mean to tell me that I'm ordered off the ranch when I came here to safeguard Jim Bolten's daughter?" demanded Fresee in white-hot rage.

"Miss Bolten will be safe here. I heard her say you could wait for her at the fence. That sounds reasonable. You don't think Bianco would bother Jim Bolten's daughter any more than he'd bother his cattle, do you?"

The thrust went home. Fresee's eyes blazed, but he succeeded in holding his tongue until he could control it. "You're makin' things worse, Velie. I'm doin' the best I can over there . . ."

"That wouldn't be much better than your worst," Velie interjected.

Fresee looked about. Others were within earshot now. It would not do to start trouble with so many influential stockmen on hand to see it. "You win with your gang, Velie. But one of these days you'll get caught without a bodyguard. Then, watch out!"

Fresee swung on his heel and walked rapidly away. Shortly afterward he rode off with his men. Velie went calmly about his business with the threat ringing in his ears.

# CHAPTER
# NINETEEN

Jane and Molly went upstairs to Molly's room where Jane had left her wraps. When Molly had closed the door, Jane sat down. Her lips were quivering as she told her friend about Fresee and his mission there.

"I can't believe Father would deliberately humiliate me," she finished. Then her fine eyes flashed. "Anyway, Fresee had no business to talk to me that way. I'm glad Larry ordered him off your ranch, and I'll tell Father so."

Then Molly and Jane talked confidentially for a quarter of an hour, when Molly remembered her duties as her mother's aid. "I must go downstairs," she told Jane. "The folks are beginning to leave, and Mother had to look after Father, besides seeing them off."

"I'm going home," Jane decided. "And Larry is going to take me."

The moon was low in the west, poising for its gentle drop behind the mountains, as Larry and Jane stood by the horses Larry had brought to the front yard. In the soft light of the stars Jane looked very beautiful, more so because of the flush of annoyance still in her cheeks and the last, flickering sparks of anger in her eyes. Her eyes softened as she looked up at Larry beside her.

"They wouldn't dare do anything to you, Larry," she said. "And I'm going to tell Father of Fresee's threat. I'm eighteen and I can speak what I think."

"I'm able to take care of myself," Larry told her. "And you mustn't tell your father anything. It will make it hard for you. I can understand how he would feel about your coming over to my party. Maybe I'm selfish, but your coming tonight was the best thing of all."

"I came because I wanted to come," said Jane slowly. "Oh, I hate this trouble, Larry. And I'm sure that Fresee has something to do with it. He winds Father around his little finger, but in such a roundabout, sneaking way that Father doesn't see it." There were tears in the girl's eyes.

Larry put his arms about her. The horses stood motionlessly with reins hanging. A breath of wind, cool and sweet, stirred the branches of the trees. "Jane, I'm not going back to college. My place now is on the ranch, helping Father. He knows it and has told Mother so. I hate this trouble, too, but it mustn't affect us, as I told you in town that night. You're eighteen and I'm twenty-two. We should know our own minds. I've known mine better than ever before since . . . the last time we met and I apologized. I love you, Jane . . . honest. There's something I want to ask you, Jane girl. But I can't unless . . . unless . . ." He looked into her eyes and faltered.

"Unless what, Larry?"

"Unless you care a little about me, Jane. If you do, I'll ask you."

"What is it, Larry?" The words came in a whisper that just reached his ears.

He held her close, and then: "Will you marry me, Jane? I love you so much I can't stand for this . . . this foolish trouble to keep us apart. Anything can happen, sweetheart, with things as they are. If you could love me a little, and wanted to . . . to . . . If we were married, Jane, wouldn't it help to smooth things out?"

"Oh, Larry." An arm crept about his neck. She drew his lips down to hers. "I'm not thinking of the trouble now, but of you. And I'm not sure of myself. Yes, I am. I do love you, Larry. But if we . . . if we . . ."

"Got married," Larry supplied gently.

"Your father never would forgive you. And mine . . ."

"They would both get over it quicker than either of us can imagine, Jane dear." He kissed her again. There was a drone of voices, a faint stamping of hoofs from the courtyard. "Nothing else matters, now that I know you love me, Jane. This is a gift, not for a birthday, but for every day of a lifetime." His voice trembled. "We are a world by ourselves, because we love each other. Nothing else counts. But you haven't said that you'll marry me. Tell me that, Jane."

There was a long moment of silence. A cheery goodbye came from the courtyard. It carried a poignant meaning to the ears of the lovely girl in Larry's arms. "I will," she murmured from his shoulder.

"That's the girl," said Larry joyously, giving her a boyish hug. "And the time for us to get married is when it'll do the most good for others." He paused and considered this. "That sounds silly," he decided aloud.

260

"I didn't mean it that way. Jane, I'll tell you something."

She looked up. Her eyes were shining wells of light. "What is it, Larry?" Already she found herself depending on him.

"Next Wednesday is the big meeting in town," he said. "Our fathers will be going in . . . all the stockmen will be going in. It's usually quite an event and lots of 'em bring their families. We can both go in. But I'm going in the day before . . . only, I am going a roundabout way. I'm going south to Great Falls for a certain document, and then . . . when we're in town . . ." He held her face with his hands. "You think it over for a week, sweetheart. If we could be married before the meeting . . . but you understand. Don't tell me anything now, Jane. Come on and we'll get started. And I sure don't have to apologize for these!" He rained the kisses on her lips and cheeks and eyes, while horsemen thundered up the bench road on their way to distant homes.

They rode up to the bench land and swung eastward across the prairie. It was little more than two hours before dawn. Larry's heart was singing. Jane hardly knew what to think, but in a week she must know. Larry's proposal that they be married so soon had both thrilled and frightened her, and finally she gave up thinking about it and gave way to the exhilaration of riding in the cool wind across the virgin plain. She had refrained from asking Larry about the trouble of this night and knew only what little Molly Owens had been able to tell her.

Far to the south of them they saw riders coming north. Larry knew this was the sheriff returning with the men he had taken down there.

"Some of our bunch!" he called to Jane.

Jane nodded and concentrated her gaze ahead. They were racing for the fence. Mile after mile, it seemed, their splendid mounts fairly flew across the prairie until they could see the group of horsemen at the gate in the fence ahead. But one of these horsemen was ahead of the others — a moving dot that was coming toward them. Soon both were able to recognize the big form of Jim Bolten in the saddle. Jane bit her lip and again that flush of annoyance came into her cheeks.

"Looks like your dad isn't taking any chances," Larry told her with a grin.

Jane reined in her horse and Larry pulled up at her side. "Maybe you'd better go back," she suggested. "Father is probably mad. I've no way of guessing what Fresee might have told him."

"Run away?" said Larry. "Not on your life. You wouldn't like me for it afterward, either. I'll face the music regardless of the tune. Let's go on and meet him, sweetheart."

They spurred their horses and in a short time Jim Bolten thundered up to them as they pulled up to meet him.

"Why didn't you come back with the men?" Bolten asked Jane in a harsh voice.

"Because Larry said he would ride home with me," Jane answered in her usual voice.

262

"But Fresee told you I'd sent him, didn't he?" her father demanded.

"It was the way he told me, Father," said Jane with an indignant toss of her head. "I won't have any man on the ranch talk to me as he did. And I want it distinctly understood that he's never to speak to me again."

"I guess you're forgetting that I'm your father and he's my foreman," stormed Bolten, darting an angry glance at Larry. "Did you order Fresee off the ranch?"

"I did. And what's more, we want him to stay off."

"Since when have you been running the KT?" Bolten sneered.

"I was running it when I told Fresee to beat it," Larry snapped.

"Listen, you young whippersnapper," said Bolten wrathfully, "we've got trouble enough without your trying to stir up more. Your father can tell you that, if you've got sense enough to see it."

"I've got sense enough to see that it isn't going to help matters any for Fresee to come on our range," said Larry in a ringing voice. "Every man in the outfit hates him, and he's not wanted."

Bolten sputtered with rage. "Why, you . . . you . . ." He turned on Jane. "Ride on to the ranch," he ordered.

"I'll wait and ride with you, Father," said the girl in a determined voice that her father had never heard her use quite the same before.

He looked at her curiously. "You're going to disobey me again?" he said, lowering his voice.

"I've never deliberately disobeyed you," said the girl. "But you are paving the way for me to do so by acting as you have tonight."

Bolten looked at her as if he could hardly believe his ears. Then a sudden change came over him. He looked long at Larry. "All right," he said, biting off his words, "we'll go home." He whirled his horse.

"Good night, Larry!" Jane called as she touched her mount with her heels.

"So long," sang Larry, his musical voice seeming to follow her as she rode away with her father.

Jim Bolten and his daughter rode through the gate in the fence, passed the men there, who followed after them, and continued on to the ranch house without speaking. Jane was thinking of the sound of Larry's voice when he had left her, of what he had told her this night, of the look in his eyes, his arms about her, his kisses — and of the thing he wanted her to do. She had never quite known until that night on the platform outside the dancing pavilion in Pondera how much she thought of him. Now she knew she loved him, and wanted him. She almost came to a hasty decision as they rode into the courtyard of the Double B.

"I'll be in to talk to you in a minute," said Bolten sternly as they dismounted.

"I'm almost too tired to talk now," said Jane. "I'm going to bed. You can talk to me when I come down later."

"You'll talk with me now! What I've got to say won't keep."

Jane hesitated, looking at him as a man came for the horses. *All right*, she decided, *I might as well have it over with*.

She went into the house and took off her coat and riding cap. She was standing by the glowing coals in the fireplace when her father entered.

"Fresee says you made a fool of him, or tried to, in front of people over there." Bolten scowled.

"He made a fool of himself, if anything," said Jane. Then her eyes flashed. "Listen, Father, are you taking sides with this Fresee against me?" she asked sharply.

"I have to stand behind my men, as you know," Bolten evaded.

"And do you have to do that at your daughter's expense?" Jane demanded. "Do you have to humiliate me before others to soft-soap your men?"

"I'll not have you talking to me like that," Bolten flared.

"And I'll not have Fresee, who is nothing but a little more than a common hand, talking to me as he did tonight, or to any escort with me," said Jane, looking her father squarely in the eyes. "I'll not have him talking to me at all, and I shall be sure to tell him that the very next time I see him. I think you're forgetting, Father, that I've grown up. I'm no longer a child. And I'm not taking orders from any subordinates on this ranch."

Bolten was taken aback by the fire in her speech, but a glint of admiration came into his eyes. "I'll speak to Fresee myself," he said in a softer tone. "I think that young Owens has been putting stuff into your head.

**265**

You're just the age to listen to such talk from the likes of him."

"That's unfair and I'll not listen to any more of it," said Jane with spirit. "He was man enough not to talk about Fresee behind his back, or anyone else, for that matter."

"Well, young lady, there's one thing you will listen to," said Bolten, his eyes narrowing. "You'll not go to the KT Ranch again. If you do, I'll send and have you brought back by force, if I have to fight the whole sneaking outfit! And you'll stay away from young Owens! If he's such a friend, and you want to keep his hair slick, you'll keep away from him."

"Father, that's a threat!" cried the girl, her face white. "And that Fresee threatened him tonight, too! You cannot order me to stay away from my friends so long as they are my friends! I'll refuse to obey! You're just as much to blame for this trouble as Mister Owens, from all I hear, and —"

"We'll not talk about that," her father interrupted angrily.

"You brought it up," Jane flashed. "You can at least keep your feuds out of the house. I won't listen to any more." She walked briskly to the stairs.

"But you'll be sensible enough to remember what I've said, I hope," Bolten flung after her. Then he went out to interview Fresee some more. He was fighting mad. It didn't improve his humor any to realize that he had to deal carefully with his foreman.

Jane went to her room. She didn't light the lamp. She looked out the windows at the stars, dimming in the hour before dawn. Then she fell upon the bed and burst into tears.

Larry joined the sheriff and the men on the bench above the ranch house and rode down with them. Rowan asked about Lafe, and Larry told him his father was better.

The sheriff appeared greatly disturbed. He looked at Larry sharply several times, as if wondering how much the youth knew. For Rowan was much irritated because the fact that Bianco — if it really could be Bianco — was in the vicinity had been kept from him. He considered that it was Lafe's first duty to acquaint him with this new turn in affairs. The circumstances that the most noted and feared rustler and bandit from the border to the line was in his county without his knowing it rankled in the official's mind. Why, people would laugh at him!

"Go in and find out when I can see your father," the sheriff told Larry when they dismounted at the barn.

"I don't think Mother will let him see anyone until the doctor says it's all right," said Larry. "But I'll go in and ask, Sheriff."

Sheriff Rowan encountered Stan Velie in the courtyard. All of the guests had left and the injured men had been brought into the bunkhouse. "Doctor here yet?" asked the sheriff crisply.

"Expect him any minute," replied Velie.

"How is Lafe? Is he very badly hurt?"

"I don't think so. He sprained his back, and it may be worse than he lets on. But I don't think he's seriously injured. It hurts him like fury to sit up, but the fact that he can sit up shows that nothing is broken, doesn't it?"

"I suppose so," said the sheriff doubtfully. "You know, Velie, this is a queer business. Was the leader of that bunch of raiders really this Bianco?"

"We have very good reason to think so, Sheriff. You heard about Bud Davis, of course?"

"Yes, and I did Lafe a favor by keeping quiet," grumbled Rowan. "But . . . did Bianco do that?"

Velie nodded. "He named Bianco before he died."

"Then I should have been told," the sheriff protested. "I should have been notified at once. Of course, I'm only the sheriff of this county and not its dictator, but I should have been told of such an important thing as this without delay."

"Lafe had his reasons for wanting to keep it quiet," Velie said soberly. "He'll tell you about it himself. You would have been notified at once if it would have done any good. Suppose you wait until you see Lafe and let him explain it to you."

"It's what I'll have to do," said Rowan. "But I'm losing time. Has Brower gone back to town?"

"The Fowlers took him in on their way home. He said to tell you he supposed you would be staying over and he had to be at the bank this morning."

"Of course," snorted Rowan.

Larry came out of the house and walked over to them. "Father's asleep," he told Rowan, "and Mother wouldn't think of waking him. She believes the best thing he can do is sleep and rest. You can have my

**268**

room, Sheriff, to snatch a few winks until you can see him."

"No, I'll go in the bunkhouse," said the sheriff. "But let me know as soon as I can talk to him. It's important, and I've got to get back to town to . . . well, as soon as I can."

"I'll call you," Larry promised.

A quarter of an hour later, Jones arrived with the doctor. When the doctor found Lafe asleep, he nodded his approval. "I understand there are some wounded men. I can tend to them until he wakes up," he told Sarah Owens. "When that time comes, let me know at once."

Larry sat in the big chair in the living room. His thoughts were racing madly. What had he done? Had he been rash on the spur of the moment? Then he pictured Jane's face in the starlight, her lips, her eyes, heard the soft voice, and thrilled at the memory of her arms about his neck, of their kisses. Yes, he loved her. But this hasty marriage! It had seemed so necessary, so sensible out there in the shadows, in the cool, sweet wind, while he had held her close, felt the warmth of her, and her soft hair against his cheek. She had said she would marry him. Jane was not the kind of girl to say and do these things if she did not mean them. The wonder of it! He had no doubt but that his father would approve. He might not approve of what was practically an elopement at first, but he would forget it in time — and not such a long time, either. Jim Bolten would be madder than a hornet. Well, Larry could take care of a wife and Bolten would have to like it sooner or later.

That was that. Larry gave himself up to dreaming, and fell asleep.

When he woke, he found his mother had put a blanket over him. The sun was shining brightly, the beams slanting across the carpet from the windows, bringing out the vari-colored pattern. He looked at his watch. They had let him sleep until ten o'clock. He went out to the kitchen and found that Mary O'Neil had kept the coffee on the stove and had some breakfast for him. Molly came in.

"How's Dad?" he asked anxiously.

"He's comfortable, so long as he doesn't move," said his sister. "He sprained his neck and the doctor said he would have to stay in bed maybe a week or more. The doctor couldn't find anything broken. He left some medicine and strapped father's back. He's attended to the men who are hurt in the bunkhouse. Sheriff Rowan is upstairs."

"He would be," said Larry. "Stay in bed for a week? Why, the Association meeting is a week from now . . . six days to be exact."

"Oh, you should forget that meeting," said Molly impatiently. "It's that Association business that's started all the trouble we're having."

"It doesn't take much for some people to start trouble," Larry observed. "Where's Jones?"

"I haven't seen him. Asleep in the bunkhouse, I suppose."

"I'll leave it to you to see he gets some breakfast when he gets up," said Larry dryly.

270

"Don't worry, there's a cook out there with a stove and everything," Molly tossed back at him.

Upstairs, Lafe was looking intently at the grave features of Sheriff Rowan. That official's expression was puzzling. It might best be described as one of bewilderment commingled with doubt. As he stared out the window from his place by the bed, he seemed to be searching for the solution of the problem thrust upon him.

"Do!" exclaimed Rowan. "Why, I'm going to round up every able-bodied man on the range and get that scoundrel. I'll comb the badlands from here to Missouri. But there's one thing you can do, Lafe. Send some men to the brakes to keep a look-out."

Lafe shook his head. "I'm not sending any of my men into the brakes . . . not yet, anyway. Do you know how long it'll take you to raise the kind of posse you're talking about? The 'punchers have beat it for the winter range in the Falls and other towns. Bolten and I are the only ones that're keeping full crews. We haven't enough between us to do what you say you're going to do."

"You mean to say you won't help?"

"I won't help kill off my men, if that's what you mean. That's what it would amount to. What would Bianco's spies be doing while you were getting your posse together? He'd know every move you were making and he sure wouldn't be where you looked for him. You're wondering whether I'm down and out." Lafe smiled. "Well, I'm playing up to this back of mine because it's the sensible thing to do. But I'm going to be on hand there next Wednesday. There's a lot more to this business than you think, but, believe me, I'm not a fool. That fall didn't hurt my brain any."

Rowan sat frowning, but he ventured no comment.

"I'll make a deal with you, Sheriff. Don't get mad when I tell you that I think I can handle this thing. The only way Bianco can be caught or stamped out is by a trick. I'm going to play the game with him. It's going to be dangerous, but that's to be expected. You keep quiet about this thing, and afterward you can say that we framed up the whole business together. I'll see you get the credit that's coming to you, and that'll make you sheriff another term . . . maybe more than one."

The sheriff pondered this while he looked at the face in the pillows. He had great respect for Lafe Owens. He knew that if the cattleman retained his post with the Association, he could get another term as sheriff, or more than one. "The news of this trouble out here last night is bound to get out," he said. "Then they'll come running to me and wanting to know why I don't do something about it. What am I going to tell them?"

"If anything gets out, it'll just be rumor," Lafe replied. "No one will be able to confirm it. My men won't talk, and I don't believe the Double B crowd will talk. I have good reason to know that Bolten won't let 'em talk." He paused to let this sink in. "Now, how are they going to confirm the rumor if you steer 'em off? You can say you came out here to the party and there was a scrap. Lay it off on the trouble between Bolten and me. What happens at the meeting will have nothing to do with it. I'm going to bait this cut-throat Bianco and we're going to get him. Your first play is to take my

272

tip and help me by doing what I say. I don't feel much like talking, but I'm talking straight."

Rowan thought for a long minute, while silence reigned in the room. Finally he got up from his chair. "I'm going to trust you, Lafe," he said in a tired voice. "You're not the kind to trifle with a man who's tried to be your friend. In fact, it looks like that is all I can do. When will you have some more to tell me?"

"The day after the meeting," Lafe answered readily.

"That's definite enough," said Rowan with a pleased expression. "I'll be getting along back to town."

Sarah Owens came into the room shortly after the sheriff had gone. "The doctor's riding back to town with the sheriff," she said.

"Well, Sarah," said Lafe, "I'm going to send a couple of men to the Falls with the spring wagon to get a wheelchair."

"That'll be fine," agreed his wife. "Then you can get around the house and out on the porch while we're having this good weather."

Lafe smiled while she fussed about the bed and arranged his pillows. He was not sending for the wheelchair for any of the reasons his wife had mentioned.

# CHAPTER
# TWENTY

When Sheriff Rowan had told Lafe Owens that news of
the trouble on the KT range would leak out, he had
been right. The peculiar thing about it was that the
news that leaked out was not new at all, but a rumor.
There was but one popular conception of the trouble,
accepted by all, and absolutely wrong — there had
been an open clash between the KT and Double B
outfits at the Owens Ranch. The Double B had tried to
break up the party. Jim Bolten and Lafe Owens had
engaged in a fist fight. Fresee and Velie had been at the
point of gun play. The sheriff had succeeded in calming
the participants and restoring order. The feud was sure
to erupt again at the annual meeting of the Teton
Cattlemen's Association. Such was the situation
prevailing in Pondera during the few days preceding the
big meeting.

Three days after his fall from his horse, Lafe Owens
sat up for a little while. The wheelchair was brought
from Great Falls and the next day the stockman
insisted that he be put in it. His repeated assertion that
it didn't hurt much was belied by the white face, the
clenched palms, and the tightly pressed lips.

Meanwhile conditions on the range were normal. Lafe made no special preparations in anticipation of another raid soon. He felt that Bianco would await the outcome of the meeting. He did not tell his wife what he was planning, but he did say: "I felt all along that this feud would break out again. Bolten thinks he is strong enough now to fight me with any kind of weapons. He isn't. I've got to show him that and settle this business for once and for all. I'm not going to be here forever, Sarah. Someday this ranch will belong to Larry. I don't propose to leave him an unsettled feud as part of his patrimony. And I don't propose to set him the example of backing down and giving in to the enemy. When I'm through, Mother, the feud will be dead and buried, without mourners."

Even Sarah had to acknowledge the wisdom of settling the trouble for good. She had just a vague inkling of the trend of his mind when he said: "I can't get it out of my head that this feud business isn't the main issue." He refused to answer questions or say more on the subject, and he swore her to secrecy regarding even as much as he had told her.

On Monday, two days before the day of the Association meeting, Henry Brower sent a message asking if there was anything he could do in town by way of arranging for Lafe's comfort when he came, or otherwise. To this Lafe replied: "Manage to inspect every stranger who comes into your bank yourself."

This last message caused Brower considerable worry. He began to wonder if the outlaw, Bianco, might not have some design on the bank. Time and again he stood before the new vault and time-lock system that had been installed but the previous year. The bank was in the center of town, and there were men in the various resorts all night to spread the alarm if an attempt were made to blow open the vault. Moreover, he did not keep a large amount of cash on hand. He finally dismissed his fears, but he kept two lights burning at night instead of one, and he watched for strangers, suspecting that Lafe expected the outlaw leader to send spies to town and that some of them might visit the bank on one pretext or another.

Monday night Lafe announced he would go to town the next afternoon. This was so he might rest the night and morning before the meeting and thus not arrive wearied by the ride in the spring wagon, which had been converted into something of a camouflaged ambulance. Lafe was to lie on mattresses and quilts until the town came into sight. Then he was to sit on the seat of the buckboard that was to follow with Sarah Owens and Molly.

Larry announced that he and Jones would go in early in the morning to make the necessary arrangements for Lafe's accommodation at the hotel. As a matter of fact, they left Monday night, with Jones going directly to Pondera and Larry riding south to Great Falls at a furious clip, there to obtain a fresh horse and endeavor to get up to Pondera by the time of his father's arrival. He left the arrangements in town to Jones, explaining carefully what was required.

But Lafe had momentarily failed to anticipate Bolten's move. The Double B owner also decided to go to town the day before the meeting, after a hurried circuit of much of the east half of the range. The result was that Bolten came riding at a fast pace from behind when Lafe was but fairly started on his way and the Double B owner saw his rival lying in the spring wagon and stopped to inquire how he felt.

"I'm favoring my back," was Lafe's curt answer.

But it was now impossible to carry out the original plan and ride into town sitting in the seat of the buckboard. The wheelchair was lashed on the rear of the wagon. Lafe's sense of the dramatic prompted him to make another swift decision. He had intended to try to walk to the hall, with support, of course; now he decided to go to the meeting in the wheelchair.

"I'm going to kick all of Bolten's props out from under him," he told Stan Velie, who was driving the wagon. "If it's a case of stealing the other fellow's thunder, all the better."

Lafe had been quick to note that only one man rode to town with Bolten. He considered it significant in more ways than one that this man should be Fresee. He had glanced at Fresee once and only when he had felt the small, glittering eyes upon him. Lafe's glance had not been one to comfort anyone. He had ordered his own outfit to stay on the range while he was gone. Velie was to return to the ranch that night as a precaution against a raid in Lafe's absence, although Lafe did not believe this precaution would be necessary.

Bolten had refused point-blank to allow Jane to go to town. Her mother had tried unsuccessfully to change his mind. There had been a coolness between the father and daughter since the affair of the party. Bolten assumed that Jane's aloofness and preoccupation was the natural result of his talk with her after her return from the KT Ranch. But her mother believed that something else was in the wind, and she expected Jane to tell her when the time should come. Jane could have told no one anything, for she did not know her own mind.

After her father had left for town with Fresee, Jane had her horse saddled. It was her custom to ride twice each day, regardless of weather conditions, except when a blizzard was raging. She took a canter in the early morning, and in the late afternoon or evening she was usually in the saddle for more than an hour, frequently for two or three. On many of these rides she had met Fresee, had spoken to him briefly when he had reined in his horse and swept off his hat. But, since the party, she had not seen him close enough to have him attempt to speak to her. She had even avoided looking in his direction when she saw him. But his cunning black eyes had followed her whenever she was anywhere around. Bolten had spoken to him about Jane, and Fresee had merely nodded. He had been careful that his employer hadn't seen his sneering smile as he turned away. Now, for the first time, Jane began to think about these frequent meetings and her face flushed with anger as she conjectured if the meetings had not been engineered by Fresee. If this were true, every such meeting was nothing less than an insult. If Larry knew . . .

278

Jane reined in her horse atop a swell of the prairie and stared into the west where the sun was sinking in a blaze of glory. She remembered vividly the look of intense hatred and malice that Fresee had flashed at Larry when the youth had announced that he would ride home with her. She remembered the diabolical gleam in his eyes when Larry had ordered him off the ranch. She knew Fresee was unscrupulous, ruthless, and cruel where his personal affairs were concerned. The slightest bit of insubordination brought down the fury of his wrath upon the offender. She had seen him in the white heat of almost uncontrollable rage when he didn't know she was watching him. And on the morrow, he and Larry would be in town. If they should have words, with Fresee ready to take offense at anything . . .

A feeling of panic assailed the girl. Insofar as Fresee was concerned, anything could happen, but he would be clever enough to protect himself from the law. Self-defense was an alibi that was easily proven in a country where men drew and fired in the wink of an eyelash. When she was much younger, Fresee had amused her with his displays of pistol practice. The rapidity with which he drew his weapon and his unfailing accuracy were uncanny, she thought. The more she thought, the more worried she became. If she could only ride to the KT Ranch and extract a promise from Larry not to go near Fresee or speak to him, but Larry had said he would be going to town early, and he was going by way of Great Falls.

Jane's face flushed again and she thrilled. "Larry, boy, I love you," she said aloud, her soft-spoken words slipping smoothly away on the vagrant wind. A frightened look came into her eyes. She had to make a decision — this night! By this time next day she could be Larry Owens's wife, or she could be at home, still Jane Bolten, loving him more than ever, and he could be in town, or on his way back, safe, or . . . ?

Again came that dreaded thought. Then the power of reasoning seemed to leave her. Her head went up to the wind, her eyes flashed, and the red lips whitened as she pressed them tightly together. She struck out at a ringing gallop across the plain for home.

Through the breast-high waters of the Teton ford, Larry Owens swam his horse against the current. As he was climbing the slope toward the opening in the trees, he saw the forms — little more than clear-cut shadows — of five riders slip past, bound westward. These, he decided at once, were some of Bianco's men going to town to be present on the day of the meeting.

He dismounted and stole out the opening to where he could see riders, but none of the figures in the saddles might be Bianco himself. Larry went back to his horse. He led the animal to the edge of the fringe of trees and waited until the horsemen were well out of sight. He had no wish to be followed over the long stretch of open country ahead.

All that night Larry rode, and at sunup he was in the city in the great bend of the Missouri. He put up his horse and soon made an arrangement for a good, fresh mount for the ride up to Pondera that day. He was at the courthouse at opening time and soon had the document for which he had come.

Back across that flowing sea of gold he rode, northwestward this time. He did not feel weary from his night ride, nor did he feel the lack of proper sleep. He thrilled with hope as he patted his coat over the breast pocket wherein was the marriage license. But now that this preliminary was dispensed with, he felt his first quavers of doubt as to the soundness of the move. If Jane were willing — of which he was not sure — would there not be others who would misunderstand? Some would be careful not to understand. If it were known, there would be talk. He thought more and more of Jane's position. He loved her; he intended to marry her. But hadn't he been impetuous in proposing marriage immediately? He half hoped Jane would not come, but he knew, if she didn't, he would be bitterly disappointed. They would have to talk it over again, perhaps. But the day was glorious, with the sun filling the world and a cool, sweet breeze laving the plain. Larry's heart sang and he whistled as he rode. His was youth, abundant health, a certain, enviable patrimony someday to come, long years to live — and he was in love. He flung the doubts from his brain with a single shake of his head and tickled his mount with the spurs.

At sunset he was in Pondera. Jones met him at the livery.

"Not here yet," said his friend. "You look like you'd found a fat poke or something. I've made all the arrangements for 'em when they come. Any news?"

For a wild moment, Larry was tempted to draw Jones into the office and tell him everything. He caught himself just in time. "None that I'm ready to give out," he said cheerily. "But I may need you on personal business tomorrow."

"*Humph*," grunted Jones.

"Takes two humps to make a camel," Larry bantered. "Say it again because you're on the wagon. C'mon and get a soda."

While they were taking their refreshment, Larry told Jones about the five riders he had seen across the river ford the night before. Jones listened and nodded his head when Larry had finished.

"I saw 'em," he said to Larry's surprise. "Spotted 'em as they came in. Two from the south, another from the north, and a pair from the west . . . like they'd just happened along. I was up and around most of the night. I'll point 'em out to you when I get the chance. They don't look none like mama's darlings. Took to the stud tables after they'd put up their horses and been sleeping all day. Bolten and Fresee are in."

Larry looked at him in surprise. "Came in a day ahead, too," he said thoughtfully. "Look here, Harry Jones, who else came with them?"

"Two was the crowd. And I reckon the pair of 'em are enough."

Larry considered this gloomily. If Jane and her mother had been coming in, they would have come with Bolten. So Jane wasn't coming. Suddenly Larry laughed. It was Jones's turn to appear astonished.

"Just think of some last year's joke?"

"If I did, the joke's on me. Harry, after Dad and the folks get in, and I've had some supper, I'm going to bed."

His manner puzzled Jones, but evoked no comment.

When Lafe Owens drove into town, Larry and Stan Velie helped him from the wagon and practically carried him upstairs to his rooms. Many stockmen already were in town and Lafe greeted all he saw with cheerful words and mien. None knew what the effort cost him and the indomitable willpower it required. So the word went out that Lafe was not nearly as badly hurt as the rumors had it.

Lafe's first act in town was to send for the banker. He and Brower were in conference for nearly an hour. Then Lafe, Sarah Owens, Molly, and Larry had supper in the upstairs sitting room that had been turned over to the KT owner.

True to his word, Larry went to the room assigned to Jones and himself as soon as he had eaten his meal. He sat on the edge of the bed and told himself he was a fool. Whatever had possessed him in that hour after the party when he had held the rendezvous with Jane? But now that the element of uncertainty had entered into their relations, Larry found he loved her more than ever — more than he had suspected. Bolten had put in some words against him, of course. That was to be expected. But it was Jane's words that counted.

Larry expected Jones to come in, and, when an hour had passed with no sign of him, he undressed and went to bed. It seemed to Larry, afterward, that he had hardly closed his eyes when he suddenly woke, sitting up in bed with someone shaking him.

"Keep quiet," said a voice in the darkness that he recognized as that of Jones. "You'll have to dress by the light from the window. They're probably watching these rooms."

"Who's they?" Larry muttered sleepily. "What's up?"

"That's what we're going to find out," said Jones, "if you'll get a move on. It's those five pretty boys from Bianco's camp. They're not playing cards and they're not drinking. I can tell that something's in the wind. I've been watching 'em all night. Get a jerk on, Larry, it's two in the morning."

Larry dressed hurriedly by the light of the stars that shone through the window. In a short time they were feeling their way down the rear stairs and left the hotel by the back way. Jones took the lead and hurried Larry across the street to the resort where he had had his trouble with Bloat Simpson. This place had been a hang-out of the Double B men. Jones led the way through an open space between two buildings to the rear of the resort. He pointed to a flight of steps outside the building that led to an upper floor, partially concealed from the street by the high false front with its gaudy sign. He drew Larry into the shadow.

"They have all been up there, one or two at a time, tonight," he told Larry in an undertone. "I've watched 'em like a hawk, but took care not to arouse any suspicion. They're waiting for someone. I've been up there, and there are four small rooms, two on each side of a narrow hall. Darker than midnight. I saw light from under the door of the second room on the right. The other room on that side is unlocked and made up like a bedroom. The two doors on the left are locked. I'd bet my chance for heaven that they're going to meet somebody up there, for I've been around enough to know the signals."

"Then let's get in that room that isn't locked," Larry suggested.

"And let 'em walk in on us? It won't . . ."

A shaft of yellow light struck across the shadows as the rear door of the resort opened silently. Five men slipped out through a width just sufficient to permit the passage of their bodies. Then the light was blotted out.

Larry and Jones crouched in the deep shadow cast by the next building while the men climbed the steps slowly and carefully, avoiding any noise. Four of the men were large; one was of comparatively slight build. They opened the door at the top of the steps and disappeared.

Larry pressed Jones's arm. "C'mon," he whispered.

They crept to the other side of the building, past the rear door. Looking up, Larry pointed to the light in the second window — the one nearest the front. The first window was dark. As they looked, the shade was pulled down at the window from which the light shone.

"All set," Larry whispered.

He turned back to the steps and they went up. The door at the head of the flight was not locked. Larry opened it stealthily with his left hand, for his gun was in his right. The short, narrow hall was dark, but light filtered through the crack under the second door on the right. They entered on tiptoes and closed the door behind them.

Larry felt along the wall until he came to the first door. He turned the knob a fraction of an inch — another, and another until he had the door open. The murmur of voices came from the other room where the light was burning. Larry stopped short with his foot on the threshold of the room he was about to enter. They heard a voice that carried sharper than the others.

"I'll do the picking! I know the stock!" Then there was silence, and again the murmurs were heard, less distinctly than before.

Larry pinched Jones's arm and Jones nudged him in return. The angry voice they had heard belonged to Fresee!

Instantly the thought came to Larry that if Fresee was in there with four of the men from the badlands — as he most certainly was — there was one of the original five missing. As if in answer to this thought, the other door suddenly was flung open. A dim light flowed into the hall as Larry stepped into the empty room. Jones was not so quick, and, as Larry whirled, a form hurtled through the air, there was a dull sound of impact, and Jones went down in a heap.

Larry went through the door in a single leap striking with his gun barrel. It found its mark on the head of the big, shadowy form looming over Jones. The man went over backward with a crash. The light glazed from the opened door of the other room as Larry dragged Jones into the empty room and kicked the door shut. He found the knob, braced his weight against the door, and almost cried out as his fingers closed on the key in the lock. He turned it instantly.

The man who had been felled was down and out. Boots shuffled in the hall and there were muttered exclamations. "Keep still!" said a gruff voice.

Larry kept his weight against the door and in another moment there came a shattering impact as one of the men in the hall hurled himself against it. Larry felt the door weave. But it held. He stepped back and his gun spit fire twice as two shots rocked the silence.

The bullets ripped through the flimsy panels of the door, ranging upward, as he had intended. He leaped aside, but the answering volley he expected did not come. Instead, there was a queer rattling of the doorknob. Jones was coming to and Larry dragged him to the window. The window was nailed down. Keeping his gun ready, Larry felt about for something with which to break the panes. His hand came in contact with a chair in the dark at the side of the window. He slipped his gun in its holster and smashed the window with the chair.

Jones was getting up. "They're in the hall," Larry told him in a whisper. "I've got the door locked. You better?"

"I'm all right," Jones grunted. He looked out the window. Below was a scattered heap of old lumber. "No chance to jump," he said. "What's that?"

He was looking at the door, and, when Larry turned, he saw the red tongues licking at the bottom and the hinge side of the door. The hall was silent save for a faint crackling. The outlaws had used the lamp's oil to fire the place.

Larry made the door in three steps and turned the key. "Get away from the window light," he called softly to Jones. He turned the knob and jerked. But there was only a slight give. The door had been tied, probably to the knob of the door across the hall.

"Listen!" cried Jones. "They want us to get caught so we'll have to explain, and we can't explain. We know too much now. Get away a minute!"

He swept Larry aside and tried the door himself. From below now came a hue and cry. "Pull that door as hard as you can!" Jones commanded. "I can see the rope against the fire. Pull the door!"

Larry grasped the knob and pulled with all his strength. Jones's gun roared in the room as he shot between the door and the jamb. There was shouting and men could be heard coming up the steps outside. The fire was burning briskly. Another minute and it would have a start that could not be overcome. Jones shot through the narrow crack again, and twice again. The door came open suddenly, nearly felling Larry, as the rope was split by bullets.

Jones leaped over the flames with Larry after him. He threw his weight against the door across the hall — the second door on that side. The lock gave way like so much tin. Once inside the room, Jones shut the door, and Larry sprang to the window. It was down but there were no nails to hold it. The moonlight came in on this side and Jones was tying blankets and sheets from the bed. Both of them pulled the bed to the window, and tying the end of the improvised rope to it was the work of moments.

"Smother it!" a roaring voice in the hall commanded. "Get the mattresses. Keep that water coming!" They were fighting the fire out there.

Jones threw the rope out the window. "Go ahead," he ordered, motioning to Larry.

"You first," said Larry.

"Great guns! This is no time to be polite!" cried Jones as he swung out the window and disappeared. Larry saw him drop halfway down. As Larry went over the sill, his last glimpses of the shadowy interior of the room showed a form bursting through the doorway. In another moment he dropped.

Men were running through the space between the buildings. None stopped to see who they were in the semidarkness. They might have been two men who had taken a room over the resort for the night, for all the others knew.

"Look for Fresee," said Larry. "No . . . wait!" He caught Jones by the arm. "He won't be with the mob. He's too clever for that. Come on."

He led the way hurriedly behind the buildings, away from the animated scene at the rear of the resort. Looking back, they could see no flames shooting from the windows or door upstairs, which showed that the fire was under control. Despite the excitement at the resort, the rest of the town was undisturbed. It could be left to the resort proprietor to see to that. Such places suffered enough notoriety as it was.

Larry led the way between two buildings and across the street. They entered the hotel by the back way and crept up to their room. Larry lighted the lamp. Then he sat on the edge of the bed and watched Jones light a cigarette. His gaze was cool and calculating, then it fired with an inspiration.

"Harry," he said softly, "Fresee is in on this Bianco business. You heard what he told those fellows tonight. Said he knew the stock. That means he's picking out the cattle for Bianco to steal. And you can bet that rustler is stealing from the Double B as well as trying to run off our stock. Fresee is the one who got Bolten all heated up over this Association business. He's the one who brought the feud to life! If we can clean out Bianco, we can clean out Fresee at the same time, and Dad'll tend to Bolten."

"I've had some such idea all along," said Jones dryly.

"And I believe Dad suspects it, too. Listen, Harry, I've got to be in town today. There's another reason aside from being here with Dad and I don't feel that I've the right to tell you. But you could be away, for a time anyway . . . if you're not too tired."

Jones looked up quickly with a wry smile. "You're trying to get out that it wouldn't be a bad idea for me to jog down the south side of the river and try to get a line on where this quintet of bad medicine hits for when it leaves town, I take it."

"You have it. But . . . if you go . . . don't take any chances, Harry. If anything happened to you, I . . . well, maybe you can guess how I'd feel. But it seems the right thing to do." His brow wrinkled in thought.

290

"Well, don't pat yourself on the back none for thinking up something original. I'd already made up my mind to do that little thing. But I've got a better chance to find out something down there than you think. Bianco sent those men in to stay during the meeting. That fifth man who came up afterward and pounced on me must have seen us. They know we've got 'em spotted. One or maybe all of 'em will go back *pronto* with the word to send in somebody else. That's why I've got to get started. I'll have a chance at 'em going and coming, maybe. Anyway, I can see where they go in and come out of the badlands. That'll be a start. I've got a hunch this thing is coming to a head sooner than quick. Your dad's got a card in the hole. I'm going."

When he was again alone, Larry saw the wisdom of Jones's words. He saw, too, that Fresee was double-crossing his employer. He had doubtless been months in planning this coup. Some of his men must be in the plot. The dead cowpuncher, Remy, had been an outsider, and Remy had been shot in the back. It was a long time before Larry slept, fully clothed.

# CHAPTER
# TWENTY-ONE

Larry was out at daylight. He found the street deserted and soon learned by cautious inspection that no severe damage had been done to the upper floor of the resort building where the fire had been started. The fire seemed such a senseless piece of business, in the cool gray of the dawn, that Larry doubted if Fresee had had a hand in it at all. For that matter he could prove nothing against the Double B foreman. And now Larry also doubted the wisdom of the move in sending Jones to watch for the outlaws in the badlands. In this cooler moment it looked as if he had evaded this errand himself. He thought less about Jane Bolten, too. She had become, for the time being, a secondary consideration in view of the startling new development. At the barn he learned that some riders had left earlier in the morning. The barn man's memory was hazy regarding their appearance or anything they had said. He didn't even know how many had gone. They had given him some money, saddled their own horses, and left. "Members of some outfit out east, I suppose," he conjectured. But Larry believed they were the quintet from the river brakes.

After breakfast Larry told his father of the happenings of the night before. His father listened with eyes glistening to what he thought was a confirmation of his own hunch. But when Larry told of Jones's mission, he shook his head.

"That was bad business," he said, shaking his head. "I didn't want . . ."

"I should have gone myself, or have gone along with Harry at least," Larry put in.

"No. I don't want Bianco to know I'm trying to locate his hang-out. And young Harry Jones won't be any match for that outfit. The chances are they've got him by this time . . . caught him, I mean. But we'll have to let that part of it go until after this meeting today. When the time comes, I'll show you how to get this cut-throat of a Bianco and Fresee with him. Maybe it'll wise Bolten up." The old stockman's eyes fired. "I'm going to put some sense in him or break him forever on this range!"

Old Lafe's instructions were brief and to the point. Stan Velie had gone back to the ranch and Larry was to be his father's right-hand man. The meeting was called for two o'clock in the same hall where the special meeting had been held.

By noon of this day the hotel lobby and the street just outside swarmed with stockmen. North reported to Lafe upstairs that the west end was represented solidly. Robertson and other influential east-end stockmen were there. Amberg was in from the far eastern rim of the range. Bolten was active, mixing with both factions, and in a new mood that reflected cheerfulness and confidence. He had the manner of a man who was holding a card up his sleeve. Fresee was not in evidence, although it was known he was in town.

But Lafe was not concerned with Fresee or his activities at this time. His whole thought was of the meeting. His every move had been carefully planned. For, to his way of thinking, the feud and all that was to come hung upon the action to be taken by the members of the Association this day. Not for a moment did he lose sight of the fact that small details — little things — counted mightily with the men of a wild, open country such as those with whom he had to deal. Nor did he discredit Bolten's activity on the east range. Lafe Owens had never wanted anything more in his life than he wanted re-election to his position as president of the organization he had built.

By one o'clock the sidewalk and street in front of the entrance to the hall where the meeting was to be held was packed. Rumors, insidiously started by Bolten and his closest adherents, circulated freely. Talk persisted to the effect that Lafe, at the last moment, intended to withdraw as a candidate owing to his incapacity, that he had been brought to town on a bed in a spring wagon, and sheer willpower alone made it possible for him to attend the meeting. Bolten was cunning in his praise. Lafe was game. He wouldn't mind if Lafe were elected, even if he was not in shape to attend to the Association's business.

Thus had Bolten changed his tactics, with the sly whispering of Fresee in his ears. Fresee appeared here and there. He had nothing to say further than he was working for the Double B and naturally would like to see his employer honored. It seemed no more than right, but it wasn't his business to meddle in such an important matter. In this way the wheels were oiled for what Bolten firmly believed would turn out a victory.

By ten minutes to two practically all the members were in the hall. Sheriff Rowan, with his staff of regular and special deputies, was on hand to see that none went up the stairs except those who belonged in the hall. The crowd, which included many hands from the ranches, was well ordered. There seemed no prospect of trouble, and both Lafe and Bolten had taken steps to assure peace.

At five minutes to two a mighty cheer went up as Lafe Owens appeared. He was in a wheelchair, waving his hand to the crowd, calling cheerfully to acquaintances. Larry and three stockmen were with him and a hush fell over the throng as the chair was lifted up the stairway, step by step. The old centaur's appearance in the hall was the signal for another outburst. And then Lafe waved to them from the platform; his eyes, roving over the sea of faces, sparkled with their old fire. He rapped vigorously on the table at his right side for order. "The secretary will read the minutes of the last annual meeting," he announced in a clear voice that contained no note of weakness.

The preliminaries began and, as was usual, were soon concluded. Lafe noted that the seating arrangement this day was different than ever before. A division of the range was represented in the seating of those from the west end on his right and those from the east end on his left. Bolten was in the front seat almost in front of Lafe on the left.

Lafe made a report of the affairs of the Association, the conditions on the range, and market activities in a strong voice, referring frequently to notes. He made no mention of rustling or the presence in the district of the notorious outlaw, Bianco.

"And now," he concluded, "the most important business before this meeting is the election of officers to serve for the next two years. First in order are the nominations for president."

As he looked down at them from under his bushy brows, they seemed to forget that he was seated in a wheelchair. The power of his personality belied his infirmity.

Fowler, the most powerful of the west-end stockmen, rose quickly. "I nominate Lafe Owens to carry on the good work he has done for the last twenty years," he said in a ringing voice.

"I second the nomination!" called North as several rose to do likewise.

This brought a round of cheering and those on Lafe's left stirred uneasily in their chairs. Jim Bolten's face wore a puzzled frown. This was all too simple. It showed over-abundant confidence. He could see those about him glancing at him. But it wasn't his move. He raised a hand to the left side of his chin that was evidently a signal.

It was George Robertson who now took the floor. Lafe was not surprised. He admired it as a show of loyalty of a friend for a close associate. "I nominate Jim

Bolten," said Robertson in a voice that carried outside the windows. "He has been a loyal member and worker of the Association for the last twenty years. This range has been naturally divided by two great ranches, the Double B and the KT. The eastern half feels that it is entitled to a president at least once in that length of time. Twenty years is a long time for one man to serve in this important position. We believe Lafe Owens is entitled to a rest, especially since he . . . is not too well at present." He avoided Lafe's eyes as he sat down.

It was the east end's cue to cheer, which the members of the faction did lustily. But the cheering lacked spontaneity. The nomination was speedily seconded by several of Bolten's followers.

Lafe Owens now spoke. "In asking this election," he said slowly, "I point to my record. I don't want my ranch referred to as a dividing point. I don't want any division of our range whatsoever." He looked at Amberg and those with him in the rear of the room as he said this. "A division of the range would spell disaster, don't forget that. We cannot split and stand as we have before. I resent the implication of the membership being divided with a candidate for each faction. I think of the organization as a whole, and have its best interests at heart as such. Because I'm in this chair, don't get the impression that I'm not well, as a member hints. We've all had men laid up for a spell after falls from horses, and ranch owners aren't immune." He concluded with a smile that was contagious. He was succeeding in making a joke of his injury.

Bolten heard murmurings behind him and he rose immediately. He faced about so he could see his audience. "Every man here knows that while there has been no open declaration to that effect, there has been a division of the range for some time. In a way, the east end is not so well protected as the west. I consider that in working for the Association the way I have, I'm entitled to more than idle consideration. What is more" — his voice swelled as he warmed to his subject — "I object to any conditions on the range being kept from the members. Everything is not as smooth as our present president would have us think. No mention was made of the trouble on the KT range a week ago. I happen to know that rustling is being attempted right now and that it's a time when the leader of this organization should be up and doing something to stamp it out. Maybe Lafe Owens will tell you about it. If he doesn't, I will!"

Bolten sat down heavily and a wave of excitement swept over the crowded room. Those who knew nothing of what had taken place the night of the party looked at each other in surprise and then looked askance at Lafe Owens. There was a glimmer of triumph on Bolten's face. Lafe had bought protection as well as he and it was up to him to explain. The mere fact that there had been trouble was enough to gain Bolten's first point. It might be enough!

With the eyes of all on him, Lafe Owens smiled faintly. "I'd rather you'd tell 'em in the first place, Jim," he said quietly.

Bolten sat as if stunned. Lafe had cleverly set a trap for him and he had stepped into it with both feet. As he saw the serene look on Lafe's face, he forgot Fresee's wise admonition to hold his temper. He rose angrily.

"All right, Lafe Owens, I *will* tell 'em!" he cried, whirling on the startled audience. "If Owens won't tell you the truth, *I will!*" he shouted. "There's been rustlin' goin' on for some time . . . since the blizzard. For the first time in twenty years this range is threatened and threatened as it has never been threatened before! Why? Bud Davis, one of the KT's 'punchers, was shot down and killed in the blizzard by the cattle thieves. He identified the leader before he died. Owens told me so himself. Was this news given out? Do you know who is headin' this drive on our stock? You've heard rumors about the raid on the KT a week ago when men were killed and wounded. Do you know who did it? I know who did it, and Lafe Owens knows who did it. I'll tell you who did it . . . it was Bianco!"

Members rose to their feet almost as a man as the name thundered in their ears. They stared at each other and at Lafe Owens, open-mouthed. It couldn't be possible! Only those few who already knew kept cool.

Bolten was holding up a hand for silence. "I told you this was a time for action! My stock's been raided, and so has the KT's. I defy Lafe Owens to deny it!" He turned on Owens with flashing eyes.

There was a dead silence. Then: "I have lost no stock," said Lafe firmly.

"Because you paid to get your stock back!" shouted Bolten. "You did lose a hundred head, same as me, at the time of the blizzard. You can't deny it without lyin'. Now tell the members how we got 'em back and remember that no matter what you say, I'm goin' to come clean!"

Lafe had listened to Bolten's hot words with an unperturbed calm and this had the effect of calming the members and lending much weight to his words when he spoke. "It's true there have been raids on the KT and the Double B," he said frankly. "In the first raids stock was run off the KT and the Double B. This stock was returned. I have good reason to believe the raids were the work of Bianco. But his activities were confined to the two ranches mentioned and did not affect other properties. There must have been a reason for this, aside from the fact that our cattle were ranging near the badlands where they could be run off easier than on the open range." Lafe paused and looked thoughtfully at his opponent. "I don't know why my cattle were returned. It still has me guessing. But maybe Jim Bolten will tell you why his stock was returned."

"Because I bought Bianco off with twenty thousand dollars in cash to prevent more trouble!" Bolten cried, shaking his fist at Lafe. "And you did the same thing to get your cattle back!"

Lafe rapped sharply with the gavel for silence. "If I bought Bianco off, why did he raid my range the second time?" he demanded sternly.

Bolten was inarticulate with rage for several moments. But now he had charged into it, had told most of what he knew, and he lost all sense of finesse. He stepped into the aisle with arms waving. "The only answer I can give to that, men, is that Owens didn't play the game square with this devil, Bianco. My foreman led a bunch of my men to help run the raiders off the KT that second time. It looks to me as if our president had intended to hush this business up because he didn't feel capable of dealing with the trouble. I'm not sayin' anything against Lafe in a personal way, but I think it's time he stepped down as president of the Association. If you elect him, you'll be putting your OK on rustlin' on this range, and, once it gets a good start, nobody can tell where it'll end."

"If you were president, how would you stop it?" Lafe shot in a ringing voice.

"I'd . . . I'd . . ." Bolten hesitated and glared. "That's passin' the buck!" he flared. "I'm not goin' to tell my plans and have you grab 'em. I think the fact that you tried to keep this business quiet will be enough to show the members the handwriting on the wall!"

Then the members witnessed an important and impressive sight. Old Lafe gripped the arms of his chair, lowered his feet from the rest below, and stood erect. His features were pale and grim with lines of strength standing out, it seemed, in stern relief. "I don't believe there's a man in this hall, outside of you, Jim Bolten, who would believe I intended to keep this matter quiet. I told all of the details to Fred Fowler and George Robertson the night of the second raid . . . told them everything except the news that you had paid that money to Bianco. I preferred not to tell the Association anything unless I told them all. I had no particular wish to tell them that you had bought Bianco off . . . to use that fact, perhaps, as a weapon. Therefore, I let you tell it." He paused, noted every eye upon him and every ear listening eagerly. "Bianco solicited twenty thousand dollars from me as he did from Bolten. I refused to pay! I can prove it. And to keep the trouble confined to my ranch alone, until after this meeting when I could better cope with the situation, I, as chairman of the directors of our bank, endorsed the loan of twenty thousand dollars to Bolten to buy Bianco off. And here's the note, with my initials on it, that Bolten signed at the bank!" He drew a slip of paper from an inside pocket and held it aloft.

A world of red whirled about Bolten's head. "It's a trick!" he shouted hoarsely. "Everybody knows I'm good for a twenty-thousand-dollar loan. The note didn't have to be endorsed. It was a trick to save the bank because the bank's wobbling right now!"

"The security for your loans would be none too good with Bianco tearing your ranch to pieces!" thundered Lafe. "I expected something like this when I heard that you told Brower you'd 'break his tin bank,' if he didn't let you have the money without the sanction of the directors and without stating the reason for soliciting the loan. To show that the bank is sound, I've sent for one hundred thousand dollars in cash and it'll be on deposit and in the vault there tomorrow." He was looking straight at Steve Amberg and those other newer members from the far eastern end of the range. "The KT is behind the bank, lock, stock and barrel, and . . . if you want to bring about a division of the range as you've hinted . . . I can say that the whole west end is behind the bank."

There was a mighty cheer at this that was not confined to the west-enders alone.

"You're usin' the bank as a club!" Bolten fairly screamed.

"There aren't many men killed on the range with silver bullets!" Lafe retorted. "I'll use any means at my disposal to keep this range intact and to protect the members of this Association. We will throw any personal feelings aside at a time like this. I hereby pledge myself to stamp out the Bianco gang after my re-election. My plans are made and in the hands of Sheriff Rowan. We have worked for the best. I hardly believe that this Bianco will wait for the worst!"

"Talk . . . all talk!" Bolten roared above the cheers.

"If there are no other nominations, we will vote for president," Lafe announced, pounding the table with the gavel.

Bolten held up a hand and spoke in a hoarse voice to the men on his side of the room. "The east end will vote solid!"

"The Association will vote by ballot!" Lafe thundered.

The hall was in a turmoil as the paper slips were distributed and each man wrote the name of his choice on the slip given him. A member from the east end and a member from the west end were called to the platform. One held the box containing the collected slips; the other drew out one at a time, announced the name written thereon, and passed the slip to the secretary for verification and recording.

Lafe remained standing. He didn't even keep track in his mind of the number of votes he was receiving. He saw Bolten's look grow blacker and blacker. Then the ordeal was over.

The secretary rose, cleared his throat, and announced: "For Lafe Owens, seventy-one, and for Jim Bolten, fifty-five votes."

Lafe sat down amid cheers.

Jim Bolten was on his feet instantly, his face purple, his arms upraised and his fists clenched. "There will be an East Teton Cattlemen's Association within a week!" he shouted. He stamped down the aisle. "You fellows from the east, follow me!" he commanded from the rear of the hall.

All but eight on that side of the room rose and crowded out behind their leader. Robertson stood irresolute. "I nominated Jim and I reckon I'll have to trail with him," he said slowly in the hush. Then he went out. Amberg and the east-enders with him stayed in their seats.

"We will proceed with the examination and election of the other officers," Lafe told the secretary.

All the officers then serving were re-elected unanimously.

# CHAPTER
# TWENTY-TWO

Bolten's shouted words and the cool, clear voice of Lafe Owens had carried to the crowd in the street. The throng was an excited, milling mass, controlled with difficulty by the sheriff and his men, when the irate Double B owner stamped out of the building with his followers at his back.

"Lafe Owens is president!"

"The Association's busted up!"

"The range is split wide open!"

Cries went up on all sides as Bolten and his followers pushed their way through the crowd on their way to the hotel. Since the insurgents were in sight and the other members of what had been the cattlemen's organization were not, the mob massed in front of the hotel for a glimpse through the windows at the turbulent scene within. Fresee was now at the side of his employer, slyly gaining his ear, his eyes darting everywhere. With a smirk on his lips, he carried an air of triumph.

It was Robertson who finally brought order out of chaos. He admonished the other east-enders to refrain from airing their troubles and got Bolten off to one side.

"This won't get us anything," he said, shaking his friend by the shoulders. "You're just making a spectacle of yourself. Cool down. You can't manage this outfit by swearin' and actin' mad. We've lost that bunch of Scotchmen out east and it was that bank business that did it. You can't count on me, Jim, unless you're ready to show some sense. Pull yourself together and I'll tell the bunch you'll have something to say to 'em later in the afternoon. Go to your room until you've got hold of yourself."

Bolten bit his lip to stem the tide of vigorous profanity. He knew Robertson was speaking sensibly. "All right," he decided. "You get the word around that our bunch will meet in the hall at five o'clock. And I sure want to see that Amberg upstairs." He ceased speaking as a man touched his arm.

It was the teller from the bank. "Can I see you a moment, Mister Bolten?" he asked respectfully.

Robertson turned away. "You can say what you've got to say," snarled Bolten.

"Mister Brower wishes to see you at the bank," said the teller.

Bolten frowned. What was this, now? He had no business at the bank. Perhaps it was about the twenty-thousand-dollar note. "I'm very busy," he grumbled. "I guess Brower can wait a while."

"He said he would like to see you in his office right after the meeting, Mister Bolten," the clerk persisted.

"Same as giving orders, eh?" Bolten said angrily. "Well, you tell him . . ." He paused, pursing his lips. "No . . . I'll be right over. You tell him that."

The teller bowed slightly and went out as Bolten beckoned to Robertson. "Brower wants to see me. News travels fast in this town. I'm going over to the bank and find out what kind of an underhand game he figures to play. I want to know where I stand in every way."

"Well, don't antagonize the bank," Robertson warned. "We're all in the same boat when it comes to finances. I mean us east-enders."

"Don't blame me for anything," Bolten growled. "If Brower's got any scheme in mind, you can lay to it that Lafe put it in his head."

But Robertson had a worried look as he passed the word among the east-enders to gather in the hall at five o'clock. He, too, wanted to see Amberg and he was waiting until the stockman should appear.

"You want to see me?" Bolten demanded as he thrashed into Henry Brower's private office in the rear of the bank.

"Sit down," said Brower politely, indicating a chair in front of his desk. The banker seemed to radiate a debonair mood this afternoon. He wore a white flower in his coat lapel.

"All decked out as if for a wedding," snorted Bolten. "Guess that cash deposit of Lafe's perked you up a bit."

"We didn't need it," said the banker cheerfully. "It's merely to strengthen confidence in the institution you saw fit to attack." An aloofness came into his manner. "You do not seem to think very much of this bank, Mister Bolten."

"Thanks for the handle to the name," said Bolten sarcastically. "As I'm probably your best customer, I reckon I'm entitled to a show of respect. What was the general idea in Lafe's waving my last note in front of the meeting?"

"He did that, I believe, to protect himself," Brower said coolly. "Incidentally I'll have to call that note, Mister Bolten."

"Yeah?" Bolten's eyes widened. "You want the money . . . now?"

"We have considerable of your paper which is payable on demand," said Brower. "We are calling that paper in, Mister Bolten. Oh, I don't say that we require the money right now, but we will have to have it within, say, forty-eight hours." He smiled complacently.

Bolten sat as if stunned. He seemed unable to believe his ears. "You . . . you're calling . . . my paper?" he stammered incredulously.

"We are, unfortunately, compelled to take this action," was Brower's reply. "You can, as you intimated the other day, probably secure accommodation at some bank in Great Falls or Helena. We are allowing you time to do so, of course."

Bolten leaped to his feet in another spasm of rage. "This is another underhanded move!" he cried. "Owens was belly-aching about me working under cover, now, what's *he* doing?"

Brower shrugged and passed a sheet of paper across the desk. "Here is a list of your obligations and the amounts due, Mister Bolten. I, of course, am not alone responsible for the bank's action."

Bolten glanced at the sheet and stuffed it in an inside pocket. "You goin' to swing this club over everybody in the east end?" he asked with a sneer. "This isn't banking business. It's a play to help that snake of an old Lafe to break me. But you can't do it, and, if the wool wasn't thicker than a pair of blankets over your eyes, you'd see that! This is plain dirt, Brower."

The banker ignored the insult in the other's eyes and tone. "All the loans this bank makes are made on the basis of adequate security," he said. "There is more loaned to east-end stockmen, as you now see fit to style yourself, than to the stockmen in the west. With the prospect of rustling operations, cattle security automatically becomes uncertain. That would be the case in any event. But, in such case, the bank would endeavor to assist in stamping out the rustling. It would try, at least. But with the eastern half of the range separating from the western half, the dubious nature of your security out there becomes a certainty. There isn't room for two protective stockmen's associations on this range. If you were not so bull-headed and stubbornly set on your own personal desires, you'd acknowledge this. Acting as you are, the bank does not want your business. And you may just as well know here and now that this bank can easily survive the loss of all the east-end business. That's all I have to say to you, Mister Bolten, and it won't do you any good to try to abuse me or any of the directors. So you can get it straight, I'll tell you that we're dumping you overboard. I guess you can understand that."

Bolten was on his feet, his face purple with suppressed rage. "You're nothing but a fop mouthpiece for Lafe Owens!" he managed to get out. "You haven't got a mind of your own. You're . . . why, you're a jumping-jack with Owens pulling the string. Have been all along, but I've been just dumb enough to be paying enough attention to my own business to take you for what you want people to think you are. You are —"

Brower rose suddenly and stepped briskly around the desk to confront the stockman. "That's enough!" he said sharply, his eyes snapping. "You have no further business here unless you're prepared to take up your paper. When you come in again, you can attend to your business through the front window. You're the only man who has ever come into this bank and insulted me, and you're not going to have the chance to do it again!"

Brower threw open the door and motioned to Bolten to leave.

Whatever Bolten saw in the banker's eyes, it kept back the flow of expletives and profanity that was on his lips. He passed Brower with his eyes narrowed to slits, swept out of the bank, and charged for his room in the hotel like a bull, looking neither right nor left. In the lobby he signaled to Fresee and the foreman followed him upstairs.

"Owens is using the bank," snarled Bolten as Fresee shut the door. "They've called my paper. It's all good as gold, but I've got to go to Great Falls or Helena and make new banking arrangements." He calmed down somewhat. "Fresee, do you suppose Bianco intends to lay off my stock? You know, now that I think about it,

I've never heard anything about his word being any too good . . . and I haven't even got his word!"

"I don't think he'll bother us," said Fresee. "I told you I didn't believe Owens had kicked in, and that last raid proves I was right. And he wouldn't have told it at the meeting if he wasn't able to back up what he said. I looked for this bank move, too."

"Then why didn't you say something about it?" Bolten demanded, and was sorry he had asked the question.

"I just guessed at it," replied Fresee smoothly, "and it isn't up to me to be telling you about finances. My work is on the range."

"That's so," agreed Bolten, mollified. It was best that Fresee shouldn't get the idea in his head that he was too important. "Well, I'll have to start south this very night. I'll have to be in the Falls in the morning and maybe go on to Helena by train. I can't lose any time. I'll have to put off the organization of the east association until I get this bank thing straightened out. And while I'm at it, I'm going to fix it for the whole east end."

"There's just one thing maybe I should say, although it's just a guess," crooned Fresee. "You understand, I'm thinkin' and guessin' because I've got your interests at heart. I'd have to have or I wouldn't have a job long. But . . . maybe this Owens has tried to queer things in the south. Maybe he thinks he can fix anything with money."

This opinion, instead of making Bolten angry, caused him to become thoughtful. He pursed his lips and remained silent for a spell. "He'd have to try to queer the whole east range," he said at length, "and those big fellows down there wouldn't stand for it. They won't let any feuds or Association jobs interfere with good business. They'll probably jump at the chance to get in up here, for they've tried to buy that bank a couple times. No, if Lafe Owens tries that, I reckon he'll find he isn't such hot stuff with the big guns."

"He's sort of a big gun himself," Fresee observed.

"Go keep a look-out for that double-crosser of an Amberg from the east edge of the range," Bolten ordered. "I want to see him as soon as he pulls away from that meeting. You can guess the inside of his play, I reckon." Bolten finished with a sneer. He didn't see Fresee's eyes flash.

"They're Scots out there and Owens used his bank club," the Double B foreman observed.

"All right, get out and keep an eye open for him," Bolten snapped. "And tell Robertson where I am. I want to see him, too."

With Fresee gone, Bolten got what he wanted — which was half an hour alone. He paced the room thinking, thinking harder than he had ever thought in his life. He realized many of his mistakes and bit his lip as he thought how cleverly Lafe had led him to his downfall at the meeting. He was no match for the older stockman when it came to wits, to plotting. Moreover, for the first time he was genuinely incensed at Fresee, and he wondered with puckered brows if he hadn't listened too much to his own disadvantage to the whisperings of his foreman; he even began to doubt

Fresee's loyalty and this startled him. He might have known that he couldn't win the coveted presidency of the Association, on which he had set his heart for years, by threats. Confound his temper! But the main subject of his thoughts in this half hour was his threat to form a new organization. He had to carry it out, now that he had made his declaration. And he had overlooked the mighty factor of the dollar. He was no match for the KT owner in lands, stock, or general wealth. It did no good to think of this important weapon Lafe had used now. He was kicked out of the bank! He would have to appeal to southern bankers for help. Suppose they refused him? The sweat broke out on Bolten's brow and he mopped it with his big bandanna handkerchief. He would have to start for Helena this very night — before sunset, if possible. And then Bolten paused in the center of the room, struck by an idea. He couldn't call off the meeting of the eastern stockmen, but he believed he had fallen on a way to postpone it! That was it, postpone it! And now he also had an argument to present to Amberg and the group from the far east end.

He lighted a cigar and sat down, his face glowing with satisfaction. When there came a rap at the door, he called out cheerily: "Come in!"

It was impossible for him to resist a flash of anger when he saw Amberg, but in a moment his face had cleared and his look became almost benign. "Sit down, Amberg," he invited, motioning the rancher to a chair. "Steve, whatever made you fellows desert us today? Now, remember, you don't have to tell me unless you want to. But it got my goat, of course, and I'd like to know."

Amberg shifted uneasily in his chair but steadied immediately and looked Bolten straight in the eyes. "We're a bunch of small stockmen out there . . . just starting out . . . and we can't take any chances. We are not like you big fellows who can do as you please. And we believe in sticking to the ship when it's sailing along all right."

Bolten nodded affably. "Sensible, too. But you could have told me any fears you might have had and I would have wiped 'em out." He leaned forward in his chair. "You know the club Lafe Owens is trying to hold over some of you . . . er . . . smaller stockmen. It's a money club. He showed his hand today. Now, so long as the east end is going to break away from the present organization, we've all got to stand together. The old Association couldn't do you any good, 'way out east there, with the new organization in between. You'd be cut off, don't you see? Oh, this isn't a threat, it's common sense."

Amberg's expression was puzzling, but Bolten saw that he had the east-ender thinking. "You might be caught between two fires out there," he suggested with a wave of his cigar. "If trouble came along and your stock was raided, you couldn't expect us to help you, if you didn't belong. Now listen . . . this isn't a threat. It's just suggesting a possibility. Honestly, I don't believe the rustlers would bother you, because your outfits aren't big enough . . . yet. But if they did . . ." He gestured with his cigar again. "We'll forget that because

**314**

I don't think there's any such chance. And I'd be in favor of helping you out . . . if we could. Now there's another matter, Amberg, which I think is at the bottom of this bolt. By the way, have you joined the west-enders?"

"Not yet," said Amberg. "In fact, we haven't been asked to join because we belong to the old Association already."

Bolten nodded. "That's right," he agreed. He was pleased, though, to hear Amberg use the word "old" in connection with the matter. "Now for this business, Steve." He leaned forward and tapped Amberg on the knee. "I saw it coming, but I couldn't make a move because I didn't know if Owens would spring it or not. It's the matter of money." He saw Amberg's eyes light with instant interest and knew he was on the right track. "With our own organization it will be necessary for us to have our own banking arrangements. I am going to Helena this very night to make the necessary preliminary moves. Now Owens said the KT was behind this bank here and so on. That's all right. Every ranch in the east end will be behind our new banking connections. And don't forget the Double B is no slouch. I have assets and plenty of 'em . . . so have Robertson and the others. And the southern banks will be tickled to death to get in up here. They've been trying to get in for years. Now we can protect you, Amberg, just as well as the tin bank here. For our connections will have a hundred times the capital and assets that Brower's outfit can command. Think that over."

It was plain that Amberg was thinking and thinking hard. "We'll think it over," he told Bolten in sudden decision.

"Good!" exclaimed Bolten, beaming and holding out his hand. "Now, I'm going to postpone the first meeting of the new organization until I can get our financial arrangements made, and, in the meantime, don't make any moves, Steve. We'll give you the protection you need."

"I guess we'll be going back right away, anyway," said Amberg, rising and reaching for his hat.

When Robertson came in a few minutes later, he found Bolten pacing the room, an unlighted cigar in his mouth, his eyes glowing.

Bolten swung about sharply. "Anything new?" he asked.

"The meeting is over with the same old crowd in the lead. Our bunch is going to stick, but . . . well, did Amberg come up?"

"Why did you hesitate?" Bolten demanded. "Yes, Amberg came up, and I'll tell you about that later. Why the but?"

"Some of the boys think we ought to have a little more time to organize . . . decide on officers and all that sort of thing. Of course, you'll be president, and . . ."

"Just the thing I intend to do!" exclaimed Bolten. "I'm goin' to postpone the meeting until I can get this financial matter fixed up. Of course, we'll have to have some time. Tell you what you do . . . get some of the boys up here and I'll explain matters to 'em and we'll postpone our meeting a week or two. Amberg and his crowd are goin' to stick, sure as thunder. I told 'em they'd get no protection out there if they didn't and that I'd attend to financial matters."

"Not so bad," grunted Robertson. He was impressed by Bolten's enthusiasm. "Well, it won't take us long to have a kind of directors' meeting."

Within a half hour the meeting had been held and the east-enders were starting for their homes. Amberg and his friends were the first to go. Bolten was attending to business matters in connection with his trip south and Fresee was dispatched back to the Double B.

Lafe Owens was closeted in his room with Sheriff Rowan and several of the most prominent of the west-end stockmen. This conference was also attended by Brower from the bank.

Lafe Owens was talking. "I made public that statement that I was putting this cash into the bank because I felt sure it would reach the ears of Bianco. If no one else gets word to him, Fresee will. I'm betting on a hunch that Bianco will raid the bank. We'll be ready for him. I've an idea as to the range out by my place, too, and that's why I'm asking for men to filter in out there for the doings. Now, my cards are on the table."

There followed a conference of some length during which plans were laid for ridding the range of the notorious outlaw who had invaded it. Then the sheriff, Brower, and the stockmen filed quietly out to put the plans into immediate operation.

Meanwhile, Fresee, riding eastward like the wind, looking back over his shoulder frequently, suddenly swerved from the road and dashed into the trees along the river. He waited, looking up and down the road from the shelter of the trees for some little time. Then he walked his horse downriver to a shallow ford. He crossed there and emerged cautiously on the south bank. Again he inspected the lay of the land. It was nearly sunset before he started eastward on the south side of the river at a fast gallop. Very often he grinned and his eyes were sparkling pinpoints of light. He would not have grinned, and his eyes would have changed their expression, had he known that a rider was waiting atop a ridge at the edge of the badlands toward which he was racing.

# CHAPTER
# TWENTY-THREE

After helping his father to his room, Larry had gone to the barn to see that the horses were all right. He paused to chat with some of the stockmen who were leaving town and waiting for their mounts to be saddled or teams hitched up. As he turned to leave the barn, a rider thundered in the rear door. He looked over his shoulder casually, stopped short in his tracks, and whirled. The rider stopped near him, looking down at him.

"Jane!" he cried as though he could hardly believe his eyes.

The girl swung quickly from the saddle, her face white, and confronted him. "Larry! You're . . . all right." Slowly the color came into her cheeks, and she looked away, tapping a boot with her riding crop. She looked very beautiful then, trim in her riding habit, wisps of hair peeping from her cap, her cheeks flushed, lips like cherries, eyes dancing.

He took her hand in both of his. "You came," he said in a tremulous voice. "I was afraid . . ." He was suddenly cognizant of the curious eyes about him. "Go into the office in front," he said, "while I look after your horse. Hurry!" She left him as he led her mount to a stall and quickly unsaddled it and tied it.

Then he hurried to the office and found her sitting on the bunk there. He was beside her in a moment, his arms about her, his lips pressed to hers. "I was afraid you wouldn't come, and I guess I couldn't have blamed you if you didn't."

"Oh, Larry, I was afraid something might happen between you and Fresee. I know how he hates you. He wants to kill you. I saw it in his eyes . . . I've seen it more than once. I . . ."

"Never mind, Jane, we've got to get out of here. There are too many around and your dad or somebody from the ranch might see us. Come on."

He took her arm and led her quickly out of the barn to the rear door of the hotel where they entered. In the narrow hallway leading to the lobby in front he halted. "Wait till I take a look in front before we try the stairs," he said excitedly. He walked quickly to where the stairs were, glanced into the lobby, and beckoned to her. In a minute they were up the stairs and Larry drew her into an unoccupied room and closed the door softly.

"Jane," he murmured softly, and for some moments he held her in his arms. "You came."

"I made up my mind last night," she said, with her head on his shoulder. "Father forbade me to come and it was late before I could get away from the ranch. Oh, Larry, what are we doing?" She drew back and looked into his eyes. Her fine, long lashes seemed touched with dew.

**320**

He put his hands on her shoulders. "When I was riding back from the Falls with our . . . our paper . . . I wasn't sure, but now that you're here, I know. I don't care about anything but you, Jane. I want you today . . . now . . . this afternoon. Was it just because you thought Fresee and I would have trouble that you came? Tell me, Jane."

She didn't look at him now. He could feel her tremble.

"Was it, Jane?" he asked softly.

"Larry . . . oh, I don't know. I came because I wanted to come." She looked up at him suddenly and he put his arm about her shoulders as he patted her cheek. She put her lips against his hand. "I'm just wondering, Larry, if . . . if we're doing right," she whispered.

"I love you, Jane, and you said you loved me. You gave me your promise and that's a sacred thing. I think it will help things if we get married, although we don't have to let anybody know . . . yet. Once we're married, we can't lose each other . . . don't you see? But it's for you to say."

Her arms crept about his neck. "I . . . I wonder if I'm just afraid? I want you, too, Larry. I . . . wouldn't want anything to happen to . . . to . . ." She ceased talking, her lips quivering.

He held her close and kissed her. "Then I don't see how we can do anything wrong," he said earnestly. "We can go to the justice and I'll ride back with you. You can make some excuse at home for being away, or even tell your mother. Maybe it'll help to stop all this trouble,

Jane. But I'm not thinking of the trouble. I'm only thinking of you, sweetheart."

Now that he held her in his arms again, the doubts that had assailed him vanished. They loved each other — they could do no wrong. It was their right!

She was stroking his hair. "Do you know where Father is?" she asked.

"I think they're having a meeting . . . the east-enders. The Association's split, Jane. Your father is starting a new one for the east range. But that mustn't make any difference to us. It's one reason, maybe, why we shouldn't wait."

"All right, Larry, dear, we'll do it!" she said, giving him a hug.

Some moments later Larry, excited and eager, opened the door and stealthily peered out into the hall. It was deserted. He stepped quickly to the head of the stairway and looked down. The way appeared clear. He motioned to Jane and she was with him in a moment.

They descended the stairway with Larry in the lead and turned into the hall leading to the rear door. Larry quickened his pace and they almost ran to the rear entrance. When they were outside, Larry looked down at his bride-to-be with a grin of boyish triumph.

He led Jane along behind the buildings until they reached a small, white shack that fronted on the street. He rapped smartly on the rear door. They waited breathlessly, looking at each other almost in fright. Then they heard noises inside and finally the door was opened and two gray eyes and a white beard showed through the crack.

"Hello, Judge," Larry greeted. "Are there many people in there?"

The justice swung the door wide. "Come in, the crowd's just left," he said in a querulous voice. He was small and spare and old, this justice. "And if there had been a crowd in the front room, we could use the back room, even if there is a bed and a kitchen stove in it." He closed the door after them.

Jane's eyes were wide and she was rather white. She put a hand on Larry's arm.

"Judge Nelson, can you keep a secret?" asked Larry.

"I've been known to fergit things," replied the justice, fingering his beard. "I reckon I could fergit 'bout you two if I had to."

"That's it. Jane and I want to . . . get married."

"Wall, thet's no trick a-tall," boomed the old man. "You got the license?"

Larry produced it immediately, and the justice adjusted his glasses and scanned it. "Seems all right, Larry. You got the ring?"

"The . . . the ring?" Larry gasped. Jane's hold on his arm tightened as he looked at her blankly. "I . . . never thought of it," he confessed with a flush.

"Thet's all right," said Nelson. "I learned long ago in this prairie country thet a man's gotta be prepared fer anything. Now you jest wait here." He shuffled out into the front office while Larry and Jane stared at each other.

In a few moments he was back with two boxes. "I keep 'em in stock." He grinned. "Now this box has the best ones, and . . ."

"Never mind the other," said Larry quickly.

"I thought so," said the old justice. "Wouldn't be like Lafe's boy to want anything but eighteen carat in a wedding ring. Now, Jane, let me try one on till we get one thet fits." The third ring fitted perfectly, and he handed the small band of gold to Larry.

"Now you two want to go out front? Every couple I've ever married in here has had good luck." He peered back and forth at them out of his watery gray eyes.

"This is all right," said Larry. "I expect it's just as binding and we can step out the back way again. We're doing this on the sly, Judge."

"Thet's just as binding, too. But you got to have a couple witnesses. Oh, don't git scairt. I'm always able to tend to these things. Hugh Mathieson and Merle Thompson are out front. I'll bring 'em in. They'll be tickled to death to be in on the secret and they wouldn't say a word so's they could have the laugh on folks afterward. You just wait."

Larry stood holding the ring, looking down at it. When he looked up, Jane's cheeks were rosy red. He kissed her quickly, and then the justice entered with the two grinning witnesses. Jane stepped a little behind Larry.

"No, step out here beside your man, Jane. I'm shore glad I'm the one to marry you two for I've known your paws and maws since doomsday."

It seemed hardly a minute before the ceremony was over and Larry was kissing, first the ring on her finger, and then her lips.

"It's allers customary to kiss the bride," the old justice pointed out, and he and the two witnesses kissed Jane on the cheek.

As simple as this, thought Larry, his eyes glowing. He handed the justice a yellow-backed bill. "That ought to cover it," he said.

"You'll have to sign," the justice said, "and I'll give Jane the paper she wants."

This formality was soon over and Mr. and Mrs. Lawrence Owens slipped out the rear door into the glory of the prairie sunset. Although they could not know it, Jim Bolten was galloping south at the moment, and Lafe Owens was complaining because Larry hadn't shown up.

"Jane!" exclaimed Larry, taking her hand. "We . . . we did it!"

To his astonishment his wife leaned her head on his shoulder and burst into tears. He had no thought of being seen. He just held her and kissed her hair, until she looked up at him and raised her lips.

"Forever's a long time, darling," she whispered.

"It can't be too long for me, Jane," he said tenderly, and kissed her. "And now we've got to fix it so we can eat in the hotel kitchen where nobody can see us and start back. Leave it to me."

They hurried back to the hotel and succeeded in getting into the kitchen. Larry fixed it promptly, as he had promised. "You wait here," he told Jane. "I'm going upstairs to see Dad and arrange it so I can ride back to the ranch right away. And I'll find out if your dad has gone back." He was gone in a moment.

When he reached his father's room, he found him eating with Stan Velie and his mother.

"Takes you a long time to get around," growled Lafe. He was not in good humor despite his victory. "You look excited. What you been up to, Larry?"

"I did a little gambling and won," his son replied. This did not sound like lying to him. "I've had a bite and I'm going to ride on to the ranch . . . unless you have something for me to do."

"Gambling!" snorted his father, while Stan Velie grinned. "Well, I suppose you've got to learn when to stop so's you'll know when to stay away from it. If you run across Jones anywhere, take him to the ranch where he belongs."

The youth caught the significant look his father gave him and nodded.

"Where's Mister Jones been all day?" Molly Owens asked.

"Oh, you want to know," said Larry, raising his brows. "And what'll you give me if I tell you?" He laughed as his sister shot him an angry glance. "The east-enders' meeting over?" he asked Lafe.

"Didn't have any," said Lafe in a satisfied tone. "Got cold feet, I reckon. Bolten had to go south, so I suppose Fresee's gone home. We'll stay in town tonight."

Larry hastened to the kitchen where a meal was prepared for Jane and him. "We've got half an hour," he told her. She nodded toward the two women in the kitchen, one of whom came immediately with food and the other with a big pot of savory coffee. Both women wore broad smiles.

"Kind of edging around old Lafe, ain't ye, Larry," said the one who poured the coffee.

"What's your name?" Larry demanded.

"You don't have to ask me my name, nor Anna's, either, and I can tell gold when I see it . . . 'specially if it's on a girl's finger!"

Larry and Jane looked at each other in dismay and Jane hastily put her left hand below the table. Then Larry carefully peeled two ten-dollar bills from his roll and laid them on the table. "I've heard of folks forgetting things for less than that," he said significantly.

"Oh, we wouldn't have had to have that, Larry." Anna laughed. "Not with you and Jane. You can lay your last white chip we won't tell, and we wish you a barrel of luck. Shake."

"Jane, we better hurry and eat and get started before everybody pegs us," Larry said, and grinned.

Shortly afterward they were in the barn. Larry got their horses with the aid of the barn man. As they mounted, he pressed a five-dollar gold piece into the man's hand. "Needn't bother to mention that there were two of us," he drawled. "Just me, understand?"

"That's all I saw," agreed the barn man as they rode out the rear way.

They slipped around the town through the timber until they had left it behind. Once on the open prairie they let their mounts out and raced in the dying sunset with a cool, sweet wind freshening.

"Didn't know it cost so much money to get married, Jane!" called Larry with his flashing, boyish smile.

"Are you sorry?" she flashed back.

"Am I? Just rein in a minute . . . close."

The horses, anxious to go, bobbed their heads and snorted at the delay. And then they were off at a ringing gallop over a field of cloth-of-gold, with the purple buttes far ahead, and the shadow of the river to their left. The wind sang in the grasses and a bridal veil of golden dust floated behind them. "Who cares?" cried Larry as he threw a kiss to Jane.

# CHAPTER
# TWENTY-FOUR

As Fresee raced through the gathering dusk for the badlands, the figure on the ridge vanished. It was Jones who cautiously led his horse down the steep slope into the timber at the edge of the plain. The night was falling fast after the long twilight of the prairie country. When Fresee galloped past, Jones mounted and followed closely within the shadows of the trees.

The other men who had returned from town had ridden in daylight and he had been unable to follow, nor had he cared to risk looking for the trail they had taken into the wilderness of the brakes for fear that a look-out would spot him and perhaps shoot him down or capture him in an ambush. He had suspected another messenger after the meeting, but had been startled to recognize the small figure of Fresee on the big horse. As it was, he didn't care if all he discovered was the place where Fresee entered the badlands. He had no doubt but that the Double B foreman was headed for Bianco's rendezvous.

By this time Fresee's caution, insofar as possible pursuit was concerned, had fled. He pushed his horse to the utmost and Jones thrilled as he realized he could catch the Double B foreman if he wished, for Jones had one of those mounts that are rarely encountered, even in a region of fine horseflesh.

The mantle of night came down and the first brave stars hung out their signals in the purple canopy of the sky. Jones shortened the distance somewhat between himself and the man he was following, a thing he now could do with safety. And then Fresee slowed his pace suddenly and a few moments later disappeared.

Instantly Jones drove in his spurs and dashed down the line of naked trees. Fresee had disappeared so suddenly that he couldn't judge the spot where he had entered. When he thought he was near this place, he reined in and brought his horse down to a walk, searching for a trail leading into the wilderness of twisted ridges, gaunt trees, scrawny pine, buck brush, deadly quicksand soap holes, and gravel patches.

Then he saw by the starlight what appeared to be a huge rock. Instinctively he cut close into the shadow of the trees and brush, halted, and dismounted. A look-out, if one was stationed at the entrance, would be looking for a horse and rider. Jones was a trailer by instinct. He crept forward afoot, and, as he had expected, he saw an opening behind the rock. He went ahead foot by foot with his gun in his hand and found a worn trail, well concealed from the open plain. Here he hesitated. This might be only one of many such blind trails. Would Bianco spare men for all these trails? Would he expect attack from that direction? With Fresee associated with him, it would be certain the Double B foreman would get word to him if attack were threatened from the other direction. All this would give the rustler chief confidence and a sense of safety. He and his men might have been there for months, might have hidden there for weeks, anyway. It was open country for miles southward, a great far-reaching plain where no cattle grazed. Jones had come up that way. There was no water and no ranches clear to the Missouri.

He rose. Nothing happened. He shoved his gun in its holster and strode back to his horse. Mounting, he rode boldly back and around the rock, and proceeded along the hard trail. Except where scrub pine and high ridges made deep shadows, he could see for some little distance ahead, as the cottonwoods, alders, and poplars were leafless. The starlight aided him. But he again kept his gun in his hand. For some distance the trail led straight toward the river. It widened constantly and many smaller trails led into it. Then, when Jones had concluded it was going to lead to a ford, it turned east. On the riverside, to Jones's left, there were a succession of gravel patches and the deadly soap holes of quicksand with their alkali crusts. But there were trails leading toward the river, too. On the opposite side, toward the south plain, were ridges, dark ravines, scrub pines, and other timber. It was the wildest and most dangerous wilderness of badlands Jones had ever seen.

Now the trail turned off to the right, climbed around a high ridge, and led through a level stretch of gaunt trees. After climbing another ridge and flattening out again, the trail swung again toward the river. In less than a minute, Jones reined in his mount with a smothered exclamation. In the distance fireflies were winking. Lights! Jones drew a long breath. He was nearing the rendezvous. At either side of the trail ahead were dark blotches denoting ridges or pines. He was a considerable distance from the lights and came to an immediate decision. He rode forward swiftly, the lights becoming steadier and more distinct, until he reached the shadows where he found a ridge on his right, toward the plain, and a thick growth of firs on his left, toward the river. Here the trail was in complete shadow. He walked his horse. The trail curved to the left and ended abruptly at the edge of a large clearing.

Jones checked his horse just in time to avoid riding into the clearing. Thrills raced up and down his spine. In the open space were a number of cabins and lean-to shacks, corrals, horses, cattle! There were several clumps of firs. The lights came from the windows of the cabins. Jones thought he now knew why he had not encountered any look-outs or guards. From the cabins came a wild medley of sound. Shouting, singing, catcalls. The band was in the midst of carousal. This was in Jones's favor. But Bianco and Fresee would not be participants in the drinking spree and they were the two he wanted to find out about.

Directly ahead, between Jones and the cabins, was a clump of firs. There were cattle standing about this clump. While Jones knew he could not approach it on foot, for range cattle are not accustomed to men on foot, he knew he could approach it on his horse. This he decided to do. He put aside the thought of attempting to ascertain the brand on the steers. The KT cattle had been returned; none had been taken since; no other stock losses had been reported. It followed that, since Fresee was associated with Bianco, these must be Double B steers that Fresee had aided the rustlers to steal.

He rode forward boldly, walking his horse, and reached the clump of firs without disturbing the cattle. Here he dismounted and found he was at the rear of the cabins. Another piece of luck. The noise seemed to come from the two largest cabins, while to the left was a much smaller cabin with no window in the rear. There were no cattle in the space behind the cabins. The din of the revelry accounted for that.

Jones slipped quickly to the rear of the smaller cabin. One well acquainted with the youth would have noticed a queer change in his demeanor during the hour and at this time especially. His moves were cat-like, his eyes sparkled with fire, he radiated an intangible alertness and eagerness — a Jones totally different from the youth people ordinarily met. He stole around the corner of the small cabin on the side away from the larger cabins where the celebration was in progress. As he expected, there was a window. He crept along the wall until he reached it. The window was closed save for a space of possibly a quarter of an inch at the bottom where the sill fitted imperfectly. A piece of gunny sack had been used as a curtain, but there was a worn spot in the corner where the fiber was wide apart and through which Jones could dimly see two forms. One was large, the other slight. That was enough. Bianco and Fresee were together.

Jones whirled about, his gun whipping into his right hand, seemingly of its own accord. He fairly hurtled to first one corner of the cabin and then to the other. No human being was abroad. He returned to the window, stooped, and glued his ear to the crack at the sill. What he heard came in snatches when the voices were raised.

"Don't wait! Tomorrow night's the time, before they know what's ... have a chance to ... hundred thousand cash." It was the voice of Fresee.

"I'll attend to that." It was Bianco speaking.

"And I'll ... raid on the KT ... draw attention ... how do I know ..." The rest of Fresee's words were lost.

"Don't be a fool!" Bianco thundered.

Jones straightened, moving to the side of the window, his back against the wall of the cabin. There had been no sound. Perhaps he sensed a vibration in the air. But a man was there before him!

The silence was as complete as the stillness of the air after the vibrating echo of a bell has died away.

"Wha's idear spyin' on chief?" The question was put in a thick throaty voice that nevertheless carried.

An instant later the heavy barrel of Jones's gun crashed against the side of the man's head. He went down, but with a screech that could be heard all through the rendezvous. Jones was running like mad for the clump of trees where he had left his horse. It seemed incredible to him that events could take place with such swiftness. Behind him there was a cracking of guns; bullets whistled past him; the night air was filled with shouts — and the thundering voice of the arch-rustler giving orders. And yet Jones told himself he might have known that Bianco would have trusted lieutenants who would not be indulging in drink. Men of the stamp that followed Bianco sobered quickly on alarm.

Jones gained the shelter of the clump of firs, dodged through them, flung himself on his horse, and was off at a mad gallop for the edge of the clearing and the trail.

"Major!" he cried in his horse's ear. "Let's go!"

But already he could hear the pound of hoofs behind him. He made the trail and dashed into the protecting shadow. But here he was at a disadvantage. He didn't know the ground he was traveling. All he could do was to give his mount its head and trust to the gallant animal to keep the trail, traversed but once. He could hear his pursuers behind him. On the open prairie they probably could not catch him, but in his present predicament he was fighting two disadvantages: he was on a strange trail, and he couldn't very well out-distance both horses and bullets. He decided to swerve from the trail when he came to the first open space, separating him from the river.

When he thundered into the open at last, he eased his pace and deliberately turned off the main trail to the right. The sounds of pursuit had become more and more distinct. His mount slid down a short gravel slope toward a cleared space. The going looked good and Jones turned in the saddle to look behind. Almost in the next moment he lurched forward with the horn of his saddle prodding him painfully. He nearly had been thrown over his horse's head. A glance showed a creamy sheet stretching from under Major's back. The animal was vainly trying to get its forehoofs out of the mud. Jones's heart stood still. It wasn't mud or gumbo. Unknowingly he had leaped into a soap hole!

Already the struggling had ceased. Jones was leaning backward as his horse's head went steadily down. Down! The deadly sucking sands were drawing the animal to its death, headfirst! Jones could see the whole ghastly surface of the soap hole quivering as if shivering in glee at the claiming of another victim — two victims.

The hot instinct of self-preservation surged through Jones's mind and body. It was the work of a few moments to secure the rope that he always carried suspended from his saddle horn. He looked behind and sighted what appeared to be a stump or a large rock. There was no time for delay. The wide loop hissed over his head and shot forth. It settled over its objective and locked. He felt his stirrups touch that terrible, quivering surface, and jerked his feet free. There was a queer, sobbing choking in his throat. Holding the rope in his left hand, he pulled the gun with his right. He would not let his horse suffer the most horrible of all deaths in the quicksand.

The tears streamed down his cheeks. "So long, Major!" The gun blazed twice, sending two bullets into the horse's head.

Jones rose in the saddle, poised on the dead animal's back, leaped, and drew himself a few feet across the shallow sand to the safety of solid ground. Just as he gained it, the rope gave way. He staggered off to a clump of bushes and lay down. The horse's head and

**336**

shoulders were under. The hind legs in the shallow sands at the edge of the mire were drawn forward swiftly. The sands, defeated of one prey, were not to be robbed of the other. Jones watched, horror-stricken, as the carcass disappeared.

"Down there somewhere!"

Jones squirmed back under the brush as riders, who had heard the shots, came down the slope. He saw them come — five of them. They stopped at the foot of the slope.

"Look!" It was a voice he did not know. "See that soap hole shivering! That's where he ended up, whoever it was."

The men walked to the edge of the bog. "See that!" cried one. "The last bubbles. And look! Here's where he roped this rock tryin' to get out, and the rope slipped on him!"

"Let's get out of this," said a gruff voice. "Gives me the creeps. For one, I can use a drink right now."

Evidently the others of the band felt the same way about it, for they hurried to their horses and were gone up the slope in a short space.

Jones lay still, fascinated by the ghostly gray of the soap hole, calm and serene now — satisfied! He looked up at the stars, his lips pressed so tightly that they were a thin line of white. He was safe, absolutely safe. But at what price!

When the sun rose in its glory after the dawn, a figure staggered into the courtyard of the KT home ranch. It wavered and swayed; hatless, coatless, gun and gun belt gone. It was Jones. His eyes were bloodshot, and, when Larry Owens came running out of the house to catch him before he could fall, he failed to recognize him.

"So . . . long . . . Major!"

Larry carried him upstairs and put him in his own bed.

It was Molly Owens who fretted about with such restoratives as were at hand. It must have been a subconscious knowledge of the extreme importance of the information that he possessed that resulted in Jones's opening his eyes within an hour.

Jones held out his hand and Molly grasped it in both of hers.

"Get Larry," he said.

When she had gone, Jones turned on his side and buried his face in the pillows. But when Larry and his sister returned, he was lying with his eyes on the ceiling.

"Take this." Larry offered to put the glass to his lips.

But Jones sat up in bed. "I reckon I can handle it. Don't go away, Miss Molly. Go over there by the window where I can see you easy. We've kidded around somewhat, but I like to look at you. You're a square-shooter. What is this stuff, Larry?"

"That's brandy," said Larry. "I was going to look for you last night, but . . . where was I to look? Tell you the truth, Harry, I didn't know just what to do. I've sent for every man on the north range, including that hard outfit from Canada to . . ."

"Never mind." Jones smiled. He looked at Molly, who had flushed and gone to her station by the

**338**

window. "I reckon you better stay and hear what I got to say," he said. Molly nodded.

He downed the brandy, sputtered, and gasped for breath. "If that's . . ." He handed the glass to Larry. "I'm not a weakling," he protested. "The thing that got me was the way I lost . . . my horse. Now, listen."

Looking through the window into the warm sunlight, he described his experiences, told every detail of what had happened from the time he left town. "Gimme a cigarette, Larry," he concluded.

Larry hastened to comply. "I'll start for town at once," he said in great excitement. "If they're going to try it tonight . . ."

Jones turned on him with an almost ferocious expression in his eyes. "You'll do nothing of the sort!" he cried. "I'll go to town. My part is there. Your part is here on the ranch. Get these men of yours ready. You'll need 'em tonight. I'll sleep till . . . well, three hours, say, and then I'll be on my way. I'll have to borrow . . . a horse," he concluded as an afterthought. "And, Larry, listen." He remained silent for some time. "I knew more of this from the start than I can tell you now."

Larry regarded his friend thoughtfully. "All right," he said finally.

Jones smiled at Molly Owens. "I'm still the mystery man," he said softly.

In another two minutes he was asleep.

# CHAPTER
# TWENTY-FIVE

The old cowtown of Pondera lay in shadows. An idling breeze stirred little curls of dust in the one main street — little spirals that rose lazily and drifted to merge into veils. It was long past midnight. To all outward appearances the town was dead, as, indeed, it should be at this time. A single lamp burned over the vault in the bank.

All about were deep shadows — shadows of buildings, shadows of trees, and in this dead hour other shadows, smaller and moving, appeared. There had been a faint sound of horses' hoofs, and now men were at the rear of the bank, others slipped to the front corners to serve as look-outs, still others formed a cordon about the building. Bianco knew his business and was taking no chances in his attempt to get the rich treasure that Lafe Owens had stored in the vault as a lure.

The men in the rear of the bank were working now. Sounds came from back there, but there was no one abroad to hear them. In a short time the sounds ceased; the rear door, perhaps secured none too carefully, had been forced.

**340**

A few notes of a night bird's song trembled on the breeze. Three men quickly slipped into the bank. One form was large and bulky — Bianco. The two others were expert cracksmen and each carried a bag of tools. The night air seemed to be vibrating. The look-outs and guards were tense, ready to give instant alarm in THE event anyone appeared. The shadows in the bank moved into the cage before the steel doors of the vault. The sharp notes of the bird floated forth again. Then the clear, still night was suddenly changed into bedlam.

Red flashes of flame spurted from the deeper shadows of buildings about the bank, from the trees behind it, and from the upper windows of a house across the street. The roar of rifles commingled with the cracking of six-guns.

Bianco and his band had walked into a carefully laid trap and seemed, by the terrific fire directed at them, to be outnumbered three to one. Sheriff Rowan and Jones had outwitted the bandits to a point where it looked as if a veritable slaughter might be in prospect. One of the look-outs plunged forward on his face with a bullet in his heart at the first fire. Three of the guards toppled.

From the rear of the bank came a mighty thunder of hoofs. The horses of the outlaws had been stampeded and were heading in the direction of the street. They came plunging through the narrow spaces at each side of the bank building, knocking down several guards who attempted to make flying mounts. This momentarily halted the shooting for neither side could see where to shoot with the frightened animals about them.

In the lull Bianco could be heard roaring orders as he dashed out of the bank. With the maddened horses plunging into the street, the guns roared again. But both factions now were at a disadvantage, for it was difficult to distinguish friend from foe. The rifle firing, which came from the windows of a house, ceased entirely. The bandits had scattered up and down behind the buildings. It was impossible for them to reach the timber for the dense shadows there were fairly alive with the sheriff's men.

Meanwhile, the horses had come to a stop and were milling about or had slowed to a trot. The bandits took a chance to get to them and raced into the street. This brought another withering fire and men went down and horses as well. Sheriff Rowan came running out of the house and a slighter figure dashed out of an alley. It was Jones, and, as if it were prearranged, at this moment two other men ran out below the bank and raced toward the horses in that direction. One was the burly form of Bianco and the other was a member of the band.

Both the sheriff and Jones started in pursuit. Rowan, in the throes of great excitement, kept shouting for the outlaws to halt. The order was ignored for it could never be said that the outlaw leader was a man to surrender. Instead, he whirled in his tracks with a savage yell and deliberately ran toward his pursuers. For a man of his size he could cover the ground at amazing speed. His companion darted back into the shadows of the buildings. The whole town was now awake and people were pouring into the street.

"Bank robbers!" was the cry. In a short space both ends of the street were crowded by armed men and escape seemed cut off.

Bianco came on, his face, barely discernible in the starlight, distorted with an insane and reckless rage. He realized only too well how he had been tricked. Nothing mattered now except to kill. Thought of fleeing actually left the man's mind. The sheriff loosed his gun, the red fireflies of death playing from its muzzle.

"Watch out!" shouted Jones, choking in the swirling dust.

Bullets sang about them from bandits about the buildings. These in turn were subjected to fire from behind and had to stop shooting to conceal their locations. Rowan, Jones, and Bianco were alone in the street almost in front of the bank. The range was too great, the dust too thick for accurate shooting, but the sheriff blindly emptied his gun. In a few moments Bianco's weapon blazed. At the third shot Rowan went down.

Bianco came on toward Jones who was some little distance behind the sheriff. He fairly leaped toward his prey. In a wink of an eyelash, Jones fired, and fell over to the left on his knee as two bullets whistled past him. Through the veil of dust his gun spoke once — twice.

Bianco, within ten feet of Jones, staggered and fell backward, firing the last shot in his gun. The bullet sang over Jones's head, and the outlaw leader lay motionlessly, face upward in the dust of the street.

Jones ran to the sheriff and found he was shot high in one shoulder and in his left leg. He sheathed his gun and dragged the official to the nearby house. The bandits must have been stunned by what they had seen, and, with their leader dead, matters looked different. A man ran into the street with his hands held high. A shot came from the bank and he sprawled his length near the form of Bianco. None of the posse would have done such a thing. He had been shot down by a member of his own band because he had offered to surrender!

But the last stand of the outlaws was short lived. The sheriff's men had closed in behind the buildings and now volleys began to sweep the alleys and open spaces. Others were closing in from up and down the street and guns blazed from across the street. Suddenly there were shouts and a dozen men ran into the center of the street with their hands up. Two of these were shot down before the posse could cease firing. In another few moments the ten men — all that remained of the most desperate band of outlaws ever to invade the northern range country — were surrounded.

The crowd of citizens surged forward. Word had spread that it was the Bianco band that had tried to rob the bank.

"Give 'em the rope, and make a clean job of it!"

"Hang 'em in the dark like they deserve!"

From a window of the house the sheriff shouted hoarsely: "Don't touch 'em! Get 'em to the jail! Show some sense, citizens!"

Jones helped the wounded man back to a bed and ran down to the crowd in the street. "Don't put a black blotch on the town!" he cried. "If we have to do it, we'll defend these prisoners with our guns!"

344

"Keep back!" shouted the members of the posse as they started for the jail with the captured outlaws in their midst.

The crowd gave way before the large number of armed men that menaced them. But they still shouted, and then gathered in a mass before the jail when the prisoners had been taken there and placed in cells. There still was work to be done and Henry Brower spoke to the crowd.

"There are wounded men to be looked after instead of killing more," he pointed out.

This quieted the throng and the work of attending to the wounded — there were many — got under way. The bandits had lost heavily, but there had been losses among the sheriff's men, also, and Rowan was now being attended by the doctor. Curiously enough, the body of the arch outlaw was left lying in the street until sunup.

Before dawn Jones was speeding for the KT where he suspected the other half of the coup had been executed.

Lafe Owens, his wife, and Stan Velie had left for the ranch the morning before and had been met by Jones, who was on his way to town to acquaint the sheriff with the expected attack on the bank that night. Men had been recruited from nearby ranches in the late afternoon and early evening, for the extermination of the outlaw band. Sheriff Rowan had intended to accompany Jones to the KT Ranch, but his wounds now made that impossible.

Meanwhile, extensive preparations had been made at the KT to repel the projected raid. Since the outlaws thought that whoever had been spying on their rendezvous had been lost in the quicksand, no change in their plans was to be expected.

"This will end the rustling and the feud," Lafe had said grimly. "I see now why Bianco returned my cattle. He didn't want me sending men into the badlands. No one knows how many cattle Bolten will find missing over there when he checks up himself. Fresee must have had a good portion of the Double B outfit in the plot with him. He intended to put one over on me and make a clean-up and slope. He sent for that rustler if he ever did anything in his life."

Sid Tyler and his PT men, who Larry had hired, were brought down from the north range. The KT crew was bunched midway of the range, and many men recruited from the west-end ranches, who had already arrived at Lafe's request, were scattered the length of the range. Old Lafe did not feel able to be out on what might be a battleground that night after his exertions of the day before and his ride back from town. Nor would Sarah Owens have permitted it. But he spent an hour giving instructions to Stan Velie.

"Fresee isn't doing this to attract attention away from town," he told his foreman. "You know that would be ridiculous. He's doing it on his own hook while Bolten is away."

As it came about, most of Lafe's instructions were ignored that night. Not intentionally, but because events took place with such rapidity, and there were so many unexpected moves, that action unsuspected was imperative. It was an hour after midnight, sometime before the start of the tragedy in town, when three separate bands of riders swept across the KT range toward a herd of 200 shorthorns that had purposely been planted within easy striking distance. In less than ten minutes one of the most disastrous clashes in the history of the Teton range was on.

Sid Tyler with his fighting PT men dashed in from the north. Larry with the regular KT men came from the west, while Stan Velie with the men imported from other ranches rode madly from the south. In an amazingly short space the herd and the raiders were surrounded.

The raiders, taken by surprise by this lightning move, were the first to shoot. Their guns blazed as they mingled with the cattle, scattering them in every direction. The KT forces returned the fire with deadly fierceness. Two score cattle went down; men on both sides toppled from their saddles and the night was hideous with the bellowing of the steers, the shouts of the combatants, and the staccato of gunfire. Then the raiders tried to break through the line drawn about them. In less than a minute they found this was an utter impossibility. Several were shot down. They converged in the center and ceased firing, holding their hands aloft. Only one made the last desperate break for liberty. With his guns blazing, this man of diminutive stature raced for the opening.

Both Stan Velie and Larry recognized him. "Don't fire!" roared Velie, as he and Larry tore away from the others to cut the reckless rider off. The rider fired at both of them, and then one of those timely accidents occurred that often decides fates and battles and careers. The fugitive's horse stumbled and threw its rider over its head. It was a matter mere of moments before Velie and Larry were on the ground close to the fallen rider. The man on the ground crouched and fired point-blank at Velie who fell on his side. Two spurts of flame streaked from Larry's weapon and the raider yelled and dropped his gun.

"Shooting's too good for you, Fresee!" Larry cried. "I'm going to save you for the rope!"

Fresee was clasping his shattered right wrist with his left hand, rocking to and fro on the ground, cursing with pain and rage. But Bianco would get him out of this mess. He calmed suddenly.

Men were raising Stan Velie. His whole left collar bone was shattered and the bullet, ranging upward, had torn away part of his jaw. It was Sid Tyler who effectively administered first aid.

"Get him to the ranch quickly as you can," Larry commanded. "And herd that bunch of range crooks to the bunkhouse."

"Look out!" came a hoarse cry.

Larry leaped with a bullet singeing his left ear. He was on Fresee instantly with the ferocity of a tiger. When he rose, he had the man's gun.

Fresee had recovered the weapon with his left hand and had made one last try to kill the man he hated. His throaty laugh held the men about spellbound until Larry jerked him to his feet. "Get his horse and tie him

348

in the saddle!" he cried in a voice none ever had heard him use before. It was the voice of old Lafe himself, ringing on the night air with the wild lust of battle. "You've done one thing, Fresee. You've cleaned this range with blood. And you're going to pay for it with a broken neck!"

Tied in the saddle, hatless and torn, dripping blood, Fresee laughed that weird, uncanny laugh that made them shiver as they started for the ranch.

# CHAPTER
# TWENTY-SIX

When they arrived at the ranch, they found Lafe up and waiting for news of what had taken place. Larry marched Fresee to the front porch that was flooded with light from the open door within which Lafe sat in his wheelchair.

"Here he is, Dad," said Larry in a hard tone. "The ringleader."

Lafe peered at the prisoner under frowning brows while Fresee sneered. Then, without speaking a word, Lafe motioned them away. As they were leaving, however, the rancher called: "Come back when you've locked him up, Larry!"

Fresee had held his bandaged right hand behind him. Inwardly he had an instinctive fear of letting men see he would never shoot again. He walked willingly enough to the storeroom in the big barn where they locked him in.

Larry left the two men who had accompanied him on guard before the door and Jerry, the barn man, hung a lantern conveniently near. It would be two hours before daylight.

Larry returned to the house and in the living room told his father everything that had happened. Lafe listened gravely. It had been a costly business. Suddenly he appeared to have aged as Larry recited the details of the clash.

"It's the end," was his comment when Larry had finished.

Hoof beats sounded in the courtyard. "That must be Velie," he said. "Have him brought in. We'll send him upstairs. Send a man on the fastest horse in the barn for the doctor."

With Velie being cared for in the house, and the prisoners herded in the blacksmith shop under heavy guard, the wounded were brought in and put in bunks in the bunkhouse. There were eight of them only, for the raiders had lost heavily. Tyler had lost one PT man and had six wounded. Of the men recruited from other west-end ranches, three were dead and four wounded. The KT suffered most of all with five dead and three wounded. Men looked at each other grimly as the figures were computed. The range would long remember this tragedy. There were angry, ominous mutterings with Fresee's name mentioned frequently.

"No, boys," said Larry sharply. "There'll be no lynching. It's bad enough as it is without such an ending."

At sunrise Jones arrived on a lathered horse with the news of what had occurred in town. He reported to Lafe, and the stockman merely nodded and dismissed him. He went upstairs to Larry's room for an hour or two of sleep that he needed badly.

Larry rode away eastward when the doctor came. In a little more than an hour he was back and Jane was with him. He turned his wife over to Molly and the two went up to Molly's room.

Men were arriving at the ranch by now, Brower from town and several west-end stockmen. Six KT men, after having been instructed by Jones in minute detail, left for the rendezvous in the badlands to make sure the cattle there bore the Double B brand. Later they reported that this was the case.

At one o'clock, Jim Bolten arrived. His face was pale as he mounted the steps and confronted Lafe Owens who was in his wheelchair on the porch.

"Lafe, is all this true that I hear?" he asked abruptly.

"Larry, bring the prisoners," Lafe ordered, ignoring the Double B owner's question.

As Larry hurried away, Bolten took off his hat and mopped his brow. Then he stared steadily at Lafe, who was looking off across the distant pasture lands. Then Lafe called: "Sarah!" His wife came quickly to the door. "Bring a chair for Mister Bolten," said Lafe.

By the time the Double B owner was seated, a group of men came around the corner of the porch, escorted by a bunch of KT cowpunchers. They formed a semicircle about the steps with Fresee in front. Fresee's eyes were snapping. He held his right hand behind him.

Lafe spoke to Bolten. "I'm turning over your men to you . . . all except Fresee. And I don't reckon you want him." He motioned to Larry. "Put those eight 'punchers aside. They're free."

With only Fresee facing him, Bolten leaped from his chair. "What is this, Fresee? What have you done?"

"Followed out your instructions." Fresee leered.

Bolten hurled himself down the steps, but Larry grasped him to restrain him. The big man's face went red and blue by turns. It was some moments before he could speak.

"You're a liar!" he shouted. "You lie and you know it!" He trembled and his hands clenched. "You're a skunk!"

"Yeah?" Fresee sneered. "Ask your men there."

Bolten whirled on the eight cowpunchers. "Did you hear me give any such instructions?" he roared.

There was no answer.

"They're afraid to talk, now that we didn't get away with it," said Fresee with his jeering laugh.

Bolten looked up at Lafe Owens. His face was white as chalk. "Lafe, do you think I did this thing?"

Lafe removed the pipe from his mouth. "No, Jim, I don't. Come back up on the porch."

"You hear?" cried Bolten, shaking his fist under Fresee's nose. "You hear? You . . . you . . ." He sputtered in his emotion.

"Only thing he could say," sneered Fresee.

"He won't feel so good when he finds out that Bianco and most of his gang are dead up in Pondera, and that the others are in jail . . . where he's going . . . and have started to talk," said Lafe.

Fresee's eyes flashed, but he grew pale. "That should worry me," he managed to say.

"It'll worry you when you come up before twelve real men for trial and hear the noose wished on your neck," said Lafe dryly. "Larry, take him away and tell those others to clear out."

"You can't trick me!" Fresee shrieked as they took him away.

Bolten tried to speak, but couldn't. He was overwhelmed.

"Listen, Jim," said Lafe quietly, "you've done a lot of listening to that skunk the last two or three years, haven't you?"

"I . . . trusted him," Bolten snapped out.

Lafe nodded. "And he's been stealing your cattle. There's a bunch of fine steers in the badlands now where he and Bianco had 'em cached. Don't stare. It's a fact. You can see 'em with your own eyes. You never counted much of your stock yourself, did you?"

Bolten failed to reply, but the look in his eyes told plainly that what Lafe suggested was true.

"He must have known this Bianco and sent for him," said Lafe. "Or Bianco happened along and he got in with him *pronto*. You had a 'puncher shot in the back the second raid on my place, remember? The one who got lost in the badlands time of the blizzard and saw Bianco? Well, it was Fresee who shot him. He knew too much."

Bolten took off his hat and rubbed his hand through his thinning hair. Then he swore. "Did you know this all along?"

Lafe shook his head. "Wasn't dead sure of it until, well, you might say yesterday and today. Jones!" he called. "Jones!"

In a few moments Jones appeared in the doorway.

"How many head do you reckon there are of Double B stock in the badlands?" Lafe asked.

354

"I should judge about five hundred," Jones replied as Larry appeared behind him.

"Jumping Jupiter!" Bolten exclaimed. "And the bank in the Falls is sending up two men to verify my count before they'd take up my paper. I'd've been in a fine mess!"

"And Jones," said Lafe, "you saw Fresee in Bianco's hangout when you sneaked in there? And heard them talking and planning all this?"

"That's right . . . and lost a fine horse getting the information."

Bolten stared at him stupefied.

"There's something you men ought to know," said the youth. "My real name is Louis Cilin. I am connected with the Southern Association at headquarters in Miles City. I got a tip Bianco was headed up this way and took a chance and came up. I can use my share of the reward money. Maybe I'll get it all." He took out papers and tobacco. "I did for Bianco, although I was lucky, at that."

Larry and the two men stared at him in surprise as he smiled.

Then Larry pushed Harry Jones aside and came out on the porch, leading Jane.

Bolten started to his feet. "Jane!" he cried. "Why aren't you home with your mother?"

"She's home with her husband." Larry smiled. "Jane and I were married the day of the big meeting."

Both Lafe and Bolten gripped the arms of their chairs, white-lipped. "Is . . . that true?" Bolten gulped.

Jane held out her hand with the thin band of gold on its third finger. "Yes, Daddy," she said in a low voice.

"And you didn't tell me?" said Bolten incredulously.

"I told Mother," was the reply.

Bolten turned to Lafe, who was looking hard at Larry. "Did you know?" he demanded.

"Not till this minute," replied Lafe grimly. "And I've a good notion to horsewhip him!"

Jane put a hand on Lafe's shoulder as Sarah Owens and Molly came out smiling. "He's a nice boy, Dad-in-Law, and said you'd get over it soon. You will, won't you?"

"Oh, he did, did he?" Lafe scowled. "Said I'd get over it soon, eh? Well, what he don't know would fill a lot of books!"

Jim Bolten was grinning from ear to ear.

"By the way, Dad," said Larry casually, "since you gave me the right quite a while ago, I'll have to write a check at the bank tomorrow for a wedding tour. Maybe we'll go East and that'll take quite a bit . . . and Jane'll have to have some clothes . . . five thousand *might* do it. But, if we go short, I'll draw."

Henry Brower laughed in the doorway.

Lafe and Jim Bolten looked at each other. "I wouldn't want to stop Jane from gettin' some new clothes," drawled Bolten with a twinkle in his eyes; "'specially since I don't have to pay for 'em."

Jane put her arms about his neck and kissed him on the cheek.

"Nobody ever heard me welsh." Lafe grinned. "Congratulations, Larry. And you've got a good girl, remember, and if you don't treat her right . . ."

"Don't be joking, Dad . . . this is serious," Larry said as they shook hands.

"Jim," said Lafe in an earnest voice, "this feud thing, as they call it, is all foolishness. I wanted to end it once and for all . . . especially on account of Larry. That's why I did some of the things I did."

"Lafe, reckon we better tear down that fence between our places so folks won't have any doubts about our being friends," said Bolten. He rose and held out his hand.

"Larry, help me stand up!" Lafe commanded.

Then the two men met for the first time in years in a hearty handclasp, and the Owens-Bolten feud was ended.

"Now, I'll have to send those two bank robbers back . . . if Brower says it's all right," said Bolten.

"Any time you need a loan, you know where to come." Brower smiled.

"And I know you'll make a good president of our Association, Lafe," said Bolten.

"And I reckon you'll make good as the next one," Lafe boomed.

"As the bride's father," said Bolten pompously, "I hereby announce that the wedding celebration will be held on the Double B!"

The stars were out, riding the fleecy, white ships that drifted in the night sky. A wind, soft and sweet with the tang of Indian Summer, laved the grasses and stirred the branches of the trees. An owl cried from its perch down by the river, and was answered by a coyote in the distance of the plain. Stillness, strange nocturnal whisperings, shadows that took form and vanished — a throbbing world of mystery waiting for the moon.

Louis Cilin — Harry-From-Nowhere — and Molly Owens were in the yard with her dainty quirt.

"I reckon so," was the dreamy reply.

"I . . . hate to see you go, Louis," said Molly softly.

"I hate to go myself," was the answer.

"Then why go?" Molly murmured.

"I'm no longer a man of mystery, Molly, and girls hate just the . . . the usual, do they not?"

"Not necessarily."

"You know, Molly," he said casually, putting an arm on her shoulder, "I believe Larry and Jane had the right idea."

"You mean in not telling anybody about it?"

"No, I mean in getting married. It must be nice to be married, and have someone to work for . . . someone to love all the time. Maybe I'm pretty stupid in the way I'm putting it, but perhaps you understand."

"Yes, I understand." He could barely catch her words.

"Sometimes I think they were setting us an example."

"And if they were?"

"Molly, I believe we love each other. I hope it isn't all one-sided with me on the one side. Is it?"

She looked up with a little laugh. "Larry said you had my goat," she said happily. "You've got more than that, Louis . . . for . . . it isn't all one-sided."

For a long time he held her in his arms before he kissed her. "Do you think we could make it in time to go along with Larry and Jane, sweetheart?"

"Yes, if you're a good manager," she whispered.

"I'm going to try to be one all the rest of our lives," he said joyously.

After a long time they went into the house.

# About the Author

**Robert J. Horton** was born in Coudersport, Pennsylvania. As a very young man he traveled extensively in the American West, working for newspapers. For several years he was sports editor for the *Great Falls Tribune* in Great Falls, Montana. He began writing Western fiction for *Adventure* magazine before becoming a regular contributor to Street & Smith's *Western Story Magazine*. By the mid-1920s Horton was one of three authors to whom Street & Smith paid 5¢ a word — the other two being Frederick Faust, perhaps better known as Max Brand, and Robert Ormond Case. Many of Horton's serials for Street & Smith's *Western Story Magazine* were subsequently brought out as books by Chelsea House, Street & Smith's book publishing company. Although virtually all of Horton's stories appeared under his byline in the magazine, for their book editions Chelsea House published them either as by Robert J. Horton or by James Roberts. Sometimes, as was the case with *Rovin' Redden* (Chelsea House, 1925) by James Roberts, a book would consist of three short novels that were editorially joined to form a "novel". Other times the stories were serials published in book form, such as *Whispering Cañon* (Chelsea House, 1925) by James Roberts or *The Man of the Desert* (Chelsea House, 1925) by Robert J. Horton. It may be obvious that Chelsea House, doing a number of books a year by the same author, thought it a prudent marketing strategy to give the author more than one name. Horton's Western stories are concerned most of all with character, and it is the characters that drive the plots rather than the other way around. It is unfortunate he died at such a relatively early age. Many of his novels, after Street & Smith abandoned Chelsea House, were published only in British editions, and Robert J. Horton was not to appear at all in paperback books until quite recently.

**ISIS** publish a wide range of books in large print, from fiction to biography. Any suggestions for books you would like to see in large print or audio are always welcome. Please send to the Editorial Department at:

**ISIS Publishing Limited**
7 Centremead
Osney Mead
Oxford OX2 0ES

A full list of titles is available free of charge from:

**Ulverscroft Large Print Books Limited**

**(UK)**
The Green
Bradgate Road, Anstey
Leicester LE7 7FU
Tel: (0116) 236 4325

**(Australia)**
P.O. Box 314
St Leonards
NSW 1590
Tel: (02) 9436 2622

**(USA)**
P.O. Box 1230
West Seneca
N.Y. 14224-1230
Tel: (716) 674 4270

**(Canada)**
P.O. Box 80038
Burlington
Ontario L7L 6B1
Tel: (905) 637 8734

**(New Zealand)**
P.O. Box 456
Feilding
Tel: (06) 323 6828

Details of **ISIS** complete and unabridged audio books are also available from these offices. Alternatively, contact your local library for details of their collection of **ISIS** large print and unabridged audio books.